Millie + Mabel's Afterlife Adventure:

Spectral Sleuths

KATHERINE HASTINGS

vinci BOOKS

Vinci Books

vinci-books.com

Published by Vinci Books Ltd in 2026

1

A CIP catalogue record for this book is available from the British Library.

Paperback ISBN: 9781036716462

The EU GPSR authorised representative is Logos Europe, 9 rue Nicolas Poussion, 17000 La Rochelle, France contact@logoseurope.eu

By Katherine Hastings

Spectral Sleuths

Millie and Mabel's Afterlife Adventures

Immortal Hearts

Into the Light

Awakened Light

Eternal Light

The Wilder Widows

The Wilder Widows

The Wilder Widows: Wilder Ever After

The Wilder Widows: Walk on the Wilder Side

Door Peninsula Passions

The Other Half

The Other Room

The Other Plan

Rescue Ops Romance

Colombian Chemistry

Sicilian Savior

Russian Rescue

Daggers of Desire

In the Assassin's Arms

Beneath the Assassin's Touch

By the Assassin's Side

Also by Katherine Hastings

Riches to Ruinville

The Big One

The Arch Pirate

A War Within

Chapter One

MABEL

I grabbed a flat, smooth stone from the edge of the dock and wound my arm back.

"What are you doing?" my best friend, Millie, asked from her spot beside me.

"Nothing." A mischievous grin spread across my face. "Just seeing if I can still nail a good skip."

But that wasn't true. I wasn't aiming for skips—I wanted a huge splash to drench my best friend. I hurled the stone with all my strength, targeting the spot right in front of her perfectly pedicured toes.

Instead of a satisfying splat, the stone hit the surface and took off, a small whirring blur that skipped perfectly seven times before sinking without a sound.

"Wow!" Millie exclaimed. "Seven perfect skips! Nice work!"

I groaned, planting my hands on my hips. "I wasn't trying to skip it. I was trying to splash you."

Millie let out a soft laugh. "I know, Mabel. We've been friends for ninety years. I can always tell when you're lying."

Unwilling to give up, I tried again, but as I tried to spike it into the water right in front of her, the stone just skipped a perfect, flawless series of hops across the pond's surface. I tried again. And again. My frustration grew with each failed attempt.

Her soft, grey curls moved in the gentle breeze. She looked over, her plump cheeks swelling with the smile that deepened the wrinkles around her eyes. "Are you done yet? I don't think Heaven will let you soak me since I don't want to be soaked right now. You know, Heaven. It always gives you exactly what you want."

I did know Heaven. Perfectly perfect Heaven we'd been living in for months of endless bliss... the kind of flawless paradise that was slowly driving me insane.

"Except I *want* to soak you! And this damn rock just keeps skipping off perfectly like I'm a freaking rock skipping champion!"

I tossed the last stone in my hand, watching it once again take off perfectly. Exhausted from my attempts, I flopped down on the dock beside her. "What's wrong with me, Millie? We have everything we could ever want with just a thought. We can paint masterpieces, learn any instrument, go anywhere we want with just a blink. Why can't I seem to be excited about it? What's wrong with me for not loving this endless perfection all the time?"

"There's nothing wrong with you," Millie said, her silver eyebrows furrowing slightly. "You're Mabel. You were never one for perfection. I know you're restless here, and Heaven can be a little… predictable," she said, then she opened her hand and with one big blink, a piece of chocolate cake appeared it. "But for all its constant happiness I know can irritate you, at least there's endless cake… and *no* calories."

She grinned widely, her eyes lighting up as she looked at the plate. She took a bite, moaning with pleasure as she savored the taste. "Here. Have some cake. It will make you feel better."

I leaned forward and took a bite, the perfect flavors of the best cake I'd ever had filling my mouth. But in Heaven, everything I put in my mouth was the best thing I'd ever had, and instead of being excited for the perfect blend of chocolate and sweetness, I just felt more irritated.

I slung an arm around her shoulder. "Maybe Heaven is sometimes frustrating for me because I still feel like I don't belong here. Honestly, I'm still not sure why they let us into the good place. You know, back on Earth, we got into a heck of a lot of trouble."

"Oh yes we did. Kinda worried we'd end up down there." She pointed a chocolate-covered finger at our feet, and I burst into laughter.

I grinned at the memories. "I gotta admit, when I was fading away, I started to panic that Heaven had a list of all the things we'd done, and we were gonna get a big fat door slammed in our faces."

Her blue eyes widened. "Oh, that list would have been very, very long."

She pulled a face, and the two of us burst into laughter as memories of our legendary mischief invaded my mind.

"Like that time in third grade when Jenny called you an ugly troll, so I put gum in her hair?"

Millie started laughing. "Or that time sophomore year that Jimmy and his friends were tormenting you about your botched haircut, so I copied his handwriting and wrote a sappy love letter to the most popular senior girl, oh man, what was her name? Lacy? Lucy? I forgot. But then I slipped it in her locker, and she read it aloud to all her friends? Oh my word, everyone teased him the whole year even though he was constantly screaming he didn't write it." She leaned in, whispering as a sly smile lifted her lips, "And only you and I know he wasn't lying. He didn't."

"It served him right!" I frowned, remembering the hell that little brat had put me through. "I wanted to drop out of school he was bullying me so badly."

Her sly smile grew into a full one. "He was too busy getting tormented himself to torment you after that. I had your back. I had it then, and I had it when your jerk of a husband cheated, and we got payback by hacking his email and forwarding his boss all those horrifyingly disgusting emails he wrote to his assistant and got him fired for sleeping with a subordinate."

Her eyes glistened and mine lit up too, remembering his total and utter devastation when I'd left him, and then he'd lost his job and his side chick all in one fell swoop. And he'd thought he'd accidentally sent the emails to the whole staff and never once figured out it had been us.

I slung an arm around her shoulder. "You had my back, and I had yours. Best friends for life."

"And afterlife," she noted, gesturing to the celestial world around us.

Best friends for afterlife we were. We'd met in a foster home when we were only three years old, and the two of us had been closer than sisters ever since. We'd become each other's family growing up as we navigated a world without our own. We chose each other as family, creating a bond stronger than if we'd merely been blood relatives. Both notorious pranksters, we'd had our share of mishaps, but I'd loved every minute of our unpredictable lives causing mischief and sharing endless laughter over all the trouble we got ourselves into.

A warm breeze, always the perfect temperature, rippled across the water. I closed my eyes and leaned back on my hands, my toes drifting in the cool pond while the sun warmed my face.

Another perfect moment. Dying at ninety-one in my nursing home had its perks, apparently. Millie had gone first, and I'd held her hand when she'd left, my grief so profound that my heart gave out only a few hours later. They called it a heart attack. I called I a broken heart. We'd been best friends for almost nine decades, and now here we were, together again, forever and ever, enjoying nothing but bliss.

Wonderful, beautiful, incredibly *boring* bliss.

At first, Heaven had been exhilarating, a non-stop adventure of discovery and wish fulfillment. But as the days wore on, the luster began to fade. Everything was perfect, yes, but that perfection came at the cost of challenge, of risk, of the very imperfections that had made life on Earth so thrilling.

"I guess I miss the unknown." I sighed, looking out at the still water. "Half the fun of doing things is not knowing if you're going to succeed. Like when we tried surfing the other day, the waves were perfectly calibrated. No wipeouts, no fear, no fun. Every painting we do turns out perfect, just like always. Where's the challenge in that? I picked up a violin last week and even though I'd never touched one in my life, I was playing like I deserved a spot at the head of a symphony. I wanted to go cliff diving back on Earth for the rush, but here, there's no rush when you know you're completely safe. No adrenaline, no thrill. That was the whole point."

"I suppose you're right," Millie said quietly, her smile fading a little. "Not much risk of dying when you're already dead. But, at least we have each other."

That simple statement soothed me as I recognized that even though I didn't seem cut out for this endless perfection business, at least the one thing I never wanted to change was getting to spend eternity with Millie.

I gazed at my friend's face, so familiar and yet so different from the one I'd known as a child. Despite the decades that had weathered us both, turning our once-brown hair to grey, her eyes sparkled with the same mischievous gleam I remembered from my earliest memories.

When we landed in Heaven, they explained we'd look like we did at our happiest. Some folks turned back into their twenty-something selves, but Millie and I only rewound a couple of decades. Apparently, our seventies were peak happiness—free from husbands and jobs, just the two of us in our little house, gardening by day and binge-watching by night.

We sat in comfortable silence for a moment, but I could feel the restlessness building inside me again. I looked around at the peaceful spot away from all the other souls that we'd chosen for our morning routine. In Heaven, things worked similar to Earth. We had homes, and each home was constructed to the exact specifications of our deepest desires. Some people had mansions, others had cabins on a lake, and others, like Millie and me, had a little stone house surrounded with gardens that we shared together, since being together is what made us happiest. An exact replica of the house we'd been so happy in on Earth decades ago.

We lived in our homes and could venture around Heaven, simply blinking ourselves to any place we'd like. There were cities filled with people and music, jungles for those who liked to explore, oceans to sail on, mountains to climb, horses to ride, and basically any of our heart's desires could be fulfilled with just a simple thought.

Well, almost all of them. Heaven never served up the kind of challenge that made life worth living. "You know, does this endless perfection ever get…" I paused, looking around to make sure no soul or angel was around to hear me. "Boring to you?"

She finished chewing her bite of cake. "You mean Heaven?"

I nodded. "Yeah. Like, I really miss all the trouble you and I used to get up to, but you can't do that kind of stuff up here. It's Heaven. Letting the air out of someone's tires because they cut you off in traffic isn't a thing. There's no traffic. And no one to cut you off. No one to piss us off so we can get our well-earned revenge on them. It's just perfect all the time, and I guess I kinda miss the thrill of our shenanigans. Our little adventures we used to go on."

She nodded. "You know, I miss it too. I don't want to complain because Heaven is, well, Heavenly, but yeah. I wouldn't mind getting into a little bit of trouble again. Some M&M Mischief as we called it when we were kids." She grinned her mischievous smile I'd seen more times than I could count, but then it fell. "But we can't, can we? I don't think that's a thing in Heaven. I think our prankster days are done. We only gave people a hard time because they deserved it. No one up here deserves it, so we'd be the jerks if we just went around causing trouble for them."

My frown deepened. "Well, I guess it's just you and me living for eternity in Heavenly bliss."

She blinked and a margarita appeared in her hand. "We may not be able to get our kicks causing trouble anymore, but at least we can do this."

She handed me the drink and I laughed. A moment later, another margarita appeared in her hand. We clinked them together then went back to our peaceful morning by the pond.

After several tranquil hours together, we strolled back toward our house. Our joints no longer ached, and our bunions no longer throbbed. With our walkers a thing of the past, we enjoyed spending much of our time walking around just enjoying the sights of Heaven. When we reached the little village square, familiar souls greeted us.

"Beautiful day!" Arthur called from a swing set.

"It always is," I replied with a wave, unable to keep a hint of weariness from my voice.

"Hi, ladies!" Edna said, and I looked over to see her and several of her friends sitting at a sidewalk café indulging in a pizza overflowing with toppings.

"Hi!" We waved back, then continued greeting our fellow Heavenly inhabitants as we continued our stroll back to our little stone house.

As we continued on, a commotion caught our attention. Nick, a soul we'd met shortly after arriving, was embracing Natalie.

"You're back!" Natalie squealed. "How was it on Earth? Did you help many souls?"

"It was wonderful," Nick beamed. "I helped so many people cross over."

I stopped abruptly, causing Millie to bump into me. "Earth? Did he say he was on Earth?"

Without waiting for Millie's response, I dragged her over to the pair. "Sorry to interrupt," I said, "but did you say you were on Earth? How is that possible?"

Nick's smile faded slightly. "Oh, I was there as a

Crossing Guard. We help confused souls transition to the afterlife."

"Like the person who helped us cross over when we died?" Millie asked, her eyes wide. "I remember just staring at my corpse watching Mabel sobbing over me trying to get back in to go back to her. It was awful. But then someone showed up and explained to me about Heaven, and I was able to let go."

"Yes. Those are Crossing Guards," Nick said. "And I was recently on assignment to be one for a month. I just got back."

My curiosity piqued. "So, you get to spend a month on Earth, and in exchange, you help souls cross over?"

"Yes, exactly," he said. "We go down in shifts, and when a person dies and doesn't immediately ascend, as a Crossing Guard, we get a little notification that there is a stuck soul, and we blink over to help them. It's very fulfilling."

Natalie smiled a wistful smile. "Being a Crossing Guard is a wonderful gift to give the newly departed. I've done it twice. It's an important task to make sure delayed souls don't get stuck on Earth and end up haunting people or something."

My eyebrow arched. "You can… haunt people? That's a thing?"

Nick's brow furrowed. "Well, yes. It's a thing. A *bad* thing obviously. Most souls either head north or south, but some refuse to let go and remain on the Earthly plane. Unfinished business. Fear of where they are going. There's lots of reasons, but it's obviously frowned upon to linger, so our jobs as Crossing Guards are to make sure those souls move on quickly."

"Mmmhmm. I see." I pursed my lips together, my mind reeling with ideas. "So, just to clarify, if you're a Crossing

Guard in ghostly form, could you, I don't know, say, haunt someone while you were down there?"

He scrunched his brow further. "Haunt someone? Why on Earth would I want to haunt someone?"

I waved my hand. "No, no. I'm not saying you would, or that anyone should, of course, but just… could you?"

He shrugged, still looking perplexed by my question. "I, uh… I guess? I mean, it's not easy, or even possible for most ghosts on Earth to manipulate the living world, but I suppose it's possible since we're in ghost form down there, and there are ghosts who have figured out how to manipulate the world around them. Moving things, making noises, even appearing as apparitions. So, yes. I suppose that would be possible." Then he lifted an eyebrow. "But not recommended."

"No, no, of course not." I chuckled, wafting my hand. "I was just curious. My curiosity is always getting the best of me. So, how does one become a Crossing Guard?"

Nick appraised me with a wary eye then finally answered, "You need to apply at the Office of Celestial Affairs. They're quite selective."

Millie shot me a look, but I stayed her with my eyes. "Okay, well, welcome back, Nick. I'm sure we'll see you around now. And good job on helping all those stuck souls. Huzzah to you."

"Thanks," he said, but his suspicious eyes still watched me with concern as I grabbed Millie's hand and shuffled her off behind me.

Once we turned the corner, I spun around, my insides bubbling with excitement as I gripped her shoulders. "We both said we're bored up here and we miss playing tricks on people. What if we sign up to be Crossing Guards and then… we go haunt people!"

Her eyes went big. "What? You're joking!"

I practically bounced in my skin. "No! It would be hilarious! There are a few people who pissed us off in life we never got around to paying back, so what if we paid them a friendly little visit and… haunted them! Oh, Millie! It would be hilarious!"

Fear flickered in her eyes. "I don't know, Mabel. Don't you think we could get in trouble?"

I waved a hand at her. "We won't do anything bad. Just have a few laughs at their expense. And we can spend some time on Earth watching people do bad stuff for a bit to break the monotony of this constant perfection. Like living in a real-world television show! Oh, Millie! It would be a blast!"

She chewed on her lip. "What if we get in trouble for doing that and get sent to…" she leaned closer, pointing at her toes as she whispered, "the bad place? They never explained to us how they know who is good and who is bad. Maybe we'll get in trouble, and they won't let us back up! I mean, I'm bored too, but I don't want to go to…" she whispered again, "the bad place."

"Psht," I said, shrugging off her worry as I'd always done when we were alive. "We'll be fine. We're not going to kill anyone. Just go down to Earth, have a little fun like the old days, and, I guess, help a few souls while we're there. It's a win win!"

Worry deepened the familiar creases on her face as she stared at me, and then after glancing around at the picture-perfect world around us, she quirked a half smile. "It would be kinda fun to see what's going on down on Earth and maybe check in on a few of those people still remaining on our naughty list."

I slung an arm around her shoulder. "Exactly! Let's do this, Millie. You with me?"

She looked up at me, then with a soft shake of her head, she laughed and said, "I was with you for ninety years in life, and you know I'm with you in death. I'm in."

"Yes!" I pumped a fist in the air and hurried us back to our house to make a plan to join the Crossing Guards and get ourselves back to Earth for a little well-earned M&M Mischief.

Chapter Two

MILLIE

We stood in front of the looming marble doors of the Office of Celestial Affairs, my hand pressed tight to my chest as if to keep my heart from leaping out. Funny thing about being dead: you still feel like you've got a body. My chest still thumped when I was nervous, my breath still sped up when I was scared, and I even got butterflies in my stomach. All three were happening right now as I braced for the trouble ahead.

"I think I'm having a heart attack," I whispered. "They're going to know our plans are dubious, and a trapdoor is going to open up and drop us straight to the bad place!"

Mabel peered down at me from behind her dark-rimmed glasses, all five-eleven of her towering over my five-three. "You can't have a heart attack, Millie. Our hearts may still beat for whatever reason Heaven keeps them going, but you're already dead."

I bumped her with an elbow. "You don't know that! We

never did fully read the welcome manual. Maybe we can die again and like, *poof* out of existence for good!"

Mabel chuckled, her sharp, intelligent eyes sparkling with mischief. "Relax, Millie. We're here to ask a few questions, fill out an application, and maybe, just maybe, get a little excitement back in our afterlives. Nothing to worry about."

I bit my lip, glancing around at the grand entrance. The Office of Celestial Affairs was as majestic as the rest of Heaven, with towering columns, sparkling fountains, and angels flitting about, their wings shimmering in the sunlight. Despite the tranquility, my nerves refused to settle.

"We don't have to do this if you don't want to," Mabel said, knowing full well that I was ready to pass out from worry. "I know I'm always the one pushing us out of our comfort zones and coming up with hair-brained plans, but as always, the choice is yours. If you want to go home and enjoy eternity with nothing but sunshine and perfection, I'll understand, and we'll turn around now. But if you want to shake things up with me a bit and get into a little mischief like old times, I really think we can pull this off."

"And you don't think we're going to go to the bad place if we get caught?"

"If we get caught, I'll take the blame and you'll be innocent. I won't let you go to the bad place."

I frowned. "But if you get sent to the bad place without me, then I'll be alone here in eternity worrying about you… living a life without you. That's worse than any fate. I'd rather be in the bad place together."

Mabel's face softened with my words. "Aw. I would rather be in the bad place with you than alone in Heaven too. But we'll be fine, Millie. I promise. We always land on our feet. Let's just go in and find out more about this whole

Crossing Guard business, and then we can decide what's next together. How does that sound?"

"Alright. Let's do this." I sighed, trying to steady my breathing as I straightened my pink hat.

I'd spent an hour choosing an outfit I thought would be appropriate for a meeting with angels. My Sunday best pink skirt suit and a strand of lovely pearls and matching earrings I'd blinked into existence. If we were going to deceive heavenly bureaucrats, I figured I should at least look respectable doing it. Mabel, on the other hand, had made no such effort to impress and wore her usual slacks and button-down cardigan, looking like she was heading to the library rather than a celestial con job.

Mabel gave me a reassuring pat on the back as we pushed through the grand doors and stepped into the building. My pangs of anxiety quickened as we approached the reception desk.

An angel with flowing golden hair and a serene smile greeted us. "Welcome to the Office of Celestial Affairs. How can I assist you today?"

Mabel stepped forward with that unwavering confidence she'd had all our lives. "Hi, we're interested in becoming Crossing Guards. We heard we could apply here."

Her smile widened. "Of course. It's a noble duty. Please take a seat, and someone will be with you shortly."

We thanked her and found a pair of plush chairs near a window overlooking more of Heaven's beauty, the lush landscape stretching as far as the eye could see. As we waited, my mind raced with a thousand thoughts. What if they saw through us? What if they knew our true intentions?

Mabel seemed unfazed, casually crossing her arms and

reclining against the seat. "You need to relax, Millie. Think of this as our next great adventure."

My body vibrated as I bounced my leg, then I forced it to remain still, trying to absorb some of her calm. "I know, but I can't help but worry. We're not the best candidates for this job. We're not exactly saints."

She smirked. "I don't think being a saint is in the job description. And hey, we were good enough to get into Heaven somehow, so we can't be all that bad. You know, we were pretty good people as a matter of fact."

I snorted. "Yeah, says the woman who took the tires off that guy's car and left it on blocks in his driveway."

She poked a finger at me and whispered, "Quiet! We don't want the angels to hear! And hey. He had it coming. He was speeding down the street so fast every day he almost killed that little boy and his dog. I was just teaching him a lesson. Justice." She lifted her chin higher.

"I suppose. You're right. Our mischief was always well-intentioned. It's not like we ever bullied anyone who didn't deserve it."

Her shoulders straightened, making her seem taller than she already was. "Exactly. We were like… Robin Hood. We stood up for the little guy."

"Well, you did most of the standing up and going toe to toe with people. I just worked behind the scenes," I admitted, since it was usually Mabel who caused the most trouble since I was always too chicken to get caught.

"You did your fair share of shenanigans too."

"Yeah, but mine were sneaky. No one ever knew it was me. You were the brave one who would look people right in the eye while you stood up to them. Like that time you—"

She lifted her hand to stop me midsentence then jutted her chin toward the angel behind the reception desk. Out of the corner of her mouth, she whispered, "We probably shouldn't be talking about all the bad things we've done in front of a literal angel."

I slid my fingers across my lips like a zipper and nodded.

We sat in silence for a long while, then an angel with a clipboard came down the hallway and approached us. "Millie and Mabel? Follow me, please."

We exchanged a quick glance and stood up, following the angel down a corridor lined with intricate tapestries depicting scenes from various afterlives. The angel led us to a spacious office, where another angel, this one quite handsome with a chiseled jaw, bright blue eyes and ebony hair, sat behind a large, ornate desk.

"Welcome," the angel said, gesturing for us to sit. "I'm Kafziel. I understand you're interested in becoming Crossing Guards?"

Mabel nodded enthusiastically. "Yes, we are. We want to help souls transition smoothly. It sounds like a very fulfilling role."

Kafziel's piercing eyes seemed to look straight through us, and I squirmed in my seat. "It is indeed a vital task. Tell me, why do you want to become Crossing Guards?"

Mabel launched into her rehearsed speech. "We're so grateful to be here in Heaven and we want to help in any way we can. We've spent our entire lives, and now our afterlives, helping each other as well as other people in need. We've seen how much a guiding hand can mean to someone. We want to extend that help to others."

I nodded along, adding, "We want to give back and make sure no soul feels lost or scared. I remember how I felt in those moments after I passed. I just stood there beside my body trying so hard to get back in it. I didn't want to leave Mabel, and even though I felt the pull to leave my mortal life, I couldn't make myself do it. But then the kindest man, Abe, showed up and told me all about Heaven and that Mabel would meet me here when it was her time. He helped me let go and transition, and I want to help someone else the same way."

The words tumbling out of my mouth weren't entirely untrue. I *did* want to help souls cross over. Abe had done that for me. But I left out the part about what we planned to do between those beautiful moments of helping those souls.

Haunting people.

Kafziel studied us for a moment, then pushed up from his desk and walked out without a word.

"They know." I trembled in my chair, whispering so loudly I may as well have been screaming.

"Shhhh," Mabel hushed. "They don't know! He's just… I don't know what the heck he's doing but they don't know. We were perfect."

"They are *angels!* They can probably read our minds, and he knows we're full of crap! Oh my God. We're going to Hell."

"We're not going to Hell," she argued back. "Just stay calm. If you act like you're guilty, they'll think you're guilty."

"I *am* guilty! You and I both know we only want to go to Earth to shake things up a bit and haunt people, and we're using this Crossing Guard thing as a cover! We're guilty and they know we're guilty and we're going to Hell. Where we probably belong!"

She reached out and took my hand, calming me down with the simple touch. "Hey, hey, hey," she soothed. "We're fine. We haven't done anything wrong. And you know what, they would be lucky to have us as Crossing Guards. We're kind, we're understanding, and what newly deceased person wouldn't want to see these mugs moments after they die." She grinned widely. "We're friendly and fun, and I bet we'd actually do a great job. And yeah, maybe we'd have a little fun between crossings, but we're good for this job. Trust me, Millie. We're gonna be fine. We've got this."

She took a big breath and nodded for me to take one with her. Together we exhaled, and I let the tension slough off my shoulders.

"You okay?"

I nodded. "Yes. Sorry. I spun out for a second there."

"You've got me to grab the wheel. Always have, always will."

She squeezed my hand and I smiled, memories of the number of times she'd calmed my easily frazzled nerves filling my mind. Mabel was always cool in any situation, and I tended to spin like a top at the slightest upheaval. It was part of why she was such a treasured person to me. Like a security blanket she could wrap me up in with just one smile.

Kafziel opened the door and walked back behind his desk, sitting down and steepling his fingers as he looked at us.

My heart pounded against my chest so hard I was certain he could hear it.

He cleared his throat. "I believe you two would make excellent Crossing Guards."

Mabel squeezed my hand tight. "You do?"

"Yes. I've reviewed your files, and I don't see anything to contradict the job description." We nodded earnestly, and Kafziel continued, "There are a few formalities. You'll need to sign these forms and undergo a brief training session. Are you prepared for that?"

"Absolutely," Mabel said, her eyes gleaming with excitement, and I nodded so hard my neck would have hurt if I could still feel pain.

He leaned back in his chair and his full lips lifted into a half smile. "Then welcome to the Crossing Guards."

The anxiety bouncing around inside me nearly burst out my skin as I smiled and said, "Thank you, Kafziel. We won't let you down."

"Good. Then follow me for processing and we'll get you assigned."

We followed him to a different room then filled out the forms, and Kafziel provided us with a detailed overview of our duties. I tried to focus on the responsibilities and the rules that applied to being Crossing Guards, but my mind kept drifting to our secret plan. Could we really pull this off without getting into serious trouble?

After several hours, we completed the paperwork and training overview. Kafziel stood up and lead us to a different room, this one a large, empty room with an ornate door marked "Earth."

"Is that how we get there?" I asked, pointing at the door.

Kafziel nodded.

"Are we going... now? Today?" Mabel's eyes got wide.

"Well, we are actually a little slow on volunteers at the moment. It's a lot to ask souls to leave the warm and wonderful world of Heaven to endure the pains and sorrows down on Earth. If you're up for it, you can start your assignment now."

I looked to Mabel for reassurance, and by the light illuminating in her expression, I knew the answer that was popping out of her mouth.

"Yes! We are ready!" she said.

He looked to me. "And you?"

With a deep breath, I gave him a nod. "I'm ready."

A stern stare passed between us. "Remember, this is a noble task, and I trust you'll take it seriously."

"We will," I answered honestly. Even if we did manage to get into a little trouble on the side, I wouldn't shirk my duties of helping souls move onto their next life.

"Normally, Crossing Guards operate individually, but we've seen in your files that you two can't be separated."

She and I looked at each other, then looked back at him giving him a confirming nod.

"So, we will only give you one beacon and the two of you will function as one. Where one goes, the other goes, and when the beacon flashes blue to alert you to a soul in need, you'll travel to them together."

"Okay, so we stay together," I said, glad for that because there was no way I was going back to Earth without Mabel.

"Here is the manual you can refer to if you have questions, and if you get in any serious trouble, you can also press your beacon and an angel will come down to assist you. Remember, it's imperative you help these souls move on to their next journey. If they refuse to go, they become lost souls and if they stay too long…"

I remembered his words in our training. "They will get reaped and cease to exist," I said, then swallowed over the lump in my throat hoping we didn't fail any of the souls that would cross our paths.

"Good luck, ladies. Your temporary shift is two weeks, and then your beacon will go off to direct you back to a door on Earth that opens to this one. At that time, we'll check in and do an evaluation to see if you are up to this task on a more permanent basis. I hope to hear only good reports."

Again, that accusatory glance passed between us, and I

could swear he knew we were up to no good, but instead of grabbing us by the hair and casting us to Hell, he just gave a sharp nod and walked over the door.

"Safe travels."

He opened the door and I squinted against the blinding white light.

Mabel bounced on her toes, her enthusiasm infectious. "This is it. Here we go. Ready, Millie?"

I took a deep breath, trying to quell the butterflies in my stomach, a potent mix of excitement and dread bubbling up inside of me. "As ready as I'll ever be."

We stood before the door, the reality of our plan sinking in. Mabel was practically glowing with excitement, while I felt a mix of fear and anticipation.

"Just think of it as our next big adventure," Mabel said, her voice filled with confidence. "What's the worst that could happen?"

I shot her a nervous glance. "You really want me to answer that?"

She laughed, and despite my fear, I couldn't help but join in. "We've got this, Millie. Together, we can handle anything."

I nodded, feeling a surge of courage. "Alright. Let's do this."

We took a deep breath, and with a final, shared look of determination, we gripped our hands tight together and stepped through, ready to embark on our newest adventure.

Chapter Three

MABEL

Hand in hand, Millie and I stepped through the glowing doorway, the brilliant white light enveloping us. A swirling sensation overcame me as the world around us shifted and morphed.

The next thing I knew, we were standing in the midst of a bustling city street, cars whizzing by and people rushing past in a blur of motion. The sounds and smells of the urban chaos hit me like a tidal wave after the tranquil serenity of Heaven.

"Whoa..." I exhaled, looking around in awe. It had been months since I'd experienced the frenetic energy of Earth, and decades since I'd been in a big city.

Millie clutched my arm, her eyes wide. "This is... overwhelming."

"Isn't it great?" I grinned, soaking in the sights and sounds. "I'd almost forgotten what the real world felt like."

As I watched the frenzy of people rushing to and fro, I stood and absorbed everything happening around me at once. Heaven's tranquil beauty was undeniable, but there was an intensity to Earth, a vibrant energy that couldn't be replicated in the afterlife.

These people weren't just existing—they were truly living. Chasing dreams, following passions, making every second count. I envied the urgency in their steps, the determination etched on their faces. Each one was on a journey, navigating the ups and downs, the triumphs and heartbreaks that made the human experience so brilliantly messy... and utterly wonderful.

In Heaven, emotions were in a constant, unchanging state.

Happiness.

Pure, unwavering happiness.

But here, emotions flickered across expressions like a kaleidoscope. A couple holding hands radiated pure joy; a businessman barked into his phone, frustration furrowing his brow; a child's peals of laughter cut through the noises like a bright burst of sunshine. Every soul was a living, breathing masterpiece, their canvases painted in vibrant strokes of love, anger, hope, and every emotion in between.

I'd almost forgotten the raw experiences of the real world and how it felt to be truly alive. Heaven's perfection was incredible to be sure, but part of me craved the bitter to appreciate the sweet—the struggles that made the triumphs so incredibly rewarding.

As I watched a tired mother scoop her giggling toddler into an embrace, I realized what I'd been missing in my afterlife. The struggles, the heartaches... they were the balance to the eternal bliss that made you appreciate the good times… made them taste that much sweeter.

In that moment, I vowed to soak in every second of this adventure. To appreciate the chaos, the passion, the dizzying rush of the human world in a way I'd taken for granted before. This was the greatest gift—a chance to experience life anew, to let it etch itself upon my soul once more.

A car flew by close, shaking me from my nostalgic musing and nearly hitting me. I threw a fist in the air. "Watch it, buddy!"

The driver, of course, couldn't hear my protest. In fact, no one on the crowded street seemed to notice us at all.

"Hey… they can't see us!" I said, looking around at the crowd completely oblivious to our presence. "This is so weird."

Millie waved at a man on the sidewalk, and even though to me she looked like a flesh and blood human, he paid her no mind. "We're invisible! Cool!"

"I love this!" I lifted my hands in the air and started spinning around, my grin stretched wide across my face as I absorbed the wonders around me. I made another spin, and my eyes flew open as a taxicab sped straight toward us.

"Look out!" I screamed to Millie, reaching out a hand to grab her, but before we could leap out of the way, it drove right through us. I stumbled back in surprise, glancing down at my still intact body as it sped away.

"Are… are we hurt?" Millie patted herself, checking for injury.

I did the same, then looked up and smiled. "Hey! We're already dead! Nothing down here can hurt us! Heck yeah!"

Millie shuddered, her face scrunching. "That felt weird. I didn't like it. That's going to take some getting used to."

"Yeah, that was weird. But better cars can go through us than us being pavement pancakes right now." Though it didn't hurt us, I also didn't like the sensation of the car passing through me. I jutted my chin toward the sidewalk.

"Maybe let's not do that again. Come on. Let's get off the street."

"Why would they put the door to Heaven in the middle of the street?" Millie asked as she followed me.

I shrugged. "I assume Heaven's been around a lot longer than cities. That door has probably been here for millennia. Wasn't a street back then."

"Good point," Millie said as we stepped up onto the curb. "Amazing to think ghosts and Crossing Guards and all that have been living among us all this time and we were never aware."

"Nick said there are some people who can see us. I always thought those people were nuts."

She nodded. "Me too. Never believed in ghosts, yet here we are. A couple of dead gals walking around on Earth."

"Well, we know we can't get run over. That's one thing we've learned. What else can we do?" I glanced over at the newspaper dispenser beside us. Experimentally, I reached out toward it and tried to grab the handle. My otherwise solid-looking hand passed through it like smoke. I frowned. "Damn. I guess we can't interact with physical objects."

"Well, that's inconvenient," Millie grumbled.

My scowl deepened. "Yeah. That *is* inconvenient. How are we going to haunt people if they can't see us, and we can't move things?"

She shrugged. "I don't know. Maybe we're not allowed to haunt people as Crossing Guards."

My shoulders slumped. "Oh man. I really wanted to go full Casper on some people who could use a little humbling. I had my eyes set on that jerk leading Russia. What's his name? We could haunt him to the point of insanity, and then when he got locked up in the looney bin, we'd have been responsible for saving the world. Like a couple of ghostly gal superheroes."

"Oh! That's a good one! Way better than mine. I only had my sights set on Howard from our nursing home. He dug up all those beautiful flowers I planted in the garden because he didn't like the way they smelled. He killed my babies." She stuck out her lip.

My eyes flashed wide as anger reverberated in my chest that someone had been giving my Millie a hard time and I hadn't known it. "Why didn't you tell me you knew who did that? You said you had no idea. I'd have given him the business!"

"We weren't on the best terms with the nurses after we broke into the kitchen and tried making pancakes at two in the morning the week before. I knew you'd go full tilt at getting revenge and probably get us in more trouble. I figured I could get him back later, but then, well, we died."

I touched her shoulder. "Well, we may be dead, invisible, and not able to touch anything, but I bet we can find some way to torment that jerk. Let's see what else we can do as ghosts, and maybe we'll find some super power we can use to get justice! We'll practice on him and then let's go save the world by haunting that psychopath in Russia. Now, to figure out what powers we have." I pressed a finger to my chin as I started running ideas through my mind.

"Like what?" Millie asked.

"Well? I don't know. Let's play around a bit and see what we're capable of."

A man came walking past, and though he hadn't done anything to deserve a haunting, I had to try out our ghostly skills. I stuck my foot in front of him, but instead of tripping over it, he just walked right through it.

"Damn it. We can't trip people," I grumbled.

"Well, it would make sense since a taxi drove right through us."

"I had to try." I shrugged.

"Oh! Hold on. Maybe we can possess people! Like get inside of them and make them do things!"

Millie's brow furrowed in worry. "I don't want to possess anyone. That sounds terrible."

"I just want to try." I looked around and found a police officer nearby writing someone a parking ticket. "I'm just going to try hopping in him for a second."

"Mabel! What if you get stuck? I don't think you should do that!"

I just grinned and trotted over to where he was leaning forward, putting the ticket under the windshield wipers. I stepped up behind him, then with a big breath, I jumped forward into him. But instead of taking over his body and possessing him, I shrieked as I plummeted straight through him, ending up face down on the pavement under the car I'd just fallen through.

"Damn it!" I shouted from beneath it.

Millie's face appeared as she peeked down beneath it. "Are you hurt?"

Grumbling, I rose up to standing smack dab in the middle of the car's hood. "No. It doesn't seem like we feel pain in this form either because if I'd have fallen like that as an old lady human, I'd have broken a hip and been on my way to the ER."

I stepped through the car and started dusting off my clothes, but then noticed no dirt had clung to me and the whole process was in vain. "Well, that was an epic fail. We can't do *anything*!" I crossed my arms and pouted. "This whole Crossing Guard business is for the birds!"

"Well, our purpose is to help souls cross over, not haunt

people, so I'm not surprised we don't actually come equipped with haunting powers."

"I know," I admitted. "It's just that when Nick said some ghosts stay behind and can haunt, I really thought we could do it too. Maybe we can if we practice a little."

I looked over at a man passing by and leaped in front of him with one last ditch attempt to possess him. "Gah!" I screamed as I tried to dive into him. Instead, I ended up on the pavement with unaware pedestrians stepping through me.

"Oh, Mabel!" Millie shouted and hurried to help me up. "What were you thinking?"

I grumbled as a woman's shoe went through my head, then I took Millie's hand, and she lifted me to my feet.

"Possession. Not a thing," I said, once again going to dust myself off then remembering it was unnecessary.

"Your haunting skills, or lack thereof, are really something, Mabel. Maybe we should just forgo the haunting thing and just do the Crossing Guard shift then go back to Heaven and stay there," Millie said.

"Even if we can't haunt, I do still like just being down here, I guess," I admitted. "It's fun watching the humans even if we can't scare the crap out of them for funsies." An idea popped into my head, and I smirked. "Wait. If we can't haunt people, that doesn't mean there may not be other cool stuff we can do. Since we're ghosts down here, I wonder if we can…"

"If we can what?" Millie asked.

With excitement fluttering in my chest, hoping with everything I had it was possible, I bent my knees and pushed off the ground, letting out a whoop of delight as I defied gravity and floated a few feet in the air. "Check it out, Millie! We can fly!"

She gasped, her hands flying to her mouth. "Mabel, get down from there! Someone's going to see you!"

I rolled my eyes. "Who's going to see me? We're invisible, remember?"

To prove my point, I drifted over to a young woman buried in her phone, waving my hand directly in front of her face. "Boo!" I screamed at her. She didn't even flinch, continuing on her way. "See?" I called down to Millie. "Completely undetectable. Come on, Millie! Try it! This is amazing!" I did a little flip, got disoriented and had to fight to steady myself. "Okay. Baby steps. Maybe just try floating up here with me."

She pursed her lips, concern tightening her face. "In Heaven, only the angels can fly. Are you sure we're supposed to be doing this?"

"I mean, I don't think we'd be able to if we weren't allowed. Maybe as Crossing Guards, we're like temporary angels? Or maybe since we're ghosts down here, it's the ghosts who can fly? I don't know why, but I'm doing it!" I tried to fly higher but couldn't get more than ten feet off the ground. It was still exhilarating to be drifting above the people below me. I practiced going higher and lower, stopping periodically to make faces at people as I hovered upside down in front of them. I stuck my tongue out at a woman talking loudly on her phone, and for good measure, I tried, and failed, to boop her in the nose.

"Come on, Millie! You're missing all the fun! We're already dead, you can't get hurt. Lord knows I've just proved that several times. Just try it, this is amazing!"

After a moment's hesitation, she bent her knees and pushed off the ground, joining me in the air. A scream escaped her lips and then turned into a nervous giggle as she hovered uncertainly.

"I'm doing it! I'm flying!" she said, then wobbled a bit and reached over and grabbed my hand. "This is so strange."

"But fun, right?" I did a little twirl, reveling in the newfound freedom of flight.

A laugh bubbled up from her chest. "Okay, yes, it's a little fun."

We spent the next few minutes spinning, twirling, and zipping through the air, putting our new abilities to the test. At one point, Millie let out a shriek as she accidentally passed through a building, ending up on the other side of the wall.

"Jiminy Josephats. I don't recommend that," she said as she rejoined me. "It's incredibly disorienting."

"Noted," I said, though admittedly, now I wanted to try it.

As we floated above the bustling sidewalk, watching the humans scurry about, a wistful expression crossed Millie's face. "I'd almost forgotten how alive this place feels. The sights, the sounds, the smells... it's all so vibrant."

"Yeah..." I inhaled deeply, catching a whiff of exhaust fumes and street food. "It's a sensory overload after Heaven's perfection."

"Don't get me wrong, Heaven is wonderful," Millie said quickly. "But there's something about the chaos of Earth that's... invigorating."

A loud honk from below made us both jump. Two irate drivers were shouting at each other, shaking their fists out of rolled-down windows.

"Geez, some things never change," I remarked dryly.

We watched, transfixed, as the argument escalated, the two men gesturing wildly. Suddenly, one of them threw open his door and stormed toward the other car, fists raised.

Millie gasped. "Oh geez, this isn't going to end well."

Intrigued, I drifted closer, positioning myself near the irate man as he reached the other driver's window. Just as he reared back his fist, I attempted to grab his arm, hoping to somehow intervene.

My ghostly fingers passed through his flesh like they were made of air.

"What the...?" I yanked my hand back in surprise, staring at it in confusion. Then I remembered I couldn't interact with anything on this plane. "Crap. I can't stop him!"

The man's punch connected with a sickening thud, and the other driver crumpled back against his seat, clutching a bloody nose.

The driver pushed open his door, coming out swinging at the man who'd just punched him. I tried again to break up the fight.

"Hey!" I yelled, even though I knew they couldn't hear me. "Cut that out!"

Millie rushed to my side, her eyes wide with distress. "Mabel, be careful!"

"They can't hurt us, and we can't do anything! We're just ghosts! Damn it!" I got in the man's face, screaming at the top of my lungs for him to stop, but he wasn't the least bit aware of my presence. "When I figure out how to haunt people, you're first on my list, you big jerk!"

But right now, we couldn't do anything other than watch the world passing us by while we were just a breath away from it all. As the two men pummeled each other, the harsh reality of our situation settled over me like a cold blanket. We were powerless to interact with the living world, mere observers in this chaotic realm.

As the fight continued to escalate, I heard a loud crash

from down the street. We gasped as we turned toward the commotion, and I clutched my chest when I saw a woman lying limp on the street beside her mangled bike.

A man jumped out of his car. "I didn't see her! Oh no! Someone call 911!"

A crowd gathered around her, and a voice called out. "She's not breathing!"

Millie and I stood frozen watching the panicked crowd. The driver paced back and forth, his hands on his head as he sobbed to his friend, who'd been the passenger. "I saw the fight happening, and I just looked away from the road for a second. I didn't mean to hit her. I didn't see her. Oh my God. Please don't let her die."

But as they started performing CPR, our eyes got wide as the soul of the woman rose from her body. She stood beside it, staring down at her lifeless corpse, the confusion etched on her young face.

"Am… am I dead? Oh my God. Is that me? Help! Someone help!" she called, but she was invisible to everyone but us.

Millie's hands flew to her face. "Oh no! She died! That young woman died!"

I stared in shock at the spirit, still trying to process the events that led to her untimely demise, and that I was, indeed, staring at the spirit of a woman who had just been alive and enjoying a bike ride only moments ago.

"What do we do? Is she ours? We're Crossing Guards. Does that mean we help her?" Millie asked, panic lifting her voice several octaves.

I glanced at the beacon on my wrist that wasn't going off. "I don't think she's ours, but I don't know if that matters? Can we help her cross? Are we supposed to just wait until this thing lights up? That's what they said, right?

Our beacon will go off when we're supposed to go get a stuck soul." I tapped the beacon strapped to my wrist like a watch, but it didn't light up.

So, unsure what to do, we just stood there, frozen.

"She's so scared," Millie finally said, her voice choked with tears as we continued watching from a distance for another minute. "Whether she's ours or not, we should go and talk to her. Oh wait! The manual! I forgot they sent us down with a manual! Let's see what it says about this."

"That's right!" I started reaching into my sweater's pocket to retrieve it, but suddenly a flash of light lit up the world around the new ghost, and from inside the glowing halo, a man stepped out and stepped up beside the newly deceased woman.

We stumbled to a stop. "Is that—" Millie started.

"Another Crossing Guard." I finished her sentence.

We stood immobile in the street watching from a distance. He slipped an arm around her shoulder, comforting her as they spoke for a minute, and then, with one last glance at her body, she nodded and reached out a hand toward him. He smiled softly as he held it, and then she disappeared in a flash of bright light, a small orb drifting higher and higher until it finally disappeared from sight. The Crossing Guard remained after she was gone, and he looked up after her for one last glance, then with a flash of bright light, he disappeared into the glowing vortex.

We stood in silent awe for a long moment, then Millie whispered, "One of us just helped that soul cross over."

"Yeah. He did. That was really something to see."

Suddenly, the weight of our new role settled over me like a sacred mantle. As I'd watched the Crossing Guard gently guide that poor woman's soul to its final rest, something deep within me shifted.

In that profound moment, the world seemed to still. The noise of the city faded into silence as clarity washed over me. This wasn't a game, or some excuse to chase the childish whims that had sent us to Earth in the first place. We had been entrusted with a sacred purpose—to shepherd lost souls and ensure their journey didn't end in aimless wandering.

"That was so sad. I... I don't know if I can do this, Mabel," Millie whispered, her eyes glistening with unshed tears.

"We can do this, Millie. I realize now that coming down here to haunt people isn't our main purpose. We have a duty to perform, and it's an important one. We're not going to fail." Wrapping an arm around her shoulders, I pulled her close. "Hey, we've got this, remember? We'll figure it out together, just like we always do."

She nodded, managing a watery smile. "Together."

As the wailing sirens of approaching ambulances filled the air, I continued feeling my newfound sense of purpose. Our adventure had taken an unexpectedly solemn turn, but I knew we were up for the challenge.

Chapter Four

MILLIE

The shrill blare of sirens faded into the distance, leaving Mabel and me standing in somber silence on the sidewalk. The weight of what we'd just witnessed—a soul tragically ripped from this world—settled over us like a heavy shroud.

"Well, after that, I could use a drink," Mabel murmured, her brow furrowed.

We may not have needed sustenance as ghosts, but that didn't mean we wouldn't enjoy a stiff drink at times like these. "Yeah. Good idea. I think I saw a bar down the street. Want to go there and conjure up a couple margaritas? Pretend it's like the old days where we'd go to happy hour together when we were younger?" I suggested, picturing the little tavern with the glowing neon sign we'd passed by during our flying experiment.

"I remember passing one, too. Want to see if we can blink ourselves into it? Kafziel said we could transport ourselves all over the place with our thoughts. We gotta practice that."

"Sure, let's try." I reached for her hand, and she gripped it tight.

But instead of going anywhere, we just stood there wearing matching confused expressions. "Um, how do we do this?"

I shrugged. "I don't know. The crash course the angels put us through covered this, but I can't quite remember the specifics. I was too busy panicking they were going to find out what we were planning and send us to Hell. Should we pull out the manual they sent us with?"

She shook her head. "Nah. I think I remember. We just have to close our eyes and think of where we want to be, and we should materialize there."

"Okay. Let's try harder. On three, we both think of sitting on the stools at the bar. 1, 2…3!" She squeezed her eyes shut, her face scrunched in concentration as I closed my eyes and braced myself for whatever may happen. But instead of the swirling vortex I'd seen the Crossing Guard use—and fully expected to appear—nothing happened..

Mabel and I opened our eyes and looked at each other.

"We're still here." She frowned.

"Seriously?" My shoulders slumped. "We are the worst ghosts ever! We can't even teleport ourselves, and I'm pretty sure they said that's a thing. And that other Crossing Guard just appeared out of thin air. Ugh. We stink at this!"

"Maybe we have to have been somewhere before to just appear there? I kinda remember them mentioning that. Crap. I'll get the manual." Mabel fished the Crossing Guard manual out of her pocket. She flipped through the pages, mumbling under her breath.

As she pored over the rules, I started to truly question if signing up to be Crossing Guards was one of the worst decisions we'd made in our lives… or afterlives in this case. I knew Mabel was restless in Heaven, and I was too, but now that we were actually down here, my anxiety boiled up to near unbearable levels.

I was always the worrier of the two of us. Which sometimes did us good when my endless worrying made us rethink a bad plan and it kept us out of trouble. But I'd gone along with this hairbrained haunting plan because it was the most excited I'd seen Mabel in months. But now as we continued failing epically as ghosts and seeing that poor girl die had made this whole Crossing Guard this all too real, I wondered if maybe we should hit the emergency beacon they mentioned, summon an angel to help us and go home, pretending this never happened.

"Ha! I got it. We have to have at least seen the place. Either in person or in photos. So, we can't just blink anywhere in the world with a thought unless we've at least seen a photo. We were trying to picture the inside of a bar we've never been to, so that won't work."

Not wanting to ruin her excitement by telling her I wanted to go home, I swallowed my anxiety like a lump of hot coal. "Can we transport ourselves to the street in front of the bar that we saw?"

"That should work. Let's think of the front of the bar we both saw when we were floating around. We have to have an actual visual, and we both saw that."

We linked fingers, and I focused my mental energy on the bar's red front door, visualizing every detail I could remember from the neon beer signs in the windows to the sign that said "Pine Street Bar" that desperately needed a fresh coat of paint.

Suddenly, a swirling vortex opened before us and pulled us in. We squealed in both fear and delight as we gripped each other tighter, then after a dizzying, disorienting journey through the bright light, we popped out of the vortex together.

"Yes! Nailed it!" Mabel pumped her fist in the air triumphantly. "We're getting the hang of this ghost gig!" Then she leaned forward, placing her hands on her knees as she steadied herself. "Oh, crap. I'm dizzy."

I teetered on my feet trying to get my bearings with what felt like the Earth moving beneath my feet. "Whoa. I feel drunk."

"Not the good drunk either," Mabel added.

After a few moments of stabilizing ourselves, we finally felt the shaking world steady.

"That was so weird." Now that I wasn't so dizzy I felt like I may topple over, I looked around at our surroundings, noting we'd landed right where we'd wanted to go. "But it worked! We're here! So, lesson number one. We can only blink ourselves to places we've seen with our own eyes. Got it."

"Let's go in the bar and take a good look around so we can pop back anytime we need a cold one." Mabel grinned and walked to the front door, pausing when she went to open it and her hand went through the handle.

"Um." I stood there, head tipped as I realized our issue. "How are we going to get in if we can't open the door? Just stand here and wait for someone to come open it and sneak in?"

Mabel smirked. "Or maybe we can do this."

Before I could argue, she stepped straight through the door, disappearing on the other side.

"Mabel!" I called, my heart rate revving up as I stood there alone on the street. "Mabel! Where are you?"

Her head popped back through the wood. "Right here! It works. Come on in!"

With my heart palpitating inside my chest, but just like we had often done in life, I put aside my worries and followed Mabel's lead. I stepped up to the door, then with a deep breath, I stepped through.

The familiar scents of stale beer and greasy food enveloped us, sparking a strange sense of comfort. We'd spent many a night in a dive bar throughout our decades together. In our youth, they'd often ended with her dancing on the bar and me finally joining her after I'd had enough cocktails to conjure up her natural bravado.

Mabel immediately made a beeline for the scarred wooden bar, and I trailed after her, sinking onto one of the tattered stools. I glanced down, noting that we didn't fall through the stools, or even the floor for that matter, and I wondered about ghost physics and why that was.

But before I could ponder the thought out loud, Mabel shouted, "Two margaritas, please!"

I started to open my mouth to remind her that he couldn't hear or see her when she grinned at me.

"Just kidding. We're invisible. Hold on. I'll conjure us up some drinks." She squeezed her eyes shut, and when she opened her eyes, her face fell. "What the hell? Why can't I make them appear?"

I did the same, closing my eyes like I did in Heaven and willing two perfectly mixed up margaritas with salt on the rim into my hands.

Nothing happened.

Realization dawned on me. "Mabel, I don't think we can just blink things into existence anymore. We're not in Heaven."

"Are you kidding me?" She smacked the bar in frustration, her hand passing through the weathered wood. "No bottomless margaritas? No endless chocolate cake? What's even the point? No wonder they have a shortage of Crossing Guards. Who in the hell wants to give up endless desserts on a whim for an existence of smelling all this delicious food and not being able to enjoy it?"

I had to admit, the prospect of being denied the sweet nectar of sugar for the duration of our stint was a bitter pill to swallow. "Well, that's certainly an unexpected downside of this gig. Maybe we should have paid more attention during our orientation. I was too busy panicking they were going to bust us for our true intentions to really listen."

Scowling, Mabel turned back toward the bar. A man on the stool beside us played on his phone and his cold beer sat unattended on the cardboard coaster. Clearly determined to seize a drink by any means possible, she reached out and grasped at the half-empty beer bottle, her fingers slipping through the glass like it wasn't even there.

"Damn it!" she spit. "I want that beer!" She tried again, her hand swiping back and forth through the bottle.

"Mabel, just give it up. We can't interact with anything on this plane. We should just feel lucky we don't fall through the ground and end up stuck in the molten core of the earth for eternity."

"I just want a sip, Millie. Is that asking too much? Just give it to me! Damn it!"

I placed a hand on my head and let out an exasperated sigh as she continued her fruitless attempts at securing us a beer. As she continued her desperate attempt to grab it, I reached out and touched her shoulder.

"That's enough, Mabel. You're stressing me out."

But then, something miraculous happened. Suddenly, her fingers seemed to catch on the bottle, sending it wobbling precariously. Mabel froze, her eyes widening in shock, and we watched in stunned silence as the bottle teetered back and forth before settling upright once more.

"Did you see that?" she gasped, whipping toward me with unbridled glee dancing in her eyes. "I touched it! I actually touched it!"

A jolt of excitement rushed through me as I studied her hands, trying to discern what sort of trick had allowed her to manipulate the physical world, if only for a moment. "How did you do that?"

"I have no idea!" She turned back toward the bar, her brow furrowed in determination as she reached for the bottle again. This time, her fingers slipped through effortlessly, as if the brief moment of contact had been nothing more than a tantalizing illusion. "Ugh, come on!"

Grunting with effort, Mabel strained and reached, swiping at glasses and bottles with increasing ferocity. Nothing. Her hands passed through every solid object, her motions growing more frantic with each failure.

"Mabel, calm down," I urged, placing a cautionary hand on her arm. "Getting worked up isn't going to—"

The instant my fingers made contact with her skin, Mabel's fingers contacted the beer bottle, and it wobbled again, ever so slightly. We locked eyes, realization dawning in twin sparks of understanding.

"Hold my hand," I whispered, awestruck. "I think… I think it works if we're touching."

She grasped my fingers without hesitation, and we turned in unison toward the bar. Channeling every ounce of ethereal energy, we extended our joined hands and pressed against the bottle. At first, we went straight through it, but undeterred, we tried again, straining with the effort of each movement.

"Come on, Millie! We've got to believe. We can do this. Together."

My face twisted with determination as we made another attempt, refusing to relent, gritting our teeth and pouring our combined focus into the task.

And then…

I felt it against my fingertips, and we both gasped as the bottle toppled over, spilling the remainder of its golden, hoppy contents onto the bar. The man jumped up from his seat, swearing at the wasted beer pouring off the bar.

"Holy crap!" I breathed. "We did it! We touched it!"

"Whoo!" Mabel shouted triumphantly. "We touched it!"

"It worked. I can't believe it worked!"

"I knew we could do it. Together, we can do anything."

We grinned at each other, then leaped up and began jumping around holding hands as we hopped around in a circle. It was something we'd done often as children, but in the last decades of our lives, our arthritic joints and achy bones wouldn't allow for such physical enthusiasm. But here we were in our aged bodies hopping and floating around the bar with reckless abandon.

"Oh, man, so awesome. Do you know what this means, Millie?" Mabel asked as she floated back down onto her bar stool.

"What?" I asked, joining her.

"We can haunt people." She grinned widely, her eyes shining with that familiar mischief I knew so well.

Even though the nervous nelly in me feared the repercussions if we followed this trail to haunting people, I could never say no to Mabel when she looked at me with so much excitement in her eyes. Her crazy ideas had often turned into the most fun and memorable moments of my life, and I hoped that perhaps this hairbrained haunting idea of hers would pan out the same way and become one of the most memorable moments of my afterlife.

My musing was abruptly shattered by a piercing beep slicing through the din. Mabel's gaze snapped to the blue blinking beacon on her wrist as the meaning dawned in her eyes.

"Oh, my. This is it. The beacon. That means… a soul needs us." Her voice was hushed, the somberness of our purpose settling over us both.

As if struck by a bucket of cold water, the thrilling adrenaline coursing through my veins turned to lead. A shiver of trepidation slithered down my spine as I considered the somber task that lay ahead—to comfort a confused spirit as they said goodbye to their mortal life.

"Oh no. I'm panicking. I can't remember anything they told us about how this thing works." I started fanning my face, my nerves crackling inside me like lightning bolts exploding beneath my skin.

Mabel danced in place, shaking out her hands as she did her little preparation dance she'd done often in life. "Okay. Okay. We got this. We got this. Okay… I forgot to too. Why didn't they train us longer! How irresponsible to just drop us down here with no supervisor!"

We looked at each other, wide eyes mirroring each other, then finally, Mabel, as usual, seemed to pull herself together first. "Okay. Okay. We have to get to this soul, but we can't use the vortex because we don't know where they are. What did they say in the training? We'd just know?"

"The manual!" I reminded her, my brain finally started to function outside the panic. "Look in the manual!"

Mabel's eyes lit up, and she opened the manual and quickly located the appropriate section, scanning the instructions with a furrowed brow. "Here it is! The distress beacon works as a guide, so we can go anywhere in the world even if we haven't been there. We just have to close our eyes and look at the beacon. It has the soul's coordinates embedded in it, and it will portal us where we need to go."

"I'm scared," I admitted, terrified of what would be awaiting us on the other end of that call.

Mabel's shoulders rose and fell in a deep breath as she steeled herself. "I'm scared too. But there is a soul out there more scared than us right now, and they need us. We can do this. Together. Ready?"

"As I'll ever be," I replied, matching her somber tone.

Unsure I was ready for what awaited us on the other side of the vortex, I took a stilling breath and remembered the sanctity of our mission and the consequences that awaited any soul we failed to usher over. We joined hands once more, but this time our palms were slick, our grip tightened by a sense of grim purpose. In silent unison, we honed our thoughts on the faint, blinking beacon, letting its gentle pulse guide us through the vortex to the lost soul awaiting us.

Chapter Five

MABEL

A dizzying vortex engulfed us as we followed the beacon's summons. The world blurred and shifted like a painting left out in the rain until, with a sickening lurch, our surroundings reformed into a secluded park bathed in inky darkness.

"Whoa..." I exhaled, trying to get my bearings.

Beside me, Millie shuddered, her arms wrapped tightly around her torso. "This place gives me the creeps."

I couldn't disagree. The park was cloaked in eerie shadows, the looming trees like gnarled sentinels guarding the secrets of the night. An unnatural hush blanketed the grounds, as if the very air held its breath in anticipation.

Someone had just died here. A shudder traveled up my spine thinking of what fate may have awaited them. I passed warm and safe in my bed, but from the eerie feeling piercing my gut, I doubted this soul had experienced such a tranquil end to their human existence.

Then, like a whisper on the night breeze, I heard it—a soft, muffled whimper slicing through the uneasy silence. Millie's head whipped toward the sound, her eyes widening in alarm when they landed upon a hunched figure near the tree line.

A young woman stood frozen beside a crumpled form obscured by the bushes. Even in the feeble glow of the moonlight, I could make out the unmistakable shape of a body, limp and motionless on the damp earth.

The whimper escaped the woman's lips again—a fragile, keening sound laced with anguish and disbelief. As we drifted closer, her outline came into focus, and the terrible realization washed over me in icy waves.

This was our soul. The one who had sparked the distress beacon's otherworldly cry for help.

Beside me, Millie's hand flew to her mouth, smothering a soft gasp of horror. "Oh, my Heavens..."

I could only nod, my voice failing me as I struggled to process the disturbing scene before us. The woman seemed so young, her face hauntingly beautiful even in her anguish. What could have ripped her from this world in her prime?

Once more, that mournful whimper pierced the night, and it was enough to snap me from my stunned trance. Steadying my nerves, I reached out and gently placed my hand on the woman's arm. Her long dark-brown hair secured in a ponytail brushed against my skin and startled me that I could feel it. Instead of my fingers slipping through her flesh like smoke as they did with humans, they gently gripped her chilled skin.

She spun around to face us, wild blue eyes meeting mine.

"Don't be afraid. We're here to help," I whispered, trying to keep my tone calm even though I felt anything but. "You're not alone."

"Who… who are you? What's happening?" Her voice quavered, edged with panic.

Millie stepped forward, her face etched with gentle compassion. "It's alright, dear. We're... friends. Guides of sorts."

The beautiful woman's brow furrowed as she peered at us. "Guides? What kind of guides? I don't understand…" Her eyes drifted back toward the crumpled form at her feet. "I… don't understand."

"We're called Crossing Guards," I explained softly. "We're here to help you cross over to the other side."

A violent shudder racked her slight frame as fresh horror bloomed in her eyes. "That's... me. I'm dead, aren't I?"

The anguish in her words cut straight to my core. Here was a poor soul ripped from her mortal life, forced to stare down at her cruel fate. The body lay motionless in a growing pool of blood, and my stomach lurched when I saw the lethal wound to her neck. This was no accident. She had been… murdered.

I spun around looking for her killer, my heart jumping into my throat thinking he could still be nearby. But instead, I saw nothing but the darkness lit only by the faint moonlight illuminating the world just enough to make out the blurred features of our surroundings.

Wordlessly, Millie moved closer until she stood mere inches away. With a soft touch, she tried to comfort the lost soul. "I'm so sorry, dear. No one should have to endure such a tragedy. What's your name?"

Fat tears welled in the woman's eyes, her lips trembling as she fought to maintain her fragile composure. "Leslie. My name is Leslie. How...how did this happen? I was just on my evening run, same as every night, and then..."

Her words fractured, shattering on a ragged indrawn breath. I could only imagine the terror that must have gripped her, the sheer visceral panic of facing one's own mortality in such a violent manner. An image flashed before my mind's eye—of this vibrant woman ambushed upon the darkened path, her life brutally extinguished before she could even process the attack.

Unbidden, fury blazed hot within my breast toward the unknown assailant that had committed such an unforgivable act. This poor girl, so brimming with youthful vitality, had been denied even the chance to truly live out her destiny. It was an injustice that struck at the very core of my being.

Before I could reign in my emotions, the words tumbled forth in a furious torrent. "What happened? Who did this to you?"

For an agonizing moment, the woman could only stare at me as if rendered mute by the depth of her shock and grief. At last, she found her voice once more, the words emerging in a tremulous whisper.

"That woman... she just... she came out of nowhere. For no reason, she..." Her breath hitched, momentarily derailing her fraught recollection as she reached up and touched her neck. "She slit my throat. It happened so fast."

The stark truth hung in the air, more horrible than I could have imagined. Senselessly slaughtered like cattle led to the killing floor—that was this poor girl's fate. A scream of impotent rage built in my throat, but I choked it down for her sake. She required my strength now, not my fury.

"Oh, you poor dear..." Millie's wavering voice was thick with tenderness and compassion. "Such a cruel, cruel injustice."

The woman bowed her head as if the weight of her anguish was too much to bear. "I'm only twenty-five. I had my whole life ahead of me. And now... now I'm just... gone. And… what happens now? I'm so scared."

Her gaze lifted, eyes swimming with unshed tears.

"I promise you, there is nothing to be afraid of anymore. Where you're going, there is peace and respite from all of this world's cruelties."

Millie picked up the thread, her voice low and soothing. "There is a place unlike anything you can fathom where your spirit will be bathed in eternal warmth and light. A place of boundless love and wonder, where all the anguish you've endured here on this mortal plane melts away like a forgotten nightmare."

The woman stared at us, lips parted in a soft 'oh' of reverence. For a fleeting instant, the fear and bewilderment sloughed from her features, leaving behind a look of hope.

"There's really an afterlife? A… Heaven?" she asked quietly.

Millie leaped at the chance to answer. "Oh, yes, dear. And it truly is wonderful. No pain. No suffering. Anything you want you can just blink into existence." Her eyes widened. "Like cake! You can just make it appear in your hand anytime you want. It's wonderful. Oh! And margaritas, and chocolate eclairs, and ice cream. Or if you don't like sweet things, you can do spaghetti or if you're into raw fish some sushi. I don't like sushi so I haven't tried Heaven's sushi, but everything you eat is the best food you've ever had, so if you're into sushi, I'm sure it's delicious. And if you like bread a nice sourdough is nice from time to time—"

I rolled my eyes, embarrassed Millie was starting on one of her anxiety-driven ramblings. "Cripes sake, Millie. She gets it. She can make things appear. We don't have to list off every food in the world." I turned back to our soul. "Sorry. She talks too much when she gets nervous."

Millie sucked the air through her teeth. "It's true. I do.

But I just meant to tell you that I know you're going to be sad leaving this world, but I promise you that the Heaven awaiting you is beyond even your wildest dreams. Everyone you've lost will be there, and some day, when it's their time, you'll be reunited with all the loved ones you're leaving behind."

She glanced down at her lifeless form. "I… I wasn't ready yet."

Millie stroked her shoulder. "I know, dear. But your time here has passed whether you want it to or not. All you can do now is take the next step and start your journey to Heaven."

"How?" she asked.

Though I wasn't entirely sure if it was the answer, I remembered seeing the other Crossing Guard help the soul pass through when they held hands. I extended my hand toward her, hovering a hair's breadth from making contact. "Just take my hand. Leave this broken, bloodied body and the cruelty of this world behind. You'll find solace and happiness in the next life awaiting you."

For a long, suspended heartbeat, her gaze searched mine, unspoken questions flickering in the depths of her soulful eyes. At last, she gave a tentative nod, squaring her shoulders as she mustered her resolve.

"Are you ready?" I asked, my hands awaiting her grasp.

"Yes..." she whispered, reaching out her hand to hover parallel to mine. "I'm ready."

Beside me, Millie beamed with pride, her radiant smile a soothing balm in the darkness that surrounded us. We didn't dare shatter the powerful moment with further words. Instead, I focused every ounce of my being, trusting my spectral instincts as I channeled our connection to Heaven, calling upon the angels to sweep this sad soul into their embrace.

Her hand gripped mine, and a soft gasp fell from her lips as my power took hold. Her edges blurred and shimmered like a mirage, then in the span of a heartbeat, her form diffused into a warm, pulsing radiance that engulfed her in a cocoon of pure, sublime energy. And then the woman's essence streamed skyward in a shimmering orb of light, dancing and twirling as it ascended toward Heaven.

Millie and I watched in awestruck silence, our hands still extended as if to cradle the departing soul in a final, tender embrace. Even as the last flickers of glimmering light winked out of sight, I could feel the residual warmth of her energy clinging to me like a lingering caress.

"That was..." Millie's voice emerged as a whisper, her eyes still fixed upon the star-covered sky where the woman's spirit had disappeared.

"Beautiful," I finished, my own voice hushed with wonder.

For a long moment, we simply stood there, allowing the weight of the experience to settle over us. In the span of mere minutes, we had borne witness to the most intimate and profound of transitions—the passage of a soul from the mortal realm to the eternal.

It was a responsibility that should have left me trembling with trepidation. After all, who was I to guide a spirit through such a monumental crossing? Yet, as I replayed the woman's final moments in my mind's eye, I couldn't help but feel a swell of pride and purpose.

We had offered her solace in her darkest hour, a lifeline of hope to cling to as she navigated the emotions and aftermath of her own death. Our presence, even though it wasn't the reason we had come here, had meant everything to her in that final moment of her time on Earth.

Millie turned to me, her eyes bright with unshed tears and a fierce, determined glint. "We did it, Mabel. We really did it."

I nodded, a smile tugging at the corners of my mouth. "We did. And you know what? I think we're going to be pretty damn good at this whole Crossing Guard gig."

She laughed a soft, happy sound that dispelled the last lingering shadows of sorrow. "I think you're right. Who would've thought, huh? You and me, a couple of mischief-makers turned soul shepherds."

"Stranger things have happened," I said, bumping my shoulder against hers in a playful gesture. "And who said we can't be soul shepherds *and* mischief makers. I mean, we can manipulate some things in the earthly realm now."

My eyebrow raised and she caught my meaning. We dissolved into a fit of giggles, the tension of the moment dissipating like mist beneath the sun. It felt good to laugh, to remember that even in the midst of such somber duties, we could still find joy and levity in each other's company.

Millie looked around, and her face soured as she looked down at the corpse of our friend who'd now moved on. "Can we get out of here? This is really unpleasant."

I nodded, ushering her away from the grisly scene. "Yes. Our work here is done. Let's go."

"Where should we go next?" she asked as we walked away.

"I know where we can go now." A mischievous smile lifted one corner of my lips. "How about we visit Howard at our old retirement home and get a little justice for your plants."

"Oh, Mabel. We can't," she whispered as if someone may hear us.

"We have nothing to do until this beacon goes off again and another soul needs our help. I say we go have a little fun with the unfilled time we've got down here. That was our original plan after all."

I waited for her to go through the motions of worry that always prefaced our adventures, and then finally, I saw the familiar flicker of excitement in her eyes.

"Well, I suppose a little harmless haunting couldn't hurt. Just nothing so bad it can get in trouble with the afterlife authorities... right?"

I grinned widely. "Howard's getting a haunting."

She looked nervous at my words, but then she grinned back at me. "Okay. Let's do it."

My smile stretched across my face as it matched hers. We both glanced back up to the starry sky above us to pay tribute to our poor soul one last time, then we grasped hands and thought of the nursing home we'd called home for years—the nursing home an unsuspecting Howard was waiting in for a couple of pissed off ghostly gals.

Chapter Six

MILLIE

Moments later, we found ourselves standing in the familiar hallway of Shady Oaks Retirement Home. The overwhelming scent of antiseptic and potpourri flooded into my nose, bringing back a rush of memories.

"Oh, man. I forgot how much they love that horrible potpourri here." I scrunched my face.

"I definitely don't miss that. Blech." Mabel scrunched her face as well. "It smells like a bad car air freshener in here. We'd better hurry up and haunt Howard quick so we can get the hell out of here. Let's go find him." Mabel rubbed her hands together, her eyes glinting with mischief.

I nodded, a nervous flutter dancing inside my belly. We crept down the hallway, peeking into rooms until we spotted Howard sitting in his favorite armchair in the small lobby, engrossed in a book. My mind flashed back to the times he had been cruel to me. He was always such a grump to everyone, but it seemed he had a particular mean streak to all the women in the home. Making fun of our clothes, our hair, our bodies. Like he thought he was some catch and he was stuck in here with all us "rotting corpses" as he often said. It'd been one thing to make fun of me, but when I remembered finding my cherished flowers ripped from the ground tossed in a wilted heap, anger started building in my chest. Picking on me was one thing but going after them was another.

"Okay. What's the plan?" I asked as we stood in front of him. "The only skill we have was kinda moving that beer bottle."

"Watch this," Mabel whispered, her face scrunched in concentration as she focused on the book in Howard's hands. She strained and grunted, trying to make it fly out of his grasp, but the book remained firmly in place. Undeterred, she tried again, this time targeting the lamp beside him. It wobbled slightly, but Howard seemed oblivious to the disturbance.

"Ugh!" Mabel grunted in frustration.

"Remember, for some reason, we could only move that bottle when we touched. Like we combined our energy or something."

"That's right! Okay, let's try it and see if we can smash this lamp and scare the crap out of him."

I placed my hand on Mabel's shoulder, lending my energy to hers. I felt it, that small current flowing through us like two rivers converging into one. Together, we channeled our focus on the lamp, willing it to move. It shook more violently, finally drawing Howard's attention. He glanced up, confusion etched on his weathered face, but it shook for only a second than stopped. He looked at it perplexed for a moment then returned to his book.

Mabel's shoulders slumped as her arms fell to her sides. "I gave it all I had and it barely moved! It's too big. But still! That lamp wiggled on its own. He should be terrified right now. Why isn't he running out of the room screaming?"

I shrugged. "It was barely noticeable. A wind could have wobbled it more. Too easy to explain away in your mind."

"This is harder than I thought," Mabel muttered, frustration evident in her tone.

"Maybe we need more practice," I suggested, though admittedly I felt defeated by our lackluster results. I hated to admit how much I wanted to see terror in his eyes as he raced from his room screaming it was haunted. No one would believe him, of course, and my revenge would be complete in him being the laughingstock of our retirement home peers.

Lost in thought envisioning him getting laughed at everywhere he went as he muttered on about his haunting, I almost missed the flicker of movement in my peripheral vision. I turned to see an older lady standing beside a nurse, casually blowing air across her face. The nurse didn't seem to see the little woman blowing in her face, and continued swatting in front of her as if she could bat away the gusts. Frustrated, she got up and moved seats. The little woman followed her and began her gentle blowing once more, much to the frustration of the nurse.

"Mabel, look," I whispered, pointing at her. "I think that woman is a ghost."

"What? Where?" Mabel slowly turned to where I pointed.

"Where is that breeze coming from. I can't get away from it." The irritated nurse stood again and stomped off while the little ghost with the head of tight grey curls giggled as she left.

"Is she… haunting this place?" Mabel asked with a gasp.

"I… I think she is. And she was able to blow on that nurse's face and make her think there was a breeze following her. She can do things!"

Without a hint of hesitation, Mabel started toward her. "Okay. She must be one of the ghosts they were talking about. The stuck souls! We gotta meet her."

"Mabel, wait! We don't know if she's friendly!" I clutched her shirt, yanking her back toward me.

Mabel turned and looked at me, her eyebrow inching up. "Are you scared of ghosts, Millie? Because I hate to break it to you, but we *are* ghosts."

I hated to admit deep down I *was* scared of the ghost. Even though she was right, and we were ghosts ourselves, it was still surreal and scary knowing there was a spirit haunting this place.

Mabel pressed a hand on my shoulder and squeezed. "She can't hurt us, remember? We're dead."

I bit my lip then nodded, and it was only a second later brave Mabel spun back toward her and called out "Hey! Ghost! Who are you?"

"Oh, geez," I breathed, terrified to see the woman look up at us, surprise registering on her slightly translucent features.

"You… you can see me!" She grinned and moved toward us. "Hello there. I'm Hazel. It's been awhile since I've seen another ghost around here."

"Well, she seems friendly enough," I whispered to Mabel.

Mabel and I exchanged a curious glance, then I stayed behind Mabel who strode right toward her without a hint of caution in her steps.

"We're Mabel and Millie," Mabel explained.

"Oh, wait. I remember you two. You just kicked the

bucket a few months ago. I thought you moved on? Haven't seen you around. What are you doing back here?"

"We did," I said quickly. "We went to Heaven and have been up there ever since, but we volunteered to come back down and be Crossing Guards to help newly departed spirits pass on."

"Oh, you're one of those goody two-shoes." She rolled her eyes. "Yeah, I've seen your kind come and go over the years when they come to pick someone up."

"Didn't you get a Crossing Guard when you died?" I asked, wondering how she fell through the cracks.

She crossed her thin, frail arms. "Yeah. I had one, but I wasn't interested in going. Told her to buzz off."

Our jaws dropped in sync. "Whoa. So, you just said no and sent your Crossing Guard away?"

"They can do that?" I whispered to Mabel.

"Apparently," she whispered back. "Let's hope none of ours try to pull that crap. I don't want that guilt sitting on my shoulders."

Hazel shrugged. "Yeah. She tried like hell to get me to go, but I didn't trust her. How did I know she was telling the truth about Heaven? Seems made up to me. Too good to be true, you know?"

"It's not made up, Hazel. We've been there. Seriously. You can trust us. You know us, right? Know we wouldn't make this up?"

She tipped her head, studying us. "Yeah. I remember you. I think. You were... nice? Funny? The memories are a bit fuzzy now, but I remember watching you cause trouble here. Made me laugh."

"Wait. Years?" I asked, my eyes widening as her words registered. "Did you say you've been here for *years*? Hazel, that's dangerous. The longer souls stay on Earth, the more they... fade."

Hazel's expression shifted, something vulnerable flickering across her face. "The other Crossing Guards passing through for pickups sometimes saw me and they warned me about that. Said I'd lose myself if I stayed too long. I thought they were exaggerating. Trying to scare me into leaving." She looked at us, fear creeping into her eyes. "But you two... you were always honest when you were alive. At least, I think you were. It's hard to remember now. Everything's getting harder to remember."

"They weren't exaggerating," Mabel said gently. "It's real, Hazel. We heard about it in our training too. Ghosts who refuse to move on don't just stay the same forever. They start losing pieces of themselves."

Hazel was quiet for a long moment. When she spoke, her voice was barely a whisper. "It's happening faster now. I have been forgetting things. Little things at first—what year it is, how long I've been here. But lately..." She looked down at her hands. "I know I had a daughter. But... I can't remember her face anymore. Can't remember her name. I know she existed, I know I loved her, but the details are just... gone. And it's getting worse. Every day, I lose a little more."

My heart clenched. "Oh, Hazel."

"And I feel hollow now," she continued, the words tumbling out now. "Like I'm just going through the motions. The haunting used to be fun, gave me purpose. But now... I don't even know why I'm doing it anymore. I just… am. It's like I'm becoming... less. Less than I was."

"That's the fading," Mabel said gently. "You're losing yourself, Hazel. Bit by bit, you're disappearing. And if you wait too much longer..."

"What happens?" Hazel asked, fear creeping into her voice.

I chose my words carefully. "The angels didn't tell us much—just that souls who linger too long eventually fade completely. They become mindless echoes, and that's when reapers come for them. To clean up what's left."

"Reapers?" Hazel's voice trembled. "They weren't making that up?"

"No. They weren't lying to you. Reapers are real, but we don't know exactly how they work or how long it takes for them to come," Mabel admitted. "The angels were vague about it. Something about maintaining balance between the living and the dead. But they made it clear—once a reaper comes for you, there's no Heaven waiting. You're just... erased."

Hazel's face paled. "I've felt something lately. A presence. Dark and cold and... wrong. It's been getting stronger, coming more often. At first, I thought I was imagining it, but..." She wrapped her arms around herself. "It's real, isn't it?"

"I think that's a reaper," I said softly. "It senses when a soul has faded too far. And Hazel... the fact that you're feeling it more frequently means you're running out of time."

"But I've been dodging it," Hazel protested weakly. "I can keep hiding, can't I?"

Mabel shook her head. "For how much longer? And Hazel, even if you could dodge it forever, do you really want to keep fading? Keep losing more of yourself until there's nothing left of who you were?"

Hazel's eyes filled with tears. "I'm scared. I don't remember why I stayed. I think... I think I had a reason once, but I can't remember what it was. And now I'm losing everything that made me me." She looked at us desperately. "What if I'm too far gone? What if Heaven won't take me?"

"Heaven will restore you," I said firmly though honestly, I didn't know for sure. I just trusted that Heaven made life perfect, and it *had* to fix her if we got her there in time. In my gut, I believed my next words were true. "All those memories you're losing? They'll come flooding back when you cross over. You'll remember your daughter's name. You'll remember her face. You'll remember everything that made you you. That's what Heaven does."

"And you know us," Mabel added. "You watched us when we were alive. We're not the 'follow all the rules' types. If we're telling you this is serious, it's because we believe it."

Hazel bit her lip, her eyes moving between us. "I don't know... I've been here so long. Moving on to the unknown... it's terrifying."

"I know it's scary," I said softly, "but trust me, Heaven is more amazing than you can possibly imagine. No more running, no more hiding, no more fading. Just endless joy, love, and... well, cake!"

Mabel shot me a look, rolling her eyes. "Really, Millie? The cake again?"

I shrugged sheepishly. "What can I say? It's a big selling point."

To my surprise, Hazel let out a small, watery laugh. "You know what? Cake does sound pretty good right about now. I haven't tasted anything in years. Can't even remember what it tastes like anymore." Her smile faded. "I can't remember a lot of things anymore."

"Then let us help you remember," Mabel said gently. "Let us send you to Heaven, Hazel. Get yourself back.

Before it's too late. And one day, when her time comes years from now, you'll see your daughter again."

Hazel looked between us, tears streaming down her translucent cheeks. "That dark presence... I felt it this morning. Closer than ever before. I'm running out of time, aren't I?"

We nodded solemnly.

She drew in a shaky breath, then squared her shoulders with visible effort. "Alright. I'll do it. I'm tired of feeling empty. Tired of forgetting. If Heaven can give me back who I was..." Her voice broke. "I want to remember my daughter's face again. And I do want to see her again someday. I don't remember her, but deep down, a mother's love never fades."

I couldn't contain my emotions, tears pricking at my own eyes. "You will, Hazel. I promise. When you get there, you'll remember everything. And it will be wonderful."

Mabel stepped forward, her voice thick. "You're making the right choice. Heaven is pretty damn amazing. Way better than fading away alone in a nursing home."

Hazel managed a small smile. "Okay. Okay, I'm ready. Help me cross over before I change my mind. Or before I forget why I agreed in the first place."

As I stared at this ghost who'd been stuck here for years, slowly losing herself piece by piece, I felt a profound sense of purpose. We'd reached her when no other Crossing Guard could. We'd saved her—not just from the reapers, but from the horrible fate of forgetting who she was entirely.

This was what being a Crossing Guard was all about—helping lost souls find their way home before it was too late.

"So, how do I do this?" she asked, her eyes searching our faces.

"Well, we take your hand and then—"

"Wait!" Mabel interjected, a spark of inspiration lighting up her face. "Before you go, could you teach us some of your haunting tricks? We could really use some pointers. Like that air thing you were doing to mess with that nurse. That was cool. What else can you do?"

"Oh, I've learned a little of this and a little of that."

"Can you teach us some stuff? We want to play a little prank on Howard."

Hazel chuckled, a knowing twinkle in her eye. "Ah, I see. Howard can be a bit of a pill, can't he? I've been haunting this place for years, so I know all about his antics." A smile tugged at the corners of her mouth. "Well, I suppose I could share a few secrets."

"Why in the hell didn't you haunt Howard?" Mabel asked. "You picked on that poor nurse when Howard was ripe for the haunting!"

She shrugged. "Oh, I've messed with him a few times, but he wasn't here when I was alive, so I don't have any real beef with him. That nurse, though…" She clenched her fist and snarled. "Oh, she has it coming."

"Yeah, she's a real jerk," Mabel said, nodding. "Never liked her much."

"She hated me," Hazel said. "Left me sitting in my diapers once for two whole days because I mouthed off to her. She is so sweet in front of the management, but behind closed doors, she's a complete psychopath. I've been trying to haunt her the hell out of here. But she writes off everything I do to her as 'her imagination'. It's maddening."

"Man! I always heard this place was haunted, but nothing ever happened to me so I thought it was bull pucky. But now I know it was you! Damn. I kinda wish you'd have haunted me when I was alive so I could have seen some of it." I paused. "Although, back before I was a ghost, you probably would have scared me to death, so I guess thanks for not haunting me."

Hazel chuckled. "You two never bothered me at all so you didn't have it coming."

"So, tell us, Hazel. What all can you do?" Mabel asked eyes sparkling with mischievous anticipation.

Hazel cracked her knuckles, a sly smile spreading across her face. "Alright, girls. Before I head off to eat this endless cake you're telling me about, let me show you how to haunt."

We squealed with excitement, gripping each other's hands and hopping up and down while Hazel smiled back at us. Over the next few hours, she patiently guided us through the intricacies of ghostly manipulation. We started with the basics, focusing on moving small, lightweight objects.

Mabel scrunched her face in concentration, her tongue poking out as she tried to make her ghostly fingers solid enough to nudge a paperclip across the table. "Come on, you little bugger," she muttered, her fingers twitching with effort.

I couldn't help but giggle at her intense expression. "Mabel, you look like you're trying to lay an egg."

"Or crap her pants," Hazel whispered, chuckling.

She shot us a playful glare. "Hey, don't break my concentration! I've almost got it!"

The paperclip wobbled slightly, then fell still. Mabel let out a frustrated huff. "Okay, so maybe I don't got it."

Hazel chuckled, shaking her head. "It takes practice, ladies. Don't get discouraged. Okay. New tactic. Try working together, combining your energy. Maybe you aren't ready for solo manipulation, and you said it worked when you did it before. Let's see how that goes."

Mabel and I joined hands, focusing our combined energy on the stubborn paperclip. Mabel poked at it with her finger several times, going straight through, but then, it began to slide across the table, picking up speed.

"It's working!" I cried out, and we cheered it on like spectators at a horse race.

"Go, little paperclip, go!" Mabel hollered.

It fell off the table with a *clink* and we turned to each other, embracing as we hopped up and down.

"Okay. Well, that answers that. You two are stronger together. From now on, you move objects together."

Mabel and I looked at each other, then she slung an arm around my shoulder. "We were stronger together in life, so it makes sense we're stronger together in death."

"Now, some ghosts can eventually learn to move objects without touching them at all—pure telekinesis. See, we're just concentrated energy now, right? When we physically touch things, we're focusing that energy into our hands to make them solid enough to interact with objects. But telekinesis is about projecting that same energy outward, away from your body, and using it to push or pull things from a distance."

She gestured toward the paperclip on the table. "Instead of making your fingers solid to touch that paperclip, you'd focus your energy around the paperclip itself, like creating invisible ghostly hands wherever you need them. It's much harder because you're not just making one part of yourself solid—you're extending your essence beyond your form."

"Whoa. That sounds cool," Mabel breathed out and I nodded in disbelief. "So you can move things from anywhere?"

Hazel nodded her head. "I've heard of spirits who can fling things across rooms with just their minds, but it takes tremendous practice and energy. Most ghosts never master it. I sure haven't. The few who do learn it say it's exhausting—like trying to lift something heavy with your actual hands, except the 'hands' are made of pure willpower projected through space."

Mabel's eyes lit up. "So, we could do that? Like fling things around the room? Make chairs float and fly around?"

"Eventually, maybe. But that's a lot more advanced than you're ready for. For now, focus on perfecting your physical manipulation skills. You need to master making your touch solid before you can even think about moving things from across a room. Let's see what else you two can move together," Hazel said, glancing around the room at all the available objects.

We started moving heavier and heavier things including pushing a chair a couple of inches. Our confidence grew with each success, then we moved on to other skills. Hazel taught us how to create eerie whispers and cold spots, and I couldn't wait to try these tricks out on an unsuspecting Howard.

"Mwuah ha ha ha," Mabel bellowed as I held her hand. Her voices echoed in the room, faint but I knew that if a human had been in there, they would have heard her.

"Wow. You two are better at that than I am. I can't get above a really indistinct whisper."

"Yeah, I was always a loud one." Mabel grinned.

"Now, for the pièce de résistance," Hazel announced, a twinkle in her eye. "Manifesting apparitions."

"Whoa! Like appearing to humans?" My jaw went slack. "You can do that?"

She closed her eyes, her form shimmering and flickering

like a candle flame. Then she opened her eyes and said, “Ta da!”

We furrowed our brows. “Wait. What happened? You just stood there and flickered like a candle.”

Her eyes lit up as she laughed. “Oh yeah! You can see me already, so of course it looked like nothing happened. *But* if you weren’t ghosts like me, you would have seen me!”

Mabel’s jaw dropped. “Holy guacamole! For real? That’s amazing!”

I nodded, awestruck. “Okay, how the heck do you do it?”

Hazel grinned, clearly enjoying our reactions. “Well, humans can’t see me *completely*. From what I can gather from their reactions, I’m more like a mist, not a full body. Like a creepy, ghostly apparition.”

“Appearing to humans? So cool,” Mabel breathed. “How? How do we do it? I wanna do it!”

“It’s all about visualizing your essence, then projecting it outward. Like this.”

She demonstrated again, her ghostly form blinking in and out of visibility like a faulty light bulb.

Mabel rubbed her hands together, determination etched on her face. “Alright, let me try.”

She squeezed her eyes shut, her face turning an alarming shade of purple as she strained to manifest.

“Mabel, breathe!” I reminded her, stifling a laugh.

She let out a whoosh of air, her shoulders slumping. “Dang it! I thought I had it. Did I flicker?”

“Nope. Nothing,” Hazel said, and Mabel grumbled and crossed her arms.

I tried my hand at manifesting, but all I managed was a faint flicker that could have easily been mistaken for a trick of the light.

"Try it together," Hazel said.

Mabel and I gripped hands, then together, our concentration scrunching both of our faces, we gave it everything we had. But this time, instead of a big improvement when we joined forces, there was barely a flicker between us.

Hazel patted Mabel's shoulder reassuringly. "It took me months to get that one, so don't be frustrated if you don't master it right away."

Mabel pouted, her bottom lip jutting out. "But I want to do that one to Howard! Really scare the crap out of him."

"At least we have some tricks, and now we know what's possible, so we can keep practicing. Don't get frustrated."

Mabel inhaled a deep breath, straightening her shoulders. "Okay. Let's keep trying."

Together we practiced everything Hazel had taught us, getting faster and faster at moving objects and creating voices and cold spots. We still struggled with the creating apparitions, but I knew with a little time, we would master that too.

What a strange turn my afterlife had taken. When you were dying, fear gripped you—would it hurt? Would I simply cease to exist? Was there even an afterlife, and if so, which direction would I be heading? If only I could go back in time and tell myself not to be scared, tell all these people on Earth that if you're a decent person, there's nothing to fear. The afterlife is incredible, and with a best friend like Mabel by my side, mine promised even more adventure than we'd had while living.

Lost in my thoughts, I almost didn't notice when Hazel suddenly stiffened, her eyes darting around the room. "Oh no," she whispered, her voice trembling. "A reaper. It's coming again. It feels… closer this time."

A wave of icy fear washed over me, and I instinctively

reached for Mabel's hand. She gripped mine tightly, her own face etched with apprehension.

"Hazel, you need to move on. Now," Mabel urged, her voice steady despite the palpable tension in the air.

Hazel nodded, her eyes brimming with a mix of gratitude and fear. "Alright. I'm ready."

"Thank you for your help, Hazel," I said quickly, my fear growing as I sensed the darkness closing in on us. "Now, just take our hands and you'll move on."

Hand in hand, Mabel and I focused our energy on guiding Hazel's spirit to the light. I could feel the reaper's oppressive presence approaching, the darkness clawing at the edges of my consciousness. But as we concentrated on Hazel's essence, I felt a warmth emanating from our joined hands, pushing back against the encroaching shadows.

Slowly, Hazel's form began to shimmer and dissolve, her features softening into an expression of peace. "We'll see you up there soon, Hazel," I whispered, my voice thick with emotion.

With a final, grateful smile, Hazel vanished in a burst of radiant light, her spirit ascending to the heavenly realm that awaited her. As the last traces of her essence faded away, I felt the reaper's presence receding, the suffocating darkness dissipating like smoke on a breeze.

Mabel and I stood there, hand in hand, marveling at the profound significance of what we had just accomplished. "We did it. Again," Mabel murmured, her voice hushed. "We saved her."

I squeezed her hand, tears of joy and relief pricking at the corners of my eyes. "This is what we're meant to do, Mabel. Helping lost souls find their way home."

"Just think," Mabel said. "If we hadn't been naughty and come to haunt Howard, we never would have stumbled onto Hazel. And chances are, one of these times, a reaper would have extinguished her. We truly are making a difference down here."

My heart swelled to bursting. "It was fate. Or maybe it was more." I glanced up at the Heavens, starting to wonder now if this was pure coincidence or if somehow, Heaven had given us a little nudge.

Mabel slung an arm around my shoulder. "Well, now that we've done such a good deed and helped a bonus soul move on, I think it's the perfect time to balance out all that good with a little bit of M&M trouble. Let's go practice out our new skills on Howard."

I grinned as excitement bubbled up inside me. "Let's go have our fun, Mabel. We've earned it."

Trying to push aside my fear of celestial retribution for breaking the rules, I set out with Mabel to hunt down the man who'd cut down my beloved flowers in their prime.

Chapter Seven

MABEL

It had been three days since we'd arrived at Shady Oaks. And for three days, we'd tried unsuccessfully to scare the pants off Howard. We'd been just a couple of pests annoying that bitter old man, but I wanted to see real fear bloom in his eyes for what he'd done to my Millie's flowers.

Our beacon had only gone off twice in that time, so we'd hurried off to help those two souls move on. One had been an elderly woman ready to pass on without hesitation, and the other had been a man in his twenties in a motorcycle accident. It had taken a little coaxing to convince him to leave this mortal world behind, but he'd eventually agreed, and we'd watched him float to the Heaven we knew waited for him above. Both experiences had been incredibly satisfying, though still sad to be sure. After our assigned souls had moved on, with nothing else to do, we'd kept trying to haunt Howard.

Moving through the nursing home, we popped in and out of every room looking for him. Finally, we spotted him in the common room, settled into his favorite armchair, a newspaper open on his lap. He seemed engrossed in the article, oblivious to the world around him.

"Okay, Millie," I whispered, a mischievous grin spreading across my face. "Let's start with something simple today. Warm ourselves up. How about a cold spot."

Millie nodded, her eyes sparkling with anticipation. We gripped hands and focused our energy on the space around Howard, willing the temperature to drop. At first, nothing seemed to happen, but as we concentrated harder, I noticed Howard shiver slightly, pulling his cardigan tighter around himself.

"It's working!" I exclaimed, my excitement building. "Now, let's try moving the newspaper."

We walked over and channeled our energy to allow us to touch the paper. The pages began to tremble as we tried our best to shake it, and Howard's brow furrowed in confusion. He reached out to still the paper, but as soon as his hand touched it, I managed to get a good grip on it, yanking it out of his grasp, sending it fluttering a few feet away.

Howard's eyes widened, and he glanced around the room, trying to figure out what had caused it to fly away. Millie and I giggled, trading the same look we'd shared since childhood whenever we were up to no good. "Did you see his face?" Millie asked, her laughter only I could hear echoing through the room. "He looked so confused!"

Emboldened by our success, we decided to take things up a notch. We focused on the lampshade beside Howard's armchair, grabbing it together and shaking the shade. At first, it only wobbled slightly, but as we poured more energy into our efforts, the lampshade began to sway back and forth, casting eerie shadows on the walls.

Howard's eyes darted to the lamp, his expression a mix of fear and disbelief. He reached out to steady the shade, but as soon as his fingers brushed against it we surged our energy together in a massive push causing the bulb to flicker and go out, plunging the corner of the room into darkness.

"What in the world?" Howard muttered, his voice trembling.

Millie and I exchanged a triumphant look, our palms cracking together in a high five as we burst into laughter.

"Oh, man. I so wish we could get that astral projection power working. I would love to see the look on his face if you and I appeared right in front of it!"

We'd tried dozens of times unsuccessfully to manifest ourselves, and I grumbled that the one thing I wanted to do seemed the most difficult to master.

"Let's try something else," I suggested. "Let's give him the eerie whisper again. I don't think he really heard voices last time. Let's give it all we got and try to freak him out."

Millie grinned, and we focused our energy on the space near Howard's ear.

"Howard..." I dropped my voice several octaves to sound menacing, drawing out the name in a haunting cadence. "Howard...we're watching you..."

Howard straight up, his face paled, and he shot up from his chair, his eyes darting around the room in a panic. "Who's there?" he demanded, his voice quivering. "Show yourself!"

Millie and I dissolved into another fit of giggles, then I cleared my throat and tried again.

"Howard, you are a baaaaaad man. You killed Millie's flowers. We know it was you. Now we're coming to kill youuuuu…" I let the last word drag out until I saw true fear bloom in his eyes.

"It's working! He can hear me!" I practically squealed with delight as I watched Howard stumble around the room, searching for the source of the whispers, his movements becoming more frantic with each passing moment. He tripped over a chair and tumbled to the ground, moaning as he gripped his hip.

I sucked the air through my teeth. "Oops. I hope he didn't just break a hip." I paused looking up to the Heavens, now worried maybe they were watching me, and I'd gone a bit too far.

"Oh, no! Is he hurt? Did we do that? Are we gonna get sent to hell if he breaks a hip and dies in the hospital? You know a broken hip is the kiss of death for the elderly! Did we just kill Howard?" Millie's voice inched up several octaves as panic set in.

Howard rolled over onto his knees then stood up, and Millie and I exhaled a sigh.

"Oh, thank God. We didn't break his hip. We aren't murderers," she breathed.

I felt the same relief wash over me. Haunting was supposed to be funny. A little payback for those who deserved it. But doing something that injured someone or got them killed? If Heaven was watching, which I hoped they weren't, it was a risk even I didn't want to take.

"Yeah. Maybe we should ease up," I said, as I stared at Howard standing in the middle of the room, his chest heaving, a sheen of sweat glistening on his brow.

"I must be losing my mind," he muttered, running a shaky hand through his thinning hair. "I could have sworn..."

We watched him limp off down the hall, glancing back toward us then shaking his head before he disappeared around the corner.

"Come on, Millie," I said softly, placing a hand on her shoulder. "I think we've done enough for today."

Millie nodded, and together we passed through the walls and into the hallway.

"We're getting better at this," Millie remarked, a small smile playing on her lips. "But maybe we should be a bit more careful with our haunting. We don't want to cause any real harm. We got lucky that time. He could have really hurt himself when he fell. You know old people bones are brittle."

I agreed, realizing that with our newfound abilities came a responsibility to use them wisely. We had the power to bring a little mischief and excitement to the world of the living, but we had to be mindful of the line between good natured fun and genuine harm.

"You know, Millie," I mused, "Now that we're figuring out how this all works, but being a ghost pretty great. Sure, we've got a lot of responsibility with the whole Crossing Guard thing, but it's pretty fun being back down here, isn't it?"

Millie chuckled, nodding in agreement. "I'll admit, I was pretty nervous coming down here with you, but you're right. It is fun to get a little change of the constant perfection of Heaven. But we do need to be careful going forward if we decide to haunt people. I don't think they'll welcome us back with open arms if we accidentally scare someone to death." She gave me a warning look. "And I'm going to be mad at you for eternity if we get tossed down there and I never get anymore cake."

I laughed and draped an arm around her shoulder. "Don't worry, Millie. We'll be careful. I'm not going to lie. I'm craving some cake too. Do you remember your twelfth birthday when our foster mom forgot about it and you didn't get anything, so we snuck into that bakery and I stole you a coconut cream cake?"

Her eyes lit up. "Oh, my favorite! Yes. That was quite a birthday!"

We walked through the halls, reminiscing about our past adventures and speculating about what the future might hold. It was easy to get lost in the comfort of our friendship, the familiarity of our banter. For a moment, I almost forgot about the weightier aspects of our new existence.

But as we turned the corner, the familiar beep of our distress beacon shattered the lighthearted atmosphere. Millie and I exchanged a somber glance, the levity of the previous moment evaporating like mist in the sun.

Another soul in need of our assistance, waiting for us to guide them to the afterlife.

I met Millie's gaze, a silent understanding passing between us. With a deep breath, we focused our thoughts on the beacon, allowing its urgent pulse to guide us through the vortex once more.

As the world rematerialized around us, we found ourselves standing in a dimly lit alley, the damp pavement glistening beneath the faint glow of a distant streetlamp. The first thing that struck me was the coppery scent of blood hanging heavy in the air. And there, just a few feet away, stood the ghostly form of a young woman, her figure positioned above her lifeless body, a pool of blood forming from the would opening her neck.

There was no doubt in my mind… this was another murder scene.

"Oh no," I breathed, my voice trembling as I took in the heartbreaking scene before us. We weren't in a nursing home helping a soul excited to leave their broken body behind, or at a car accident that had claimed another life, but it was just that. An accident. Instead, once again, we found ourselves staring at a beautiful young woman cut down in her prime. There was something truly unsettling knowing this death was intentional. Senseless. Cruel. Her future stolen by the brutal actions of an unknown assailant. And like that first soul we'd been sent to, it made it so much harder to bear.

"Not another murdered young woman." Millie swallowed hard, her face etched with sorrow and anger.

Steeling myself against the wave of emotions, I approached the woman with Millie close behind. "Hello," I said softly, keeping my voice gentle and reassuring. "We're here to help you."

The dark-haired woman turned, her blue eyes wide with fear and confusion. "That's me. I… I'm dead. I died. Why? Why would someone do this to me?"

She started sobbing, and my heart clenched as I stared at the confused woman's spirit, her mortal body at her feet on the cold pavement beside a smelly dumpster as if she was nothing but garbage.

As we began the delicate process of comforting the distraught spirit, I couldn't help but feel a growing sense of unease. Two murdered girls in such a short span of time. It was a chilling pattern that set me on edge.

While Millie soothed the woman's fears and began explaining the wonders that awaited her in the afterlife, the gears started turning in my mind.

Same age. Same dark hair. Same blue eyes. Both incredibly beautiful.

I glanced at the slice across her neck.

Same kill signature.

A flicker of unease skittered down my spine as I knew the answer to the question bouncing around in my mind.

There is a serial killer at work here.

"Excuse me," I interrupted Millie as she continued

listing off every type of cake she'd tried in heaven. "I don't want to bring up the horrible memories, but can you just tell me, was it a woman who killed you?"

Tears welled in her eyes. "Yes. It was so dark, but I'm sure I saw a woman. I was just taking this shortcut home like I always do. I heard a sound, and as I turned to look, I felt something across my neck and then…" She glanced down at her lifeless body and whimpered.

"But you saw a woman?" I asked again.

She nodded. "Yes. For just a second. She grabbed my hand as I died and dragged me a few feet over by these dumpsters and then ran away. Why would she do this? I was so young and had so much going for me. I just got a new promotion. Had a first date with a wonderful man. I… how did this happen?" She dissolved into tears again.

"Did you get a good look at her? Any distinguishable features?"

She shook her head. "No. It was so dark. Her face was hidden by the shadows, and I only saw her back as she dragged me in my last moments, but it was a woman. I'm sure of that. She… she killed me."

The tears flowed freely, and Millie comforted her, giving me a warning look not to keep upsetting her.

"I'm sorry, I just needed to know. Please, don't think on this tragedy any longer. You're going to a better place now. I promise."

As we worked to bring peace to yet another lost soul, a fierce determination took root in my heart. I knew, with a certainty that defied logic or reason, that I wouldn't rest until we got to the bottom of these heinous crimes.

Standing there, watching the young woman's essence ascend to the heavens, I felt a weight settle upon my shoulders—a burden I knew I was meant to carry. In life, I had always been the defender of the downtrodden, the champion of the bullied and oppressed. I had faced down countless jerks and bullies, using my wits and my moxie to bring them to justice.

But this? This was different. Staring at the lifeless body of an innocent soul cut down in her prime by a faceless killer, I realized that the stakes had never been higher. This wasn't just about settling scores or righting petty wrongs. This was about something far more profound, far more urgent.

This was about saving lives.

A cold fury gripped me as I pictured the killer stalking her next victim, plotting to snuff out another bright light in this world. The thought of more senseless deaths, more families shattered by grief, more futures stolen away in the blink of an eye... it ignited a fire within me, a blaze that couldn't be quenched by anything short of justice.

I made a silent vow, there in the stillness of that blood-stained alley. I would not rest, would not falter, until the killer was brought to justice and the world was made safe once more.

After the young woman's soul faded into the Heavens, I pointed at her body and looked at Millie. "This is the work of a serial killer. The crimes are too similar for it not to be. And she's still out there, Millie. Walking free, probably looking for her next victim."

My friend shuddered, wrapping her arms around herself as if to ward off a sudden chill. "You're right. But what can we do? We're just a couple of ghosts."

A fierce, determined fire ignited within me, blazing hot and bright against the darkness that threatened to encroach. "I don't know. But I'll be damned if I'm going to stand by and let that monster claim another innocent life."

Millie's eyes widened. "Mabel, are you suggesting what I think you're suggesting?"

"I am." I squared my shoulders, meeting her gaze with unwavering conviction. "We're going to find out who did this, and we're going to make sure they never hurt anyone else ever again."

For a long, tense moment, Millie simply stared at me, her expression unreadable. I could practically see the gears turning in her mind, weighing the enormity of what I was proposing. But then her worried eyes hardened, and I saw my own grim resolve mirrored in her eyes. In that moment, I knew that we would stop at nothing to unravel the mystery of these murders. We would use every spectral trick in our arsenal, every ounce of our ghostly cunning, to track down the killer and bring them to justice.

Lifting her chin and straightening her spine, she gave a determined nod. "Alright. I'm in."

A fierce grin split my face as I reached out to clasp her hand in mine. "Partners in crime-solving."

She returned my smile, her grip tightening around my fingers in a silent pledge. "Partners in crime-solving," she echoed.

"We're gonna be like *Murder She Wrote*, *Columbo*, and *Cagney & Lacey* all rolled into one!" I declared, my voice ringing with determination. "Heaven help whoever did this because they've got a couple of vengeful spirits on their tail now."

As we stood there in the hushed stillness of the alley, our hands entwined and our hearts united in a common purpose, I couldn't help but feel a flicker of grim satisfaction.

The monster who had so callously snuffed out a vibrant young life had no idea what was coming for them. Millie and I had spent a lifetime honing our skills in the art of mischief and mayhem. Now, we would channel those talents toward a far nobler cause—bringing a killer to justice and ensuring that no more innocent souls met such a brutal, untimely end.

Our focus would remain on the lost souls that needed our guidance, but in the quiet moments between crossings, we would pool our otherworldly resources and begin the hunt. We would stop at nothing until the perpetrator was unmasked and made to face the consequences of their heinous crimes.

The game was afoot, and Heaven help anyone who dared to stand in our way.

Chapter Eight

MILLIE

Two days had passed since we'd helped the murdered woman's soul move on to the afterlife. While we passed the time between crossings, Mabel and I found ourselves sitting in a quaint café, pretending to sip on imaginary coffee, all the while lamenting our inability to conjure up a heavenly slice of cake.

"I miss the endless buffet of desserts in Heaven," Mabel grumbled, poking at our counter neighbor's scone with her ghostly finger. It moved a little, but the diner beside us didn't seem to notice.

With a sigh, I stared at the dessert case filled with food we couldn't eat. "What I wouldn't give for a big ol' slice of devil's food cake right about now."

"When we get back, I'm going to conjure up a feast that will spread out across our entire dining room. My mouth is practically watering just thinking about it. How long until we go back?"

"Seven days," I answered.

"Man, time is passing by quick," Mabel said, then her

face fell as she glanced down at the counter. "And how are we going to find and stop a murderer in only seven days? We haven't even figured out a single extra clue."

The mention of our self-appointed mission sobered me up instantly. We'd been racking our brains for the past forty-eight hours, trying to figure out where to start in our quest to bring the murderer to justice. But as two old ladies whose only experience with crime-solving came from binge-watching television shows and reading murder mystery novels, we were coming up woefully short on ideas.

"We're not giving up," I said, gently touching her arm. "We just need to think harder about where the heck to start our investigation."

"You know," Mabel mused, tapping her chin thoughtfully, "on *Murder, She Wrote,* Jessica Fletcher always seemed to stumble upon clues just by talking to people and poking around town."

I raised an eyebrow. "And how are we supposed to interview people when no one can see or hear us?"

Mabel waved a dismissive hand. "Details, details. The point is, she always cracked the case in the end."

"Yeah, after like ten more people died," I countered, shaking my head. "I don't think we can afford to wait for the bodies to pile up before we catch this psycho."

We lapsed into silence, each of us lost in thought as we tried to channel our inner detectives. The café bustled around us, the living going about their day, blissfully unaware of the two ghostly grannies plotting to take down a serial killer in their midst.

Suddenly, Mabel perked up, her eyes widening as she stared at the television mounted on the wall behind the counter. "Millie, look!"

I turned to see a news report flashing across the screen,

a somber-faced anchor delivering the latest update on a developing story.

"...the body of a young woman was discovered in Oakwood Park early this morning, posed in what authorities are calling a 'disturbing and ritualistic manner.' The FBI has been called in to assist local law enforcement, and sources say they are investigating a possible connection to four other recent murders in the area..."

Mabel and I exchanged a knowing glance, the pieces clicking into place in our minds. Oakwood Park. That was only a few blocks from where we'd found the last victim's soul.

"It's got to be the same killer," I breathed, a chill running down my spectral spine. "And four other bodies? We only know about two. What are the odds of another murderer stalking women in this town?"

Mabel nodded grimly. "And did you catch that part about the body being posed? That's got serial killer written all over it. And why didn't our beacon go off?"

She tapped at her wrist.

"Maybe that soul was assigned to a different crossing guard."

"Damn it! We missed out on being there to get more clues!"

We leaned closer to the TV, straining to catch every detail of the report. The anchor droned on about the increased police presence and the need for public vigilance but offered no new information about the killer's identity or motives.

As the segment ended, Mabel turned to me with a determined glint in her eye. "We need to get to that crime scene. If there are any clues to be found, that's where they'll be."

I hesitated, uncertainty gnawing at my gut. "I don't know, Mabel. What if we mess something up? Contaminate evidence or something?"

She rolled her eyes. "We're ghosts, remember? It's not like we're going to leave fingerprints or tracks in the mud. Besides, we may not be able to interview people because we're ghosts, but we can walk right through the crime scene tape and listen in on their investigation without anyone being the wiser."

I had to admit, she had a point. With a nod of agreement, we closed our eyes and focused on Oakwood Park, willing ourselves to the location burned into our minds from the news report.

A dizzying swirl of energy engulfed us, and when we opened our eyes again, we found ourselves standing at the edge of a densely wooded area. Yellow police tape cordoned off a section of the park, uniformed officers milling about as they secured the perimeter.

Mabel and I exchanged a glance, steeling ourselves for what lay ahead. We strode forward, passing effortlessly through the barrier and into the heart of the crime scene.

The first thing that hit me was the overwhelming sense of dread that hung heavy in the air, a palpable darkness that seemed to cling to every blade of grass and gnarled tree root. It was the kind of feeling that made the hairs on the back of my neck stand up, even if I was already dead.

As we drew closer to the center of the activity, the body came into view—a young woman, sprawled unnaturally across a park bench, her limbs twisted into a macabre pose that twisted my gut into a knot.

"Oh God, I'm going to be sick," I said, though I didn't know if vomiting was possible in my deceased state.

We stopped and stared in horror at the grisly scene, but

it wasn't just the positioning of the body that made my spectral blood run cold. It was the face—a face I recognized all too well, even in death.

"Mabel," I choked out, my voice barely above a whisper. "That's her. The woman from the alley. The one we helped cross over."

Mabel's eyes widened in horror as the realization sank in. "But... but how? We saw her die in that alleyway. How is her body here?"

A sickening thought wormed its way into my mind, and I fought back another wave of nausea. "The killer must have come back for her. Moved the body after we left then posed her like this. Disgusting."

Mabel cursed under her breath. "If we had just stuck around a little longer, we could have caught the sicko red-handed. Scared her into turning herself in or something."

Guilt twisted in my gut like a knife. She was right. We'd been so focused on helping the victim's soul that we hadn't even considered the possibility of the killer returning to the scene. If we had just waited, hidden ourselves and kept watch...

I shook my head, forcing the recriminating thoughts aside. There was no use dwelling on what we could have done differently. The past was the past, and we had to focus on the present—a present where were hunting a killer, and I wouldn't rest until she was behind bars.

"We can't change what happened," I said, my voice steady with determination. "But we can sure as hell do everything in our power to stop this monster before she strikes again."

Mabel nodded, a fierce light burning in her eyes. "Damn straight. And the first step is figuring out what clues we can get from this crime scene."

We moved closer to the body, weaving unseen through the swarm of FBI agents and forensic technicians who buzzed around like worker bees. Snippets of conversation floated past us, and we tried to gather as much as we could.

"...no signs of a struggle, just like the others..."

"...strange ritual elements, possible occult significance..."

"...still waiting on the ME's report, but preliminary COD looks like exsanguination..."

So many conversations were happening around us it was impossible to focus on just one. Mabel and I exchanged a bewildered glance.

"I feel like we need a pause button so we can listen to each conversation one at a time so we can understand what the heck they're talking about," Mabel muttered, her brow furrowed in concentration.

I hummed in agreement. "Okay. Keep listening, but let's look for clues ourselves."

I scanned the scene for anything that might stand out, anything that could point us in the right direction. But all I saw was a jumble of evidence markers and cryptic scrawls in the investigators' notepads, none of it meaning a damn thing to my untrained ghostly eyes.

A group of people in blue jackets with *FBI* marked in yellow on their backs stood a short ways from the body discussing the case.

"Oh, the FBI! They know their stuff," Mabel said, then started toward them.

We walked up behind them, still keeping a bit of distance, and listened in. They huddled together, their voices low and urgent as they compared notes and theories.

"What do you think, Agent Sadler?" one of the agents asked, a tall man with a neatly trimmed beard. "Another victim of our mysterious surgeon?"

The young, mid-twenties brunette agent with a haunted look in her eyes, responded with a grim nod. "It looks that way. The precision of the cuts, the removal of a different body part—it all points to someone with extensive medical knowledge, and it matches up with the other victims. All killed with the same slice to the neck. All found posed in a place somewhere other than where they were killed. All missing a body part. All beautiful young brunettes with blue eyes. It fits the pattern, don't you think, Agent Nelson?"

Agent Nelson, a grizzled older man with a stern expression, gave a curt nod. "Good observations, Sadler."

She lifted at the small praise, her shoulders straightening up as she smiled. "Thanks. I know we're gonna catch this guy. You can count on me to do whatever it takes to get this sick son of a bitch."

"Good." He grunted his response, then his voice took on a cutting edge as he added, "Just try not to almost blow anyone up in the process this time."

Agent Sadler visibly flinched at his words, her gaze dropping to the ground as she seemed to shrink under the weight of his criticism, like a popped balloon letting out all the pride that had swelled up her shoulders only a moment ago. The other agents exchanged knowing looks, their expressions ranging from pity to disdain.

"Come on, Nelson," the petite blonde agent interjected, her tone softening. "It's been a month since the incident. Sarah's been through enough."

Nelson scoffed. "Tell that to the agents who almost died because of her reckless behavior. She's lucky to still have a badge after that stunt."

Sarah remained silent, her shoulders hunched as if trying to make her already slight frame as small as possible.

It was clear that the incident still haunted her, the guilt and shame etched into the lines of her face.

Mabel and I exchanged a glance, our hearts going out to the young agent.

"Enough. Let's focus on the case," the petite blonde said, then turned the conversation back to the crime.

As the agents continued to theorize about the killer's motives, speculating about a surgeon with a God complex and the significance of the missing body parts, Sarah seemed to withdraw even further into herself. She kept her eyes fixed on the ground, as if trying to avoid the judgmental gazes of her colleagues.

"Did you hear that?" Mabel whispered, her eyes wide with a mix of excitement and disbelief. "They think the killer is a man. A surgeon."

I nodded, my face set in a grim line. "But we know that's not true. The victims' souls told us themselves—their killer is a woman."

Mabel's fists clenched at her sides. "We have to tell them. Somehow, we have to make them see that they're barking up the wrong tree."

"But how? We can't exactly communicate with them."

Mabel's face twisted in frustration. "I don't know. Man, this is awful. We're going to have to solve this ourselves since the FBI seems to be going in the completely wrong direction!"

"So, how do we do that?" I asked, completely unsure what next steps to take.

Mabel stared at the body, then cringed. "I think we need to go examine the body ourselves and see if we can find anything they missed."

My eyes flashed wide, and just thinking about getting

close to the horrible scene sent another wave of nausea climbing up my throat. "What? Go next to it? No way!"

Mabel tossed her hands in the air. "Well, these yahoos seem to be screwing the pooch, so I don't see any other options. We need to go look."

"Ugh, no. Please no." I glanced at the body still a couple dozen yards from us. "I don't want to get any closer."

"Come on. We'll do this together. We have to stop this monster from doing this again, and if that means we need to get up close and personal with that body, then that's what we have to do. Come on, Millie. Let's get this over with."

With horror and fear crashing inside me, I stilled my nerves and took her hand. We walked slowly toward the body. Agent Sadler and the fellow agents had returned to the corpse and were examining it.

"He cut the neck here with one quick slice," Agent Nelson said.

"She," I corrected with an eye roll, even though they couldn't hear me.

Agent Sadler looked over her shoulder in our direction, then her sharp voice caused us to jump. "Hey! You two! What the hell do you think you're doing in my crime scene? You're contaminating the evidence!"

We stood stunned and wide-eyed face to face with the fierce-looking woman, her dark hair pulled back into a severe bun and her eyes blazing with the kind of intensity that could make even the most hardened criminal quake in their boots.

But it wasn't her imposing demeanor that made my jaw drop. It was the fact that she was staring directly at us, her gaze locked onto our ghostly forms like a heat-seeking missile.

Mabel and I gaped at each other, our mouths opening and closing like a couple of landlocked fish. This wasn't possible. We were invisible to the living, intangible specters that could pass through walls and walk unseen among the masses.

So how on earth could this woman see us?

As if reading my thoughts, the agent's eyes narrowed, her hand twitching toward the holster at her hip. "I said, what are you doing here? This is an active crime scene, and you're contaminating my evidence."

Mabel and I remained frozen, our minds spinning with the implications of this impossible encounter. We'd spent the past week growing accustomed to our ghostly existence, secure in the knowledge that we were hidden from the prying eyes of the living.

But now, as we stood there under the piercing gaze of this formidable FBI agent, one thing became crystal clear.

The game had changed, and we were in for one hell of a ride.

Chapter Nine

MABEL

"You can see us?" I blurted out, staring at the beautiful FBI agent in disbelief. Beside me, Millie's jaw had dropped open, her eyes wide with shock.

Agent Sadler narrowed her eyes at us. "Of course, I can see you. You're standing right in the middle of our crime scene!" She turned to her fellow agents, gesturing toward us with an exasperated wave of her hand. "Would someone get these two old women out of here?"

Her colleagues exchanged confused glances, their brows furrowed as they looked in our direction. A tall man with brown, short hair spoke up, his voice hesitant. "Uh, Agent Sadler? What are you talking about? There's no one there."

She let out a sigh. "I'm talking about these two old ladies who walked right into our crime scene!" She pointed at us, her eyes hard as she glared. "Who the hell let them in here? Just someone please get these whackos out of here."

The agents continued staring at her, then passing shifty glances back and forth.

"Sarah, hon. There is no one there. We have no idea

what you're talking about," the small, blonde female FBI agent said, her voice tipped with worry.

Sarah looked at us again, staring as if to confirm what her eyes were seeing.

"Uh, hi." I waved awkwardly. "We're ghosts, and I, uh, I think you're the only one that can see us, and I hate to tell you that you're starting to look crazy to your FBI pals."

Millie gave a shy wave. "Hi."

Her eyes widened in disbelief. I could practically see the gears turning in her mind as she processed the situation.

Millie, ever the peacemaker, stepped forward with her hands raised in a placating gesture. "Listen, Sarah, we know this is confusing, but we can explain. We're not actually old women. We're ghosts, and it seems like you're the only one who can see us. You need to stop telling people you're seeing old ladies."

Sarah's face paled, and she took a stumbling step backwards. I couldn't help but notice the slight wobble in her movements, as if her balance was off-kilter. She quickly caught herself, but the momentary clumsiness wasn't lost on me.

"Sarah, are you okay?" the little blonde agent asked again as Sarah stood staring at us bewildered.

She pointed at us. "You… you can't see those two old ladies?"

The male agent snorted and whispered to the blonde woman under his breath, "She's officially lost it. Oh, how the mighty have fallen."

Sarah recoiled at his words, glancing at us and then back at the agents all looking at her with worried and perplexed expressions.

"Sarah, you're really worrying me," the blonde agent

said, ignoring the whispers between her colleagues. She seemed to be the only one genuinely concerned for Sarah.

With one last glance at us, she stared directly into my eyes as if to confirm we were, without question, real.

I gave her a pleading look. "Play it off as a joke! Hurry! You sound nuts!"

Sarah stared at me in disbelief for one long moment then took a deep breath and exhaled it with a laugh. "Ha! I'm kidding! I really had you guys going there!"

She continued her nervous, awkward laugh as the other agents stared at her with a mix of pity and confusion.

"A joke," she said quickly, her cheeks flushed with embarrassment and anger. "Duh, you guys. It was a joke. Guess it went over your heads. Well, uh, I think our investigation here is good. I, uh, I got to run back to the office. Gotta look up some ideas I've got. I'll, uh, I'll catch you guys back there."

Millie and I watched silently as Sarah spun away from her colleagues and started hurrying through the park toward the parking lot.

As she left, a couple of the male agents began their whispering again about how Sarah used to be the one to watch and now she'd be the one to get the boot, and when they started laughing, Sarah's hurried footsteps faltered for a moment, and I knew she'd heard their callous words.

She stiffened her back and kept on.

Millie and I stayed behind for a few moments, and we heard the agents talking more freely as she passed out of ear shot.

The muscular male in his early twenties leaned in closer to his colleague, his voice low but still audible to my ghostly ears. "She's been off her game ever since the incident. I heard the higher-ups are considering pulling her from the field entirely."

The tall agent with the short, brown hair shook his head, his expression a mix of pity and frustration. "She used to be the rising star of the bureau, but now? It's like she's a completely different person. Jumpy, erratic, making rookie mistakes left and right. Can't lie though, after how arrogant she was that she was the best, it's kind of funny to watch her completely fall apart."

"Stop you guys," the little blonde agent said, halting their conversation with a glare. "Leave her alone. She's been through a lot."

I glanced at Millie, seeing the concern etched on her face. We both knew that Sarah was struggling with more than just our sudden appearance. There was a story here, a painful one, and it seemed to be affecting every aspect of her life.

"What do we do?" Millie asked. "She can see us. But that poor girl. Everyone thinks she's nuts. I think we need to talk to her."

I nodded. "We do have to talk to her. She's the only one that we can tell the killer was a woman. We've got to go after her."

Millie and I started after Sarah, following behind her and waiting until we were far enough away from the judgmental crowd to say anything so we didn't make her look more nuts if she turned to talk to us.

"Ghosts?" she hissed under her breath as she continued rushing from the embarrassing scene. "Now I'm having hallucinations about ghosts from my concussion? Great. Like the residual headaches and balance issues aren't enough. Now I've got to hallucinate ghosts in front of all my colleagues." She tapped her forehead. "So embarrassing!"

We caught up to her and I got closer, then whispered, "Hate to break it to you, sugar, but we're as real as it gets. Well, as real as ghosts can be, anyway."

Sarah spun toward my voice and looked right at us, then shook her head vehemently, her expression a mix of panic and disbelief. "Crap. I'm still seeing them. I really need to call my neurologist and admit that I'm having side effects from the blast. This can't be good."

As she hurried away, she continued mumbling to herself, her voice low and strained. "This isn't happening. It's just another side effect from the concussion. It has to be."

Millie and I exchanged a worried look. Concussion?

As if reading our thoughts, Sarah continued her muttered monologue. "I should tell someone about these hallucinations. The dizziness, the headaches, the clumsiness... and now I'm seeing and hearing things that aren't there. Ghosts?" She squeezed her temples, cringing. "I can't believe that just happened. I'm going to be the laughing stock at the office."

"We're not hallucinations, hon," Millie said sweetly. "I'm sure this must be a shock, and we're sorry we didn't know you could see us, so we caused that embarrassing scene for you back there. But we're real. We're ghosts, and for some reason you can see us."

She slowed her steps for a moment but refused to look back, swearing under her breath. "That's it. My career is done. They're gonna find out I have issues now and shove me behind a desk or send me packing. My life goal is over because I made *one* stupid decision. Ugh!" Her footsteps sped with her anger, her head down and her shoulders hunched.

I felt a pang of sympathy for Sarah. It was clear that she was struggling with more than just our ghostly presence.

She seemed to be carrying the weight of some past trauma, some mistake or failure that had left her doubting herself and her abilities.

Millie, ever the nurturing soul, reached out a comforting hand, forgetting for a moment that we couldn't actually touch the living. "Sarah, please, listen to us. We're not hallucinations. We're real ghosts, and we're here to help."

Sarah kept walking, pointedly ignoring us as she approached her car. I could see the tension in her shoulders, the way her hands trembled slightly as she fumbled with her keys.

Desperate to get through to her, I blurted out the one piece of information that I knew could make a difference in the investigation. "The killer isn't a man, Sarah. It's a woman. We know because we've spoken to the victims' ghosts."

That got her attention. Sarah froze, her hand hovering over the car door handle. She slowly turned to face us, her expression guarded but curious. "What did you just say?"

Millie jumped in, excited Sarah stopped to acknowledge us. "The FBI is looking for a male suspect, but we know for a fact that the killer is a woman. The victims told us themselves."

For a moment, I thought we had her. I saw the flicker of doubt in Sarah's eyes, the way her brow furrowed as she considered our words. But then, just as quickly, the skepticism returned, and she shook her head.

"No, this is crazy. I'm not listening to a couple of figments of my imagination. I need to focus on the real investigation, not some fantasy concocted by my malfunctioning brain."

With that, she wrenched open the car door and climbed inside, slamming it shut behind her. As the engine of her dark blue sedan roared to life, Millie and I watched helplessly.

"Should we climb in with her?" I asked.

Millie hesitated then shook her head. "I'm worried we'll scare her more, distract her, and cause her to crash. I think we should stay put."

I nodded, visions of us causing the confused agent to veer off the road and meet her end in a fiery crash filling my mind. I then imagined us getting the beacon to help her soul move on… and how ironic it would be that it was us who caused her death in the first place being the Crossing Guards to help her accept it. "Yeah. Let's not accidentally kill the one person who can see us."

She drove away, leaving us standing in the parking lot.

"Well, that could have gone better," I sighed, rubbing a hand over my face.

Millie nodded, her expression thoughtful. "She's struggling, Mabel. Not just with the idea of us being ghosts, but with something else. Something deeper."

I thought back to the whispered comments from Sarah's colleagues, the way they had dismissed her so easily, as if she were a joke to be tolerated rather than a valued member of the team. It seemed that whatever mistake or trauma she had recently experienced, it had left her reputation in tatters.

She was the best of the best, the agents had said. Top of her class. The shining star of the FBI. The daughter of a legend. That's what they were saying about her back there. And now, because of some incident that had happened, she'd been reduced to a laughingstock.

I felt a surge of determination well up inside me. Sarah needed our help, whether she wanted to admit it or not. She needed someone to believe in her, to support her, to help her find her way back to the brilliant agent she once was. And we needed her to help us stop the killer sending beautiful young souls to Heaven well before their time.

"We can't give up on her, Millie," I said firmly. "She's our best chance at catching this killer and preventing more innocent lives from being lost. We need to find a way to get through to her, to convince her to work with us."

Millie nodded, a small smile playing at the corners of her mouth. "I have a feeling that Sarah is going to need us just as much as we need her. She just doesn't know it yet."

As we stood there in the parking lot, watching the dust settle in the wake of Sarah's departure, I couldn't help but feel a flicker of excitement mingled with determination. This was shaping up to be our most challenging and important mission yet.

Chapter Ten

MILLIE

Mabel and I navigated our way through the bustling city streets, passing effortlessly through the throngs of unaware humans. Our mission was clear: find Sarah and convince her that we were real, that we were here to help her solve this terrifying case.

As we made our way toward the FBI office, Mabel turned to me, her expression uncharacteristically serious. "Millie, we've got to find Sarah and make her believe us. Those poor women, cut down in their prime by some twisted killer... we can't let it happen again."

I nodded, my own features set in fierce determination. "I know, Mabel. Sarah's our best hope at stopping this monster. With her FBI smarts and our ghostly intel, we could crack this case wide open."

Mabel's eyes sparkled with a mix of mischief and resolve. "Plus, it'll be fun to see the look on her face when she realizes we're the real deal. I bet she'll freak."

I couldn't help but chuckle at my friend's irreverent humor, even in the face of such dire circumstances. It was one of the things I loved most about Mabel—her ability to find light in the darkest of times.

"Let's just focus on finding her first," I reminded gently.

"Oh, there! That's it!" Mabel pointed to the FBI building. We hadn't been able to transport ourselves there since we'd never seen it, instead having to blink ourselves to the bar we'd gone to when we first arrived and then navigate the streets the rest of the way.

We phased through the walls of the FBI building, pausing when we got inside.

"Should we go through the security scanners?" I asked, staring down at the line of people waiting to get through.

Mabel rolled her eyes. "We're ghosts, Millie. We don't need to go through the scanners. Although, I wonder if they would go off if we did?"

Mabel pushed off the ground and flew just over the heads of the people waiting in line, then dipped down and went through the scanner. Nothing happened, and she floated back to me, frowning.

"Damn. Would have been funny if it went off. I could have spent the whole morning going back and forth and making it beep on people."

"Mabel," I scolded. "We've got a serious task in front us. We need to focus on finding Sarah and not playing pranks.

She stiffened. "Right, right. You're right. Okay. Where to start?"

I shrugged, "I guess we just start checking everywhere."

We moved through the lobby, starting on the first floor, our eyes scanning the sea of desks and agents for any sign of Sarah. We went floor by floor, poking our heads into meeting rooms, break areas, and even the restrooms, our search growing more frantic with each passing moment.

"Where could she be?" Mabel grumbled, her brow

furrowed in frustration. "It's like trying to find a needle in a haystack, except the haystack is a labyrinth of bureaucracy and bad coffee."

Just as I was about to suggest we try the next floor up, I caught a glimpse of a familiar face through the opened door of an office barely larger than a cubicle. "Mabel, look! There she is!"

"Holy crap," she said, staring at her with wide eyes. "We did it! Man, we are some seriously good detectives!"

I glanced at her, chuckling. "Well, she is an FBI agent and this is the FBI office, so it's not exactly rocket science to figure out where she may be."

Mabel shrugged it off. "Still. It's a big building, and we did it. We rock! Let's go talk to her."

Relief flooded through me as we waltzed into Sarah's office, our smiles bright with excitement. "Sarah! Thank goodness we found you!"

Sarah lifted her head from the stack of papers on her desk, and her eyes widened in a mix of shock and horror, her mouth falling open in a silent gasp.

"Oh, no," she groaned, burying her face in her hands. "The hallucinations have started again."

I stepped forward, my voice gentle but insistent. "Sarah, please listen to us. We're not hallucinations. We're real ghosts, and we're here to help you catch the killer."

Sarah shook her head vehemently, her fingers threading through her hair in agitation. "No, no, no. This can't be happening. Please don't be happening." She peeked up at us then cursed under her breath. "It's happening. Oh no, I'm gonna have to call that neurologist. Crap."

Mabel moved closer, her expression earnest and imploring. "You're not losing your mind, Sarah. We're as real as the nose on your face. Well, minus the whole we're ghosts and your nose is part of your real human face thing, but you get the gist."

She actively ignored us, lifting her papers in front of her face to block the view.

"We're still here," I said, peeking over the papers.

She spun around in her black office chair muttering to herself as she held the paper closer to her face in an attempt to block us out.

"Sarah, you can't ignore us," I pleaded. "I know this must be scary, and you've got to be so confused, but we're here to help you stop that serial killer. You have to believe we're real so you can listen to us and realize the investigation is going in the wrong direction. Please, Sarah. It's important you listen to us and let us help you before another innocent woman dies."

I choked up over the last word remembering the sadness and pain of finding those poor spirits beside their bodies, the palpable darkness surrounding their deaths feeling like it may crush me.

"This is nothing but a symptom of my concussion. They aren't real, they aren't real," she whispered on repeat.

"This is going to be harder than I thought." Mabel crossed her arms with a huff. "How in the hell can we help you solve this murder if you can't accept we're real?"

Sarah continued ignoring us and pretended to read her papers.

For the next several minutes, Mabel and I bombarded Sarah with theories, insights, and pleas for her to believe us. We recounted our conversations with the victims' spirits in vivid detail, describing the killer's gender, the way she had seemed to attack them without warning, the chilling efficiency of her murders.

Sarah, clearly still convinced that we were mere figments

of her imagination, tried to ignore us, burying herself in her work with a stubborn set to her jaw. But Mabel and I were nothing if not persistent.

"Sarah, please," I begged, my voice cracking with emotion. "Those women, they died in terror and pain, their lives snuffed out by a monster in human skin. We can't let their deaths be in vain. We have to stop her before she strikes again."

Mabel nodded fervently, her own features etched with determination. "Millie's right, Sarah. This is bigger than all of us. We have a chance to make a real difference here, to bring justice to the victims and their families. But we need your help to do it."

Sarah's resolve seemed to waver for a moment. I could see the war raging within her, the desperate desire to believe battling against the cold, hard logic of her rational mind.

But then, just as quickly, the walls slammed back up, and Sarah's expression hardened once more. She leaped to her feet, marched over to the office door, and closed it with a decisive click.

Whirling around to face us, she hissed, "Enough! I don't know what kind of mental breakdown I'm having, or what kind of head injury I got that can cause such vivid hallucinations, but I need you two to go away. You're not real, and I can't keep indulging these delusions."

Mabel and I shared a frustrated look, our determination to convince Sarah only growing stronger in the face of her stubborn disbelief.

"But we are real, Sarah," I insisted, my voice rising with a touch of desperation. "And we can prove it to you."

Mabel's face lit up. "Wait! That's what you need. Proof!"

Sarah looked between us, her arms crossed tight against her dark black blazer. "How? How do the hallucinations in my mind intend to prove to me that they are real?"

Mabel and I looked back and forth, then I saw the familiar glint in Mabel's eyes meaning she had an idea. "I've got it! Millie, go stand behind Sarah."

I quickly obliged, positioning myself at Sarah's back. Mabel turned to Sarah, a playful challenge in her tone. "Okay, Sarah. Put your hand behind your back and hold up some fingers."

Sarah rolled her eyes, her arms crossing over her chest in a defiant stance. "This is ridiculous. I'm not playing along with my own hallucinations."

But Mabel was undeterred. She arched an eyebrow. "Scared to find out we're real and you're wrong?"

Sarah's face tightened. "I'm not scared."

"Then prove it," Mabel challenged. "Hold some fingers up behind your back and I'm going to show you that we can see them."

"Fine," she huffed.

Millie looked behind her back and motioned to me it was three fingers.

I grinned. "Three. You're holding up three fingers. And I know this because there is a ghost behind you who can see what you're doing. So, now you must accept we are real and we can get down to business of catching a killer!

Sarah furrowed her brow then tipped her head. "Wait a minute. That... that doesn't prove anything," Sarah said, looking at me with a challenging gaze. "You're just a projection of my own mind. Of course you would know how many fingers I'm holding up because *I* know how many fingers I'm holding up."

Mabel's brow furrowed, realizing the flaw in her plan. "Damn. She's right."

We looked at each other, our collective minds searching for a way to prove our existence when I grinned. "Hold on. Watch this and tell me that this is in your mind."

I floated over to her desk, and biting my lip, used all my energy to push the papers on her desk. My hand went right through. "Dang! Hold on. I'm still trying to get the hang of this."

I tried again and failed. Sarah stared at me with an arched eyebrow and a confused expression.

"Hold on. I'll help," Mabel rushed to my side, gripping my hand tight as we combined our energies.

"Watch this," I said confidently, then with all the energy I had, I focused my fingers on the papers and gave them a swat. They lifted off her desk and fluttered to the ground.

"Ha!" I shouted triumphantly.

Mabel whooped and gave me a high five. "See! Ghosts!"

Sarah's eyes flashed wide. "How… how did…"

"Because we're ghosts, girl!" Mabel grinned wide.

Sarah, still refusing to give in to this new reality where she could see specters, shook her head. "No. That was a gust of wind or maybe just my imagination. Part of the hallucination."

We let out a collective sigh. I started to lose hope we'd ever convince Sarah we were real, but then, another idea struck Mabel, and her face lit up with renewed determination. "Fine. Then we'll show you something that your mind couldn't possibly know ahead of time and something you can't explain away so easily."

"Like what?" Sarah's eyebrow lifted with the question.

"Yeah, like what?" I asked, excitedly.

"When was the last time you were outside of this office?" Mabel asked.

Sarah shrugged. "I don't know. A couple hours ago."

"So, then it's safe to say your mind couldn't know everyone and everything out there right now, correct?"

She nodded. "I guess so. Okay. Correct."

"Then Millie and I are going to go out there and look around and come back in here and tell you everything we see. Step outside, see it's all real, and you'll know we're not just in your head."

Sarah twisted her lips but finally jutted her chin at the door. "Fine. Go."

Mabel's face illuminated with the challenge, and she motioned for me to follow her. We phased through the office wall into the busy hallway beyond. Agents hurried past, engrossed in their own tasks and conversations, completely unaware of the two ghostly observers in their midst.

Mabel and I began calling out details about the passing agents, our voices carrying through the wall to Sarah's office.

"Ooh, look at that guy with the mustache," Mabel remarked, pointing to a portly agent waddling by. "He's got a big ol' ketchup stain on his tie. Bet he had a burger or hot dog for lunch." She paused, her eyes closing as she moaned out, "Mmmm. Oh man. A hot dog. That sounds so good right now."

She opened her hand, squeezing her eyes shut as she sucked her lip between her teeth while she concentrated.

"What are you doing?" I asked, perplexed.

"Trying to will a hot dog into my hand," she answered, grunting with the energy she put into the failing attempt. Finally, she let out her held breath. "Damn it! No luck. Ugh. I want a hot dog!"

"Focus, Mabel," I said with a shake of my head.

"Right." She turned her attention back to the bustling agents moving around the office building.

I chimed in. "There. That woman with the red hair. She's got a run in her stockings. Right on the back of her calf."

We continued our running commentary, describing the quirks and details of the unsuspecting agents in the hallway and the bullpen just around the corner. At one point, a young man stumbled, sending a flurry of papers flying into the air. Mabel and I couldn't help but laugh as he scrambled to gather them up, his face turning a brilliant shade of red.

After a few minutes of our impromptu narration, we heard the office door open behind us. Sarah stepped out into the hallway, her eyes searching the area with a laser-sharp focus. She glanced around, taking in the scene that we had just described in vivid detail.

"See?" Mabel said with an air of arrogance. "I told you that we were real. Everything we've described to you that you didn't know yet is here in living color. Guy with ketchup on his tie. Runs in stockings. Clumsy guy with dropped papers." Mabel kept pointing out all the details we'd rattled off to Sarah through the door.

"How... how would I know all that?" she whispered, her voice trembling slightly. "That information wasn't in my mind. It's impossible for me to have hallucinated it."

Mabel and I exchanged a triumphant grin. "Like I said before, because we're ghosts, girl," Mabel declared. "Bona fide spirits from the great beyond. And we're here to help you catch a killer."

Sarah retreated back into her office then leaned back against the wall, her hand pressed to her forehead as she tried to process this extraordinary revelation. "I… can't explain this. There's no other explanation then—"

"Then we're ghosts! In the flesh!" Mabel opened her arms wide and grinned, then dropped her arms and shrugged. "Well, I guess not in the flesh because, well, even though we look solid, we're ghosts so we don't actually have real flesh. But you know what I mean."

I offered a few comforting words knowing she must be incredibly overwhelmed. "I know this is hard to believe, hon, but it's true."

"It can't be," Sarah argued, shaking her head. "Ghosts don't exist."

Mabel grumbled. "Man, how are we ever going to catch a killer if we can't make you believe that we died and we came back here to help you?" Her eyes lit up. "Wait! You're the FBI! You can look people up on your computer, can't you?"

Sarah nodded. "Yeah. Of course."

A sly smile lifted Mabel's lips. "Then why don't you go over there and look us up. You'll see then that we lived once, we died a few months ago in our nursing home, and then you'll have to accept we're real."

"Oh! Great idea!" I clapped. "That's so smart, Mabel!"

She took a little bow. "Why thank you, Millie. Well, Sarah? What do you say? Ready to accept you've got a couple ghostly grannies to help you close this case?"

Sarah twisted her lips as she looked between us, then she tossed up her arms. "Fine. I'll do it. What are your names and birth dates?"

We rushed after her as she headed to her computer, and we rattled off all our information as her fingers tapped against her keyboard. Hovering over her shoulders and looking at the screen, I held my breath as I watched my photo appear along with my birth and death date.

"What?" Sarah breathed.

Mabel pointed at the screen. "Ha! See? That's Millie!"

She looked at the photo and then back at me. Still

seeming to resist this irrefutable proof, she typed in Mabel's information. A moment later, Mabel's photo popped up on her screen with a birth and death date.

"See? Just like we said." Mabel crossed her arms and arched an eyebrow. "You finally ready to accept the fact and admit that we're ghosts?"

Sarah looked up at us, her eyes wide as I saw the acceptance forming within them as she whispered, "Holy crap. You're real."

"We're real, and we're gonna help you catch a killer!" Mabel grinned.

I didn't know what to say, so I just gave her a sheepish wave. "Hi."

"I think I'm gonna pass out," she said, and I watched the color drain from her face.

Chapter Eleven

MABEL

"Ghosts. Real ghosts," she whispered in disbelief as her eyes darted between us.

As the shock of our ghostly revelation settled over Sarah like a heavy fog, I couldn't help but empathize with her. Her world had just been turned upside down, and I could only imagine the thoughts racing through her mind. How would I have felt when I was alive finding out that ghosts were real?

Sarah slumped back in her chair, her eyes wide and unfocused as she looked back at the computer screen displaying our obituaries. "I can't believe this," she whispered, her voice trembling slightly. "Ghosts. Real ghosts."

"She doesn't look well," Millie whispered to me as Sarah kept staring at us repeating her words.

The pale color in her face mutated to a bright red, and I knew she may pass out.

"Quick, Millie! Let's make a cold spot and cool her down. She looks like she's gonna pop!"

Together we grabbed hands and sent a cool rush over

Sarah. The drastic change in temperature seemed to snap her out of her trance, and slowly the normal color returned to her face.

"You okay?" Millie asked. "If I were alive and some ghosts showed up, I'd be a wreck too. Just take a few moments and breathe. Everything is going to be okay."

Sarah finally stopped repeating her words, and after a deep breath, she looked at us and said, "Why me? How can I see you?"

We both shrugged. "Honestly, we have no idea. We heard that some humans can see ghosts, but you're the first one that we've encountered. And by your reaction, we can assume this is a new thing for you?"

She nodded. "Definitely. I have never *ever* seen a ghost before you two."

"Strange," I said, wondering why she could see us.

Suddenly, Sarah's face lit up with a sort of recognition. "You know, as I'm sitting here trying to piece this all together, I can't help but think about something that happened last month. Something that, perhaps, is the reason I can see you both."

"What is it?" I asked, and I leaned in closer to hear the answer as well.

"I'm not sure if it's the reason, but if I were doing an investigation, I would certainly consider it notable information. Last month, I was in an accident. It's where I got the concussion that I thought was giving me hallucinations."

We continued listening as she went on.

"Well, I had a concussion because I was in a blast that sent me flying across a room and into a brick wall. I hit my head hard enough that I actually stopped breathing. I was dead for several minutes before one of my colleagues resuscitated me. Is it possible that because I was dead for a short while that's why this is happening?"

"Very possible," I agreed. "It would certainly make sense. And you haven't seen any other ghosts?"

She shook her head.

Millie pinched her lips, thinking. "That makes sense though. Sprits who refuse to move on start to fade. Lose themselves, essentially. And then reapers come for them, so there aren't a lot of ghosts walking around down here. We've only seen a few stragglers in our stint as Crossing Guards."

"Crossing Guards?" Sarah asked.

"Yeah. That's what we are and it's why we know what we know about your case." I went on about our jobs here on Earth and how things like ghosts and Crossing Guards and reapers worked. We then told Sarah all about finding the two murdered girls and how they both said they were killed by a woman.

"Wow. This is so much to take in," Sarah said softly.

"I know it is, hon." Millie went to touch her shoulder, but her hand went right through.

"And as much as we'd love to stand here and regale you with tales of the afterlife, we have a killer to catch before they strike again."

"And you really want to help me solve the case?"

Millie nodded, her smile gentle and reassuring. "That's right, Sarah. We've seen the pain and suffering this killer has caused, and we can't just sit by and watch it happen. We want to work with you, to use our unique abilities to bring them to justice."

I stepped forward, my expression serious. "I know this is a lot to take in, Sarah. But please, trust us. We're on your side, and together, we can stop this monster before they strike again."

Sarah took a deep, shuddering breath, her eyes flickering between Millie and me. I could see the gears turning in her mind, the last vestiges of doubt and disbelief crumbling away in the face of our undeniable presence.

Finally, she nodded, a small, hesitant smile tugging at the corners of her mouth. "Okay. Okay, I believe you, you're ghosts. I believe you know facts about the killer that I don't. And I believe that the three of us can stop this monster."

We had done it. We had convinced Sarah of our existence, and now, we could finally get to work on solving this perplexing mystery. I let out a whoop of joy, pumping my fist in the air. "Yes! The dream team is officially assembled. Watch out, killer, because Mabel, Millie, and Sarah are on the case!"

As the reality of her new partnership with a pair of meddling ghosts fully sank in, Sarah's eyes widened, and she let out a soft, disbelieving laugh. "I can't believe this is happening. I'm working with ghosts. Real, actual ghosts. If someone had told me this morning that I'd be teaming up with a couple of supernatural crime-solvers, I would have laughed them out of the room."

I grinned widely. "We may not be professionals like you, but we've watched a *lot* of mystery shows in our many decades on earth, and we've got the insider track with the information we got from the souls this sicko took. We'll help you in any way we can, and I know that together, we can stop these killings and lock this murderer up before she can send us one more soul to cross to the other side."

Sarah nodded, the determination settling over her features like a mask. "Okay. Okay, let's do this. But first things first—we need to set some ground rules. I can't have you two popping in and out of existence willy-nilly, especially not in front of my colleagues. It makes me look like I'm insane. When I'm with other people, you're quiet."

She passed a warning glance between us.

Millie and I exchanged a sheepish glance, remembering our earlier faux pas at the crime scene. "Right, of course," she agreed. "We'll be more careful from now on. The last thing we want is to jeopardize your reputation or your investigation."

Sarah let out a long, slow breath, the weight of her newfound reality settling over her like a heavy cloak. "This is going to take some getting used to. But if you're right, if you really can help me catch this killer... then I'm willing to give it a shot." She straightened her shoulders, the fire of determination burning bright in her eyes. "Alright, then. Where do we start? You said you have information on the killings?"

I nodded eagerly. "You bet your badge we do! First things first, the killer is a woman."

Sarah furrowed her brow. "The FBI profilers are convinced we're looking for a man, a surgeon or doctor with medical training."

I snorted. "Well, they're barking up the wrong tree. Our ghostly witnesses were very clear on that point. The killer is definitely a woman."

Sarah leaned forward, her hands clasped tightly in front of her. "Interesting. I couldn't quite figure out what made them so certain it was a man. They said because the person had to be strong enough to move the bodies, but I thought that there were plenty of ways for a woman to accomplish it so we shouldn't rule it out. But, I guess I just went with what they said since I don't want to be sticking my neck out right now after…" she paused and shook her head. "Nevermind. So, it's a woman. Did they mention anything else? Any information or clues that could be helpful? Did they give a description?"

Millie shook my head, her shoulders slumping that we had no description to hasten our capture of this criminal. "No. No description. We didn't know to ask the first one, and the second one we did ask, but she said it was a woman though it was too dark in the alley to make out her features."

I lifted my finger. "But they did say she used some kind of wire to do the deed. Not a scalpel like the cops think. A wire... thingy."

Sarah's eyes narrowed as she processed this new information. "A wire… thingy? That's an odd choice of weapon. But it could explain the precision of the wounds, the clean cuts."

Sarah's lips twisted as she contemplated our words. "Interesting. With the clean, precise cut, the Medical Examiner thought the murder weapon was likely a scalpel. It's part of why the BAU made a profile that led to a surgeon."

"Nope. A wire," I said decidedly.

She paused for a moment, her mind racing with the implications of our ghostly intel. Then, a look of determination settled over her features, and she stood abruptly from her chair.

"We need to talk to the medical examiner," she declared, already reaching for her simple black purse. "If the murder weapon isn't a scalpel, she might be able to tell us what it could be."

As Sarah prepared to leave, I couldn't help but notice the slight tremble in her hands, the way her fingers fumbled with the buttons of her coat. It was clear that our presence, and the reality of her new supernatural situation, had shaken her to the core, but other than the small giveaway, she did an excellent job steadying her shaken nerves.

Millie, always the keen observer, picked up on Sarah's unease as well. "Hey, you okay there, agent? You look like you've seen a ghost. Well, I guess you have, but you know what I mean."

Sarah let out a shaky laugh, running a hand through her hair. "I'm fine. It's just... this is all so surreal. And after what happened last month, I just…" She paused and shook her head. "A few months ago, my biggest worry was proving myself to my colleagues, showing them that I had what it takes to be a top agent. Then the incident happened, my career is in shambles, and now I'm talking to ghosts. I'm just struggling to wrap my head around it."

"You mentioned a blast? What happened, Sarah?" I asked.

Her voice took on a distant quality as she continued, her eyes unfocused as if lost in a painful memory. "I was so eager to make a name for myself, to live up to my father's legacy. He was a legend in the bureau, you know? I thought I had to be perfect, to stand out head and shoulders above the other new recruits to live up to his reputation."

We waited quietly for her to go on.

Sarah heaved a heavy sigh, her shoulders slumping under the weight of her words. "I made a mistake. A big one. I was chasing a suspect, and I got too close. Ignored protocol, rushed in without backup. I thought I could handle it on my own, that I could be the hero."

She let out a bitter laugh, shaking her head at her own foolishness. "I was wrong. The suspect had a bomb, and I got trapped inside with him. My team was working on a way to rescue me when it went off... I was too close. The blast threw me against a wall, and I hit my head. Hard. A few of my teammates were almost killed, but luckily, they were just out of range when it exploded. If they'd have come even seconds earlier to save me though…" Her voice drifted off. "What a stupid mistake. My stupid, arrogant decision almost got myself and three other people killed."

Millie and I exchanged a worried glance, our hearts aching. "Oh, Sarah," Millie whispered, her voice soft and comforting. "That must have been terrifying."

Sarah's voice wavered as she continued, her eyes glistening with unshed tears. "I was dead, for a few minutes. They brought me back, but the damage to my reputation was done. Several coworkers were hurt. I had a severe concussion, and the bureau... they've lost faith in me. My colleagues, my superiors—they all see me as a liability, a reckless agent who can't be trusted."

My face hardened with resolve as I lifted off the ground, moving closer to Sarah. "Well, that's just a load of hooey! So you made a mistake, big deal! Happens to the best of us. What matters is that you learned from it, and you're still here, fighting the good fight."

Millie nodded in agreement, her own determination burning bright. "Mabel's right, Sarah. You've been given a second chance, and we're here to help you make the most of it. Together, we can solve this case and prove to everyone that you're the brilliant agent we know you are."

Sarah looked up at us, a glimmer of hope flickering in her eyes. "You really think so?"

"We know so," I said firmly, my ghostly hand coming to rest on her shoulder. I used all my energy to manifest a whisper of a comforting touch. "And I bet if we can bring this killer to justice, the FBI will have no choice but to see you as the capable, amazing agent that you are. Now, let's go talk to that medical examiner and see what she can tell us about the murder weapon."

Sarah nodded, a smile tugging at the corners of her mouth. "Okay. Let's do this."

As we left the office, Millie and I followed alongside Sarah, and I couldn't help but feel a surge of pride and purpose. We were more than just meddling spirits now—we were partners in this investigation, united in our goal to stop a killer before she could strike again.

Chapter Twelve

MILLIE

As we stood outside the door to the medical examiner's office, anticipation buzzed in the air. Sarah knocked twice then strode in like she was familiar with this place. Mabel and I hurried along behind her, and we practically vibrated with excitement to be along for our first official FBI investigation.

"Don't you feel like we're on one of those CSI shows we used to watch?" Mabel whispered to me.

"Oh! Yes!" she said excitedly. "Like that one where they had the fancy lab and—"

Sarah shot us both a look and we quickly caught the meaning. We had already broken the first rule of our new partnership.

"Sorry, we'll be quiet," Mabel said, and I gave her a sheepish look.

"Hi, Dr. Chen," Sarah started, then she froze when she saw a young woman with short, dark hair and tortoise shell glasses. "Who are you? Where's Dr. Chen?"

She looked up from the autopsy report she was studying,

and her warm, brown eyes met Sarah's. "Oh, hello. I'm Dr. Rina Patel. I'm filling in for Dr. Chen while he's out of town at a conference."

Sarah scrunched her brow, clearly taken aback by the change in personnel, but she quickly regained her composure. "Nice to meet you, Dr. Patel. I'm Special Agent Sarah Sadler. This is—" She started to point toward me, and in that moment, remembered we didn't exist to the rest of the world, so she froze, eyes wide as she stared at Dr. Patel.

"Keep talking or you'll look nuts again!" Mabel whispered.

Sarah shook her head slightly and kept on. "Uh, this is a surprise. I wasn't expecting to see someone other than Dr. Chen."

"Nice recovery," I whispered, giving her an encouraging thumbs up.

Sarah didn't look at me and kept her gaze fixed on Dr. Patel. "I called a bit ago to let them know I was coming down. Thank you for taking the time to meet with me. I have some questions about the murder weapon in our serial killer case."

Dr. Patel nodded, a thoughtful expression on her face. "Funny you should mention that," she said, then hesitated and trailed off before adding more.

"Funny why?" Sarah asked, picking up on the same thing.

After hesitating for a moment, she responded. "I, uh… I've been reviewing Dr. Chen's findings, and I've noticed some…" she paused, searching for the right word, "inconsistencies in his reports on the wounds."

I exchanged a glance with Mabel, my eyebrows shooting up. "Inconsistencies? This just got interesting."

"What kind of inconsistencies?" Sarah asked, stepping a little closer as she crossed her arms.

Dr. Patel froze up, a flicker of uncertainty crossing her face. "I don't want to get Dr. Chen in trouble," she said, her voice low. "He's my superior, and he has far more experience than I do. I don't know if I'm comfortable questioning his findings until he gets back. Maybe I'm wrong."

Sarah's expression softened, and she took a step forward. "Dr. Patel, please don't worry about protecting Dr. Chen's ego if you've found something important. I need to know, and sometimes a fresh set of eyes can catch something new. Your insights could be the key to solving this case and bringing a killer to justice, and I really don't want to wait until Dr. Chen returns. We've got a killer on the loose and the longer they are out there, the more chance they have of killing again. Please, don't worry about getting in trouble for stepping on toes. Just tell me what you know."

Dr. Patel took a deep breath, then nodded. "You're right. Thank you, Agent Sadler." She turned to her computer, pulling up a series of images from the previous murders. "Look here, at the edges of the wounds. See how they're more jagged and irregular than you'd expect from a scalpel?"

Sarah leaned in, her brow furrowed in concentration. "You're right. They are clean, but they don't quite look like clean, surgical cuts."

Dr. Patel nodded, encouraged by Sarah's interest. "Exactly. And look at this." She pointed to a close-up of one of the wounds. "See that faint discoloration? It's a residue of some kind, but it doesn't look like any surgical lubricant or antiseptic I've ever seen."

I moved in closer, my nose practically pressed against the screen. "Ooh, a mystery residue! This is getting juicy!"

Sarah shot me a quick look that warned me to get back, then turned to Dr. Patel, her eyes alight with curiosity. "What do you think it could be?"

Dr. Patel shook her head. "I'm not sure yet, and I don't want to speculate without evidence. I've sent a sample to the lab for analysis, but it'll be a few days before we get the results back."

Sarah frowned, clearly frustrated not to get an answer immediately. "And the murder weapon? If it's not a scalpel, what do you think it could be?"

Dr. Patel pulled up another image, this one showing the wound from a different angle. "Based on the irregularities in the cuts and the unusual residue, yes. Something thin and strong, capable of making precise cuts but leaving behind a distinct signature. I've been considering alternative theories, looking into tools that could mimic the precision of a scalpel but leave behind a different kind of trace evidence."

"Any chance it could be a wire?" Sarah asked, and I shot Mabel a look as we both held our breaths, waiting to find out if this investigation was finally going to head our way.

Dr. Patel pushed her glasses back up on her nose and looked at Sarah with a stunned smile. "Wow. Great eye. I was thinking we might be looking at some kind of wire. Great observation, Agent Sadler."

Sarah stood a little taller at the compliment.

Mabel gasped, her hand flying to her mouth. "A wire! Just like the victims said!"

I nodded, a grin spreading across my face. "Now we're talking. That's proof Sarah can use to take this investigation in the right direction."

Sarah turned to Dr. Patel, her expression serious. "Thank you for bringing this to my attention, Dr. Patel.

Your findings could be the break we've been looking for in this case."

Dr. Patel smiled, a hint of pride in her eyes. "I'm glad I could help, Agent Sadler. I'll let you know as soon as I have the results back on that unknown substance."

"Please do. It was nice to meet you, and I think you're an asset to the FBI." Sarah extended her hand, and Dr. Patel shook it with a wide grin.

As we left the medical examiner's office, I couldn't contain my excitement. "Did you hear that? A wire, not a scalpel! We were right all along!"

Mabel nodded, her face alight with pride. "And that mystery residue? I bet it's going to be the key to cracking this case wide open."

Sarah led us to a quiet corner of the hallway where no one could see us talking, her voice low and urgent. "Okay, so we know the killer is using a wire, which confirms what you two said. Now we need to take the next step in the investigation."

"What do we do next?" I asked, my excitement to be part of the case palpable in my voice.

"Well, killers often use weapons they are comfortable with. Something they've used or seen in their day-to-day life. Something they have easy access to. Our next step is to think about who works with wires and would be comfortable with a weapon like that."

I tapped my chin thoughtfully. "Someone who works with wire a lot. Maybe an electrician or a mechanic?"

Sarah shook her head. "No, I don't think so. The cuts are too precise, too deliberate. This is someone who knows how to manipulate wire with skill and finesse."

Mabel's eyes popped wide. "Piano wire! Didn't we see

that one show where that piano teacher killed someone with piano wire?"

Sarah shrugged. "Possible. What else? Who else uses wire. It is thin wire, not the heavy-duty kind."

We all started rattling off ideas, but none of them struck a chord. Then Mabel's face lit up.

"Wait a minute," she said, turning to ne. "Didn't you used to make jewelry back in the day? Didn't you use wire for that?"

I nodded, my eyes lighting up with understanding. "That's right! I remember using thin, strong wire to create delicate chains and clasps. It was perfect for getting precise, clean cuts. In fact, it's so sharp I cut myself on it several times." I turned to Sarah, my ghostly form practically vibrating with excitement. "Sarah, what if our killer is a jeweler? Someone who's skilled with wire and knows how to use it to create intricate designs... or deadly wounds?"

Sarah's brow furrowed as she considered the possibility. "A jeweler... that could explain the missing jewelry on all the victims. Maybe our killer is taking them as some kind of twisted trophy."

Mabel lit up with pride. "I didn't even know the jewelry was missing. See? We're on the right track now! A jeweler."

Sarah tipped her head. "It fits the evidence. A jeweler would certainly have the skill and tools to create the kind of wounds we're seeing. However, it's important we don't get blinded by theories. It's a lead, but we still need to keep an open mind about other alternatives."

I felt a surge of excitement at the prospect of a new lead. "So now what do we do next?"

"Well, we know it's wire and since the medical examiner agrees, this is the best lead we've got right now. We need to look into local jewelers, see if any of them fit the profile. But first, I need to update my boss on this new information."

I cringed. "Is this the boss that you said has lost his trust in you and almost fired you?"

Her shoulders slumped. "Yeah. That's the one."

Mabel frowned. "Darn it. Too bad we can't just follow this lead without him and then come back with the killer *and* your triumphant redemption all in one fell swoop! Bam! Take that! No one would be doubting you anymore."

"I'm an employee of the government. Unfortunately, it doesn't work like that. I can't just go off chasing leads without his approval.

I winced, wishing I could spare her. I knew how much she wanted to prove herself, to show everyone that she was still the brilliant investigator she had always been. But I also knew that sometimes, you had to take risks to get results.

"Sarah," I said, my voice soft and gentle. "I know you're worried about making another mistake. But you can't let that fear hold you back. You're a darn good agent, and you've got the instincts to match. Trust yourself and trust us. We'll be right there with you, every step of the way."

Mabel gave a sharp nod of solidarity. "Millie's right, Sarah. You've got to follow your gut on this one. And if your boss gives you any trouble, just remind him that you're the one who's going to crack this case wide open."

Sarah took a deep breath, then squared her shoulders with a determined nod. "Okay. Let's do this. Time to talk to my boss and get permission to go back to the crime scene with fresh eyes."

My eyes went big as my anxiety surged thinking about returning to that gruesome place. "We're going back to the crime scene?"

"Yep. We need to look for clues with fresh eyes. Ones

that aren't focused on catching a male surgeon. Maybe we missed something."

Mabel shimmied with excitement. "Oh, man. This really is like all those crime shows we watched. How fun to be living it. This is way more exciting than haunting people!"

Sarah furrowed her brow. "Haunting people?"

Mabel waved a hand. "Nevermind that. All that matters is we're one big step closer to catching a killer and preventing any more innocent girls from dying. If I never have to see a beautiful, young woman standing over her dead body again, it will be too soon."

I nodded along at her words, remembering that as exciting as it was to be part of an investigation, this wasn't a game. It was a noble cause… a vow we had made to get justice for those women and put an end to the senseless killings.

"Well, I guess we need to go talk to my boss now." Sarah squared her shoulders, a flicker of apprehension crossing her face. "I know he's been tough on me since the incident, but I have to believe that he'll see the value in this new information."

We followed Sarah through the FBI building up to the offices of the head honchos. She knocked twice on a door, and a deep voice bid her to enter. Sarah strode into her boss's office with her chin held high, and even though I could practically feel the nervous energy radiating off her, she headed in wearing a cloak of confidence I knew she was internally lacking.

"Sir," Sarah said, her voice steady and confident. "I have a new lead in the serial killer case. The medical examiner has found evidence that suggests the murder weapon may be a wire, not a scalpel."

Her boss, a grizzled older man with a perpetual scowl sat at his mahogany desk behind a small plaque in front of him engraved with the words *FBI Director Ted Donahue*. He looked up from his stack of papers with a skeptical raised eyebrow. "A wire? What kind of wire?"

Sarah took a deep breath, then launched into an explanation of Dr. Patel's findings. She described the inconsistencies in the wound patterns, the mysterious residue that was being analyzed and noting that each victim was missing their jewelry.

"So, what are you suggesting, Sadler?" he asked, his tone gruff but not entirely dismissive. "That our killer isn't a surgeon?"

Sarah nodded, her eyes blazing with conviction. "Yes, sir. Specifically, I believe our killer may be a jeweler. The missing jewelry from the victims, the wire as a murder weapon, the skill required to create such precise wounds... it all fits."

Her boss leaned back in his chair, considering her words. For a moment, I thought he was going to shoot her down, to tell her that she was grasping at straws. But then, to my surprise, he gave a curt nod.

"Alright, Sadler. You've got my attention. Go on."

Sarah's shoulders sagged with relief, but only for a moment. "I need to revisit the last crime scene, sir. See if there's any evidence we might have missed that could point toward a jeweler or anyone else that may be using a wire for a weapon."

Her boss's eyes narrowed, and I could see the skepticism creeping back into his expression. "You want to go back to the scene? After what happened last time? I heard you had some kind of a… melt down? Something about two old women?"

I cringed knowing our actions had accidentally put her smack dab back on her boss's radar. Mabel and I exchanged a sheepish look.

Sarah flinched as if she'd been slapped, but to her credit, she didn't back down. "I know I made a mistake making a joke at a crime scene, sir. And I'm not going to let that happen again. But I believe in this lead, and I know I can find the evidence to support it. Please, just give me a chance."

"You're on probation, Sadler. You're not even supposed to be out in the field without your Training Agent. It was a courtesy we even let you go along to observe the investigation there with the team."

"I know, sir," she said quickly. "And I wouldn't ask if I didn't truly believe in my gut that this is a lead worth pursuing. And Agent Cooper is out on paternity leave now, so I don't even have a Training Agent, and I haven't been reassigned one while he's out."

"That's because we've got four high profile cases spreading our agents thin, and we don't have the resources to assign one to you right now. We're down three other agents right now on medical leave while they recover from their injuries."

His eyebrows rose with the accusation, and with the way Sarah almost melted into the chair she shrank so low, I didn't have to be a special agent to know that he referred to the accident she'd caused last month.

"Please, sir," she said softly. "I swear I won't cause any problems. I just want to go look at the scene with a fresh perspective. That's all I'm asking."

For a long, tense moment, her boss stared her down, his expression unreadable. Then, finally, he gave a grudging nod. "Fine. Take a look at the scene. But Sadler, if you screw this up..."

Sarah nodded, her jaw tight with determination. "I won't, sir."

He leaned forward, the sternness in his expression softening. "Your father was my partner and one of the best agents we've ever seen. That's why I'm so shocked that you've made so many missteps in your first year here. You were the most promising agent we'd seen in years."

He was her father's partner? Mabel and I exchanged a look, and I knew she was thinking the same thing.

"I know, sir. And I'm truly sorry I made some mistakes… mistakes I know my father wouldn't be proud of. Mistakes that let me, and you, down." Her voice shook for only a second, but then she cleared her throat. "But I know I'm an exceptional agent and I'm going to prove it to you and win back your respect if you'll just let me follow my instincts and go after this lead."

He looked at her thoughtfully, his eyes softening. "I've known you since you were a little girl. Hell, you used to call me Uncle Ted." He chuckled softly. "And it's because of that connection, because of my partnership with your father, that you still have a job right now after what happened last month. But I mean it, Sarah. You've got to get yourself together. No more mistakes. The higher ups are breathing down my neck to sideline you, so I'm taking a huge chance having your back. My ass is on the line too if you make a mess of things. Don't let me down."

I could see her fighting back the tears, but she was too strong to let them go. "Thank you, sir. I promise I won't let you, or my father, down. You have my word."

He sat back in his chair and gave her a nod. "Then go. Report back when you have something."

As we left the office, Mabel walked up beside her. "I know you can't talk to us right now because people are watching and you'll look like a looney tooney, but I'm breaking the rules to tell you that you did an amazing job in there. Nice work, Sarah."

She didn't look at us, and kept walking, but I saw her spine straighten a little taller.

I stepped up and matched her steps. "He's lucky to have you on his team, and he knows it. You're going to crack this case, and then everyone who doubts you will be singing a different tune."

We turned a corner where no one could see us, and Sarah shot me a grateful smile, but I could see the worry still lurking in her eyes. "Thanks, ladies. But let's not get ahead of ourselves. We still need to find that evidence."

Mabel crossed her arms, a mischievous smile tipping her lips up. "Well, then what are we waiting for? Let's get out there and start hunting for clues!"

As we made our way out of the FBI building and toward the last known crime scene, I couldn't help but feel a thrill of anticipation. We were on the brink of a breakthrough, I could feel it in my spectral bones. And with Sarah, Millie, and me on the case, I knew that no killer, no matter how twisted or clever, could hide from justice for long.

Chapter Thirteen

MABEL

The park was eerily quiet as Sarah, Millie, and I arrived at the last crime scene. The police tape had been removed, and it was hard to imagine that just a couple days ago this tranquil spot had been the site of a gruesome murder. The once bustling area now seemed devoid of life, and it didn't take a detective to know why. Who would want to visit a park that had just been the scene of a grisly crime scene?

As we walked toward the picnic table where the body had been found, I couldn't shake the horrifying image of the young woman's lifeless form, displayed like some macabre work of art, her right arm absent from the posed corpse. A shudder ran through me, and I wrapped my arms around myself, trying to ward off the chill that had nothing to do with the temperature.

Millie, noticing my discomfort, placed a gentle hand on my shoulder. "It looks so peaceful now. Like a park happy kids should be playing in, but instead, all I can think about is that gruesome image of that poor woman we helped cross over."

"I know. Me too. It's tough, Millie, but remember, that's why we're here. Let that image motivate us to find the clues we need to catch this twisted killer."

I nodded, drawing strength from her words and the determination in her eyes. We had a job to do, and I wasn't about to let my own fears and doubts get in the way.

"So, what do we do first?" Millie asked Sarah, who was walking around the picnic table like a shark circling its prey.

"We just start looking."

"For what?" I asked.

She shrugged. "That's the hard part. We don't know what we're looking for until we see it. Look for anything out of place. Anything that catches your eye. There's no such thing as a stupid question when it comes to investigations, so if you see something, say something. We can all decide together if it's a clue."

With a sharp nod, I tapped my fingers to my head and gave her a salute. "You got it. We'll start searching."

Millie and I used our ability to fly so we could make quick sweeps over the area. As we were passing back and forth, I noted that the picnic table was butted right up against the sidewalk, and an idea popped into my mind.

"Hey, didn't you say that they think the killer is a man because he has to be strong enough to carry the victims?"

"Yes," Sarah said. "But I don't necessarily buy that. I'm a small woman and I know that I could figure out a way to haul a body around."

I pointed at the sidewalk. "Like choosing areas that make it easy to pull the body in with something like, say, a wagon?"

She glanced at the sidewalk and then looked up at me. "Exactly, Mabel. Now you're thinking like an agent."

I beamed with pride, shooting Millie a huge grin that she answered with two thumbs up.

Sarah paused, tipping her head. "Thinking back, every posed body was next to an easy access for something on wheels. And they wouldn't have made an indent to catch our eye because the surfaces were either paved or graveled and well-traveled from things like bikes. So, it's something we wouldn't have caught."

"Happy to help." I hovered a little higher as my pride swelled inside me. "All those episodes of *Murder, She Wrote* and *Colombo* are really paying off."

Sarah chuckled then went back to scouring the area for any overlooked evidence. Millie and I fanned out again, darting from one spot to another, peering under benches and around trees, our movements growing more and more frantic as the minutes ticked by.

"This is just like that episode of *CSI* where they found the crucial piece of evidence in the most unlikely place," I mused, my head poking through a nearby bush. "Remember? It was stuck in the gum on the bottom of a park bench."

She snapped her fingers and lifted one in an "aha" gesture. "That's right! And then they had to bring in that special gum expert to analyze it. What was his name again? Dr. Sticky or something?"

"This was *CSI* not a kid's show. I'm pretty sure the writers were more clever than Dr. Sticky when naming the doctor who examined gum."

Millie tipped her head, musing, then started laughing. "Okay. Yeah. It wasn't Dr. Sticky."

I joined her in laughter, a welcome break from the darkness of our current duty, and even Sarah cracked a smile, shaking her head at our antics.

I floated up a nearby tree noticing a natural hole that would be an excellent place for a killer to hide a clue. Prepared to discover the piece of evidence that would crack the case wide open, I stuck my head inside. But instead of a clue, a pair of dark beady eyes blinked back at me, and I realized I was nose to nose with a raccoon.

"Ahhhh!" I shrieked, flying backward out of the tree, the force of my exit enough to send me into a head-over-heels out of control spin.

"Mabel!" Millie shrieked.

I screamed as I continued flipping in a dizzying tailspin I couldn't recover from. Millie flew over, catching me by the arm and hauling me to a stop.

"Whoa!" I breathed out as my body stopped spinning, but it seemed my head was still on that wild ride while I teetered in Millie's tight grip. "Holy crap! I was out of control!"

"What the heck happened?" she asked, keeping her grip on me as if worried the minute she let go I'd start flipping away again.

"I stuck my head in the tree to look for a clue and instead, I was staring right at a raccoon! Scared the crap out of me!"

"A raccoon?" Sarah asked, rushing over.

"Yes! Totally caught me off guard, and I realize now that it probably didn't even see me, and definitely can't hurt me, but my human survival instincts not to get my face bit off are apparently still alive and well. I shot out of there so fast I lost control of my body."

Millie palmed her face then looked at me, eyebrows inching up as she said, "Why in the world would you even think that the killer would put a clue up there in the hole of that tree? It's not like she can float, Mabel. So, you thought that she dragged a body down here, worked quickly to place the posed body without being discovered, and then dragged out a ladder to climb a tree and leave a clue behind in case a ghost that can fly would come along and investigate?"

I glanced at the tree, my lips twisting as I contemplated my decision to shove my head in a tree… and Millie was absolutely right. But instead of admitting my mistake, I just shrugged and said, "Gotta be thorough. Can't leave any stone unturned or any tree unsearched."

Millie shook her head but didn't tease me any further.

"But you're okay?" Sarah asked as Millie and I floated back down to stand beside her.

"I'm okay. Thanks to Millie."

She finally released her grip. "You're welcome. You scared me. Don't do that again!"

I shook my head. "I won't. That was pretty scary." Then I paused, remembering the excitement of flipping along much like the roller coasters I'd loved when I was alive. "Although, it was the first time since we died I had any kind of adrenaline rush. In fact, it was quite a thrill! Maybe I could—"

"Mabel," Millie warned. "Don't finish that sentence. We're not doing it again."

With a grunt, I tossed up my hands. "Fine. But I'm not promising it won't accidentally happen again at some point."

She pursed her lips and gave me that familiar look I'd seen often when she knew I was up to no good.

"Murder mystery. Finding clues. Focus," she said, and I nodded, lifting my chin as I remembered the somber task ahead of us.

"Glad you're okay," Sarah said. "I'm going to go back to where I was just looking."

As she turned to walk away, she suddenly swayed on her feet, her face draining of color. Millie and I were at her side in an instant, and suddenly I felt the weight of her in my hands as we stopped her from falling. It surprised me how quickly I'd been able to manifest the ability to interact with something solid when the need arose, and as we pushed her back upright, I was grateful we'd been practicing so much.

"Sarah, what's wrong?" I asked, my voice tight with concern.

She pressed a hand to her forehead, her eyes squeezing shut in pain. "It's just a headache and vertigo spell. I get them sometimes, ever since the incident."

I exchanged a worried glance with Millie. We both knew that Sarah's concussion had left her with more than just physical scars. The guilt and self-doubt that plagued her were just as debilitating as any headache but watching her lose her balance like that was upsetting.

"Maybe you should sit down for a minute," Millie suggested. "Take a break, catch your breath."

Sarah shook her head stubbornly, her breaths deep and deliberate as she remained still, her hands on her knees with her eyes closed tight. "No, I'm fine. We don't have time for this. The killer is still out there, and we need to find the evidence to stop them."

I bit my lip, torn between my admiration for Sarah's determination and my concern for her well-being. "Sarah, I really think you should get that checked out. Those symptoms could be a sign of something serious."

She laughed, but there was no humor in the sound. "And let everyone know that I'm damaged goods? No way. I'm already fighting an uphill battle to prove myself after what happened. The last thing I need is for people to think I'm weak or unfit for duty. I didn't mention these to the doctor—I needed them to clear me for duty. They'll go away on their own."

"Okay," I said softly. "But promise me you'll take care of yourself. And if these don't get better, you'll get yourself checked out. If you're in a dangerous situation and you have one of these episodes, it could end really badly for you. You can't catch a killer if you're running on empty. Or lying in a dizzy heap on the floor."

Sarah met my gaze, and for a moment, I saw the vulnerability she tried so hard to hide. Then, with a deep breath, she pushed her hands against her thighs and rose to standing, her shoulders squared, and her jaw set with determination.

"Fine. I promise," she said, and I hoped she meant it. "The episode is over. Let's get back to work."

We resumed our search, the moment of weakness forgotten as we focused on the task at hand. I continued floating along, then took a dip under the picnic table, scanning the grass for any clues. As I floated in a circle, I rolled onto my back and found myself staring at the bottom of the picnic table… and an interesting mark carved into the wood.

"Sarah, look at this," I called, my voice thrumming with excitement. "It looks like some kind of… I don't know. Symbol."

Sarah hurried over, her brow furrowed as she examined the tiny carving. "You're right. It's definitely not part of the original design. But what does it mean, and is it from our killer, or was it here before the murder?"

Millie poked her head under and scrunched her brow as she stared at it. "You know, if we're looking for a jeweler, a lot of them use a mark similar to that and stamp it into their pieces."

My eyes went big. "Millie! That's brilliant! Is this like a signature the artist left behind to mark their crime scene like they would their work?"

Sarah tipped her head. "You know, that's not a bad thought. I'm going to take some photos and we can run them through the database to see if they show up on any jeweler's art pieces. Nice work, Millie."

As Sarah snapped a photo, Millie grinned widely and I gave her a little fist bump, then we all crawled out from under the picnic table and sat on top of it.

"Now to find out if this is just a random carving or if it's really a signature from our killer, we'll see it at the other crime scenes." She pulled out her phone, scrolling through the crime scene photos from the other cases. Her frown deepened as she zoomed in on each image, trying to make out any similar marks or carvings.

"I can't tell if there's anything like this in the other photos," she said, frustration creeping into her voice. "It's going to take forever to drive around to all the crime scenes and check in person."

Millie and I exchanged a look, a silent conversation passing between us in the space of a heartbeat. We knew what we had to do.

"Sarah, show us the photos," I said, my voice calm and steady. "If we see a picture of the crime scene, we can transport ourselves there. We'll go look for any similar marks and be back in a jiffy."

Sarah's eyes widened, surprise and disbelief on her face. "You can do that? Just... teleport yourselves to a location based on a photo?"

I grinned, a mischievous glint in my eye. "Ghost powers, remember? We're full of surprises."

For a moment, Sarah hesitated. "I don't know. I'm the

trained FBI agent. I think I should really be there doing the investigation with you."

Millie smiled softly. "We'll just go take a look, and if we find something, we'll flash back and report to you straight away. And it's not like we can cause any damage. We're ghosts, remember?"

Twisting her lips, she seemed to be weighing the pros and cons of sending two ghostly amateurs to do the job of a trained investigator.

But in the end, practicality won out. With a sigh, she turned her phone toward us, the crime scene photos displayed on the screen.

"Okay," she said, her voice heavy with resignation.

"Okay?" I asked, my voice lifting with excitement.

"Okay," she said, then her face turned stern. "But be careful. And come back as soon as you find anything."

"We will. We'll just go look around for any kind of a similar mark and blink back to you the moment we find anything."

"Sounds good. I'll wait here and keep looking for more clues."

"We'll be back in a jiffy," Millie said, then she looked at me and nodded, our faces serious despite the thrill of excitement racing through us.

With a final glance at the photo, we closed our eyes and focused on the location. The world around us blurred and shifted before the vortex opened up and pulled us in. As we materialized in the beautiful public garden where the third body had been found, I was struck by the breathtaking beauty that surrounded us.

The meticulously landscaped grounds were a vibrant tapestry of colors, with lush green grass stretching out like a plush carpet and flower beds overflowing with a rainbow of blooms. The air was filled with the gentle hum of bees and the sweet fragrance of roses, lavender, and honeysuckle. A winding path of smooth cobblestones led to a magnificent fountain at the center of the garden, its water sparkling in the sunlight as it cascaded over the intricately carved stone. It was hard to believe that such a tranquil and idyllic setting had been the scene of a brutal crime, the remnants of the yellow police tape fluttering in the breeze serving as a jarring reminder of the gruesome body that had been found posed here.

"Whoa," Millie breathed, her eyes wide with wonder. "This place is beautiful."

I nodded in agreement, my heart racing with the thrill of our newfound abilities. But as much as I wanted to revel in the moment, I knew we had a job to do.

"Come on," I said, my voice taking on a no-nonsense tone that would have made any TV detective proud. "Let's start looking for those marks."

We scoured the area, our eyes peeled for any sign of the mysterious symbol. We checked under benches and tables, behind trees and bushes, even in the cracks of the sidewalk. But each search turned up empty, and I found my frustration growing with the passing moments.

"Where was the body positioned at this crime scene?" Millie asked as we stood together looking around.

"Over there." I pointed to the fountain in the center of the garden.

"Let's go look at that again. The killer made the mark right under the last body, so it would make sense that they would make their mark closer to this one."

"Unless the last mark wasn't from the killer," I sighed, realizing that maybe it was nothing and just some mark carved by a teenager or a kid.

"Come on. Let's look again."

We went back over for a second look and started scouring the flowers and rocks around the fountain again.

Just as I was starting to lose hope, Millie let out a triumphant shout. "Mabel, over here! I found something!"

I rushed over to where she was standing, and there, carved into a rock surrounding the fountain was a small, intricate symbol, almost identical to the one we had found at the first crime scene.

"That's it," I breathed, my fingers tracing the delicate lines. "That's the same artist's mark."

Millie nodded, her face serious despite the glint of excitement in her eyes. "We need to show Sarah. She has to come see this for herself."

"Wow. We're like real detectives now, Millie. Cagney and Lacey had nothing on us." I bumped her with an elbow, and she grinned widely back at me.

With a final glance at the mysterious mark, we closed our eyes and focused on Sarah's location. The world blurred around us once more, and when we opened our eyes, we found ourselves back at the first crime scene, Sarah pacing anxiously nearby.

She stopped and spun toward us, her eyes wide as we popped back into her life. "Whoa. That was weird. You just appeared out of nowhere."

"Yeah, this whole teleporting thing is taking us a little getting used to, but it's extremely handy."

"Did you find anything?" she asked, her voice tight with anticipation.

Millie and I nodded in unison, our faces serious. "We found the same artist's mark at the other crime scene," I said, my voice steady despite the excitement that thrummed through me. "You need to come see it for yourself."

Sarah's eyes widened, her mouth dropping open in surprise. "You're kidding. You really found one?"

"Yep. It's there. No doubt now it's the killer's mark. We'll show you."

She didn't hesitate, and with a nod, she grabbed her keys and headed for her car.

"Let's go," she said, her voice filled with a newfound determination.

As Millie and I watched her climb into her car, I couldn't help but feel a surge of pride and satisfaction. We were finally making progress, finally getting closer to the truth behind these terrible crimes.

Sarah opened her window and called, "You ladies riding with me or am I meeting you there?"

We looked at each other and grinned. "We're part of a team. I say we ride with her."

Millie nodded in agreement, so we flew over and through the door, landing in the back seat.

I gave a sharp nod of my head to Sarah as she looked at us in the rearview. "Let's go catch a killer."

Chapter Fourteen

MILLIE

The sun setting over the city cast long glowing shadows across the bustling streets as Sarah, Mabel, and I walked toward the FBI building. We had spent the afternoon visiting the various crime scenes, searching for more clues that might lead us to the killer. The discovery of the mysterious symbols at each crime scene had given us a renewed sense of purpose and determination.

As we made our way through the halls of the FBI, I could sense the tension radiating off Sarah. She had been quiet on the drive back, her brow furrowed in deep thought. I knew she was still processing the implications of our findings and trying to figure out how to present them to her boss.

We had just settled into Sarah's office when her phone rang. Sarah picked it up, her expression morphing into one of surprise as she listened to the person on the other end.

"Dr. Patel, thank you for getting back to me so quickly," she said, her voice tinged with excitement as she looked at us. "You have the results of the substance analysis from the wounds?"

Mabel and I exchanged a look of anticipation. This could be the breakthrough we had been waiting for.

Sarah's eyes widened as she listened to Dr. Patel's findings, her free hand gripping the edge of her desk. "Clay? The substance found in the wounds was clay?"

A jolt of realization coursed through me, the pieces of the puzzle suddenly clicking into place. "Clay... like a sculptor would use?" I whispered to Mabel, my mind racing with the implications.

Mabel nodded, her eyes alight with understanding. "Is there any sculpting tool that would cause the kind of wounds we've been seeing? Ask her! Ask her! Wait! Put her on speaker so we can hear!" she practically bounced up and down with excitement.

Sarah rolled her eyes but then honored the demand and pressed the speaker button before relaying the question to Dr. Patel.

Dr. Patel's voice filled up the room as we listened intently. "Yes, there are several tools that could potentially match the wound patterns. Wire cutters, clay shapers, even certain types of knives used for carving and shaping clay. I can have tests run on various sculpting tools to see if any of them match the pattern of the wound and get you an exact weapon."

"That would be great. Thank you, Dr. Patel," Sarah said, giving us a little nod.

Mabel and I leaped into the air, floating in a circle while holding hands, our excitement overriding any sense of decorum. "It's not a doctor or a jeweler!" I exclaimed, my voice echoing through the room. "It's a sculptor! A different kind of artist! We're hot on the trail!"

Sarah shot us a warning look, but I could see the glimmer of excitement in her eyes. She thanked Dr. Patel for her findings and ended the call, turning to face us with a determined expression.

"A sculptor," she repeated, her voice barely above a whisper. "It makes sense, doesn't it? The way the bodies are posed, like macabre works of art. The missing body parts, as if…" She paused and her face darkened before she finished by saying, "Oh, that's a horrible thought, but what if the killer is using them to create some kind of twisted human sculpture. Each body is missing a different part, that together would create a whole once she's finished."

I felt a wave of nausea wash over me at the thought, my stomach churning with revulsion. "That's actually the most horrifying thing I think I've ever heard," I muttered, my face twisting into a grimace. "Who could do something like that?"

Mabel shook her head, her own expression one of disgust and anger. "Someone seriously messed up in the noggin," she said, her voice hard with determination. "But now we know what we're dealing with, and we're going to stop them before they can hurt anyone else. So, what do we do next? Start shaking down some artists to get some leads?"

Sarah shook her head. "Not yet. I need to update my boss on this new information," she said, rising from her desk. "If we're going to pursue this lead, I'll need his approval and support."

As we followed Sarah through the halls of the FBI, I could sense the anxious energy radiating off her. She had been through so much in the past few months, from the incident that had nearly cost her her life to the constant scrutiny and doubt from her colleagues. I knew how much this case meant to her, not just as a way to catch a killer, but as a chance to prove herself and regain the trust of those around her.

This time, Sarah asked us not to come in and distract her. We waited outside the office as she knocked on the door, her spine straight and her shoulders squared. When her boss called for her to enter, she took a deep breath and stepped inside, leaving Mabel and me to pace anxiously in the hallway.

"Do you think he'll go for it?" Mabel asked, her brow furrowed with worry. "He hasn't exactly been supportive of Sarah lately."

I bit my lip, my own doubts and fears swirling in my mind. "He has to," I said, my voice barely above a whisper. "Sarah's onto something here, and if he can't see that, then he's an idiot and who cares what he thinks."

We fell silent as we strained to hear the muffled conversation taking place behind the closed door. I could make out the low rumble of her boss's voice, followed by Sarah's measured responses. There were moments of tense silence, punctuated by the occasional raised voice or frustrated sigh.

After what felt like an eternity, the door opened and Sarah emerged, her expression unreadable. Mabel and I rushed to her side, our questions tumbling out in a jumble of words.

"What did he say?" Mabel asked, her eyes wide with anticipation.

Sarah took a deep breath, her gaze flickering between us. "He's concerned," she said, her voice tight with emotion. "He doesn't want me to make another mistake, to put myself or anyone else in danger."

Anger started flaring in my chest at her boss's lack of

faith in her, but Sarah held up a hand, cutting off my protests before they could begin.

"But," she continued, a small smile tugging at the corners of her mouth, "he's willing to trust my instincts on this one. He's giving me the green light to pursue the sculptor lead, as long as I keep him informed every step of the way."

Mabel let out a whoop of joy, pushing off the ground and doing a victory dance in the air. A surge of relief washed over me, the tension that had been coiled in my muscles finally releasing.

"He did warn me, though," Sarah said, her expression sobering. "He's the only one who has my back right now. If I screw this up, it's not just my job on the line, but his reputation as well. He's taking a big risk, trusting me after everything that's happened."

I reached out, my hand hovering just above Sarah's shoulder in a gesture of comfort. "You won't let him down," I said, my voice firm with conviction. "*We* won't let him down. We're in this together, and we're going to see it through to the end."

Sarah nodded, a flicker of determination sparking in her eyes. "Let's do this," she said, squaring her shoulders as she turned to head back to her office.

As we made our way through the main area where the other agents were working, I couldn't help but overhear the whispers and snickers that followed in Sarah's wake. They were talking about the incident that had nearly ended her career, the bomb that had left her with a concussion and a shattered reputation. They were mocking her for her supposed "hallucinations" of two old ladies at a crime scene, their voices dripping with disdain and disbelief.

I noticed Sarah's steps falter, her head dropping as the weight of their words settled on her shoulders. Mabel and I exchanged a glance, our hearts aching for the pain and embarrassment our friend was feeling.

The only agent who didn't join the growing group of malicious whisperers was the little blonde agent who'd stuck up for Sarah at the crime scene. Instead of smirking and laughing at the jokes, her sympathetic eyes followed her as she made her way toward her office.

As the snickers continued, suddenly, Mabel's expression hardened, a mischievous glint sparking in her eyes. Before I could stop her, she grabbed my hand, yanking me along with her.

"Mabel! What are you doing?"

She didn't answer, pulling me with her across the room, weaving through the desks and chairs until she reached the agent who had been leading the charge against Sarah.

With a noticeable grunt of effort and a flick of her wrist, Mabel sent a stack of papers flying off the agent's desk, scattering them across the floor in a flurry of white.

Finally, I realized what she was doing and why she'd dragged me with her. She needed our combined energy to get some well-deserved justice for Sarah.

A sly smile spread across my face as I gripped her hand tighter. "Get him," I whispered.

Mabel positioned herself behind him, then with a look of sheer determination and a burst of energy I knew she worked hard to channel, she kicked him in his behind. He stumbled forward, his arms pinwheeling as he tried to regain his balance, but it was too late. He crashed to the ground, landing in an undignified heap right next to his desk.

"Hey! You really got him good! Whoa!" I clapped. Moving papers was one thing, but knocking over a human being was entirely another and far more power than we'd ever manifested before.

"I'm pissed off! I think that helps!" Mabel answered, her attention spinning back to the agent now bending down to gather up the mess.

I couldn't help but giggle at the sight, my body shaking with building laughter. But Mabel wasn't done yet. With a mischievous grin, she reached out and tapped the cup of coffee sitting on the edge of the desk, sending it tipping over and spilling its contents all over the agent's backside.

The other agents erupted in laughter, pointing and jeering at their fallen colleague. "Looks like he's had an accident!" one of them crowed, clutching his sides as he howled with mirth. "Better change your pants, buddy. It looks like you've crapped yourself!"

I glanced over at Sarah, expecting to see her cringing with second-hand embarrassment. But to my surprise, she was fighting back a smile, her eyes sparkling with barely contained amusement.

"Tada!" Mabel exclaimed as she floated above the fallen agent, her arms wide before she took a bow.

I clapped and bounced up and down, "Well done, Mabel! Hurray! You sure showed that jerk!"

Mabel did an inappropriate thrusting gesture over the agent, causing me to break down in giggles, then I looked over at Sarah, unsure how she'd feel that we'd just essentially haunted the living. But there was no scolding stare meeting my eyes, and instead, I was pleasantly surprised to see a small smile on her face as she looked at us, giving a slight nod of gratitude.

Mabel floated upside down, stuck her tongue out at the man with the wet behind—now the laughingstock of the office—as he clamored to his feet. Then we drifted back to the ground and headed toward Sarah. As we rounded the corner into the privacy of the hallway, Sarah let out a breath, her shoulders sagging with relief. "Thank you," she said, her voice soft with gratitude. "I don't know what I did to deserve you two, but I'm so glad you're here."

I nodded, my smile stretching across my face. "We've got your back, Sarah. No matter what."

"Man, it really helps to channel the energy to interact with the world when you're pissed off. Gotta remember that for the future, Millie," Mabel said excitedly, then her face tightened with a scowl and a glare. "And when someone is picking on our girl, Sarah, that's a whole different level of anger. No one messes with the best agent in the business and gets away with it. Not when we're around. We've got your back."

Sarah's smile widened, her eyes glistening with unshed tears. For someone who came off cold and aloof, it warmed my heart to see that we'd somehow started wiggling our way into hers.

"I know," she said, her voice thick with emotion. "And I can't tell you how much that means to me. My whole life I've never really had any… friends."

"Never?" My eyes popped wide, my heart clenching at the thought of not having a friendship like I had with my Mabel. How empty and sad my life would have been without her.

She shook her head. "No. Never. I knew I wanted to be like my dad from the time I was little, so I had to work extra hard to be the best at everything so I could earn a place right here in this building." She gestured to the sterile white walls and outdated brown carpet surrounding us. "I didn't have time to play with the kids on the street or join a team. I was studying, trying to stay at the top of my class. And admittedly, I'm competitive. Working with other people isn't my strong suit, and in this line of work, most of us are competitive and cutthroat. So, I've gone at it alone, always looking for any way to push myself to the head of the class. To be smarter, faster, and more clever than anyone I'm up against. And because of that, I don't have any friends."

"You do now," Mabel said quickly. "We're you're friends. And friends always have each other's backs. And they don't ever hesitate to ask for help. And they lean on each other when they need support." She looked at me, her smile softening, and I touched my heart knowing she was speaking of our decade's long friendship. "We rely on each other, and now you can rely on us."

"Always," I said. "We have your back, Sarah. And you can trust us."

"Not to mention having ghost friends means we can secretly kick the ass of the guy who is giving you a hard time. Literally!"

Sarah laughed, her eyes shone with the new light of understanding, and I knew for the first time in her life, she was starting to understand what friendship could bring to her life. We stood there for a moment, basking in the warmth of our growing bond and the strength of our shared purpose.

"Thanks for doing that for me. It was pretty funny."

Mabel rubbed her hands together, a mischievous glint in her eye. "Well, I for one plan on continuing to haunt that jerk of an agent. He's got it coming, and I've got plenty more tricks up my ghostly sleeve."

I shook my head, but a fond smile tugged at my lips

remembering how much Mabel liked giving people their comeuppance. "As fun as that sounds, maybe hold off on that for now," I said, my voice gentle but firm. "We've got bigger fish to fry."

Sarah nodded, her expression thoughtful. "Millie's right," she said, her voice taking on a note of authority. "Our priority right now is finding this sculptor and stopping them before they can hurt anyone else."

Mabel's playful expression stiffened. "So, what's our next move?"

She paused, her brow furrowing as she considered it. "Well, I guess the first step is doing some online research and trying to find out if any sculptors used an artist's mark like the one we found. We can have it scanned into the database and search to see if it's online anywhere. Then we can compile a list of female sculptors in the area and cross-reference them to see if any have a violent history. Most serial killers don't have a criminal record, which is why they can often blend in so seamlessly with society, but we still need to run the check to cover all our bases. And then, if we don't have anything substantial, the next step would be to visit the art district and get boots on the ground with some good old-fashioned leg work."

I got excited at the thought of following Sarah around while she shook down some suspects. This really was as exciting as getting to step right into our favorite who-done-it mysteries we'd loved when we were alive.

Mabel tipped her head. "Did you guys ever find any clues at the murder scenes? Maybe now that we've got this new information, we should go back with fresh eyes and give them a once over as well."

Sarah shook her head. "Yeah, that would be nice, but

we've never found the murder scenes, only the places where she displayed the bodies. No can do."

Mabel and I exchanged a look, then I said, "Um, we know where two of the murder scenes are."

Sarah's eyes flashed big. "Wait, what?"

I nodded. "Yes. When our beacon goes off to help a soul, we get transported to where they died. Our job is to help them say goodbye to their earthly body and move on. We were transported to two different places for the last two victims. One a park and the other an alley."

"Wait. So you're telling me you know *exactly* where the bodies were when they were killed?"

We both nodded our heads.

"Oh my God! This is huge!" Sarah said, spinning on her heel and rushing toward her office. "I'm grabbing my purse and we're heading there right now!"

As we followed behind her, Mabel whispered, "I guess maybe we should have told her earlier that we know where the murder scenes are."

I whispered back. "I didn't realize they didn't know. Now I feel bad we didn't say anything."

We shared an oops look and hurried along behind Sarah. When she reached her office, she grabbed her blazer off the back of her chair and reached for her purse. A small knock at the door caused us all to spin toward it.

"Agent Sadler?" the petite blonde agent we'd seen at the crime scene said from where she stood in the doorway.

"Yes, Agent Collins?" Sarah slid her purse over her shoulder, no doubt chomping at the bit to see the murder scenes.

"I just wanted to say that I'm sorry everyone is giving you such a hard time. I heard what they were saying out there, as I know you did too, and I just want you to know that we all make mistakes, and I know that you're an amazing agent. They're just jealous, you know."

Millie and I took a small, sharp inhale, and my heart squeezed in my chest hearing someone Sarah worked with having her back.

Sarah looked taken aback as Agent Collins went on.

"Everyone was absolutely terrified of you when we all got hired together last year. Your dad was a legend here, and you were a legend at Quantico. You broke almost every record they had, and we would all talk about how nervous we were to work with you."

"You were?" Sarah asked, her voice higher than normal.

Agen Collins laughed. "Oh my God, yes! I was fangirling so hard when I met you. We all were. But those guys were threatened by you."

"Of course they were," Mabel whispered. "Because she kicks ass, and they suck."

I shooshed her, wanting to hear Agent Collins's speech.

"When you made a mistake, they jumped on you like a bunch of weak wolves who saw a chance to take down the alpha as a group. They're only acting like this because they know you're better than them, but if they can keep you beat down, maybe you'll quit so one of them can be top dog."

She stepped a little further into the office. "So don't. Don't let them make you quit. I know you're going to make some kind of an epic comeback, and I just wanted you to know that I'm totally here for it. So forget what they said, okay? You're an amazing agent. I know it, they know it, and I hope you know it too."

Sarah stood wordlessly staring at Agent Collins, then finally a small smile lifted her lips. "Thank you for saying that. It... it means a lot to me."

Agent Collins winked. "I'm only telling you the truth. I'll see you around."

"Bye," Sarah said, her voice still sounding a bit stunned.

As soon as Agent Collins left, Mabel and I rushed over to Sarah. "See! You *are* an amazing agent! She's absolutely right. Those guys are just threatened by you, and they are going to be a whole lot more threatened when you solve this case and stick it to them!"

I nodded. "They aren't even going to know what hit them. And hey. You said you don't have any friends? Well, even though we're happy to be your friends, it may be fun to make one that can be seen talking to you in public. And from what I just saw, I think you've got a great candidate right there. And let me tell you, having a best friend is the most magical thing in the world."

Mabel gave me a wink, and Sarah shrugged. "I don't know. Maybe? I wouldn't even know how to start a friendship. I'm twenty-six years old, have a criminal justice degree from Harvard and a Master of Science in Criminology from the University of Pennsylvania. I was the top of my class at Quantico, and yet, I haven't the faintest idea how to go about something as simple as making a friend."

I gave her a little wink. "Lucky for you, when it comes to friendship, we're the experts. We'll teach you what you need to know."

"Thanks, ladies. I appreciate the support. And as much as I'd love to sit here and get friendship lessons from you, we've got a murder scene to get to. Now, lead the way."

With a grateful smile, Sarah opened the door and strode out into the hallway, Mabel and I following behind. As we made our way out of the building and into the gathering dusk, I knew that we were one step closer to getting justice for our two souls who'd been ripped from this world too soon, as well as the others we hadn't gotten to meet.

As we climbed into Sarah's car and set off into the night, I bundled up all my courage to go back to the scene of the crime and face the horrors I'd felt that fateful day. But no matter what challenges lay ahead, I knew one thing for certain: with Sarah, Mabel, and myself working together, there was nothing we couldn't face. Together.

Chapter Fifteen

MABEL

The eerie stillness of the woods along the running path sent a shiver down my spine as Sarah, Millie, and I arrived at the murder site of the first victim we'd met. It seemed so peaceful, but the lingering energy of the gruesome crime still hung heavy in the air. It was hard to believe that an innocent young woman had taken her last breath in this very spot.

"Where was the body?" Sarah asked, wasting no time in getting started on her investigation.

"Right there." I pointed to the spot in the grass where we'd found the woman standing over her lifeless corpse.

Sarah wasted no time, her keen eyes scanning the scene for any clues that might still linger all these days later. Mabel and I waited nearby, staying out of her way while she worked the scene with her expertly trained eyes.

"Poor girl was just running along enjoying life and then…*bam.* Dead." I shook my head.

Millie shuddered. "It was so sad. She wasn't ready to go

at all. She said she was on her nightly run and then suddenly, she was attacked."

Sarah's head snapped up from where she studied the grass our victim had been found in. "Did she say that? Nightly run?"

I nodded, immediately picking up on where she was going. "Yes. In fact, both victims mentioned that they were in their routine. The runner said it was her nightly route, and the other woman said she took this shortcut every evening on her way home from work."

Sarah nodded, her brow furrowed in concentration. "These areas are so secluded," she murmured, gesturing to the deserted alleyway. "It's not the kind of place a killer would just stumble upon by chance. Which means—"

"They were stalked," I whispered, a shiver trembled through me, a mix of anger and sorrow. "The killer must have been watching them, learning their routines, waiting for the perfect moment to strike."

Millie looked around at the bushes and trees surrounding the path as if someone may be in there stalking us.

Sarah's eyes narrowed in tight determination. "Exactly. These weren't victims of chance the killer stumbled onto. We noticed they all looked similar. Same dark hair. Same age. Same color eyes. No doubt she picked them for a reason and stalked them, watching their routines until she could find the perfect place to kill them. A spot secluded enough she could do it quickly and leave the body for a short period until she could come back and get it. You said you spent a few minutes with the souls before they passed over, and you didn't see her, so we know she had to leave and come back. Probably to get something to transport them."

Like a bloodhound who'd caught a scent, Sarah followed her logical thinking to look for more clues. As she swept the light from her flashlight across the grass, suddenly, she froze.

Sarah crouched down, her gloved fingers tracing the faint impressions in the dirt and grass right next to where the body had been. "Look here," she said, her voice tight with excitement. "Tire tracks, narrow and shallow. It looks like some kind of wheeled cart or wagon."

Millie and I exchanged a knowing glance.

"Just like we suspected," I said. "The killer is using a wagon to transport the bodies."

"This is a solid clue. Maybe I can get impressions and figure out a brand or model of the tire and cross reference it with which wagon makers use them. Do a search for anyone in the area that's bought that type of wagon and see if any are sculptors."

Millie's face lit up. "See? This is why you're the top agent. Brilliant!"

Sarah looked up at us, her eyes flickering with excitement. Before we could discuss this new clue further, a glowing light began blinking, lighting up the darkness with its blue glow. I glanced down at my wrist, where the Crossing Guard beacon was flashing insistently.

"Millie," I said, my voice urgent. "We've got a soul to guide."

Millie's eyes widened, her gaze falling to my wrist. "But we can't leave Sarah alone out here," she protested, glancing around the darkened alley with a shudder. "It's not safe."

Sarah straightened up, a wry smile tugging at the corners of her mouth. She tapped the gun holstered at her hip, the metal glinting in the dim light of my beacon.

"Don't worry about me," she said, her voice calm and assured. "I may have been a bit of a mess lately, but I was top of my class at Quantico. I'm a perfect shot, and I can take care of myself."

Millie and I hesitated for a moment, torn between our duty as Crossing Guards and our concern for Sarah's safety. But the insistent pulse of my beacon reminded us that a soul was waiting, in need of our guidance.

"We'll be back as soon as we can," I said, then looked around once more to make sure we didn't see any dangers lurking in the dark.

"I'll be fine. Go."

Millie chewed on her lip, then gave me a nod. We closed our eyes and focused on the soul's location. The world blurred around us as we were pulled into the vortex, the colors and sounds of the park fading away.

When we opened our eyes again, we found ourselves in a dimly lit hospital room. An elderly man stood above his pale, thin body, staring at the corpse hooked up to a variety of machines. But his gaze wasn't fixed on his own lifeless form—it was on the gray-haired woman sitting in the bedside chair, her weathered hands clutching his still fingers as tears streamed down her cheeks.

The steady beep of the heart monitor filled the room, and suddenly, an explosion of commotion burst in, nurses rushing right through our spectral forms to his side.

"Code blue!" one yelled.

Another nurse with a solemn tone shook her head. "No. He's a DNR, remember? We have to let him go. And it's for the best. He was in a lot of pain."

The man's spirit remained focused on his wife, his ethereal hand reaching toward her face as if trying to comfort her while she sobbed beside him, her body wracking with grief.

"Agatha," he whispered, though she couldn't hear him. "Oh, my sweet Agatha."

Finally, he looked up to see Millie and me. A flicker of recognition sparked in his eyes, but worry creased his brow. "You're not nurses. Are you... are you here to take me away?" he asked, his voice barely above a whisper. "Because I can't leave her. Not yet. She needs me."

Millie and I exchanged a gentle look. "Yes," she said, her voice soft and understanding. "We're here to guide you to the other side, where peace and rest await. But we know it's hard to leave someone you love."

The man's face crumpled as he looked back at his wife. "I'm ready to go. I've been sick for so long. Ready to leave my broken body behind. But we've been married for sixty-two years. She doesn't know how to be without me. Look at her—she's falling apart already."

The nurses tried to take her out of the room, but she folded forward, clutching her lifeless love and clinging to him the way I'd clung to Millie when she'd left me.

I moved closer, my heart aching for his pain. "What's your name?"

"Lenny," he said, his voice thick with emotion. "And that's my Agatha. My whole world. I can't leave her."

"Lenny," I said gently, "I understand your worry. But staying here won't help Agatha heal. She needs to grieve, to say goodbye, to learn how to carry your love forward. There's nothing you can do for her now, and you can't stay here. But don't worry. You'll see her again when it's her time."

"But what if she can't handle it alone?" His eyes glistened with unshed tears.

Millie reached out and took his hand. "She's stronger than you think. You helped make her that strong over sixty-two years. And Lenny, where you're going... it's more wonderful than you can imagine. Everyone is happy, everything is perfect, and when it's Agatha's time, you'll be there waiting for her."

"Is it as wonderful as they say?" he asked, glancing between us with desperate hope.

"Better," Millie said, her voice warm with conviction. "Everyone you've lost will be there, and someday, when it's her time, you'll be reunited with Agatha for eternity. And, one of the best parts… you can conjure up cake with the blink of an eye!"

Despite his tears, Lenny let out a small chuckle. "I haven't had an appetite in months. Cake sounds wonderful."

"It is wonderful," I agreed. "And Lenny, when you get there, this sick, frail body you're in will be transformed to whatever age you were when you were happiest."

A glimmer of wonder crossed his pale, gaunt face. "Really? I can be young and handsome again?"

"You can." We smiled at each other. "We died going on ninety, but we look like we're in our seventies because that was the time in our lives we were happiest. If you were happiest in your twenties, then twenty is what you'll be."

His eyes brightened for the first time. "I was a real looker back in my day. Agatha used to say I looked like Cary Grant." He paused, his expression softening. "Maybe when she gets there, I can sweep her off her feet all over again."

"I have no doubt you will," I said warmly.

Lenny looked back at his wife one more time, watching

as she pressed a gentle kiss to his forehead. "Okay. I'll go," he whispered. "Let me just say goodbye."

My heart ached as I watched Agatha weep over Lenny's still form, and I was transported back to that devastating day when I'd sat beside Millie's lifeless body, consumed by grief so profound it had literally killed me. I remembered the bottomless despair, the feeling that life held no meaning without her. If only I'd known then what I knew now—that death wasn't an ending but a doorway, that our love would carry forward into something even more beautiful than what we'd shared on Earth. But like Agatha now, I'd been lost in the darkness of not knowing, drowning in the belief that goodbye meant forever. How I wished I could tell Agatha that her tears, though natural and necessary, were only temporary. That Lenny would be waiting, young and handsome as Cary Grant again, ready to sweep her off her feet for all eternity when her time came.

Millie and I pressed together closer, our fingers entwining as we watched Lenny walk around behind Agatha. His hand hovered over her shoulder as he leaned down and brushed a tender kiss to her cheek. "You are the love of my life, Agatha. And I'm so sorry I had to leave you behind all alone. But I will be waiting for you, my love. As long as it takes, I'll be waiting."

Suddenly, Agatha stiffened, her head raising from its place on his chest as her eyes searched the empty spaces of the room. A small smile tipped her lips, as her teary blue eyes joined the soft gesture.

"Lenny. I can feel you."

Millie squeezed my hand tighter as my throat and heart constricted at once.

"Oh, Agatha. I'm here my darling. And I'll miss you.

Please go be happy. I can't leave until I know you'll be okay."

She sat in silence for a moment, then her gaze fell back down to the body of the man she'd loved most of her life. She took his hand in hers and squeezed.

"I love you, Lenny," she whispered, her voice breaking. "I'll be okay. I promise I'll be okay until we're together again. Thank you for loving me. Thank you for giving me the most wonderful life. I'll find you again in the next one, I promise. I'll always find you."

Tears poured down Lenny's face, but instead of sadness, his face radiated with peace and joy. "She felt me," he said in wonder. "She knew I was saying goodbye."

"Indeed she did," I said softly. "And now it's time to go. You'll see her again when she's ready."

His hand hovered just above her shoulder for one more moment, then he closed his eyes and exhaled a breath. "Okay. I'm ready. How do I do this?"

"All you need to do is take our hands. We'll help you go."

With a final, tender glance at Agatha, Lenny walked over and took my outstretched hands. As the warm, welcoming light began to envelop him, Agatha suddenly looked up from his still form, her tear-filled eyes scanning the room as if she sensed something.

"I'll see you again, my love. Goodbye."

The light pulsed around him, filled with all the love and reunion awaiting him in Heaven. As he faded from view, Agatha pressed her face against his chest one more time, her shoulders shaking with both grief and a strange sense of peace, as if she truly had felt his loving farewell.

We stared at the space he'd been for a moment, and this time we didn't feel sadness in sending a soul on. He was ready, and we knew what awaited him in Heaven was going to be a welcome reprieve from the pain of his last days of existence. But still, it was a bittersweet beauty of a soul's transition—the sadness of love temporarily separated, but the joy of knowing that connection would be restored in the most perfect way imaginable. And perhaps most beautiful of all, the mysterious way love could bridge even the gap between life and death, allowing Agatha to sense Lenny's final goodbye.

As we watched Agatha saying farewell to her lifetime love, the beautiful moment reminded me why our work as Crossing Guards mattered so much—helping souls find peace. I couldn't help but think of the murdered women we were trying to help—souls ripped away before they could experience a love like Lenny and Agatha's, before they could live full lives and say proper goodbyes.

"We need to get back to Sarah," I said quietly. "There's still work to do."

Millie nodded, understanding the urgency in my voice. With a final respectful glance at the grieving widow, we transported ourselves back to the crime scene, and my heart stuttered when I saw Sarah sitting in the grass, her fingers pressed into her temples and a pained look on her face.

"Sarah! Are you okay? Are you hurt?" We whisked over to her, each landing at her side.

"Have you been assaulted? What's happened?" Millie asked, panicked, her eyes searching everywhere for an assailant.

Sarah shook her head gently, her eyes squeezing shut as she fought through the discomfort. "No, it's... it's my headaches again. I was bent over looking at a clue, and the vertigo just hit me out of nowhere."

"Oh, Sarah. I really think you should get this checked out."

Sarah's eyes snapped open, a flare of defensiveness flickering in their depths. "I can't," she said, her voice tight with frustration. "If I admit to any weakness, if I let them see me as anything less than perfect, they'll never take me seriously again. I'll be sidelined, written off as damaged goods."

"But you could get hurt if you're in a situation and these episodes strike."

Knowing I wanted her to get looked at, I used a technique I knew would resonate with a moral and protective person like Sarah. "Or you could get your colleagues hurt if you're on a mission together and this happens. And I know you couldn't live with yourself if that happened."

She looked up, her eyes filled with recognition, but then she softly shook her head. "I know. I do. But I'm not working with anyone right now that isn't already dead, so I promise I'll get this checked out if I ever think it could put someone beside myself in danger. I would never do that."

"I know," I said quickly, not wanting to make her feel bad. "We just worry about you and want you to get checked out to make sure this isn't something serious. You've been going at everything all alone for so long, I think it's time you realize you don't have to do everything by yourself anymore. You can show weakness and lean on people for help when you need it. Lord knows I do." I looked at Millie and she smiled.

I felt a pang of understanding, my heart swelling with empathy. Sarah hadn't had a Millie in her life like I had. She's never learned to trust someone else completely and know with certainty they wouldn't use it against her. "Sarah, I know it's scary to admit when you need help. But sometimes, the strongest thing you can do is to let others in, to trust that they'll have your back when you need it most."

Sarah let out a soft sigh. "Yeah. I just… I don't know how to be vulnerable without worrying someone is going to use it against me. It's scary admitting you need help, and right now in my situation with everyone staring at me waiting to fail, I just don't think I can put my neck out there any further. Unless things get worse or I feel like I'm going to put someone in danger, I just want to deal with the episodes when they happen and move on."

"Okay," I said, understanding her hesitation in admitting the aftereffects of her head injury. "Just promise us you won't hide your issues from us at least. We're here to help. And if things get worse, promise you'll get checked out."

"I will. I promise. I just need a little more time," she said then rose to standing.

"You okay?" Millie asked, her voice tinged with worry.

"Yeah. The episode is over. I'm good. How was your Crossing Guard call? Everything go okay?" she asked.

I nodded, a small smile starting as I remembered the man's joy at leaving his broken body behind. "Just helping an old man cross over," I said. "He was ready to go, and excited about the whole cake situation."

Sarah raised an eyebrow, a glimmer of amusement in her eyes. "Cake situation?"

Millie grinned, her eyes lighting up the way they always did when she talked about cake. "Oh, yeah. One of the best parts of Heaven is that you can blink cake into your hand any time you want. And any kind of cake! Plus, calories don't count so you can just eat as much as you want."

"Wow? Really?" Sarah asked. "But only cake?"

"Oh, no," I said quickly. "Anything you want really. Any

food. Any item. Anything, really. Heaven is all about getting everything you've ever wanted."

"Wow," she said, her voice tinged with wonder. "I'm amazed Heaven is actually a real thing. It's pretty humbling actually knowing for sure that this life isn't the whole shebang… that there's more to it after we're gone." She paused, biting her lip as she contemplated her next question. "Do I have to be like… religious to get there? I wasn't raised with religion, and when I looked into it as an adult, there were so many to choose from, all certain they are the only one true religion, that I got confused and just gave up. Is it wrong to ask if there is one I should join to make sure I get in?"

Millie shrugged. "We weren't religious and we got in. It seems to be more based on whether you are a good soul or a bad soul. I don't think they care much at all about what church you went to or what God you worshipped. Just if you're a good person."

"And sometimes we're shocked we got in." I snorted.

Sarah arched an eyebrow. "Oh, boy. You two weren't good people?"

Millie and I shared a giggle. "We weren't *bad* people, but we did get into a little trouble pulling pranks in our day. Apparently, Heaven is understanding about revenge work, and they let us in anyway."

She looked at us, and a flicker of worry clouded her dark eyes. "I wonder if I'll be considered a good enough person to go to Heaven."

Millie practically spit out, "You? Of course you will! You save lives for crying out loud. They'll probably roll out the red carpet for you."

Sarah's face flushed red as she smiled. "Yeah?"

"Definitely," I said. "There are a lot of retired cops and

military personnel up there. Real heroes in life and they were rewarded in death. People who took care of others seem to be quite common up there. I'm certain you'll be one of them and be up there eating cake with us someday."

"Hopefully a long time for now though," Millie said quickly. "We don't want our beacon to go off for you until you're a little, old, wrinkled, lady who dies in her bed like we did."

"And being a Crossing Guard? Is that something everyone does?"

"No. We signed up for it."

"That's so great of you. It seems like really noble work."

Millie and I exchanged a sheepish glance, our cheeks flushing with embarrassment. "Well, to be honest," I said, rubbing the back of my neck, "we didn't exactly sign up for the job out of the goodness of our hearts."

Sarah's brow furrowed, confusion etched on her features. "What do you mean?"

I sighed, a rueful smile tugging at my lips. "Initially, we only became Crossing Guards because we wanted to come back to Earth and haunt people."

"Haunt people?" Sarah's eyes widened, shock and disbelief warring on her face. "Why on earth would you want to do that?"

Millie and I shared a guilty look, shifting uncomfortably. "You have to understand," I said, my voice quiet and contrite, "Heaven is perfect. Like, absolutely, mind-numbingly perfect. For most people it's, well, Heaven. They love it. But for a couple of mischief-makers like us, well... it got a little boring."

"In life, we used to get revenge on mean people," Millie chimed in, a hint of mischief sparkling in her eyes. "You know, give them a taste of their own medicine. Stand up for the little guy to bullies and whatnot. We figured being Crossing Guards would give us a chance to keep up our old habits, but in this case, we could haunt them to get our revenge."

Sarah stared at us for a long moment, her expression unreadable. Then, to our surprise, she burst out laughing, the sound filling the air around us and breaking the night-time silence other than the chirping of crickets.

"Oh, my God," she gasped then burst into laughter. "You came here to haunt mean people? Seriously? That's hilarious! You two are something else, you know that?"

We started laughing with her, acknowledging the ridiculousness of our initial motivations on coming to Earth.

"Yep, we were just going to buzz around Earth looking for people who deserved a little comeuppance and then haunt their asses to give them a taste of their own medicine."

Sarah continued laughing, wiping tears from her eyes. "I'm having such visions of you two floating around causing trouble."

"Yeah. We did get a little haunting done to that jerk who killed all my flowers at the nursing home." Millie frowned. "I really loved those flowers. But then…"

Her voice trailed off, and I knew where her mind went.

"But then we met those poor murdered girls," I said, sobering at the memory. "And we realized that catching their killer was more important than any haunting hijinks."

Sarah nodded, her own expression turning serious. "Speaking of the killer," she said, turning back to the scene, "I think we can safely conclude that she's stalking her victims, learning their routines. She probably hides nearby, waiting for the perfect moment to strike, then comes back later with her vehicle or wagon to collect the body. The need for a wagon is proof the killer is a smaller woman. A large male could easily carry those bodies. They were all under a hundred and twenty pounds."

Mabel frowned, confusion furrowing her brow. "But we already told you the killer is a woman," she said. "Why do you need more proof?"

Sarah looked at us, her eyebrows lifting. "Because I need proof to show why I'm taking the investigation in a different direction and including a woman in my suspect list. What am I supposed to do, tell my boss that two spectral sleuths told me it's a woman? They'd laugh me out of the office, or worse, have me committed."

"Oh," I said, drawing the word out. "Yeah. That makes sense. Man. You've got a lot of red tape to go through that Millie and I don't need to worry about."

"I do. And with the extra eyes watching my every move, I can't afford to make a mistake. Everything has to be by the book."

I felt a pang of sympathy for Sarah, understanding the delicate balancing act she had to maintain between her ghostly allies and her very human colleagues. "We'll help you get the proof you need," I said, my voice firm with determination. "Whatever it takes to build a solid case and catch this killer."

Sarah nodded, gratitude and relief shining in her eyes. "Thank you," she said, her voice barely above a whisper. "I don't know what I'd do without you two."

As we prepared to leave the crime scene, a sudden realization struck me. "Wait a minute," I said, turning to Sarah with a furrowed brow. "How are you going to explain to your boss how you found these kill sites in the first place?"

Sarah's face fell, a mix of dread and uncertainty washing over her features. "Crap," she muttered, running a hand through her hair. “You’re right. I can’t exactly tell them a couple of ghosts led me here. And there isn’t any obvious evidence some passerby could call in to tip us off.”

Millie and I exchanged a worried glance, the gravity of the situation sinking in. Sarah’s career, her very livelihood, could be on the line if she couldn’t come up with a plausible explanation for her discovery.

For a long moment, Sarah stood in silence, her eyes distant as she weighed her options. I could practically see the gears turning in her head, the internal battle raging between her desire to catch the killer and her fear of the consequences.

Finally, she squared her shoulders, a new fire burning in her eyes. “You know what? I don’t care. I’ll figure something out, and if I don’t find a plausible explanation, I’m just going to go forward anyway without looping my boss in,” she said, her voice ringing with conviction.

Millie’s eyes widened, a flicker of concern crossing her face. “But Sarah, won’t you get in trouble for not filling your boss in on all this? I mean, going rogue is a pretty big deal, isn’t it?”

Sarah let out a heavy sigh, her gaze dropping to the ground. “Honestly? Yeah, it is. If they find out I’ve been withholding information, conducting an unauthorized investigation... I’m on such thin ice it could be the end of my career.”

I felt a pang of sympathy for Sarah, the weight of the decision she was facing hitting me like a ton of bricks.

“Sarah,” I said softly, my voice thick with emotion. “Are you sure about this? We don’t want you to jeopardize your whole career.”

Sarah’s head snapped up, her eyes blazing with a fierce intensity. “I’m sure,” she said, her voice steady and unwavering. "I became an FBI agent to save lives, to bring justice to those who have been wronged. And right now, every instinct in my body is telling me that this is the right path, the only path. Four girls are dead, and I'm not going to let there be a fifth if there's even the slightest chance I can stop it."

She took a deep breath, her fists clenching at her sides. "I'll do whatever it takes to catch this killer, to stop them from hurting anyone else. And if that means going rogue, if it means risking my career... then so be it."

Millie and I exchanged another glance, a mix of awe and concern. We knew that Sarah was a force to be reckoned with, a true warrior for justice. But knowing she was willing to risk her livelihood to save even just one life made my heart sing. There was no doubt in my mind with a soul like hers that someday Heaven would welcome her with open arms even if the FBI slammed the door in her face.

"Okay," I said, my voice barely above a whisper. "We're with you, Sarah. No matter what happens, we'll be right by your side, fighting the good fight."

Sarah nodded, a flicker of gratitude softening her features. "Thank you," she murmured, her voice thick with emotion. "I couldn't do this without you two."

"If ever there were two people to go rogue with, you're standing next to them. We've got your back, Sarah."

"Thanks." She smiled.

"Better to ask for forgiveness than permission." I lightened the mood with my smile. "I said that often in life."

Millie chuckled. "And we were asking for forgiveness a lot."

Sarah smiled. "I have no doubt that was the case."

"So, what do we do next?" Millie asked, her eyes searching between us.

Sarah thoughtfully twisted her lips, then that familiar look of determination returned to her face. "We know the killer is a woman, and likely a sculptor. I say we give the information to the tech crew to run the data searches trying to find a suspect with our new information, and in the meantime, it's time we pay a visit to the art district, see what kind of clues we can dig up."

I rubbed my hands together, a mischievous smile spreading across my face. "Now you're talking," I said, my voice practically purring with anticipation. "Let's go catch us a killer."

As we set off into the night led by Sarah's determined strides, I knew we were closing in on the killer. But knowing she was likely planning to strike again, I knew the stakes had never been higher, and some woman out there was depending on us to save her.

Chapter Sixteen

MILLIE

The art district exploded with colors and creativity, the streets lined with galleries, studios, and quirky shops that spoke to the artist in me. Though I'd never been talented at any of it, I'd enjoyed art during my lifetime and had dabbled in things like jewelry making, painting, and even a little ceramics. As Sarah, Mabel, and I stepped out of the car, I couldn't help but feel a sense of excitement to be in a place just brimming with art and life.

"Okay, ladies," Sarah said, her voice low and determined. "Remember, we need to keep our eyes and ears open for anything that might point us in the direction of our killer. Anything unusual, any whispers or rumors that might give us a lead."

Mabel and I nodded, our own expressions mirroring Sarah's focused intensity. We knew that this was a crucial moment in the investigation, a chance to finally get one step ahead of the twisted soul who had taken so many innocent lives.

"There's a lot of ground to cover," Sarah said, looking at our surroundings.

It was then we all noticed the couple staring at her, brows scrunched in confusion.

"Uh, Sarah. You're talking to yourself," I whispered, despite the fact they couldn't hear me.

Sarah's eyes widened and she stared back at the couple who quickly diverted their eyes and hurried away.

"Crap," Sarah whispered, then Sarah pressed her cell phone to her ear to pretend to talk on it while she addressed us in public.

"You two need to remind me not to talk to you in public. I forgot."

"Sorry," Mabel answered for us. "I got so excited about our case I forgot I'm dead and you look like a looney tooney talking to air."

"Sorry, Sarah," I said sheepishly. "So, what's the plan again?"

She continued into the cell phone. "Okay. I think the best first step is to do some discreet snooping, and I'll ask around about the artist's mark."

"Won't she know that means we found it?" I asked, my eyes glancing around at the people milling about, wondering if maybe she was one of them. Maybe one of these innocent looking people was the twisted killer right here in plain sight. A shiver traveled up my spine.

"Yeah. How are you going to not tip her off if you're flashing around her artist's mark we found at the crime scenes? Won't that just send her high-tailing it out of the country?" Mabel asked.

A smirk twitched on Sarah's lip. "I'm a professional detective, ladies. I wouldn't do something so obvious. Today my cover is that my great aunt passed away and left me behind a beautiful sculpture. I want to know the maker of it so I can commission a new one, and I'm asking around the art district to see if anyone recognizes it and can help me find the artist."

Mabel and I looked at each other, eyes lit up with pride.

"Wow!" I said, smiling. "You really are a smart one. I never would have thought of that."

"Top agent in the FBI right here, everyone! This here is the best one!" Mabel pointed to Sarah, shouting loudly to the people milling about unable to hear her.

"Mabel," Sarah shushed. "Stop it! I'm undercover!"

Mabel grinned. "Ghost, remember? You're the only one that can hear me."

Sarah's face faltered, and then she chuckled. "That's right. You both look so real to me that I forget sometimes."

"Okay," I said, the wheels in my mind spinning. "So, you can go around asking people about the artist's mark. Mabel and I can hit some of the galleries and fly right up to the sculptures undetected and look for that mark ourselves. We can also eavesdrop a bit and see if we hear anything important."

"Alright," she said, a small smile tugging at the corners of her mouth as she arched a dark eyebrow. "But stay out of trouble, you two. And meet me back here in an hour, okay?"

Mabel snorted. "Us? Trouble? Never."

But I wasn't the only one that saw the familiar twinkle in her eye. Sarah and I exchanged a look, then with a mischievous grin and playful salute, Mabel darted through the wall of a nearby gallery, leaving me to roll my eyes and follow in her wake.

For the next hour, we whizzed in and out of galleries and studios, our ears pricked for any snippet of conversation that might prove useful as we hovered near all the artists and gallery owners, listening for something, anything, that may tip our investigation toward our killer. Our invisible forms made it easy for us to duck behind red velvet ropes cordoning off the fragile sculptures and search them each closely for any artist's mark matching our killer.

"Did you check that one over there yet?" I asked as Mabel and I floated past one another in the high-end gallery near the center of the district.

"Um, not that one. I'll go look." She zoomed across the gallery, darting around the people milling about staring at the pieces and discussing all the artsy terms that never made sense to me.

"See anything?" I asked as Mabel scoured the sculpture of an extremely large naked man holding a small dog in his arms.

"Nothing yet. Man, this is a weird sculpture. Why would a naked man just be standing there holding a little chihuahua or whatever that tiny dog is? It doesn't even make sense. In fact, most of the stuff here is so weird I don't understand it at all." She looked up and pointed to the red board leaning against the wall that a group of artsy looking ladies stood discussing. "Like that is literally a 2x4 painted red and called art. *I* could do that! Hell, a five-year-old could do that."

I furrowed my brow as I stared at the red board, trying once again to figure out what was artistic about it... and failing. "Yeah, some of these are just weird. At least this one, though strange, took actual talent. It's really detailed and realistic."

Mabel searched up the statue's larger-than-real-life-sized thighs, cringing when she reached the area between his legs. "Too detailed. Cripes. I didn't need to see that so close."

I chuckled. "That would have been an interesting place to leave the artist's signature."

We started laughing, and it felt good to ease the tension of the seriousness of our hunt for a killer. If there was one thing Mabel and I always excelled at, it was finding humor no matter what had been happening in our lives.

"Hello, little doggy." Mabel floated a little higher, leaving the incredibly detailed area that had us in stitches. She reached out to gently pet the dog's head. "Nice to meet you."

Her ghostly finger passed right through the sculpture, as expected. But then she tried again, getting more frustrated with each failed attempt.

"Come on, you stupid little mutt," she muttered, now poking aggressively at the dog's nose. "I just want to boop your snoot!"

Then she floated down to the statue's muscular chest and started tracing patterns on it with her finger. "You know, I've seen pictures of muscular men like this, but I don't think I ever touched one in real life. My husband had a pot belly and boobs as big as mine."

She started tracing her fingers along the carved lines of his chest. "Could you even imagine what it would be like to have a man with a physique like this one? Maybe when we're back in heaven I should conjure one up instead of cake. Do you think they would let me do that? Like David Hasselhoff from his days in *Baywatch.* Tell me you wouldn't rather have him than cake."

"Mabel!" I scolded, rolling my eyes as she waggled her eyebrows at me. "Don't be crude!"

"What? We don't have loves in Heaven because we never found them in real life. I mean, you know… like Agatha and Lenny. We don't have that like so many other people do. Do you ever wonder if we'll get one? Like, our husbands definitely weren't our soul mates."

I crinkled my nose. "It would be more like hell than Heaven being stuck up there with them for eternity."

"But maybe our true loves just haven't… died yet?" Mabel's voice turned wistful. "Do you think one day there will be a knock on our door and there they'll be? Or are we each other's soul mates, so that means we don't get a romantic one? Don't get me wrong, I'm glad it's just me and you, but you don't have pecs like this hunk."

I contemplated her words, and though I'd never voiced them aloud, I had often wondered the same thing. Why didn't we get a love story like Lenny and Agatha's? We'd gotten married, sure, but only because back then that's what women were supposed to do. Neither of us had truly loved the men we'd chosen—they were practical arrangements more than passionate romances.

But perhaps Mabel was right. Even though our love wasn't romantic, I knew without a doubt that we were true and complete soul mates. We'd chosen each other as family when we were just children, and that bond had only grown stronger through nine decades of shared laughter, tears, and mischief. Maybe that kind of love—pure, unconditional, and unshakeable—was rarer and more precious than romance.

Still, a small part of me couldn't help but wonder if somewhere out there, our perfect matches were still living their earthly lives, and someday we'd hear that anticipated knock on our heavenly door. Maybe we'd end up as the most perfect foursome—two best friends who'd found their romantic counterparts without losing each other. The thought made me smile, even as I pushed it aside as wishful thinking.

"I mean, tell me you haven't thought about trying to conjure up a hunk in Heaven. Admit it. You've thought it."

A warm heat bloomed through my cheeks as I shook my head… and lied. "Of course not! Don't be crude!"

I'd thought about it. Many times. I just hadn't been brave enough to try it, and too embarrassed to ask the angels if we could conjure up some men to keep us company. And I'd be lying if I hadn't thought of David Hasselhoff myself, imagining transporting us to a beach in Heaven and just watching him run back and forth on it in those little red shorts all day. Mabel and I had been obsessed with him in life, and I secretly hoped maybe when he died, it'd turn out he was my great love and he'd come knocking on my door in Heaven.

She pressed her hands to his chest, pretending to play with the nipple on his swollen bronzed pecs. "Come on. I know you've thought about conjuring up a man like this. Just admit it! You want some big, muscular pecs like these. Oh man, why can't God just let me touch pecs like this just once. Now that would be a Heaven I could get into. I'm closing my eyes and pretending it's David Hasselhoff."

I was giggling at her antics when suddenly a group of chattering art enthusiasts came bustling through, their arms full of brochures and wine glasses. I instinctively scooted sideways to avoid being walked through—I absolutely hated that sensation—and crashed directly into Mabel.

The moment our bodies connected, Mabel's hands, which had been playfully poking at the statue's nipple, suddenly found purchase on its chest.

The massive statue shuddered and began to teeter backward on its pedestal.

"Holy—" Mabel started to say as she pushed off from it, lifting her hands in the air. "I didn't mean to do that!"

"Oh no, oh no, oh NO!!" I shrieked, watching the slowly falling sculpture. "Hurry! Catch it!" I launched forward to grab his arm, but without us touching each other for extra energy, my hands went right through. "Mabel! It's falling!"

"Millie! Grab my hand!" she yelled.

I lunged forward and seized her fingers just as the statue began its slow-motion plunge toward a group of unaware elderly patrons admiring a nearby painting.

With our combined energy, we flew to the other side and pushed against the statue's back with all our might. It started to right itself.

"Heave!" Mabel grunted, and I closed my eyes and pushed with everything I had. But we overcorrected, and the massive bronze man began tipping forward instead.

"Too much, too much!" I screamed, and we zipped around to the front again.

We threw ourselves against the statue, catching it before it came crashing down. But in our panic, Mabel's palm landed squarely on the sculpture's most prominent anatomical feature.

Her eyes went wide with horror. "OH MY GOD, I'M TOUCHING THE—"

"Just PUSH!" I screamed, grabbing her other hand.

Together we shoved upward, Mabel's face bright red as she tried to steady the statue while her hand remained firmly planted on its bronze manhood.

The sculpture finally settled back into place with a loud thud, and Mabel staggered back, fanning herself like she might faint. "Sweet Jesus, I touched his ding-dong!"

"Well," I said, biting back a laugh, "the Good Book does say, 'Ask and ye shall receive.' You wanted to touch a man—there you go."

Her eyes bulged. "That is *not* what I meant!" She glared upward, shaking her fist at the ceiling. "Not funny, God! I *meant* David Hasselhoff, not Bronze Bob here!"

I clapped a hand over my mouth, giggling. "Well, you got what you asked for and nearly toppled a priceless statue in the process. If Sarah were here, she'd have you booked for assault." I snorted, still laughing. "Next time, be a little more specific—ask for David Hasselhoff in the flesh. Or better yet, just ask for cake so I can have some too."

A nearby woman screamed, pointing at the now-still statue. "Did anyone else see that thing moving by itself?"

The confused crowd gathered around, trying to figure out what had just happened.

Mabel grabbed my hand. "Well, Millie, I think that's our cue."

"Agreed."

We zipped backward through a wall just as a security guard came barreling into the room, shouting, "Nobody touch the art!"

On the other side, we pressed ourselves against the cool plaster, listening to the commotion build. Mabel stifled a giggle, her shoulders shaking.

"Cake," I whispered, poking her side. "I'm telling you. Next time, just ask for cake."

With a laugh and a roll of her eyes, she said, "David Hasselhoff in the flesh first, and then cake. Come on. I think it's time we get out of here and go find Sarah."

I heard the leftover commotion of people arguing over who'd bumped the statue, so I nodded. "Yeah. Good idea."

As we floated through the district, Mabel turned to me with a grin. "You know, Millie, I'm having a blast down here. It's like we're in one of those detective novels we used to read, solving crimes and catching bad guys."

My eyes lit up. "Exactly! We're a crime-fighting duo! What do you think they would call us?"

"The Ghostly Gumshoes!" Mabel said quickly.

I grinned. "I like that! Or what about…" I twisted my lips… "Incorporeal Investigators!"

Mabel nodded, a huge smile. "Oh, that's good! Or how about…" She placed a finger on her chin. "The Spectral Sleuths."

I started laughing. "I love it! The Spectral Sleuths. That's us!"

We shared a high five, then our laughter slowly dissolved into a soft chuckle.

Mabel's face fell slightly, a wistful look crossing her features. "I'm going to miss this when we go back. And Sarah, of course. She's become such a good friend to us."

I felt a pang of sadness at the thought of leaving Sarah behind, of returning to the perfection of Heaven without her by our side. "I'll miss her too," I said, my voice soft with emotion. "But we'll see her again someday, when her time on Earth is done." I paused, cringing. "Unless we've broken so many rules that they send us straight to hell when we get back."

Mabel blew out a puff of air, waving a dismissive hand in the air. "Nonsense. We're gonna catch a killer! Who could send two sweet little old murder solving ghosts to hell?"

That worry I often had bubbled up inside me again, but as usual, Mabel eased it with her smile. "I hope so. I sure don't want to get kicked out, and then many, many decades from now, we'll see Sarah again in Heaven. And in the meantime, we'll cherish every moment we have with her."

I caught sight of Sarah walking down the street, a determined expression on her face as she approached a group of artists chatting outside a coffee shop. We hurried closer, but we didn't greet her so we wouldn't throw off her game.

"Excuse me," she said, her voice polite but firm as she held up a sketch of the mysterious artist's mark we had found at the crime scenes. "I'm hoping you might be able to help me. I recently inherited a sculpture with this mark on it, and I'm trying to track down the artist. I was hoping to commission another piece to complement it."

The artists studied the sketch, their brows furrowed in concentration. But one by one, they shook their heads, apologizing for not recognizing the mark.

Mabel and I exchanged a glance, our own disappointment mirrored in Sarah's expression. But she thanked the artists graciously, moving on to the next group with the same question.

As we watched her work, I couldn't help but marvel at Sarah's dedication, her unwavering commitment to the case. She was like a bloodhound on a scent, relentless in her pursuit of the truth.

Finally, after what felt like an eternity of fruitless searching, Sarah picked up her phone and held it to her head. "Well, I haven't found a thing. You guys?"

"No luck," I answered. "We searched all the sculptures in the district, and none had the artist's mark."

"And Mabel searched *everywhere,*" I said, and she and I exchanged a giggle.

Sarah's lips twisted in frustration. "Damn it. Then we're heading back without any leads." She looked up at a small art supply store nestled on a quiet corner of the district. "Actually, I haven't been in there yet. I'll ask the guy about the mark, and maybe we can look at the sculpting tools and see which ones fit the description Dr. Patel gave us for what would have made the marks on the wounds."

"Let's go," I said, excited to join her in her search.

Inside the store, Sarah approached the elderly shopkeeper, a kind-faced man with hazel eyes and a gentle smile. She showed him the sketch of the artist's mark, but he shook his head, apologizing for not recognizing it.

"No worries," Sarah said, her voice light and friendly. "While I'm here, though, I was hoping you might be able to show me some of your sculpting tools. I'm thinking of taking up the hobby myself."

The shopkeeper's face lit up, and he eagerly led Sarah to a display of chisels, wire cutters, and other implements. As he explained the different tools and their uses, Mabel and I remained nearby, studying each one with a critical eye.

"Look at that one," Mabel whispered, pointing to a wicked-looking wire cutter with a sharp, pointed tip. "I bet that could do some serious damage."

I nodded, a chill running through my body at the thought of it being used in a grisly way. "And those clay shapers," I murmured, gesturing to a set of small, pointed tools. "They look like they could make some pretty precise cuts."

As Sarah and the shopkeeper continued to chat, a young woman entered the store, a flyer clutched in her hand.

"Excuse me," she said as she approached the counter. "I was wondering if you might be willing to donate a gift card for a fundraiser we're holding. It's to benefit the family of Laura Ashker, the deceased sculptor. We're hosting a silent auction and could use some donations to raise money for a memorial display we'd like to put together for her. Also to send her family something to cover funeral expenses and such. I'm sure it wasn't cheap."

The shopkeeper's face softened with sympathy. "Of course," he said, his voice heavy with emotion. He immediately reached beneath the counter, pulling out a paper gift certificate and scribbling a denomination on it. "Such a tragedy, what happened to that poor girl. Shook me right to my core."

The woman nodded, her eyes glistening with unshed tears. "Yes, it was such a shock."

"Did you know her?" he asked as he put the gift certificate into an envelope."

"I did," the woman said. "We went to art school together. She was so talented, so full of life. It's just so senseless, what happened to her. Murdered. Who would want to kill that wonderful woman?"

Sarah's head snapped up, her eyes widening with interest. "I'm sorry, I don't mean to eaves drop, but did you say someone was murdered recently? A sculptor?"

The woman's face crumpled, a single tear sliding down her cheek as she nodded. "She was found beaten to death in her studio a couple months ago," she said, her voice barely above a whisper. "The police never caught the killer."

Sarah's jaw clenched, her eyes illuminating the way they did when she caught a clue. "I'm so sorry for your loss," she said, her voice gentle but firm. "That's just terrible."

The woman wiped her tears. "It's just such a tragedy what happened to Laura. She had just been awarded a Guggenheim Fellowship, which is a huge deal for any artist, but especially for someone so young. And on top of that, she had a solo show coming up at the Gagosian Gallery in New York. That's the kind of opportunity most artists dream of, and she had it all ahead of her. It's just so sad to think of all that potential, all that talent, cut short like that."

"Hopefully this helps in raising money for a worthy memorial," the shopkeeper said, holding out the envelope.

The woman thanked him, taking the gift card and

leaving the store with a final, grateful smile. As soon as she was gone, Sarah turned to the shopkeeper, her expression intense.

"Wow. A murder. That must have really shaken the art community, huh?" she said to him, and I knew she was softly fishing. "Did you know her too?"

The shopkeeper sighed, his eyes distant with painful memories. "She was a regular customer here," he said, his voice heavy with sorrow. "Always in and out, buying supplies and chatting about her latest project. She had such a bright future ahead of her, such a unique vision. It's just so hard to believe that someone could snuff out that light so brutally."

Sarah nodded, her expression grim. "I can only imagine," she said, her voice soft with sympathy. "Thank you for sharing that with me. I know it can't be easy to talk about."

The shopkeeper smiled sadly, his eyes glistening with unshed tears. "I just hope they catch the monster who did this," he said, his voice thick with emotion. "Laura deserves justice, and her family deserves peace."

Sarah's expression hardened with resolve, and I knew in that moment that she would stop at nothing to bring Laura's killer to justice. Because if her mind was in the same place as mine, the chances were high that it was the same killer we hunted.

As we left the store, Sarah pulled out her phone, her fingers flying over the screen as she searched for any information on Laura's murder. Mabel and I hovered over her shoulder, our own ghostly eyes straining to make out the details.

And then, with a gasp of recognition, Sarah zoomed in on the photo in the article about Laura's death. With her dark hair, blue eyes and striking features, she was a dead ringer for the other murdered women we had encountered.

The same age, the same physical type, the same creative spark snuffed out too soon.

"This can't be a coincidence," Sarah murmured, her voice tight with excitement. "A young, talented sculptor, brutally murdered just months before our killer starts targeting women who look just like her? I think we may have found our first victim, the one that started it all. We need to go examine the evidence they found in the initial investigation and maybe try to get to that crime scene to examine it ourselves."

Mabel and I exchanged a glance, and I felt a flutter of anxiety and excitement inside my stomach. We knew that we were on the brink of a major breakthrough, that Laura's murder could hold the key to unlocking the clue that would reveal our killer.

Chapter Seventeen

MABEL

Sarah, Millie, and I pulled up to the curb outside Laura's studio. We'd pored over all the police reports all through the night, and now Sarah wanted to try to take a sweep through the crime scene herself to see if the local police had missed anything. We made our way into the older but well-maintained apartment building, then found the door to her studio on the third floor.

"302. This is it." I pointed at the black numbers above the dark, wooden door.

The police tape had been removed, but the heavy padlock on the door made it clear that this was still a crime scene, off-limits to the living.

Sarah let out a frustrated sigh as she jiggled the lock, her brow furrowed with determination. "Damn. I was hoping maybe they'd have opened it back up by now and I wouldn't need to call the local police to let me in," she muttered, her eyes scanning for any other points of entry.

"Can we do that? Call the cops to let you in?" I asked.

Sarah glanced around the empty hallway before

lowering her voice. "It's just... my boss still doesn't know I'm this far into the investigation. I don't know how to get approval to enter the crime scene without looping him in."

Millie's features creased with confusion. "But why wouldn't you want to loop him in? Don't you trust him?"

Sarah ran a hand through her hair, a wry smile tugging at her lips. "It's not about trust. It's about the way I've been conducting this investigation. I've been following leads that are a bit... unconventional."

Mabel's eyes widened with understanding. "You mean like working with a couple of ghost detectives?"

Sarah chuckled softly. "Exactly. If I tell my boss that I've been taking advice from two spectral sleuths, he'll think I've lost my mind. He'll pull me off the case faster than you can say 'boo.'"

Millie's brow furrowed. "But don't you have evidence to back up your theories? Couldn't you present that to him without mentioning us?"

Sarah shook her head. "Some of the key pieces of evidence we've uncovered, like the locations of the actual murder scenes, I can't explain how I got them without revealing your involvement. And given my recent track record, I'm not sure my boss would be willing to take my word on faith alone."

Mabel's expression softened. "That's tough. But Sarah, you can't keep going rogue forever. At some point, you're going to need the resources and support of the FBI to crack this case."

Sarah sighed, leaning against the wall. "I know. And I will bring him in, eventually. But right now, I need to follow this lead about Laura's murder. If I bring my boss in prematurely, he might shut it down before we have a chance to prove the connection."

Millie tipped her head with a sympathetic frown. "We understand, Sarah. But remember, you're not in this alone. Mabel and I, we've got your back, no matter what."

Sarah smiled gratefully, the tension in her shoulders easing slightly. "I know you do. And I can't tell you how much I appreciate that. I just hope that when this is all over, my boss will understand why I had to do things this way."

Millie grinned. "Oh, he will. Because when we catch this killer and blow this case wide open, you'll be the star of the FBI! And he'll be thanking his lucky stars that he has an agent like you on his team."

Sarah laughed, the sound echoing off the empty hallway walls. "Let's hope you're right, Millie. But first, we need to get inside this studio and see what clues we can find. Too bad they didn't cover lock picking at Quantico."

"Well, the two of us can go in and look around no problem," Millie said, disappearing through the wall and then popping her head back out with a grin.

"I know, it's just I'm a trained detective and I may see things that you two may miss."

Millie frowned.

Sarah quickly corrected with, "Not that you two haven't been amazing detectives so far. It's just that I got a lot of training in how to search for clues."

"Spectral Sleuths," I said, lifting my chin proudly. "We decided that during this case, we're calling ourselves the Spectral Sleuths."

Sarah started laughing. "You know, I like it."

"Don't worry, Sarah, the Spectral Sleuths will go sleuthing for evidence in there!" Millie grinned.

Sarah looked frustrated, but she nodded. "Go ahead. I know I'd rather be investigating, but it's fine. You girls do your thing. I'll just wait out here and you can buzz in and out and report to me what you're finding."

I hated seeing Sarah looking sad to be left out of the hunt, and honestly, she *was* far more adept at picking up on important clues that our amateur sleuth selves, so I looked at the lock and then tipped my head.

"If you think you need more than just the eyes of the Spectral Sleuths, then let me try something." I exchanged a mischievous glance with Millie. "Remember how Hazel said some ghosts can manipulate objects without touching them. What if we tried that? Maybe I can push the tumblers from the inside."

"You want to try moving something with your mind?" Millie's eyes widened. "We've never done that before."

"Well, we've never been ghosts before either, and look how much we've learned already." I moved toward the door. "Millie, hold my hand while I try it. If we're really just energy now, maybe we can focus that energy differently like Hazel was talking about."

With my tongue poking out as I concentrated, I focused on the lock mechanism inside. "I can almost feel the tumblers," I whispered, shocked when they actually started to move. "Oh my God, it's working! I'm doing it!"

"Come on, Mabel! You got this!" Millie chanted me on.

Grunting and groaning while I gave it my all, I tightened my grip on Millie's hand. With a final, determined push, I sent a surge of spectral energy into the lock. The mechanism gave a soft click, and the lock dropped to the floor, as if by magic.

I stared at it in shock. "Holy crap, it actually worked!" I turned to face my companions, a triumphant grin lighting up my face. "Ta-da!" I exclaimed, taking a bow. "One studio, unlocked and ready for snooping."

Sarah's jaw dropped. "How the hell did you just do that?"

"This ghost we met, Hazel, said that ghosts are just concentrated energy and some ghosts can move things," I explained, still amazed. "Even send things flying around a room once they get good at it. Since we are just energy, we can focus our essence and move things without touching them. I just focused my energy on the tumblers inside the lock, and voila! Although, honestly, I never thought I'd actually be able to do it!"

"That's incredible," Sarah breathed. "So you can move things with your mind now?"

"Apparently? Though I have no idea how much I can do or if it'll work again." I looked at Millie. "We're definitely going to need to practice this."

Millie chimed in, pride evident in her voice. "Well done, Mabel! We've been working on honing our abilities ever since we crossed over, but this was a lot more than I expected us to accomplish. I can't wait to learn how you just did that and try it myself."

Sarah shook her head, a mixture of gratitude and exasperation playing across her features. "I don't know whether to thank you or arrest you," she quipped, stepping cautiously into the studio. "And let's hope I don't get caught breaking in here but come on. Let's do this."

We followed her in, and the interior was much as I had expected—a large, open space with high ceilings and plenty of natural light. Sculptures in various stages of completion lined the walls and clustered on worktables, the tools of Laura's trade scattered among them.

But there was an eerie stillness to the place, a heaviness in the air that spoke of the tragedy that had occurred here. I could almost feel the echoes of Laura's presence, the lingering traces of her creativity and passion cut short by a brutal act of violence.

"Wow. She really was talented," Millie said as she examined a sculpture of a woman that looked so realistic you'd have expected her to get up from her relaxed pose and walk away.

"It seems the art world agreed." I looked at another sculpture, amazed at how she could take clay and turn it into something so beautiful.

"Jealousy has been the cause of many deaths since the dawn of time," Sarah said. "It's very possible her recent rise is what caused her death. Our sculptor could have been jealous of her success. It would fit."

"Poor girl." Millie stared down at the blood-stained floor where Laura had met with her untimely demise. "Young and full of talent with her whole life ahead of her. So sad she got taken too soon."

"And all the more reason we need to find this killer and stop her." My jaw tightened with my resolve, and it seemed to deepen every moment we spent in the studio reminding me that Laura was a person and not just a faceless victim in this investigation. She deserved the same justice we sought for the two souls we'd help cross over.

Millie and I floated high and low through the studio, our eyes scanning every surface for any clue or detail that might point us in the direction of Laura's killer. We phased through walls and peered into drawers, our incorporeal forms allowing us access to every nook and cranny of the space.

As I drifted past a cluttered workbench, a small, leather-bound book caught my eye. I instinctively reached to pick it up, but my fingers passed through the pages as I tried to flip it open. "I can't open this damn thing. Millie, look at this," I called out. "It's Laura's guest log. She kept track of everyone who visited the studio. Come over and hold my hand and let's try to get a peek inside."

Millie floated over, and as we combined energy, I was able to flip open the book.

"There are a few entries from the week before her murder," she murmured, her finger tracing the lines of ink. "But nothing on the day of, or the day before."

I frowned, my brow furrowing as I considered the implications. "I guess the killer probably didn't sign in," I mused. "Unless it was a really stupid killer."

Sarah, who had been examining a half-finished sculpture across the room, looked up at the sound of our voices. "Did you find something?"

I pointed to the guest log. "Laura's visitor book. It's unlikely the killer signed in on the day they killed her, but maybe they visited here before. It could give us some names to cross-reference with our list of suspects."

Sarah came over and flipped through the pages with much more ease than the concentration it took me to flip even one page. "Good find," she murmured, pulling out her phone and snapping a few quick photos of the relevant pages. "I'll have the team back at the office run these names, see if anything pops."

We spent the next hour combing through the studio, searching for any other clues or evidence that might shed light on Laura's final days. But aside from a few unfinished sculptures and some scattered sketches, we came up empty-handed.

As we stepped back out into the hallway, Sarah snapped the lock back into place to hide the evidence we'd snuck inside to perform our own investigation.

"Well, that didn't tell us much," Sarah said on a sigh.

"I'll check the names on the guest book, even though the police likely already did it, but maybe we'll see something they missed."

"What about the red-haired lady?" I asked, remembering the police report had noted a couple of witnesses reported seeing a red-haired woman entering the studio on the day of the murder. Maybe we should follow up with those witnesses, see if they remember anything else about the woman they saw?"

"I'm not exactly authorized to be conducting interviews." Sarah hesitated for a moment, her brow furrowing as she considered our suggestion. I could practically see the gears turning in her head, weighing the potential risks and rewards of pursuing this new angle.

But in the end, her determination won out. "Well, I guess we're already here. May as well knock on their doors and see if they're home and have remembered anything else. I think one witness was in 309 if I remember correctly from the report. Let's see if she's home." With a curt nod, she took us down the hall and knocked on the door, her badge held up for inspection. After a moment, the door swung open, revealing a woman in her mid-thirties with paint-splattered overalls and a wary expression.

"Can I help you?" she asked.

Sarah flashed her badge, a reassuring smile on her face. "Agent Sadler, FBI," she introduced herself, her voice calm and professional. "I'm investigating the murder of Laura Becker, and I was hoping you might be able to answer a few questions about the day of her death."

The woman's face fell, a flicker of sadness passing over her features. "Of course," she said, stepping back to allow Sarah entry. "Anything I can do to help."

As Sarah stepped inside, Millie and I moved along

behind her, looking around at the artistic space. The studio was cluttered but cozy, with paintings and sketches covering every available surface.

Sarah took a seat on a battered couch, her notebook and pen at the ready. She smiled warmly at the witness, trying to put her at ease. "Thank you for taking the time to speak with me, Miss...?"

"Jacobs. Emily Jacobs." The woman settled into an armchair across from Sarah, her paint-splattered overalls a testament to her artistic pursuits. "I'm happy to help in any way I can. Laura was a talented artist and a good neighbor. What happened to her..." Emily's voice trailed off, her eyes glistening with unshed tears.

Sarah nodded sympathetically, giving Emily a moment to compose herself. "I understand how difficult this must be for you. But anything you can remember about that day, no matter how small, could be crucial to our investigation."

Emily took a deep breath, her brow furrowed in concentration. "Well, like I told the police, I saw a woman with red hair leaving Laura's studio that afternoon. It wasn't unusual though because Laura often had visitors, especially ones I didn't recognize. Customers and friends came and went pretty often, but I definitely saw a red head that day."

Sarah jotted down a note, her pen scratching against the paper. "Can you describe the woman in more detail? Her height, build, any distinguishing features?"

Emily closed her eyes, trying to picture the scene in her mind. "She was tall, maybe 5'10" or so. Slender build. Her hair was a deep, vivid red, like the color of a fire engine. It hung down past her shoulders in loose waves. We only passed each other briefly, and I didn't get a good look at her face, so unfortunately, I can't give you a clear description of her features."

Sarah nodded, her pen flying across the page as she recorded the details. "And her demeanor? Did she seem agitated or nervous?"

Emily shook her head. "No, not that I noticed. She walked with purpose, like she knew exactly where she was going."

"Anything else you can think of about her? Anything about her clothes? Body language? A scent you picked up? Any little clue could help, so think hard about anything you saw, even if you don't think it's important."

Emily pursed her lips, her eyes moving around as if searching an image in her head. Then she looked at Sarah. "I'm remembering now, the only other thing that I noticed was she must have been a painter like me because she had a ton of blue paint on her clothes."

Sarah's astute senses picked up on a clue. "Like more than a usual amount of paint on her clothes? More than this?" She waved her pen at the woman's speckled overalls.

She nodded. "Yeah. A lot more. The whole front of her outfit was basically covered in paint. She chuckled. "Must be a new painter because although we get paint on ourselves pretty often, as you can see from my appearance, it looked like she'd put more on herself than a painting."

I didn't know why Sarah's face twitched like she'd caught a scent no one else could smell, but I tingled with anticipation to discover what she'd sniffed out.

Sarah tapped her pen against her chin. "What shade of blue was it? Can you remember?"

Emily closed her eyes again, picturing the scene. "It was a bright, almost electric blue. The kind of color that really stands out."

Sarah's eyes widened, a piece of the puzzle clicking into place.

She stood abruptly, her notebook snapping shut. "Miss Jacobs, thank you for your time and your keen observations."

Emily blinked, surprised by the sudden shift in Sarah's demeanor. "I'm glad I could help. I hope you catch whoever did this to Laura. She deserved so much better."

Sarah nodded briskly. "We'll do everything in our power to bring her killer to justice. You have my word on that."

As Emily bid her goodbye, Millie and I stayed quiet, but I could barely wait for the door to close behind us when I started hounding Sarah for answers.

"What happened back there? You caught something, didn't you? What is it? What happened?"

"You got a clue out of that?" Millie asked, pushing in closer.

Sarah's lip twitched in a determined half-smile. "The paint. From the amount the woman described was covering the front of her, I think that she's our killer, and since this was a crime of passion, she didn't come prepared to kill. After bludgeoning Laura to death, our killer would have been covered in blood, and with no change of clothes, she would have been covered head to toe when she left. Unless…"

"Unless she poured blue paint all over herself to cover the blood so she could just walk out!" I said, my mouth dropping in awe of Sarah's detective skills.

Millie's face lit up. "Like the electric blue paint can we saw when we were searching Laura's studio! She was painting the walls of the bedroom!"

Sarah nodded at us, glad we were chomping onto the same bone. "Exactly. I bet our killer went here without intent to kill, something made her snap, she killed Laura, realized she was covered in blood and then saw the blue paint, covering herself with it so she could get out undetected. I think the red-haired woman is our killer."

I practically flipped in the air from the excitement buzzing inside me. "Holy crap! We're doing it! We're closing in on her. We're going to catch a killer!"

"Whoop!" Millie clapped, bouncing up and down as she grinned. "Nice work, Sarah! We knew you were the best detective for the job."

Sarah swelled with pride as she stared at us, and then she straightened her shoulders and said, "Come on. We've got work to do."

"Where to next?" I asked, following her down the hallway.

She slowed her steps and took a sharp breath. "To the office to tell my boss what I've been up to and get his permission to use the FBI's resources to hunt down this redhead."

Millie and I exchanged a glance knowing how much Sarah worried over getting her boss's approval, and not wanting to make herself more of a target than she already was at the office. But this time, she had evidence that could back her up, and two ghosts behind her as well.

After a drive across the city to the FBI offices, Sarah pulled into the parking lot. I could practically feel the nervousness radiating off her in waves.

"Are you nervous to ask him?" I said as we climbed out of the car.

Sarah sighed then pulled out her cell phone and held it to her ear pretending to talk on it. "No. I mean, I shouldn't be. I have great evidence." She arched an eyebrow. "Even if I can't explain all the steps to how I got there without looking nuts. But I guess, if I'm being honest, yeah. I'm nervous."

"Do you think he'll turn you down?" Millie asked as we followed along.

She sighed. "I don't know. I think my leads are solid and I my gut tells me I've got this right. It's just that if I'm wrong, I'm going to look like an even bigger dumbass than I already do. And I don't think my career could take that kind of hit right now."

"You're not wrong," I said quickly. "I know this is the killer. It has to be."

"I sure hope so," Sarah said. "I just wish I could solve this all on my own before I had to involve anyone else in my process."

Millie asked, "Your boss was your father's partner. It sounds like you have a good relationship, right?"

She smiled. "Yeah. He was like an uncle to me growing up."

"Then it's time for you to start trusting other people to have your back. You're always trying to do everything on your own, and sometimes you need to learn to ask for help. Like right now. You need his help, so let's take a leap of faith and trust that he's going to support your theory."

"Thanks, ladies. Getting to the agency, I was so used to doing everything on my own. But now that I'm here, it turns out I'm going to need to start learning how to fit into a team. It's not easy for me. Trusting people, I mean."

"Do you trust us?" I asked.

She looked between us then smiled. "Yeah. I trust you both."

"That's why we're here." Millie smiled. "To help you. You trust us, and that's a start. Now let's try to trust that your boss is going to trust you."

"You've got this, Sarah," I said, trying to infuse my voice

with as much encouragement as possible. "Your boss will understand. He has to."

Millie nodded. "You're not alone in this, remember? We're right here with you, every step of the way."

I watched as Sarah took a deep breath, seeming to draw strength from our words. She squared her shoulders and strode through the door into the building, her stride purposeful as she made her way to his office.

Once she reached it, she hesitated, her hand poised to knock. Millie and I hovered beside her in solidarity.

"You've got this," Millie whispered.

Sarah nodded, then rapped sharply on the door. "Sir? Do you have a moment?"

When he answered for her to enter, we followed Sarah into the office. I couldn't help but feel a surge of pride. She was taking a huge risk, putting her trust in others, and I knew how difficult that was for her.

Her boss, Director Donahue, looked up from his desk. "Sadler. Come on in. What's on your mind?"

Sarah stepped inside, closing the door behind her. "It's about the Laura Becker case. I think it's connected to our current investigation."

Donahue leaned back in his chair, his interest piqued. "Laura Becker?"

Sarah nodded, "Yes. A sculptor who was bludgeoned to death a couple months ago."

His eyes lit with recognition. "Oh, yeah. I remember hearing about that. But that wasn't an FBI case. The local police were handing that. That's a bit of a stretch trying to tie that bludgeoning death to our case, don't you think?"

Sarah shook her head. "I know it sounds far-fetched, but hear me out. I've uncovered some evidence that points to a link between the cases."

She proceeded to lay out the clues: the red-haired woman seen at Laura's studio, the mysterious blue paint that could have been used to conceal blood evidence.

When Sarah finished, her boss leaned back in his chair, his fingers steepled under his chin. "You've been busy, Sadler," he said, his tone unreadable. "Why didn't you come to me with this sooner?"

I held my breath, waiting for Sarah's response. But she didn't flinch, didn't back down. "I needed to be sure, sir. I didn't want to bring you a half-baked theory. But now, with the evidence we've uncovered, I truly believe that Laura's murder is the key to cracking this case wide open."

When Sarah finished, he let out a low whistle. "That's quite a theory, Sadler. But you know I'm going to need more than speculation to green-light an official inquiry."

Sarah nodded, her expression serious. "I understand, sir. And I wouldn't come to you with this if I didn't believe in it wholeheartedly. But the truth is, some of the evidence I've gathered has come from... unconventional sources."

Donahue raised an eyebrow. "Unconventional how?"

"Unconventional? That's one way to describe us." I snickered, and Millie elbowed me in the ribs, reminding me Sarah had made us promise not to make a peep in his office and distract her.

I shrunk a little then slid my fingers across my lips and pretended to zip them.

Sarah hesitated, choosing her words carefully. "Let's just say that I've had some help from outside the bureau. But I can't reveal my sources without compromising their safety and the integrity of the investigation."

He leaned forward, his gaze intense. "Sadler, you know I've always had your back. But I need to know that you're not going rogue and breaking any laws on me here."

Sarah met his eyes, her conviction unwavering. "Sir, I give you my word that everything I've done has been in the pursuit of justice. I'm not trying to go behind anyone's back or break any rules. I'm just following the evidence where it leads me."

He held her gaze for a long moment, searching for any sign of deception. Finally, he sighed, a rueful smile tugging at his lips. "Your old man always did have a nose for this sort of thing. Looks like the apple didn't fall far from the tree."

Sarah seemed to grow a little taller at the mention of being like her father. "I learned from the best, sir. I know I'm asking a lot right now, but I need you to please trust me that I have facts to back this up but not press me for what they are. If you have even the littlest bit of faith left in me after everything that's happened, then have faith in me now. It's a woman. A red-headed woman. I'd stake my career on it."

He spun his pen between his fingers as he appraised her, his lips tight as he twisted them back and forth. We held our collective breaths as we waited for his response, and then finally he set the pen down on the wooden desk.

"Okay. I won't ask how you know what you know, and I'm going to trust you to take this thing to the end."

Her eyes widened in surprise. "You will? I mean, you do? Trust me?"

A slight smile tipped his lips. "I've been at this for a long time. Long enough to get a sense of these things. My gut tells me that even though you can't, or won't, explain it to me, I need to trust you right now. So yes, I trust you. Go deeper down your theory about the red-haired woman, and I'll do my best to keep the brass out of this until you figure it out one way or another. Just be quick and be clean."

"Yes, sir." She stood quickly. "I won't let you down, sir. I'll report in when I have something."

"Keep me in the loop, okay? And if you need any resources or backup, just say the word and I'll do what I can."

Sarah nodded, relief and gratitude washing over her face. "Thank you, sir. I won't let you down."

With a little wink, he leaned back in his chair. "Good luck, Sadler."

When we left the office, Millie and I couldn't contain our excitement any longer. We swooped in beside Sarah, our faces split in wide grins.

"You did it, Sarah!" I cheered. "You brought your boss on board!"

Millie nodded, pride shining in her eyes. "And you did it by trusting in your team, in the people around you. That took real courage, Sarah."

I watched as Sarah's eyes glistened with unshed tears, touched by our words. I knew how much it meant to her, to have our support and encouragement as well as a man she clearly respected.

As we walked through the bullpen, I couldn't help but marvel at the change in Sarah's demeanor. She stood taller, her head held high, a new sense of confidence in her step.

I knew that the road ahead wouldn't be easy, that there would be twists and turns and obstacles to overcome. But I also knew that with Sarah at the helm, with Millie and me by her side, there was nothing we couldn't handle.

Chapter Eighteen

MILLIE

The bustling energy of the FBI office hummed around us as Sarah, Mabel, and I waited for the tech team to generate the list of red-haired sculptors in the area. Sarah paced back and forth in her office, her agitation palpable in the tight set of her shoulders and the furrow of her brow.

"I hate this," she muttered, her voice low and frustrated. "I feel like I should be out there, doing something, not just sitting around waiting for a bunch of names. The killer could strike again tonight for all we know. There hasn't been a consistent schedule."

Mabel and I exchanged a glance, and we'd known one another so long we didn't need words to convey our joint worry. We knew how much this case meant to Sarah, how driven she was to bring the killer to light. But we also knew that she was running herself ragged, pushing herself to the brink of exhaustion in her pursuit of justice.

"Sarah," I said gently, moving over to her side and placing a hand on her shoulder to stop her repetitive steps. "We know how important this is to you. But you can't keep going at this pace. You need to take a break, give yourself a chance to recharge."

Sarah shook her head, her eyes flashing with determination. "I can't afford to take a break, Millie. Not when the killer is still out there, not when there are still so many questions left unanswered."

Mabel chimed in. "But that's just it, Sarah. The tech team is working on the list, and there's nothing more we can do until they're finished. So why not use this time to let loose a little, have some fun?"

Sarah's brow furrowed, confusion and skepticism warring in her expression. "Fun? How am I supposed to have fun when there's a murderer on the loose?"

I couldn't help but chuckle at her answer. "Sarah, honey, there's always going to be another case, another mystery to solve. Another killer on the loose. But your time on Earth, it's limited. You can't spend every waking moment working or you'll miss out on all the joys and experiences that life has to offer."

Mabel nodded, her features softening with understanding. "Since we met you, Sarah, you've done nothing but work. No friends, no family, just an endless string of late nights and early mornings working. That's not living, that's just… existing."

Sarah's shoulders slumped, a flicker of vulnerability passing over her face. "I know. But this job, it's all I have. It's all I've ever wanted to do."

I tipped my head in understanding. "And you're amazing at it, Sarah. But you need balance. You need to find joy and connection outside of your work, or even at work with your coworkers, or you'll burn out faster than a candle in a hurricane."

Mabel's face lit up, a mischievous glint in her eye. "And

what better time to start than tonight? It's Friday, the city's alive with possibility, and we've got nothing but time on our hands. Let's go out, paint the town red, and show the world what the Spectral Sleuths are made of!"

Sarah hesitated, her gaze flickering between us with uncertainty. But I could see the flicker of longing in her eyes, the desperate desire for something more than the endless grind of casework and paperwork even if she couldn't admit it to herself yet.

"Come on, Sarah," I urged, my voice soft but insistent. "Take a chance, just this once. Let us show you what it means to truly live."

"I don't think so." She shook her head.

Mabel and I sighed in unison, then Mabel crossed her arms. "You know what. We're only here for a limited time, and I want to go dancing. Are you really going to deny me a night on earth shaking it with the living?"

"You two can go. I'll be okay here," she said, and her pacing started up again.

Mabel and I exchanged a glance, then I stepped to her side, crossing my arms as well. "I want to go dancing too, but we won't go without you. If you stay, we stay."

Sarah's steps slowed, and she looked at us with a flash of irritation. "You're not blackmailing me with guilt to go dancing. If you want to go, you can go."

Mabel shrugged. "I guess if we aren't going out dancing, then we'll just start a dance club here. Oh, what was that song we used to dance to back in the day? The fun one with the moves!"

"The Macarena!" I exclaimed, and instantly knew what she was up to.

As if we shared one mind, Mabel and I burst out singing off key, our bodies moving as one as we sang the annoying song and danced around Sarah's office in mirrored moves.

"You are not going to do that all night." She frowned.

We repeated the chorus, grinning at her as we started the whole dance over, getting louder this time.

For a long moment, Sarah stared at us as if she wanted to incinerate us with her gaze, but then she slapped a hand onto her forehead. "Okay! Okay! Fine! I'll go dancing if you promise never to sing that song to me again."

We stopped dancing and exchanged high fives. "Whoot!"

With a defeated sigh, Sarah grabbed her purse. "Let's do it. But just for a few hours, and then it's back to the case. Deal?"

"Deal!" we chorused.

A short while later, we found ourselves standing outside a trendy dance club, the pulsing beat of the music spilling out onto the street. Sarah fidgeted nervously, her eyes darting around the crowd of scantily clad clubgoers waiting in line, the pulsing neon lights illuminating the dark sidewalk each time the bouncer opened the door.

"I don't know about this," she murmured, her voice barely audible over the throbbing bassline. "I've never been to a place like this before. My colleagues talk about this club all the time, but I wouldn't even know what to do. Maybe we should go back to the office."

Mabel laughed, her body already swaying to the rhythm. "That's the beauty of it, Sarah. There are no rules, no expectations. You just let the music move you and see where the night takes you. Come on. We made a deal, and we're going dancing."

I nodded, memories of our own youthful exploits flooding back in a warm rush of nostalgia. "Mabel and I used to go dancing all the time back in our day. The styles may have changed, but the thrill of losing yourself in the moment, that never goes out of fashion."

Sarah took a deep breath, squaring her shoulders as if steeling herself for battle. "Okay. Let's go."

The bouncer gave her a once over and checked her ID, then we made our way inside, the pulsing energy of the club enveloping us like a living, breathing entity. Bodies moved on the dance floor, a writhing mass of sweat and lights and pounding bass. Sarah hesitated at the edge of the crowd, her eyes wide with trepidation.

"Come on. The best dance moves always come out after a couple of drinks," Mabel said, leading us toward the bar.

We followed behind her, then Sarah ordered a glass of wine and found an empty bar stool.

"Man, I wish we could have a margarita!" Mabel blinked her eyes hard as if she could somehow pull down a margarita from heaven straight into her hand.

"We've tried about ten thousand times," I said, sharing her frustration. "We don't get to eat or drink until we go back."

"But you don't need to eat or drink?" Sarah asked after taking a sip of her wine and pressing her cell phone to her ear to talk to us.

"No. Not to survive because, well, we're already dead. It's just we miss the taste of it. And in Heaven, you could eat a thousand pounds of food a day if you wanted and drink a gallon of margaritas. It's…"

"Heaven." I grinned. "And cake. So much cake! Oh, I miss the cake." I licked my lips.

"Do you two miss it?" Sarah asked.

We exchanged a look, and I took the lead on answering the question the way I knew we both felt. "Yeah. We do. It's amazing up there. But at the same time, when we were up there, we were missing all the chaos of Earth. I guess in a perfect afterlife, we could go back and forth at will and enjoy the best of both worlds."

"And can you?" she asked, taking another sip.

I shrugged. "I don't know. The closest we've come is being Crossing Guards. I guess we'll see what happens at the end of our temporary assignment. Maybe they'll let us come back down and do this again." Then my face fell. "Or maybe they'll find out what we've been up to and never let us return or worse, dump our naughty ghostly asses down in hell."

Mabel waved a hand. "You worry too much. We're crushing this Crossing Guard thing! We're going to be fine. Now, enough talk about the afterlife when we're here enjoying the living world. Come on, ladies. It's time to go dancing!"

Sarah glanced at the dance floor and softly shook her head. "I'm going to look like an idiot," she muttered, her gaze darting around self-consciously. "Everyone here is so young and cool, and I'm just... me."

Mabel snorted, her body already shimmying and swaying to the beat. "Nonsense! You're a total catch, Sarah. And besides, who cares what anyone else thinks? This night is about you, about letting go and having fun."

I nodded, hopping to Mabel's side and joining her in a lively two-step. "Come on! Let's go! We'll be right there at your side."

"Yeah, but no one else can see you two, so I'm going to look like I'm dancing all alone."

"She's right, Sarah. Dance like nobody's watching. Because in the grand scheme of things, what do their opinions really matter? Trust me. When you get to the afterlife, you're going to feel mighty stupid about all the things you were too scared to do in life and the things you missed out on. 'In the end, we only regret the chances we didn't take.' That saying is so true. So, come on. Take a chance and have some fun. You may just find you can be a kick ass FBI agent *and* have a fabulous, fun, and full life!"

Sarah hesitated a moment longer, then, with a rueful sigh, she gave one sharp nod. "Okay. Fine." She put her cell phone in her purse, finished her wine in several big swings, then followed us out onto the dance floor.

At first, her movements were stiff and self-conscious, her arms held close to her sides as she swayed awkwardly to the music. Mabel and I whooped and hollered, truly dancing like no one was watching because, in our case, they weren't. We continued shaking it at Sarah, her face cracking in smiles as she struggled not to laugh at our antics. But as the minutes ticked by, as the infectious energy of the crowd began to seep into her bones, I watched as the tension slowly melted away from her frame.

Her hips began to move more fluidly, her arms lifting and swaying with the pulsing rhythm. A smile spread across her face, tentative at first, then blossoming into a full-blown grin of pure, unadulterated joy. She spun and swayed, her laughter ringing out over the pounding beat as Mabel and I danced alongside her.

One song after another, Sarah let herself go, and Mabel and I couldn't stop grinning as we watched her cracking out of her shell like a little baby bird already itching to take flight. As another song ended, Sarah wiped the sweat from her brow and nodded for us to follow her to the bar. We danced along behind her, and when she got to the bar, she collapsed onto a stool, her face flushed and her eyes sparkling with exhilaration.

"That was amazing!" she gasped, her voice breathless with laughter. "I can't remember the last time I felt so alive, so free."

Mabel and I exchanged a triumphant glance, our collective hearts swelling with pride.

"That's what life is all about, Sarah," I said softly. "Embracing the moment, letting yourself feel the joy and the sheer, unbridled energy of being alive."

"Agent Sadler?" a familiar voice asked.

We turned to see the little blonde, Agent Collins, standing behind Sarah with a martini in her hand.

Sarah spun to face her. "Oh, hey. I, uh… what are you doing here?

Agent Collins laughed. "What am *I* doing here? I believe the question is what are *you* doing here? We come here all the time and must have invited you a dozen times but gave up because you always said no." She gestured toward a group of young agents all huddled around a table sharing beers and laughs.

The confidence Sarah exuded when at a crime scene hot on the trail of a killer dissipated as she shuffled awkwardly in front of the woman. "I, uh, I just wanted to go dancing tonight, I guess."

"Are you alone?" she asked.

Sarah glanced at us out of the corner of her eye. "Uh, yeah. I'm alone."

Agent Collins' pretty face split into a wide grin. "Well, then I guess you'd better come join us!"

Sarah rocked back as she gently shook her head. "Oh, I don't think so."

Agent Collins sighed on a smile. "Don't worry about those guys giving you a hard time before. They can be real assholes, but they can also be really great if you just give them a chance. I bet if you come and have some fun with us, and bond with us, maybe they'll stop treating you like a leper and start treating you like a teammate. Come on, Sadler. Join us."

Sarah chewed on her lip, and I decided to break the number one rule not to talk to her when she was with her fellow humans.

"Sarah, this is your chance to take a step in the right direction with your coworkers. Go. Have fun. Make friends. Mabel and I are going to help this soul cross over, and you go spend some time with people who still have a heartbeat. You can do this."

"Go get 'em, girl!" Mabel cheered her on.

Sarah hesitated for another long moment and then gave a soft nod. "Okay."

Agent Collins grinned and reached out, grabbing Sarah's hand. "Come on. First drinks on me."

As they walked away, Sarah peeked back at us over her shoulder. We gave her a thumbs up and Mabel called out, "Go get 'em, Tiger! And if anyone gives you crap, just give me a name and I'll haunt their ass!"

Sarah stifled a smile then we watched her nervously approach the group of agents, who welcomed her shocked expressions and smiles.

"Look at our girl." I sighed. "She's really coming out of her shell."

"She's so lucky to have us." Mabel crossed her arms as we watched Sarah shaking everyone's hands. "We're helping souls cross over to Heaven and Sarah cross over from being a work-obsessed loner to having some semblance of a life."

"Man, we're good at this Crossing Guard thing," Mabel said, slinging an arm over my shoulder. "And not just helping souls cross over, which we are absolutely crushing, but we're down here solving murders, stopping a killer, and helping Sarah maybe start living her life a little."

"Yeah. I guess maybe you're right. We're pretty good at this."

We watched Sarah from a distance, and I couldn't contain my smile seeing her interacting with her colleagues and smiling. As I watched her talking to her new friends, a handsome man with dark hair, a chiseled jaw, and deep dimples started talking to her, and she smiled brighter than I'd ever seen.

"Whoa. Who's Special Agent Hottie McHotterson?" Mabel let out a long, slow whistle. "Damn. I haven't seen him around the office before."

"I think Sarah likes him. Look at her blushing! I can see the red in her cheeks from all the way over here!"

"I can see his fine behind from all the way over here and I don't blame her for blushing one bit."

We shared a giggle then decided to stop spying and leave Sarah to share an evening with her living, breathing friends. As we passed by her on our way out, she glanced up at us and gave a small smile that let us know she was okay, and it warmed me all the way into my soul. I knew that our mission was about more than just solving crimes and catching killers. It was about healing, about growth, about finding joy and purpose in a world that could be so dark and unforgiving.

"Come on, Millie," Mabel said, linking her arm in mine. "Let's go float around the city and watch for people acting rude and then haunt them for a while. I really want to practice my tripping skills."

I laughed and leaned into her. "Lead the way."

Chapter Nineteen

MABEL

We burst through the wall of Sarah's office to see her hunched over her cluttered desk, her fingers pinched along-side her temples.

"Morning!" Millie sing-songed, and the sharp sound made Sarah cringe.

"Ouch," she answered, giving us each a warning stare. "Why are you so loud this morning."

"Whoa? Someone is looking a little less than enthusiastic about this beautiful morning. A bit hungover perhaps?" I teased.

Sarah shot me a look that answered my question, then took a sip of her coffee and sat back in her chair.

"So," I began, a mischievous grin spreading across my face. "How was your night? Did you paint the town red with your FBI pals? Dance 'til dawn? Kick up your heels?"

Sarah ducked her head, a faint smile tipping up her lips. "Honestly, it was... nice," she admitted. "I had a really good time, actually. It felt good to let loose a little, to not feel like an outsider for once."

"And they were all nice to you? Anyone on that list of people you want me to haunt?" I clenched my hand in a fist, twisting my face and lifting my lip in a menacing sneer.

She chuckled. "You know, they were nice. At first things were kind of awkward. I've never really hung out with them, and with everything that happened they've all treated me like a leper, but Agent Collins really helped push me to stick it out, and eventually, after a lot of awkwardness, things kinda just felt… normal. Like there wasn't this huge chasm between me and the other agents. It was… good."

Millie and I exchanged a triumphant glance, and my heart swelled with pride that we'd helped her make strides with her colleagues.

"That's fantastic, Sarah," Millie said, her tone warm and sincere. "We're so happy for you."

I couldn't resist a little lighthearted teasing, eyebrows inching up as I asked, "And what about that handsome agent you were chatting up? The tall, dark, and dreamy one with the dimples? What was his name again?"

Sarah's cheeks turned a delightful shade of crimson. "What handsome agent?"

I scoffed. "Oh please. Don't play coy. You know *exactly* who I'm talking about. The guy looks like he stepped right out of a romance novel, and I know you agree because your face was the shade of a fire engine when he smiled at you. The same shade it is now when I mentioned him."

I waggled my eyebrows and her blush deepened.

With a sigh, she answered, "His name is Agent Parker. And I wasn't chatting him up," she mumbled, her gaze fixed firmly on her coffee cup. "We were just talking, that's all."

"Uh-huh," I drawled, my grin widening. "Just talking. Sure. And I'm the Queen of England."

Millie swatted at me, her own expression a mix of

amusement and admonishment. "Leave her alone, Mabel. Sarah's allowed to have a conversation with a colleague without it being a big deal." Then she paused, leaning it. "Or is it a big deal? Did anything happen? Did he kiss you?"

"No!" She answered quickly, then cleared her throat, her embarrassment giving way to a more serious expression.

"If I were your age and single… and alive… I'd have done a lot more than kiss that man." I waggled my eyebrows again, a mischievous grin spreading across my face.

She batted a hand at me. "Anyway, it doesn't matter. I don't have time for dating right now, not with this case still unsolved. But it was nice to make some friends, to feel like I'm part of the team for the first time. Baby steps, right?"

I nodded, my own face sobering as the weight of our investigation settled back over us like a heavy cloak. "Speaking of the case," I said, my tone all business. "Did the tech guys come up with that list of red-haired sculptors yet?"

Sarah shook her head. "Not yet. They said it could be another hour or two."

"Well then," I said, exchanging a mischievous glance with Millie, "perfect time to work on our new telekinesis skills."

Sarah looked up from her coffee. "Oh no. Not in my office. I don't want you two breaking anything important."

"We'll be careful!" Millie protested. "We just need to practice a little before we need to use it for real. While you were dancing around town last night, Mabel and I did some practice around the city. We're getting pretty good at it!"

"Fine," Sarah sighed, pressing her fingers to her temples again. "But start with something small and harmless."

I spotted a paperclip on her desk. "Perfect." Millie and I joined hands and concentrated. The paperclip wiggled, then shot across the room like a tiny missile.

"Okay, not bad," Sarah said. "Try something else."

We focused on her stapler next. It shifted an inch, then two, then suddenly lurched sideways and knocked directly into her coffee mug.

"No, no, NO!" Sarah lunged forward, but it was too late. Coffee splashed across her keyboard and into her lap.

"Oh, crap!" Sarah jumped up, coffee dripping from her clothes. "It's hot!"

"We're so sorry!" Millie and I rushed toward her, then remembered we couldn't actually help clean up.

"Here, let me—" I reached for tissue, my hand passing right through the box.

"We can't even help!" Millie wailed, looking mortified. "I'm so sorry, Sarah!"

Sarah grabbed tissues herself, dabbing at her keyboard and clothes. Despite the mess, she started chuckling. "You two are like supernatural toddlers. All this power and no coordination."

"We're still learning?" I offered weakly.

"Next time, practice in an empty room," Sarah said, still smiling despite being covered in coffee. "Preferably one without electronics or important FBI agents." She finished blotting her lap, looking up at us and pointing to the brown stain spread across her crotch. "I look like I pissed myself."

"Sorry, Sarah," we echoed, each pulling a face.

As if on cue to break the embarrassing moment, Sarah's computer pinged with an incoming email. She clicked it open, her eyes scanning the contents with laser-like focus. "Got it," she said, her voice tight with anticipation. "Four names, all local, all with a history of working in sculpture."

Millie and I crowded around the screen, jostling for a better view. There, in stark black and white, were the names of our potential suspects. One of them, I knew with a sickening certainty, was the twisted soul we'd been hunting, the monster who had snuffed out so many bright young lives.

"Mira Novak, 39, MFA from Yale." Sarah read aloud, her finger tracing the lines of text. "Victoria Milton, age 45, studied at the Art Institute of Chicago, Cassandra Lee, 42, self-taught, no formal education. And Allison Hines, 37, BFA from RISD."

I felt a shiver run through my body, the names searing themselves into my brain. One of these women had to be our killer, a predator who stalked the streets in search of her next victim. And it was up to us to stop her before she could strike again.

"So, what's our next move?" Millie asked, her voice tight with determination. "How do we narrow down the list, figure out which one of these women is our killer?"

Sarah leaned back in her chair, her brow furrowed in thought. "Ideally, we'd put surveillance on all of them, track their movements and see if anything suspicious pops up. But realistically, I know I won't get approval for that, not without more evidence to go on. We're short agents right now and getting approval for surveilling four women is a big undertaking."

A flicker of excitement sparked in my chest, an idea taking shape in my mind. "You don't need approval for surveillance," I said, my voice thrumming with energy. "You have us! Ghosts, remember? We can follow these women around, watch their every move without anyone being the wiser."

Sarah's eyes widened, a mix of surprise and uncertainty flickering across her face. "I don't know, Mabel. That feels a bit like breaking the law, doesn't it? Invading their privacy, spying on them without a warrant?"

Millie shook her head, her own expression serious. "Sarah, we're talking about a serial killer here. A monster who's already taken too many lives, who won't stop until we make her. If bending a few rules is what it takes to catch her, then that's what we have to do."

I nodded, my own resolve hardening like a fist. "Millie's right. We're not breaking any laws, not really. We're ghosts, so your laws don't apply to us. We're just using our unique abilities to gather evidence, to stop a killer before she can hurt anyone else. And if that means a little ghostly stalking, then so be it."

Sarah hesitated for a long moment, her gaze distant and thoughtful as she weighed the risks and rewards of our unorthodox plan. But in the end, her determination won out, her jaw setting with a steely resolve.

"Okay," she said, her voice low and intense. "Let's do it. We'll start with just one, see what we can find before we move on to the others. I don't want us to spread ourselves too thin, not when the stakes are this high. We need to really look into these women and find out for certain which one is our killer so I can gather the evidence we need to get a warrant and go after her."

Millie and I nodded, our faces taut with the seriousness of our next task. This was it, the break we'd been waiting for, the chance to finally put our otherworldly skills to the test.

"So, who's our lucky first contestant?" I asked, rubbing my hands together with anticipation.

"Well, the background checks show nothing notable on any of them, so that's no help." Sarah scanned the list again, her finger hovering over each name in turn. "Let's start with Allison Hines," she said finally, her tone decisive. "She's the youngest of the bunch, closest in age to our victims, and her studio is the closest to the last murder scene. It's as good a place to start as any."

I felt a surge of excitement race through me, the thrill of the hunt already pulsing in my veins. "Then what are we waiting for?" I said, my grin stretching from ear to ear. "Let's go catch us a killer."

The three of us hurried out of the office and piled into Sarah's car. A short while later, Sarah pulled up outside Allison Hines' studio, a converted warehouse in the heart of the city's arts district. Millie and I sat in the back seat, the nervous energy buzzing between us.

"Remember," Sarah said, her voice low and urgent. "Just observe and report back. Don't do anything to alert her, and for God's sake, don't get caught."

I rolled my eyes, a playful smirk tugging at my lips. "Sarah, please. We're ghosts. The day we get caught snooping is the day I hang up my spectral spurs for good."

Millie nodded, her own expression serious. "We'll be careful, Sarah. Promise. And we'll stay with her tonight then find you at the office in the morning to let you know what we find."

Sarah took a deep breath, her fingers drumming nervously on the steering wheel. "Okay. Good luck, you two. And be safe. I'm going to go take a light look at Mira Novak while you're following Allison. Just tail her a bit and poke around to see if I can spot anything from a distance. You can transport yourselves to my car if you need me, right?"

We nodded. "Yep."

"Good. If I'm not here in my car, check the office first and we'll find each other."

"Be careful, Sarah." I gave her a look, and she gave a final nod.

Millie and I phased through the car door to the building, our ghostly forms gliding effortlessly through the brick and mortar walls, then we moved up the stairs to Allison's apartment.

We stopped outside for a moment, sharing a look.

"I know she can't hurt us, but I'm scared," Millie said softly. "What if there is something horrible inside when we go through those walls."

I glanced at the brick wall and my stomach clenched with nervous anticipation of what we may find on the other side.

"We'll face it together." I reached out and took her hand, then with a deep breath, we phased through the walls.

Inside, the space was cavernous and cluttered, with half-finished sculptures and piles of scrap metal scattered across the concrete floor. At first glance, Allison Hines seemed like any other artist, her lithe form hunched over a workbench as she wielded a blowtorch with practiced ease. But as Millie and I watched, our senses on high alert, I couldn't help but wonder if beneath the surface of this seemingly ordinary woman lurked a darkness that would emerge at any moment. Every second we watched her I felt like she might suddenly spin around, looking right at us and laughing her evil laugh. The image kept me on edge as we followed her around, but as the moments ticked by, our sculptor never ripped off her mask revealing the monster beneath the façade.

For hours, we followed Allison, our ghostly forms flitting silently through the shadows as she went about her day. We watched as she sculpted and welded, as she made phone calls and chatted with friends. We climbed into the back seat of her car and rode along with her as she ran errands, and we sat across from her when she grabbed a quick bite to eat at a nearby cafe.

But as the day wore on, and the sun began to dip below the horizon, we found ourselves no closer to unraveling the mystery of the red-haired killer. Allison seemed, for all intents and purposes, to be nothing more than a dedicated artist, her life revolving around her work and little else.

As night fell, and Allison retired to her small apartment above the studio and started cooking dinner, Millie and I regrouped in the darkened living room.

"I don't know, Mabel," Millie said, her voice heavy with disappointment. "I don't think she's our killer. We've been watching her all day, and there's just nothing suspicious about her."

I sighed, my own frustration bubbling to the surface. "I know. But we can't give up yet. Maybe we missed something, some clue or detail that could point us in the right direction. I say we report in to Sarah quick then come back and watch her through the night. Killers strike at night, and we don't want to give up on her too soon."

Millie agreed, so we quickly popped into Sarah's car where she was silently staking out Mia's house.

"Hi," I said as we appeared.

Sarah jumped in her seat and gasped, inhaling a piece of beef jerky. Her eyes watered as she hacked, pounding her chest.

"Oh, no! Don't choke to death, Sarah! Don't go to the light! Don't go to the light!" I said, horrified our abrupt appearance had startled her into choking on the hunk of meat.

Finally, she coughed it up, gasping with a deep breath as

she managed out, "You scared me half to death! A little warning next time!"

We shrunk in the back seat. "Sorry. It's not like we can pick up the phone and call you to tell you we're coming."

She finished coughing, then let out a breath. "It's fine. It was just bad timing right when I was about to swallow."

"Sorry, Sarah," I said softly, sucking the air through my teeth.

"Any luck?" she asked now that she'd caught her breath.

"Nothing," I said with a sigh. "She seems pretty ordinary so far. Anything here?"

Sarah shook her head. "Nothing unusual from the outside at least. But I can't get inside."

"Want us to take a quick look just to make sure there aren't any body parts laying around?" Millie asked, then cringed. "Eww. I really don't want to find body parts."

"Actually, yeah. Do you mind? We can put more time into her after you finish with Allison, but a quick look wouldn't hurt."

I gave her a sharp salute. "On it."

Millie and I moved across her mowed lawn and slipped through the walls into her house. We traveled through the dark rooms looking for anything overtly suspicious but again, found nothing other than ordinary items in an ordinary house. We peeked into her bedroom to see her sleeping in her floral, queen-sized bed, and there were no blinking neon signs above her head flashing "Serial Killer Sleeps Here." Millie and I exchanged a look and shook our heads then went back to Sarah.

"Nothing," Millie said as she slipped into the back seat.

"My gut doesn't think it's her, but I'll keep an eye on her just to be safe."

"We're going to go spend the night at Allison's just to be

sure she doesn't only allow her dark side out in the dark, and then we'll meet you at the office in the morning."

"Sounds good. Be safe, ladies."

"We will," Millie said, her face twisting with concern. "You as well."

We flashed ourselves back to Allison's apartment and found her sitting on her couch, her tabby cat curled up in her lap as she sipped on a glass of red wine staring at the television.

"Oh! *Bridgerton!*" Millie said, quickly pulling up a seat on the couch. "We died before this season came out!"

"I love me some *Bridgerton.*" I agreed and slid in beside her. "I mean, if we have to sit here all night and watch Allison, we may as well catch up on these episodes."

Millie grinned and the two of us sat beside Allison who was completely unaware of her television watching partners while she binged three hours of it. I tried several times to blink popcorn in my hands, grumbling each time I opened my eyes to find them empty. But for those few hours, we used our investigative time to keep an eye on Allison while we also giggled over the steamy scenes flashing across the television screen.

We groaned when she turned it off before the final episode, then we followed her to her bedroom where she and her cat curled up together for the night. After she was fast asleep and definitely wasn't heading out on a murder spree for the evening, we spent the next hour as she slept combing through her place, our ghostly eyes peeled for anything out of the ordinary. But aside from a frankly alarming number of cat figurines and a collection of truly shockingly dirty romance novels, we came up empty-handed.

As dawn began to break over the city, and Allison stirred

from her slumber, Millie and I exchanged a defeated glance. We had given it our all, but in the end, it seemed that Allison Hines was a dead end, another false lead in a case that grew more twisted by the day.

With heavy hearts, we transported ourselves to the office to find it empty, then we popped back to Sarah's car, which was still parked outside of Mia's house, our ghostly bodies appearing in the back seat without warning.

"Whoa. You scared me again," she said, pressing a hand to her heart. "I was kind of hovering between awake and asleep. I'm awake now. Well?" she asked, her voice tight with tension. "Did you find anything?"

I shook my head, disappointment a bitter taste in my mouth. "Nothing. Allison's clean, as far as we can tell. Just a boring artist with a boring life and a weird thing for cats."

"And really dirty novels," Millie whispered, my eyes widening. "Like… *really* dirty."

I chuckled, "Oh, come on, Millie. Admit it. You wanted to read them."

She blushed and glanced at her feet, then giggled.

"So she's a cat lover with a thing for really dirty romance novels? Nothing else notable?"

Millie shook her head. "We had to step away once during the night, though. Our beacon went off, and we had to answer the call."

Sarah's eyebrows shot up, curiosity and concern mingling in her expression. "Your beacon? You mean, you had to go help a soul cross over? In the middle of the stakeout?"

I nodded, feeling a twinge of guilt at the admission. "Yeah. It's part of the job, you know? When a soul needs our help, we have to drop everything and go to them. No matter where we are or what we're doing. It always comes first."

Sarah leaned back in her seat, her brow furrowed in thought. "I can't imagine how tough that must be. Trying to balance your duties as Crossing Guards with our investigation, never knowing when you'll be called away."

Millie let out a weary sigh. "It's not easy, that's for sure. But it's important work, and we can't turn our backs on those souls in need."

I gave a soft nod. "Being a Crossing Guard is the most important job there is. No soul is going to be left behind for the reapers on our watch. We made sure to get back to Allison's place as quickly as we could, though. Didn't want to miss anything important."

Sarah nodded, understanding passing over her features. "I get it. And I appreciate your dedication to both your Crossing Guard duties and our case. I know it can't be easy, juggling all of this."

"We'll always find a way to make it work," I said, my voice firm with conviction. "The souls we help, the killer we're chasing... it's all part of the same mission. To bring light to the darkness, however we can."

Sarah smiled, her eyes shining with a mix of exhaustion and determination. "Couldn't have said it better myself, Mabel." Sarah sighed, her shoulders slumping with the weight of our failure. "Damn it. I really thought we were onto something with this redheaded killer lead. Mia didn't leave last night either."

Millie reached out, her hand hovering just above Sarah's shoulder in a gesture of comfort. "Don't give up, Sarah. We still have two more suspects to check out, two more chances to catch this monster and bring her to justice."

I nodded, my determination reigniting like a searing

flame. "Millie's right. We're not done yet, not by a long shot. On to the next one, and the one after that, until we find the sicko who did this and make her pay for what she's done."

Sarah took a deep breath, her eyes hardening with renewed resolve. "Okay. Let's do it. But first, I need coffee. Lots and lots of coffee. I haven't done a stakeout in forever and forgot how exhausting sitting around can be."

As we pulled away from the curb, the rising sun painting the quaint neighborhood in shades of gold and pink, I couldn't help but feel a flicker of hope amidst the frustration. We had faced setbacks before, had stared down the darkness and come out the other side.

And with Millie by my side, and Sarah at the helm, I knew that there was nothing we couldn't overcome, no mystery we couldn't unravel.

The game was on, and the Spectral Sleuths were closing in on a killer.

Chapter Twenty

MILLIE

The three of us huddled together at Sarah's desk staring at the list of red-haired sculptors laying before us.

"Okay," Sarah said, her voice tight with determination as she crossed off two names. "We've got two suspects left. Victoria Milton and Cassandra Lee."

"And what if they don't show anything unusual either? What if none of them are the killer and we come up empty handed?" I asked, verbalizing the thought I couldn't get out of my mind.

Sarah let out a puff of air. "Well, I really feel like we're on the right track with our red-headed killer, so if it's not one of these four, then we keep hunting. Dig deeper. We don't quit until we find her."

"We won't," Mabel said quickly. "And maybe we have to watch these ladies for more than just a night. Maybe we've already met our killer, but she was just taking the night off."

"That's true." I poked a finger on my chin. "It's not like she's out killing every night."

Sarah pointed at the list. "Let's just stick to the plan and take the logical steps as we go, and we'll deal with what we find as we find it. Our first step is to check out these two new sculptors. Split up again, cover more ground. That seemed to work well last night."

"We'll take Victoria," I said, my voice steady despite the flutter of nerves in my stomach about potentially spending time with a serial killer.

Mabel gave a sharp nod. "You can do some light surveillance on Cassandra, see if anything pops. We can stop over later and do a casing of her place as well if Victoria doesn't prove to be our killer."

Sarah took a big sip of her coffee then set it down right on the faint circular coffee stain. "Sounds like a plan. But be careful, you two. If Victoria is our killer, there's no telling what she might be capable of."

Mabel grinned, her eyes sparkling with mischief. "Don't worry about us, Sarah. We're ghosts, remember? It's not like she can hurt us. We're already dead. *You* be careful in case *Cassandra* is the killer."

I wished I shared Mabel's confidence, and though I knew she was right, and a mortal killer couldn't hurt us, it still didn't quell the unease bubbling just beneath my surface to perhaps be heading straight into a killer's lair. But with Mabel at my side, just like I had in life, I let her confidence wrap around me like a protective blanket.

We stared at photo from the internet of the street outside Victoria's studio, closed our eyes and let the vortex swallow us up and take us there. As we appeared in front of the apartment building, I couldn't shake the feeling of unease that prickled along my spine. With only two suspects left, the chances of encountering a killer had jumped astronomically and it set my teeth on edge.

As Mabel and I once again prepared ourselves to find a

grisly scene awaiting us, we held hands and phased into her studio. The tall windows filled the room with natural light, casting a warm glow onto the wooden floors. Her sculptures, mostly inspired by the human form, were in several places around the studio area, some looking finished and others in varying stages of completion.

"No bodies," Mabel whispered as we looked around.

I let out a sigh. "Thank God. I really don't want to see what our killer has been up to with the body parts." Then a thought crossed my mind and I whispered, "Or maybe they are in the freezer?"

We shared a look and then moved to the freezer, holding our breaths with nervous anticipation as we stuck our heads inside.

"Just pizza and ice cream," I said, breathing out my sigh of relief as we pulled our heads back out.

"We didn't check the other freezers last night. We'll go back tomorrow after we finish tailing Victoria and check those out. That's a good point and I didn't even think of it."

I nodded, still hoping that we wouldn't be the ones to find anything gruesome. I couldn't even open my eyes during the scary scenes of the movies Mabel loved so much, and I didn't think I could handle living through a horrifying discovery in real life.

"Let's check the sculptures for the mark." Mabel jutted her chin toward some of the works in progress.

We investigated them all together, but none bore a mark to be seen.

"Damn. I don't think they put their mark on until they're done. Nada." She grumbled.

I frowned that we didn't have a definitive clue that would have sealed up our case without me having to see any more death or gruesome sights.

"Well, so far nothing is jumping out," Mabel said, her voice lifting to normal volume even though there was no reason for us to have whispered in the first place since no one could hear us. "I don't see Victoria though."

Just then, we heard the blow dryer fire up down the hall, so we shared a look and followed the sound. We found Victoria in her bathroom fixing her hair and applying a light coat of red gloss to her lips. She was beautiful with her long, red hair and ivory complexion, and she looked quite similar to Allison with her slender but athletic build. After she finished touching up in the mirror, she headed out of her apartment. We matched her steps, following her out to her dark blue little truck. After a short drive downtown, we followed Victoria as she went about her day, her actions so ordinary and unremarkable that I found myself stifling yawns of boredom.

She started her morning at a quaint little coffee shop, sipping a latte and chatting amiably with the barista about the weather and the latest art gallery openings. Her smile was warm and genuine, her laughter ringing freely across the cozy space.

From there, she made her way to a nearby park, where she settled on a bench and pulled out a sketchbook. For nearly an hour, she sat in peaceful contemplation, her pencil moving across the page with a fluid grace that spoke of years of practice and passion.

Mabel and I hovered nearby, unseen by the crowds enjoying a beautiful afternoon outside.

"She seems so normal," Mabel muttered, her tone frustrated. "Just another boring artist, and not the faintest hint of a psychopathic dark side hellbent on murder."

I nodded, my brow furrowed in thought. "Maybe we

were wrong about her, Mabel. Maybe she's not our killer after all."

Mabel nodded and together, we let out a frustrated sigh. It seemed we were no closer to catching our killer than we'd been this morning.

"I wonder how Sarah is faring?" I asked, now worrying that it meant she was the one who could be in close proximity to the killer.

"I want to go check on her, but until we get back to Victoria's studio, I don't want to risk losing her."

"Yeah. Good point. We'll check on her as soon as we know it's safe to flash away for a few."

Victoria left her bench at the park, so we followed along after her like little ducklings rushing behind their mother. As the day wore on, Victoria went about her errands with the same unassuming air. She browsed the shelves at a local art supply store, chatting with the owner about the latest shipment of clay and glazes. She stopped by a grocery store, filling her cart with the same mundane staples as any other shopper.

By the time she climbed into her truck to head home, Mabel and I were starting to feel like fools. We'd wasted an entire day following a woman who seemed about as dangerous as a fluffy bunny rabbit.

"Well, I guess we're probably heading back to her place for a boring evening." I sighed. "I hope Sarah's investigation is more fruitful than what kind of breakfast cereal her target likes to buy."

Mabel shrugged. "Maybe if we're really lucky, she'll be watching the last episode of *Bridgerton* so we can find out how it ends."

I lit up and nodded. "Oh, that would be perfect!"

But as Victoria pulled out of the parking lot, she drove

past her apartment toward the highway exiting the city. Mabel and I shared a look.

"She's not going home," Mabel said, glancing back toward her apartment building.

As we left the city, Victoria's happy, relaxed demeanor shifted. It was subtle at first, a tightening of her jaw, a hardening of her eyes. But as the miles ticked by, and the city gave way to winding country roads, the change became more pronounced.

"Where is she going?" I asked, the nerves in my stomach crackling like little fireworks in my belly.

"Do you feel that?" Mabel whispered, her body pressing closer to mine in the small back seat of the truck. "That darkness? Like suddenly she feels like a different person. I can't explain it."

I nodded, my body trembling with a mix of fear and excitement. "She's hiding something, Mabel. I can feel it in my bones."

Victoria's hands gripped the steering wheel with a white-knuckled intensity, her eyes darting to the rearview mirror with a furtive, almost paranoid frequency. She muttered under her breath, her words too low and garbled for even our ghostly ears to make out.

As the truck veered off the main road and onto a narrow, rutted track that led deep into the woods, Mabel and I exchanged a glance of pure, unadulterated dread.

"Mabel," I whispered, reaching over and gripping her hand. "Where are we?"

"I don't know," she said back, her eyes scanning the darkness. "This looks like some old warehouse district that hasn't been used in years."

"I don't like this."

She squeezed my hand tight. "We're okay. We're safe. We've got each other."

"I'm scared," I breathed out as the truck came to a stop outside a decrepit warehouse, its windows boarded up and its walls covered in graffiti.

Victoria killed the engine, her breathing heavy and ragged in the sudden silence. We looked at each other, and that dread settled deeper over my shoulders, crushing down on me as my previous survival instincts begged me to grab Mabel and bolt into the woods far away from the woman making my skin crawl.

"She can't see us. She can't hurt us. We have to stay with her," Mabel said, tightening her grip on my hand as if she could read my mind.

With a lump in my throat swelling larger by the second, I nodded, and we slid through the side of the truck and followed close behind as Victoria made her way inside the warehouse. The interior was dark and dank, the air thick with the stench of decay and despair.

We continued following her through the rundown factory, and she made her way through the discarded metal parts as if she had been here many times before. She headed down a hallway and when she got to the end, she glanced over her shoulder, her gaze passing right over us.

I held my breath as I looked into her eyes while she stared right through me. I knew before she even opened the door that I was staring into the eyes of a killer.

Victoria pushed open the door and stepped inside. Mabel and I shared a stilling breath, then with her gentle look of assurance, we stepped into the room together. We blinked against the darkness, only Victoria's cell phone light illuminating a small part of the room. I squinted, trying to make out the figure in the center of the room.

The lights flicked on, and like a spotlight shining on it, the sculpture came into focus, looming before us like a nightmare made flesh. It was a twisted, grotesque thing, a patchwork of human body parts and clay molded together into a human sculpture with a sick, perverse artistry.

I let out a strangled gasp, my hand flying to my mouth in horror. "Oh, my God," I whispered, my voice trembling with revulsion. "Is that... are those..."

"Real bodies," Mabel finished, barely able to speak as I shook with a mix of terror and rage. "She's been using her victims to make this... this abomination."

Even though we'd been using all our energy to hunt this killer, I still couldn't process the shock we'd actually found her. For a while, it had almost felt like we were playing a game of make believe… like none of this was real, and the hunt was just like the games Mabel and I had made up that had taken us all over the neighborhood on fake mystery solving missions as children. But there was nothing fake about the horror we'd found in that abandoned warehouse or the killer standing just beside it.

Victoria's eyes were wide and gleaming with a mad, fevered light. She reached out, her fingers caressing the cold, dead flesh with a tenderness that made my skin crawl.

"Beautiful," she murmured, her voice thick with a sick, twisted love. "So beautiful. And almost complete. My masterpiece."

"I'm going to be sick," I choked out, barely able to speak the words as my eyes remained transfixed to the sculpture I couldn't seem to look away from even though I wanted to erase its horrifying image from my mind.

Victoria's touch traced the smooth edges of skin and clay blended into one figure. The headless torso made of clay and the four limbs attached to it, bent and shaped to form what would be a romantic pose.

"Just one more piece," Victoria said, her touch moving to the head missing from the top. "And then my masterpiece is finished, and everyone will know that *I* am the most talented artist. Me."

Bile rose in my throat, my spectral form shaking with a potent mix of horror, rage, and sorrow. Those poor women, their lives ripped away, their bodies desecrated... all for the sake of this monster's twisted vision. "Mabel… I can't look at this any longer. We need to get Sarah. Right now."

She nodded, and with one last glance at the sculptural horror show, we grabbed hands. With a burst of spectral energy, we transported ourselves back to Sarah's car, our ghostly forms materializing in the passenger seat.

"Sarah!" I cried, my voice high and panicked. "Sarah, it's her! Victoria is the killer!"

Sarah's eyes widened, her hands gripping the steering wheel with white-knuckled intensity. "What? Are you sure? What did you see?"

Mabel and I tripped over each other's words in our haste to explain, our voices rising in pitch and volume as we described the horror we had witnessed. The sculpture, the body parts, the madness in Victoria's eyes... it all came pouring out in a jumble of terrified, sickened words.

Sarah's face paled, her breathing coming in short, sharp gasps. "Oh, my God," she whispered, her voice barely audible over the pounding of my own heart. "Oh, my God, we found her. We actually found her."

For a moment, we all sat in stunned silence, the weight of our discovery pressing down on us like a physical thing, my body still trembling from the aftershocks of what I'd just seen. Then, with a shake of her head, Sarah snapped into action, her training and instincts taking over.

"Okay," she said, her voice steady and calm despite the fear that flickered in her eyes. "We need to do this by the book. I can't just go barging in there, guns blazing. We need evidence, something concrete that will hold up in court."

"We have to hurry!" I said, wiggling in my seat. "She said she needs one more piece to complete it. She's going hunting again." I gulped, closing my eyes for a moment. "She has the four limbs, one from each kill. All she's missing is…"

I froze and Mabel finished. "A head. It's missing its head."

"Oh, my God," Sarah breathed.

"Yeah. Screw the FBI. Just grab your gun and let's go there right now." Mabel's jaw tightened. "Just pop her between the eyes and put that sicko down! She deserves it, and we can't let her hurt anyone else."

Sarah's eyes bulged. "You guys, I can't just go *murdering* someone."

"Not someone." Mabel lifted a finger. "A killer. A sick, twisted, disgusting killer. You'd be doing the world a favor. I bet the big guy upstairs won't hold a little murder over your head given the circumstances."

"I'm not just going to kill her." Sarah gritted her teeth. "Even though I have to admit I want to."

"So, what do we do then? She's going to kill someone else if we don't work fast!" Anxiety knotted my insides so tightly I was certain they'd burst.

Sarah closed her eyes, and I could see the battle waging between her to rush in and stop the killer right here, right now, and the trained FBI agent who knew this needed to be by the books in order to stop her for good.

"Okay. We have to do this right." Sarah's jaw clenched, her eyes hardening with resolve. "Now, we build a case. If I go in there right now without a warrant, everything we find will be tossed out. She'll go free. We gather evidence, we watch her every move, and we make damn sure that when we take her down, she stays down for good."

Mabel and I exchanged a glance.

"We're with you, Sarah," I said, my voice steady and strong. "Every step of the way. Let's catch this monster and bring her to justice."

We had found our killer, had stared into the face of evil and refused to blink. And now, with Sarah by our side and the burning fires of justice ignited inside us, we would see this through to the end.

Chapter Twenty-One

MABEL

The weight of our discovery hung heavy in the air as Sarah, Millie, and I sat in the car, our minds reeling from the horrifying truth we had uncovered. Victoria, the seemingly unassuming artist, was the twisted soul behind the murders, the monster who had been using her victims' bodies to create her macabre masterpiece.

Sarah's face was a mask of grim determination as she turned to us, her voice steady despite the gravity of the situation. "I need you two to stay on Victoria," she said, her eyes flashing with a fierce intensity. "Make sure she doesn't hurt anyone else while I work on getting a warrant."

Millie's eyes shimmered with worry, her brow furrowed in confusion. "But how are we going to get a warrant without revealing how we discovered her creepy, yucky murder lair?"

Sarah sighed, running a hand through her hair in frustration. "I don't know yet. But I'll find a way. I have to. In the meantime, you two need to tail Victoria, keep an eye on her every move. If she so much as looks at another potential victim, you intervene. Whatever it takes."

I nodded as I felt a swell of determination overcoming the fear creeping through every inch of me. "We won't let her hurt anyone else, Sarah. You can count on us."

With a final nod of understanding, Millie and I closed our eyes, focusing our spectral energy on Victoria's hidden warehouse. The world around us blurred and shifted as the vortex pulled us in, then when we opened our eyes again, we found ourselves back in front of it, but Victoria's truck was already gone.

"She's not here," Millie said, panicked. "Where is she?"

"Let's try her truck. We know how to get in that."

Millie gave me a sharp nod, and once again we held hands and willed the vortex to appear, sucking us in and making us reappear in the back of Victoria's truck, the vehicle speeding down a darkened road toward an unknown destination. Millie and I exchanged a glance of trepidation.

As the miles ticked by, and she reentered the city, she wound through the busy streets until she turned into a wooded park in the heart of it. We hit a small bump and heard a *thump* in the bed of the truck. We spun back toward the sound, and I half expected to see a body, but instead, saw a little yellow wagon bouncing in the back beside a blue tarp. A sickening realization dawned on me. Victoria was heading toward a park, a place where runners and hikers often ventured alone, unaware of the danger that lurked in the shadows, and she had the wagon with her.

"Crap," I breathed. "The wagon. That's what she uses to transport the bodies so she doesn't have to carry them."

"Oh no," Millie whispered, her voice trembling with horror. "Mabel, I think we're going on a murder."

As a lump slid down my throat at the gruesome thought, I

shook my head, my face tightening along with my fists. "We're not going *on* a murder, Millie. We're going to *stop* a murder."

As Victoria pulled into the park's deserted lot and killed the engine, Millie and I phased through the truck's walls, our spectral forms hiding us in plain sight. We watched as Victoria moved around the truck, her movements quick and furtive as she glanced around to make sure no one was watching before starting down the mouth of the trail.

With a shared look of panic, Mabel and I hurried after her, my heart pounding so hard I swear I'd have dropped dead of a heart attack if I weren't already a goner..

As Victoria made her way down the park path into the woods, Millie and I followed close behind, our ghostly forms flitting silently through the trees. She moved with a predatory grace, her eyes scanning the trails ahead like a lion hunting its prey.

But as she stalked her victim, she didn't know two specters were stalking her, and we wouldn't let her take another innocent life.

Victoria reached a spot just outside of the warm lights that illuminated the trail, and she slid into the darkness, blending into the bushes. With a quick glance at her watch, she coiled down low like a snake prepared to strike.

"This must be the route the runner takes. The other souls had routines, and I bet this woman does too." My pulse thrummed like a racecar through my veins. "This is where she plans to attack. Then she'll hide the body while she goes back to get her wagon and take it back to her warehouse when it's safe. Just like she did with the others."

Millie whimpered and started pacing back and forth. "This can't be happening. This can't be happening."

"Hey. You're okay, Millie. Just calm down. We've got

this. We aren't going to let another woman die at the hands of this psycho. Not on our watch."

With her lip fixed between her teeth, she whimpered again then joined me next to Victoria.

I leaned down in Victoria's face, my eyes narrowed as I whispered right into her ear. "I'm going to stop you. And when you are in prison paying the price for your crimes, I am going to haunt you so hard you're going to go crazy and end up in a padded cell."

She didn't hear me, and instead she glanced at her watch once more, then I saw the glint of metal in the moonlight as she pulled her wire tool from her pocket… the same tool she had used to end so many innocent lives.

And then, like a scene from our worst nightmares, we saw her. A young woman, her dark hair pulled back in a ponytail swinging behind her, her athletic form moving swiftly down the path. She was the spitting image of Victoria's previous victims, a fact that sent a chill down my spectral spine.

Millie and I exchanged a look of pure, unadulterated panic. We had to do something, had to find a way to warn the unsuspecting runner before it was too late.

"What do we do?" Millie asked, her voice high and frantic. "We can't let this happen, Mabel. We can't let her take another life. Oh, my God! What do we do? What do we do?" She started spinning in circles, her hands on her head clutching her little grey curls tight.

I tried to stay calm, but panic started to grip me as well. But then as I saw the evil glint in Victoria's smile, I knew I had to find a way to stop her. And then, like a bolt of lightning, an idea struck me.

I whispered, my voice low and urgent. "We need to

distract her, throw her off balance. Give the runner a chance to get away."

Millie's eyes widened as her panicked steps slowed, understanding dawning on her face. "Okay. How?"

I grinned, a smirk lifting my lips into a mischievous smile. "Like this."

I opened my hand, inviting Millie to take it. She gave me a brave little nod then stepped to my side and gripped my hand tight.

As the runner drew closer, her footsteps pounding against the paved trail, we moved behind Victoria and I focused all of my energy onto her crouched form. With a burst of spectral power, I kicked out, my incorporeal foot connecting with her backside as I let out a mighty, "Heeya!"

Victoria let out a yelp of surprise, her body pitching forward into the dirt. She scrambled to right herself, her eyes wide with confusion as she scanned the bushes for her unseen attacker.

"The runner is still coming! She's coming!" Millie started spinning out again.

"Then we have to stop her. Now!" I cried, my voice ringing with urgency. "Follow me!"

I grabbed Millie's hand, and we shot across the dwindling distance separating the woman from her would-be killer crawling back up to her feet in the bushes.

I pulled Millie into the center of the trail, gripping her hand as hard as I could.

"Channel our energy. We can't mess this up. Come on, Millie. Give me everything you've got!"

She closed her eyes, and I felt her energy surging through me. I tried to manifest my body in the trail in front of the woman running toward us, but even as I grunted and groaned, the best I mustered was a flicker.

"Crap! It's not working!" I spit out, breathless.

"She's getting closer!" Millie squealed.

I looked over to the bushes where Victoria had rehidden herself, and my mind raced with ideas on how to stop the inevitable.

"Quick! Stay with me!" I yanked Millie along and flew faster than we'd ever gone until I was side by side with the woman running toward her death. I squeezed Millie's hand so hard it would have hurt if we felt pain. With a deep, otherworldly boom, I channeled my voice onto the earthly plane, my voice echoing through the crisp night air.

"STOP!" I bellowed, my words carrying on the wind like an eerie banshee's cry. "TURN BACK! RUN AWAY!"

The runner froze in her tracks, her face contorting with pure, unadulterated terror. For a moment, she stood paralyzed, her eyes wide and unblinking as she stared into the darkness.

"I. SAID. RUN!" I shouted into her face, putting every ounce of energy I had into making my voice break the barrier between the living and the dead.

And then, like a deer fleeing a hunter's arrow, she turned on her heel and sprinted back down the trail, her legs pumping with a desperate, frenzied energy.

Millie and I flew after her, our ghostly forms matching her pace as we urged her onward, our voices rising in a chorus of eerie warning.

"RUN!" we screamed, our words echoing through the night like a ghostly siren. "RUN FOR YOUR LIFE!"

But the runner never looked back, her survival instincts propelling her forward, away from the danger that had lurked so close.

As the woman disappeared into the night, her form swallowed up by the darkness, Millie and I exchanged a look of pure relief. We had done it. We had saved an innocent life, had stopped a monster in her tracks.

"We did it," I whispered, my voice trembling as the reality of what we had just accomplished sank in. "We saved that woman's life, Millie. We stopped Victoria from claiming another victim."

Millie nodded, her eyes glistening with unshed tears. "I know. But it was so close, Mabel. If we hadn't been there, if we hadn't acted when we did..."

She trailed off, unable to finish the thought. I reached out, my hand finding hers and giving it a reassuring squeeze. "But we were there, and we did act. We made a difference tonight, Millie. We proved that we're not just a couple of meddling ghosts. We're a force for good, a team to be reckoned with. The Spectral Sleuths are on the case, and we're not backing down. Not now, not ever."

Even though I knew fear coursed through my oldest friend, she straightened a little taller. "We've got this."

When we were certain the runner had covered enough distance to escape the death that had awaited her just a few yards up the path, we hurried back to Victoria. She stood in the center of the path, her eyes blazing with anger as she clutched the unbloodied wire in her hand, her fury at being thwarted palpable in the air.

We had stopped Victoria tonight, but there was no doubt she was already planning to strike again, her bloodlust unquenched, her twisted desires derailed.

We had to get to Sarah, had to find a way to secure the warrant that would bring this nightmare to an end. With a burst of ghostly energy, we transported ourselves back to Sarah's car, our forms materializing in the back seat with a flash of blinding light.

"Sarah!" I cried, my voice high and urgent.

She jerked the wheel then quickly corrected. "Oh, my God. You scared me!"

"Victoria, she tried to kill again. We stopped her, but she's not going to give up. We need that warrant, now."

Sarah's face paled, her hands gripping the steering wheel with white-knuckled intensity as she pulled into her parking spot at the FBI office. "I'm trying to think of how to get a warrant," she said, her voice tight with frustration. "But without hard evidence, without something concrete to tie her to the murders, my hands are tied."

Millie let out a groan of despair as she slumped against the seat. "So, what do we do? We can't just let her keep killing while we stand behind the red tape."

For a moment, Sarah was silent, her brow furrowed in deep thought. And then, like a spark of inspiration igniting in her eyes, she sat up straighter, her jaw set with determination.

"We go to my boss," she said, her voice ringing with conviction. "I lay out every shred of evidence we have, every gut instinct screaming that Victoria is our killer, and I beg for him to trust my instincts. And we pray that he listens, that he gives us the green light to take her down."

I felt a flicker of hope spark in my chest, a glimmer of light amidst the darkness. It was a long shot, a desperate gamble in a game where the stakes couldn't be higher.

But as I looked at Sarah, her face stone cold and solemn, I knew that we had no other choice. We had to try, had to do whatever it took to stop Victoria before she claimed another victim.

Chapter Twenty-Two

MILLIE

Sarah marched with purpose down the hallway of the FBI building as Mabel and I floated alongside her. The fluorescent lights flickered overhead, casting an eerie glow on the linoleum floor as we made our way toward her boss's office.

"Do you think he'll go for it?" I asked nervously. "The warrant, I mean?"

Sarah shook her head, her eyes fixed straight ahead. "Honestly? Probably not. But we have to try. The only other thing I can think of is an anonymous tip, but they're going to track that if this case goes to trial. If I take even one misstep, every single thing we find going forward will be thrown out. Meaning even if I see Victoria there standing at the sculpture holding the murder weapon, she'll walk free."

"Yikes," Mabel said. "Okay. I can see now why you're so hellbent on getting actual evidence instead of just barging in there guns blazing."

I felt a flicker of unease at the thought of our evidence being scrutinized in court, but I pushed it aside. We had come too far to let legal technicalities stand in the way of justice.

As we approached the door to her boss's office, Sarah took a deep breath, squaring her shoulders before knocking twice.

"Come in," his gruff voice called from inside.

Sarah pushed open the door, stepping into the office with Mabel and me close behind. Her boss looked up from the stack of paperwork on his desk.

"Agent Sadler," he said, leaning back in his chair. "It's late. What brings you here at this hour?"

Sarah gave him a tight smile. "I practically live here too, sir. Part of the job."

He chuckled, but there was no humor in the sound. "Fair enough. What can I do for you?"

Sarah launched into her pitch, laying out all the evidence we had gathered against Victoria. She spoke of the clay in the wound, the murder weapon pointing to a sculptor, the victims' profiles, the mysterious red-headed woman seen near the crime scenes. But as she talked, I could see her boss's frown deepening, his eyes growing more and more skeptical.

When she finished, he leaned forward, his elbows resting on the desk. "Agent Sadler, I appreciate your dedication to this case. But what you're asking for... a warrant to search the property of a private citizen... it's a serious matter."

Sarah nodded, her face tight with frustration. "I understand that, sir. But Victoria Milton is our prime suspect. Everything points to her being the killer."

Her boss sighed, rubbing a hand over his face. "Everything except hard evidence. You have no proof that she's involved, just a lot of circumstantial theories and gut feelings." He paused, his expression softening slightly. "Look,

Sarah. Your instincts are solid. Always have been. I believe you're onto something. But my hands are tied without concrete evidence. A judge won't sign off on a warrant based on what we have."

Sarah opened her mouth to argue, but he held up a hand gently. "I'm not saying no forever. I'm saying bring me something more. One piece of solid evidence that ties her to that warehouse, and I'll go to bat for you with the judge myself. You know I will."

Sarah's shoulders slumped slightly, but she nodded. "Yes, sir. I understand."

"I'm proud of how you're handling this case," he said quietly, his eyes sincere. "Your father would be too. Even when the path forward isn't clear, you keep pushing. That's what makes a great agent. Now go find me that evidence."

Sarah sat up taller, his praise and the words about her father's pride seeming to ignite that fire inside her that his denial had diminished.

"I'll get you that evidence, sir. She's our killer. I know it."

He gave her a slight nod and brief smile, barely there, that said "I believe you. Now prove it."

As we left the office, Mabel immediately started pacing alongside Sarah. "Okay, okay, we can fix this! We need evidence. Evidence, evidence, evidence." She rubbed her chin then stuck up a finger, her eyes flashing wide with excitement. "I've got it—I'll flash to a payphone and call in an anonymous tip! You can go into your boss's office for something else, we'll call while you're in there so he hears you getting the tip and Bob's your uncle! Evidence!"

Sarah pressed her cell phone to her ear, pretending to take a call so she could talk to us. "That won't work. How would an anonymous tipster have my personal cell number?"

"Oh." Mabel deflated. "Right. Okay, what about—"

"We could call the tip line!" I suggested excitedly.

"You're ghosts. They can't hear you," Sarah muttered. "Only I can."

"Damn it," Mabel grumbled. "Okay, new plan. What if we... uh..." She looked at me desperately. "Okay, here me out! I'll possess someone and make them call it in!" she said, snapping her fingers.

I sighed, shaking my head. "You have tried several times to possess people and failed. Miserably. What makes you think it will work this time?"

She twisted her lips, thinking. "Um, maybe, I don't know, because it's like important this time? Maybe I'll succeed?"

At that moment, an agent walked by. Mabel squatted down, face tightening in concentration.

"What are you doing?" Sarah asked into her phone.

"Hee-ya!" Mabel launched forward toward the agent, but once again, instead of possessing him, she flew right through him and disappeared through the wall. A moment later, she popped back out, defeat plastered on her face.

"Right, right. Man, being dead has some serious limitations." Mabel crossed her arms, frustrated. "There's got to be something—"

Sarah suddenly froze mid-step, her eyes widening. "Wait a minute. Does Victoria even own that warehouse?"

Mabel and I exchanged a glance. "I... I don't know," I said, my voice trembling with anticipation. "But if she doesn't?"

"Then we may not need a warrant at all," Sarah finished, a slow grin spreading across her face. She spun on her heel, heading back toward her desk with renewed purpose. "Come on, let's go check the property records."

"Oh!" Mabel pumped her fist in the air. "This is exciting! And way easier than possessing people. That's freaking impossible."

We raced to Sarah's computer, hovering over her shoulder as she typed furiously on the keyboard. And there, in black and white on the screen, was the answer we had been hoping for.

"The warehouse is owned by the city," Sarah breathed, her eyes shining with triumph. "It was seized for unpaid taxes and then condemned. Which means..."

"Which means you can get permission to enter it without a warrant?" Mabel finished, her voice practically vibrating with excitement.

Sarah grinned widely. "Exactly. But damn. It's the weekend and it's late. I hope someone can grant us access. Wait. There should be an on-call facilities manager for emergencies."

"This is definitely an emergency!" I nearly bounced out of my skin. "Call them!"

Sarah was already reaching for her phone, her fingers flying over the screen as she dialed the number for the city's property management office.

"This is Special Agent Sadler with the FBI. I need immediate access to a condemned warehouse owned by the city. It's critical for an ongoing investigation. Can you connect me with the on-call facilities manager?"

She went on hold for a few minutes, and then her eyes lit up as she introduced herself again and rattled off the address of the building. We waited with bated breath as she explained the situation, her voice calm and professional despite the urgency thrumming through her veins.

"Thank you. Thank you so much, sir. I'll reach out if I have any trouble getting in."

She hung up the phone and her smile stretched wide across her face. "We did it. We have official permission to enter, and now there's no risk that anything I find could get thrown out."

"Yes!" Mabel whooped, leaping up in the air.

I clapped my hands, squealing with the news. "You're so smart! This is exactly what we needed."

"Let me just text my boss to put aside his hunt for the warrant and then let's go."

Sarah fired off a text, then we wasted no time, piling into Sarah's car and racing through the streets toward the abandoned warehouse on the outskirts of the city. As we drew closer, a sense of foreboding washed over me, a cold, creeping dread that settled deep in my spectral bones. I remembered what was in there, and I had to fight the urge to run away, never wanting to come face to face with such horror again.

But Mabel needed me. Sarah needed me. The souls of those women who'd lost their lives to Victoria needed me. I stilled my anxiety with a deep breath and calmed myself down as we pulled up outside the warehouse, its rusted metal walls looming like the jaws of some great, hungry beast. Victoria's truck was nowhere to be seen, but that didn't mean she wasn't inside, planning on how to get her next victim.

"Millie and I will go in first," Mabel said, her voice strong and protective. "Make sure the coast is clear. She can't hurt us, but she can hurt you."

Sarah nodded, her face tight with tension as she watched us phase through the car and then the warehouse walls. Inside, the air was thick with the stench of death and decay, the shadows seeming to writhe and twist with a malevolent energy.

We searched the building on high alert for any sign of Victoria. But the warehouse was empty, save for the sculpture that twisted my stomach into knots.

We phased back through the wall and then into Sarah's car. "It's clear," I said, then paused and a gulp slid down my throat. "But Sarah... the things you're going to see in there..."

Sarah's jaw clenched, her eyes hardening. "Show me."

Together, the three of us entered the warehouse, the beam of Sarah's flashlight cutting through the darkness like a knife. We made our way down the path Mabel and I remembered well, and there, in the center of the room, stood the grotesque sculpture.

I could hear Sarah's breath catch in her throat, her steps faltering as she took in the full horror of Victoria's creation.

"This is… why? Why would she do this? It's horrible," Sarah breathed.

"It takes a truly sick mind to think this is art. Clearly Victoria is a seriously messed up psycho," Mabel said as we all stood shoulder to shoulder.

"I didn't even know such darkness existed in the world," I said, struggling to breathe as I diverted my eyes. "Is this enough evidence now that you've seen it?"

But before she could answer, a blue light flashed against the darkness.

I glanced at Mabel's wrist. The Crossing Guard beacon, its light flashing with urgent insistence.

Mabel and I exchanged a glance, our faces tight with guilt and regret. We couldn't leave Sarah, not now, not with a killer still on the loose. But the beacon's call was like a siren song, a pull that we couldn't ignore.

"Sarah," I said, my voice trembling with apology. "Mabel and I... we have to go. Just for a moment. There's a soul that needs our help."

Sarah tore her gaze away from the sculpture, her eyes wide with shock and confusion. "Right now?"

Mabel nodded with an apologetic look. "We'll be quick," she promised, her voice low and urgent. "We won't let you face this alone."

Sarah shook her head quickly, stiffening her shoulders as she gave us a look that said she understood. "I'll be fine. Go."

We gave her a thankful smile, then with that, we were gone, the warehouse fading away as the beacon's light engulfed us in its ethereal glow. We found ourselves in a hospital room, the steady beep of a heart monitor filling the air as the body of an old man lay in the bed, his face pale and drawn.

His soul stood above his corpse, confusion etched on his face.

"Hello," I said, moving to his side. "We're Mabel and Millie and we're here to help you cross over."

"Please," he whispered, his voice thin and reedy. "I'm scared. I don't know what comes next."

Mabel and I exchanged a glance, our hearts heavy with the weight of our duty. We knew we had to help this soul cross over, to guide him to the peace and rest that awaited on the other side. But even as we spoke the words of comfort and reassurance, even as we told him of the wonders awaiting him, our thoughts were with Sarah, alone in that warehouse of horrors.

But instead of taking our hands and crossing into his afterlife, he continued with a barrage of questions about Heaven that we continued answering.

“We have to get back,” Mabel whispered out of the corner of her mouth, her voice tight with urgency. “Sarah needs us.”

“I know,” I whispered back, but the old man’s spirit remained, his questions and fears pouring out in an endless stream of words.

He asked another round of questions. “Tell me what it’s like in Heaven. Will I see my wife again? What about my parents? Oh! My dog! Will my dog be there? He died when I was twenty, so many, many years ago. Has he just been waiting up there for me all this time? And what about golf? I used to love to golf when I was younger. Will there be golf? Will I be fit enough to golf again?”

I could feel my patience wearing thin, the urgency of our mission pressing down on me like a physical weight. And then, much to my surprise and very unlike my caring nature, I felt something snap inside me.

“For the love of Pete,” I growled, my voice low and fierce. “Just cross over already. Your dog. Your parents. Your friends. Golf. All there. It’s great and grand and perfect and you’re wasting your time here when you could be there. There’s cake waiting for you on the other side, all the damn cake you could ever want. But right now, we have a friend who needs our help down here, and we can’t waste another second standing here answering your incessant questions which will be answered by the angels awaiting you up there! So go. Go to the other side. Please.”

I held out my hands, feeling a bit guilty for cutting his transition short, but deep down I knew what waited for him was much better than the scene of this dark hospital room standing beside a body that had passed its prime years ago.

The old man’s eyes widened with shock and then, understanding. With a final nod of acceptance, he took our hands and faded away, his essence dissolving up into the warm, welcoming light of the afterlife.

Mabel and I wasted no time, our ghostly forms blinking back to the warehouse in a flash of spectral energy. But as we materialized in the shadowy depths of the room where we'd left Sarah, our hearts seized with a terror unlike anything we had ever known.

There, in the center of the room, stood Victoria, her eyes wild with madness and fury. And in her hand was the cold, hard grip of a gun pointed at Sarah.

Sarah's eyes met ours, wide with fear and desperation. But even in the face of certain death, even with a killer's gun aimed at her head, she managed to give us a small, almost imperceptible nod.

A nod that said *I trust you. You'll get me out of this. We're in this together.*

And in that moment, I felt a surge of love and fierce, unshakable determination washing over me. Victoria might have the upper hand now, might think she had Sarah cornered and outmatched.

But she had no idea who she was dealing with.

No idea of the power, the unbreakable bond, that tied us together.

No idea that the Spectral Sleuths were standing behind her and prepared to do anything in their power to save their friend.

Chapter Twenty-Three

MABEL

Time slowed as we stared at the scene with Victoria's gun pointed at Sarah. Her eyes met ours, wide with fear and desperation, but in that split second, I also saw that familiar stubborn fire, a silent plea for us to trust her.

"FBI! Drop the weapon!" Sarah shouted, her voice steady despite the terror that must have been coursing through her veins. Her hand hovered over the gun in her holster.

Victoria's eyes narrowed, a cruel smile twisting her lips. "I don't think so. You're in no position to give orders, Agent. Drop that weapon. Do it slowly."

I glanced at Sarah, noticing the pale sheen of sweat on her forehead and the slight tremor in her hands. Realization dawned on me—Sarah was experiencing one of her headaches, the lingering effects of her concussion. That must have been how Victoria managed to get the drop on her.

I cursed myself for not pushing her harder to go to the

doctor, and instead let her walk right into this deadly situation.

"Victoria Milton," Sarah said, her voice strained but determined. "You're under arrest for the murders of Laura Becker and at least four other women."

Victoria laughed, a harsh, grating sound that sent shivers down my spine. "Under arrest? I don't think so. Now unholster your gun and drop it on the floor." Sarah remained unmoving, and Victoria shouted, "Drop it!" in a tone so sharp and powerful, all three of us jumped.

Sarah took a deep breath, her gaze never wavering from Victoria's face as she slowly pulled her gun out of the holster, gently setting it on the ground next to her feet. "It's over, Victoria. We have all the evidence we need to put you away for life. The sculpture, the victims' DNA, your twisted little trophy collection... it's all here. Just put down the gun and we can stop this madness now. Get you some help."

Victoria's eyes blazed with a fevered intensity as she spoke, her voice trembling with a mix of rage and desperation. "Help? I don't need *help.* You don't understand," she spat, her gaze darting between Sarah and the sculpture. "No one ever understood my art, my vision. Behind my back, they all mocked me, dismissed me, said I was no good."

She began to pace, her movements erratic and jerky, like a puppet on tangled strings. "I poured my heart and soul into my sculptures, spent years honing my craft, perfecting every line and curve. But did anyone ever appreciate my work? Did anyone ever see the beauty, the truth, the raw emotion that I poured into every piece? No."

Her voice rose, taking on a shrill, almost hysterical edge. "Then she called me a hack, a failure, a washed-up has-been. She said my work was lifeless, soulless, devoid of meaning or purpose. But she was wrong. They were all wrong."

"Who called you a hack? Laura Becker?" Sarah asked, her voice eerily calm despite the tenuous situation.

Victoria whirled around, her eyes locking onto Sarah's with a terrifying intensity. "Laura Becker," she spat the name. "The darling of the art world, the rising star that everyone fawned over. She was everything I wasn't—young, beautiful, celebrated. I overheard her at an art show, and do you know what she said when she was with her friends staring at *my* sculpture? She had the audacity to call my work garbage, to say that my sculptures looked nothing like reality."

"So, you killed her?" Sarah asked, keeping her talking.

Victoria's face contorted with rage, her fingers tightening around the gun until her knuckles turned white. "Flat. Lifeless. Boring. That's what she called my art. She didn't know I was even there standing in the group as she mocked my work in front of everyone at that gallery."

Her voice dropped to a whisper, her eyes distant and unfocused. "I followed her back to her studio that night to confront her. To tell her how badly her words had hurt me. I watched her through the window as she worked on her latest piece. And as I stood there, watching her, seeing the way she moved, the way she breathed life into her art... I realized that she was right. My sculptures were lifeless. They were empty, hollow shells of clay and metal and stone."

My stomach twisted as I thought about Laura working on her sculpture, completely unaware a killer watched her through her window. My skin prickled as a shiver moved down my spine.

"I knocked on her door, but instead of confronting her about how horribly she'd made me feel, I asked her for…

help. To teach me what she had that made her so special and me so… not."

Victoria's voice softened, and her arm started to lower, the gun's trajectory no longer leveled with Sarah's head. I saw Sarah's gaze flick to the gun. But before she could make her move, Victoria's arm snapped up as the gun trained back on Sarah while a twisted smile spread across her face.

"But when we looked at her sculptures and I pushed her to tell me her technique so I could try to capture the same realism in my own, do you know what she said?"

Sarah didn't answer, instead remaining motionless in the face of true insanity.

With a soft laugh, Victoria said, "She told me I didn't have the natural talent she did. That she couldn't teach me how to be an artist because it's either something you have or something you don't. And I… didn't have it."

A sadness flooded her eyes as she recollected the moment, and there was the tiniest part of me that felt sad for her. An entire life dedicated to her art only to realize she could never be as good as someone like Laura.

"I begged her to teach me, but then she asked me to leave. I begged her harder to just tell me how she did it. How did she accomplish at so young what I'd been trying to accomplish my whole life? She wouldn't tell me. She just kept saying I didn't have it and that I should leave. And when I begged one more time, she called me a washed-up hack and to get the hell out. She pushed me to the door. And then it just… happened. It wasn't a conscious decision. It wasn't a choice I made. Suddenly her metal sculpture was in my hand, and blind rage exploded through my arm as I slammed it into the side of her head."

I gulped, closing my eyes against the brutal image.

Victoria's closed eyes snapped back open and locked on

Sarah's, a manic gleam dancing in their depths. "And then I hit her again. And again. And again. Over and over, my body no longer my own to control as my rage and anger seemed to take over every inch of me. And then it happened. As I stood there, covered in her blood, I saw the truth. I saw the beauty in death, the purity of the human form stripped bare of all pretense and artifice. And in that moment, I realized that she was the key to unlocking my true potential. She was the muse I had been searching for all along."

She gestured wildly to the grotesque sculpture behind her, her voice rising to a fevered pitch. "Don't you see? This is my masterpiece, my magnum opus. This is the culmination of everything I have ever worked for, everything I have ever dreamed of. This is my tribute to Laura, my love letter to the woman who showed me the way, who unlocked the true depths of my artistic soul. A masterpiece that no one else will ever be able to trump. She didn't think my sculptures were realistic enough?" She waved a hand at her monstrosity. "Tell me *this* isn't realistic? Tell me *this* isn't beautiful. Tell me *this* isn't a masterpiece that will finally make everyone remember my name while they forget hers. This time, *I'll* be the one getting all the recognition."

Sarah's face was a mask of horror and disgust, her eyes wide with shock. "You're sick, Victoria. You need help."

Victoria shook her head, a twisted smile spreading across her face. "No, Agent. I don't need help. I need to create. And that's exactly what I've been doing, with each and every one of my victims. Creating the most realistic, beautiful sculpture all an ode to my muse, Laura." She waved a hand toward the sculpture behind her, the grotesque patchwork of human body parts and clay. "Isn't it stunning? The perfect recreation of the woman who started it all, the one who made me realize my true potential. With just one more finishing touch, my masterpiece will be complete. And once I have it cast in bronze, it will stand forever—the most realistic statue anyone has ever seen. They'll marvel at my genius, and finally, they will know the greatest talent of all has been standing in front of them, unseen, all along."

"You killed all those women, Victoria. For this. They were innocent victims."

"Victims? They weren't victims. I immortalized them," she said as if it made the most sense in the world. "You see, Agent, true art is about capturing the essence of life itself. When I killed Laura Becker, I saw beauty in death that I had never seen before. But one body, one life, it wasn't enough. It couldn't capture the complexity, the diversity of human experience."

Victoria paced closer to us, completely unaware of our presence. I glanced at the gun by Sarah's feet, wondering if we could lift it to her the moment Victoria turned away again. But was that too risky? Would that decision get Sarah shot if we didn't move fast enough? My nerves jangled like live wires, sending jolts of panic through every fiber of my being.

Victoria continued her deluded explanation for her horrifying crimes. "Each woman I chose represented a different aspect of Laura, a different facet of her beauty and vitality. I needed each piece from a different woman because each one lived differently, moved differently, experienced the world uniquely. By combining these parts, I'm not just recreating Laura—I'm creating the ultimate tribute to female beauty and strength. A patchwork of perfection, each piece lived in and loved and ultimately sacrificed for a greater purpose."

"You slaughtered innocent women. That's what I see." Anxiety clamped around my chest, afraid Sarah might say the wrong thing and set off the unhinged woman aiming a gun at her. But instead of getting angry, Victoria just chuckled. "You're not an artist. Of course you wouldn't understand. The art world… they'll see my vision. One woman alone couldn't embody all these qualities. But together? Together they form something transcendent. Something divine. Don't you see? This isn't just art. It's apotheosis. I'm not just a sculptor—I'm a god, creating life from death, beauty from tragedy."

"You killed innocent women, cut off their body parts, posed them like disturbing sculptures, and tried to create a human sculpture with their pieces. You're not a God. You're a monster."

Anger flashed in Victoria's eyes for a moment before it receded, and she smiled. "I'm not a monster, Agent. You can't see it now, but you will. I created art even in the remains of the sacrifices to my masterpiece. I didn't just discard them like common trash. These women, they gave so much to my vision. They deserved to be honored, to be transformed into art themselves. Even the way I sculpted their corpses with such care, such attention, is a celebration of the part they contributed to my masterpiece. These poses, they're not just art—they're epitaphs. Living sculptures that tell the story of each woman's sacrifice. They force the world to see these women as I saw them: as vessels of beauty, as components of a greater vision. And now, all I need is the perfect face to complete my masterpiece. A face that can bear the weight of all this beauty, all this sacrifice." She tipped her head, looking at Sarah with an unnerving stare. "A face like yours, Agent. You could be the crowning glory of my greatest work. Don't you want to be part of something eternal?"

She stepped a little closer, and though I knew Sarah was preparing for a fight, I could see the waver in her stance, her balance still off from her episode. She blinked fast as if trying to reset her brain to stop the vertigo that came on so suddenly.

"You have beautiful bone structure. Lovely lips. Hypnotic blue eyes. Gorgeous dark hair. I don't know how I didn't see it before. You're quite stunning, Agent."

Sarah shot us a look, and my eyes widened as I realized where Victoria's deranged mind was wandering.

"Millie, we have to do something. She's spinning out. She's going to kill Sarah."

Millie remained frozen next to me, and I knew her well enough to know that the fear coursing through her was enough to paralyze every muscle in her body. I'd seen it happen before, and I couldn't have her freeze up on me now.

"Millie!" I shouted, and she jumped. "Don't panic. We've got this, but we are going to have to save Sarah together. Take a deep breath. With me."

Millie looked at me, eyes wide with terror, and together we took a deep breath in, and then out, and then in, and then out.

As Millie and I worked on getting her anxiety under control so we could fight this villain, Victoria continued trying to rationalize her murder spree with her warped sense of reality.

Victoria's red-glossed lips curved into a smile. "I was sad to have damaged Laura's head in the attack—it would have made the perfect addition to my sculpture. I've searched for the right final piece, and though I thought I lost it tonight, I see now that was for the best. The perfect ending to my creation… might be you."A surge of panic twisted my stomach with desperation. We had to do something, had to find a way to stop Victoria before it was too late.

I turned to Millie, my eyes wide with urgency. "We have to help her," I whispered, my voice trembling with fear. "Sarah's in no condition to fight, not with her headache and vertigo. We can't let Victoria hurt her. We can't wait anymore. She's going to make her move."

Millie nodded, and I saw her quiet strength starting to slip into place like sliding a cloak of confidence over her terrified body. "Okay. Together," she said, her voice low and fierce. "We'll use every ounce of power we have, every trick in our arsenal."

With a rush of adrenaline, I prepared myself for most important task I'd ever faced.

Save Sarah's life.

"Millie, we need to use our telekinesis to create a massive distraction. I mean a huge one."

"But we've never done more than move a few things."

I looked at her and though I wasn't sure where it came from, I knew deep down our powers wouldn't fail us. "We've got this."

She took a breath then gave one sharp nod.

Steadying my nerves, I clenched my jaw tight. "Sarah, get ready to run for cover when things start flying. We've got you."

She gave me a quick glance and a slight nod, then Millie and I gripped hands tight. This wasn't like moving a paper-clip or unlocking a door—this was everything at once. I could feel Millie's energy flowing into mine, our combined essence burning like a furnace as we prepared for the most difficult thing we'd ever attempted.

"Together," I whispered, and we both closed our eyes, pouring every ounce of our spectral power into the room around us.

I felt our energy stretching, reaching out like invisible arms toward every object scattered throughout the studio. The tools, the sculptures, the broken bits of clay and metal —I could sense each one, heavy and resistant. My ghostly form flickered as I strained to make contact with so many items at once. My essence wrapped around each one, and I could feel the shape the weight of them all as I prepared to move them at once.

"It's working," Millie whispered. "Stay strong, Mabel."

I shook with effort as I started to slowly lift them. "I can't hold them all," I gasped, feeling our combined power wavering.

"Yes, you can," Millie squeezed my hand tighter. "We can. For Sarah."

I looked at the killer staring at our friend with violence in her gaze. I saw Sarah start to falter, her façade as the tough, unbreakable FBI agent shattering as she struggled to stay upright.

We've got you, Sarah.

With a surge of determination, I felt our energy explode outward like a dam bursting. Every object in the room shuddered, then lifted into the air simultaneously. The effort was overwhelming—like trying to juggle a dozen bowling balls while running a marathon.

Then, with a burst of spectral energy that left us both trembling, I sent them flying, hurling the entire arsenal at Victoria with all the force of a ghostly hurricane.

Victoria screamed, her arms raised to shield her face as the objects pelted her from every angle.

"The sculpture! Tip the sculpture! She won't let it fall! It will distract her!" I shouted, remembering our incident accidentally tipping a sculpture in the museum. Together, Millie and I spun all our energy toward the horrifying creation. With a burst of willpower, we pushed it. It started teetering back and forth.

"No! It's falling!" Victoria screamed, racing through the flying objects to steady her beloved sculpture.

Sarah took advantage of the distraction, grabbing her gun from the floor as she dodged the barrage of flying objects, rolling to safety under a table. With a quick flip, she popped it onto its side and ducked behind it.

With her sculpture steadied, Victoria dropped to the floor beside it, covering her head. "What the hell is going on?"

"Get her, Millie! Get her!" I shouted, another rush of power surging through us for a moment as a whirlwind of objects swirled around Victoria huddled in a ball. But then, our power started to deplete, the items began dropping to the floor with thuds, echoing off the empty walls.

Victoria peered up, then crawled up to her feet. "How did you do that?" she hissed, her eyes scanning the room for Sarah. "What the hell was that? Where are you?" She shouted the last words, spinning around the room, her gun pointing everywhere she turned.

"Don't answer her, Sarah," I said. "She doesn't know where you are. Just stay down while we handle this. You're in no condition to fight. Just trust us."

Knowing trusting anyone but herself was nearly impossible for Sarah, I hoped that she would heed my words as I looked at Millie. "We need to get Victoria's gun."

Millie nodded. "Okay. If we do it together, I think we can knock it out of her hands."

"Sarah, when you hear us shout, that means we've

disarmed her and you can pop out and get her. Just stay down until we give the signal!"

Sarah remained quiet where she hid behind the table, and I crossed my fingers she'd let us help her and not follow her past patterns of trying to accomplish everything by herself. She was having a dizzy spell and that meant she wouldn't have solid aim. She needed to trust us now more than ever.

Millie and I walked up to Victoria as she moved across the open room one slow, predatory step at a time. "Where are you, Agent?" she hissed.

"On three, Millie. We grab it and we throw it as far from her as we can."

Millie nodded. "Okay. One, two… three!"

Together we wrapped our spectral hands around the gun, eyes squinting with determination as we grabbed it. With a mighty pull, we ripped it from Victoria's hand and sent it sailing across the room.

As it clanked against the stone floor, I shouted, "Now, Sarah!"

Sarah popped up, gun trained on Victoria as she shouted, "On the ground! Now!"

But instead of obeying the sharp command, Victoria screamed, launching herself at Sarah while Sarah let off a shot.

It grazed Victoria's shoulder but didn't stop her from landing on Sarah like a feral cat, clawing and screaming as she wrestled for her gun.

"No!" Millie screamed as the two women rolled across the floor, jockeying for position.

"Sarah's in no condition to fight!" I spit, knowing that during her spells, just standing was difficult, not to mention fighting for her life. As they rolled around, Victoria grabbed a sharp sculpting tool from the floor that we'd sent flying around during our initial attack. My heart leaped into my throat when she sliced Sarah's arm with it.

Sarah cried out and knocked it from Victoria's hand, then continued struggling against the woman fighting her for her gun with pure, unadulterated rage. They thrashed and writhed, the weapon wavering between them as they fought for control, their bodies intertwined in a desperate struggle. The gun wavered between them, the barrel dancing dangerously close to Sarah's face as Victoria fought with the strength of a woman possessed.

But Sarah was a skilled agent, her muscles honed by years of rigorous training and her mind sharpened by the heat of countless battles. Even with the lingering effects of her concussion, she refused to give in, refused to let this twisted killer claim another victim.

My mind reeled with the possibilities of how to intervene, but everything I thought of like throwing things at them or trying to help Sarah wrestle the gun away could accidentally give Victoria the edge if we slipped up for even a second. Then the one thing I knew would give Sarah the edge she needed and startle Victoria long enough for her to take control popped into my head.

I turned to Millie, my body quaking with urgency. "We have to manifest, to show ourselves to Victoria. She'll be terrified and lose her focus, giving Sarah the time she needs to overtake her."

Millie hesitated for a moment, her eyes wide with uncertainty. "We've never been able to fully materialize before."

But as we watched Sarah fighting for her life, as we felt the love and devotion that tied us together as friends and partners, I knew that we had to try. "We can do this, Millie. Together."

We stood beside the two women fighting for control of the weapon, and I caught Sarah's pleading gaze for a second before her eyes narrowed and she returned all her energy to the fight.

"Get ready, Sarah," I said as I slipped Millie's hand into mine. We focused all our energy, all our friendship, our love, our connection into the space between us. We remembered Hazel's words and pictured ourselves becoming solid, becoming real, our spectral forms taking on the weight and substance of the living.

And then, with a blinding flash of light and a rush of spectral energy, we felt our ghostly bodies solidify, our incorporeal forms becoming tangible and real.

As Victoria straddled Sarah, the barrel of the gun slowing inching toward Sarah's face, Victoria's eyes widened, her face twisting with shock and horror as she caught sight of us floating above her.

"What the hell?" she gasped, her mouth falling open as she blinked rapidly at Millie and I, our ghostly forms shimmering with an otherworldly light, our eyes blazing with a fierce, protective love.

"Get away from her," I snarled, my voice low and threatening. "Now!" The world rumbled from the force of my ethereal growl.

Victoria stumbled backwards, her grip on the gun slipping. Sarah seized the opportunity. With a burst of adrenaline-fueled strength, Sarah wrenched her arm free from Victoria's grasp, her elbow connecting with the killer's chin in a sickening crack. Victoria's head snapped back, her grip on the gun loosening for a fraction of a second.

It was all the opening Sarah needed.

In one fluid motion, she rolled to the side, her hand closing around the grip of the gun and tearing it from

Victoria's grasp. She sprang to her feet, her stance wobbling for a moment before she steadied it, the weapon trained on the killer's chest as she towered over her, her eyes blazing with a fierce, unwavering determination.

"Don't move," Sarah growled, her voice low and dangerous. "It's over, Victoria. You've lost."

Victoria stared up at her, her face a mask of shock and disbelief. She opened her mouth as if to speak, but no words came out, only a strangled, animal-like whimper.

And then, like a puppet with its strings cut, she collapsed back onto the floor, her body going limp as the fight drained out of her. The madness that had driven her, the twisted obsession that had fueled her reign of terror, seemed to flee in the face of Sarah's unbreakable resolve.

Victoria's face crumpled, her eyes filling with tears of rage and despair. "No," she whispered, her voice broken and defeated. "No, it can't end like this. My art... my vision... It's not complete."

Sarah kept the gun trained on Victoria, her expression grim and determined. "Victoria Milton," she said, her voice ringing with authority. "You are under arrest for the murders of Laura Becker and four other women. You have the right to remain silent. Anything you say can and will be used against you in a court of law."

Victoria stared at her sculpture for a long moment, and then her teary eyes found their way back to us where we flanked Sarah, floating just beside her. "Are you… real?" she asked, ignoring Sarah's attempt to read her her rights.

"Real enough to kick your psycho ass." I crossed my arms, lifting my chin high,

Millie mirrored the motion and gave a sharp nod with her head. "And the ones who are *so* going to haunt your sick ass in prison."

As I felt our physical forms wavering and morphing back into our invisible ones, I smiled one last time at her. "This won't be the last time you'll be seeing us, sweetheart."

Victoria's eyes flashed with fear as we disappeared back into the veil separating the living from the dead. Sarah called for backup after she finished reading Victoria her rights. With Victoria's hands securely cuffed behind her, Sarah stepped far enough away from her that she couldn't hear her and turned her back to her so she couldn't see us talking, then let out a weary sigh.

"Thank you. Thank you both so much. I don't know what would have happened without you."

All three of us glanced at the horrifying statue, and no doubt we all shared the same thought of what Sarah's fate would have been if we hadn't intervened.

"We've got your back, Sarah. I'm just so glad this is over. You did it. You caught her."

"*We* did it," Sarah corrected. "If it weren't for my Spectral Sleuths, we'd still be hunting down a deranged surgeon."

Millie shook her head. "Nah. You would have figured this out on your own. I know you would have."

Sarah shrugged. "Maybe. But I definitely wouldn't have had as much fun as I did with you two at my side."

My heart warmed as Millie and I squished together closer. "Aw. And to think you believed we were a hallucination and tried to get rid of us."

Sarah blew out a puff of air. "Yeah. I really thought I was losing my mind from my head injury." She pressed her fingers to her head, squinting tight. "And after tonight, I think it's time I stop trying to hide this and come clean to my team. I was in real danger tonight because of it, and I don't want anyone else to be in danger because of my selfish actions."

"I think that's a smart idea, Sarah." Millie smiled softly. "You really need to get that taken care of so you can come back to fight these killers at full strength."

The sounds of distant sirens filled the air, echoing through the empty room.

"Time's up, Victoria," Sarah said, walking back over to her. "We've got enough to put you away for life."

A tear slid down Victoria's cheek as she looked at her warped creation one last time. "I just wanted people to remember me. To celebrate my work the way I know it should have been celebrated."

"Oh, they'll remember her, alright," I snorted to Millie. "When they're doing episodes of *Why Women Kill* and she gets her turn, people will remember her for sure, but not for her art. They'll remember her because she was a psycho killer."

Millie nodded in agreement, then smirked. "A psycho killer *we* helped catch!"

We turned to each other and a *slap* echoed through the room as we high-fived.

"Could you imagine if they had the real story?" Sarah chuckled then held up her hands like she was reading a marquee. "The title would be: Two ghosts and a brain scrambled FBI agent take down serial killer."

As we started to laugh at the ridiculousness of our situation, the tension and anxiety from the days leading up to catching our killer started sloughing off us.

Victoria watched Sarah, now looking like she was talking to herself. "They're there, aren't they? You're… you're talking to them. The old ladies. I… I didn't imagine them?"

Sarah's laughter petered off and she glanced at us, realizing she'd slipped and started talking to us in front of Victoria. Instead of admitting it, she looked at Victoria with a dismissive shrug. "What old ladies?"

"I'm going to tell everyone what I saw," Victoria said, her eyes narrowing. "If you don't let me go, I swear it. I know you've got two ghosts or something working with you. It explains what happened in the park too!" Her eyes lit up with that realization then they narrowed again. "I'll scream it from the rooftops that you've got ghosts doing your dirty work. Let me go and I'll keep your secret."

Sarah chuckled. "Actually, you'll be screaming it from a jail cell not the rooftops. And you think I'm worried about you telling anyone about what you *think* you saw? Your… hallucinations?" She snorted. "A woman so cracked and warped she convinced herself that murdering innocent women and piecing their parts together like a sculpture is art. By all means. Talk away. You'll just sound even nuttier than you already are."

Victoria screamed and fought against her cuffs for a moment before slumping forward in defeat.

Sarah picked up her phone, pretending to take a call as she stepped out of hearing range of Victoria again.

"Oops. I forgot she was listening for a second there."

"That's why you made the rule we don't talk to you in front of humans. Whoops." I sucked the air through my teeth then stopped and grinned. "But now I think it's kind of funny because she can't figure out if we're real or if she's gone crazy."

"I know how she feels," Sarah chuckled.

We joined her, and I almost couldn't believe how far we'd come from that first day we'd met her.

"Well, we did it," Millie said to us, stepping in closer.

"We caught her, and we vindicated those poor women she killed and stopped her from killing another."

"And me." Sarah blew out her breath. "With my episode happening, I know she could have killed me. Without your amazing intervention, I would have been the next soul making your beacon start flashing."

My stomach twisted with the thought. "No way. You're just getting started, and you're just learning how to live. Even though we will have a blast together in Heaven someday, it should be many, *many* decades from now when you're a little old lady just like us."

She smiled. "Didn't you say that when you get to Heaven you become the age of the time you're happiest in your life? You two were happiest in your seventies, so you look seventy?"

"That's right," Millie said.

Sarah smiled wider. "Then I won't look like an old lady when I'm up there in Heaven with you. I'm going to look exactly like I look right now because this is the happiest I've ever been, and I know that even though I'll have a great life, nothing will ever be able to top the time I got to work with the Spectral Sleuths."

My throat tightened as I choked back the tears. "Oh, Sarah," I breathed, and I heard Millie sniffle.

As the sounds of shouting officers filled the warehouse and our time to talk to Sarah openly before they arrived was coming to an end, we pulled her in for a hug, our spectral powers surging so we could make contact and squeeze her tight. As the three of us stood hugging each other, I felt a sense of profound relief wash over me. We had done it. We had faced down the darkness and emerged victorious, our love and our partnership stronger than ever before.

Chapter Twenty-Four

MILLIE

The warehouse was a flurry of activity as FBI agents and local police officers swarmed the scene, their voices rising in a cacophony of shouts and commands. Victoria Milton, the twisted sculptor who had terrorized the city, was being led away in handcuffs, her face a mask of defeat and despair.

Beside me, Mabel and Sarah stood watching, their expressions a mix of relief and exhaustion. We had done it. We had faced down the killer and emerged victorious, stopping her from taking one last victim and cutting a young life too short.

But as the adrenaline of the moment began to fade, I noticed Sarah's face growing pale, her breathing shallow and uneven. She swayed on her feet, one hand reaching out to steady herself against the wall.

"Sarah?" I asked, my voice lifting with concern. "Are you okay?"

Before she could answer, a familiar voice rang out across the warehouse. "Agent Sadler!"

We turned to see Sarah's boss, Special Agent Donahue,

striding toward us. Sarah straightened up, her jaw clenching as she braced herself for the confrontation.

"Sir," she said, her voice steady despite the disorientation I knew she fought to contain. "I can explain—"

But Agent Donahue held up a hand, cutting her off mid-sentence. "Explain what, Sadler? How you single-handedly tracked down a serial killer and brought her to justice? How you risked your own life to save countless others?"

Sarah blinked, confusion and surprise flashing across her face. "I... I thought you'd be angry, sir. She got the jump on me and..."

Agent Donahue shook his head, a small smile tugging at the corners of his mouth. "Angry? Sadler, I'm proud of you. Damn proud. You trusted your instincts, followed the evidence, and never gave up, even when everyone else had their doubts. Me included."

Sarah's eyes widened, a flicker of hope and relief sparking in their depths. "Thank you, sir. That... that means a lot, coming from you."

Agent Donahue's expression softened, his gaze growing distant and thoughtful. "You know, back in the day when I had the privilege of working with your father, he was one of the best agents I ever worked with. Not just because of his skills, but because of the kind of teammate he was."

Sarah nodded, her eyes glistening with unshed tears. "He always said that the job was about more than just catching bad guys. It was about having each other's backs, no matter what."

Agent Donahue smiled, his own eyes growing misty with memory. "Exactly. And that's what made him the best damn partner and agent anyone could have asked for."

Sarah took a deep breath, her shoulders squaring with

determination. "About that, sir. There's something I need to tell you. Something I should have told you a long time ago."

Agent Donahue's brow furrowed, concern etching itself into the lines of his face. "What is it, Sadler?"

"I've been having… episodes," Sarah said, her voice quiet but steady. "Headaches, vertigo, ever since the explosion. I didn't want to say anything because I was afraid it'd give you just one more reason to sideline me, that I wouldn't be able to prove myself."

Agent Donahue's expression softened, understanding dawning in his eyes. "Sadler..."

"But I realize now," Sarah continued, her voice growing stronger with each word, "that proving myself means nothing if I'm putting my team at risk. I had an episode tonight, and it's why Victoria was able to get the jump on me. It's one thing to put myself in danger, but if I have an episode out in the field, if I can't be there for my teammates when they need me..."

She trailed off, her eyes flicking to me and Mabel. I felt a surge of pride and love, my heart swelling with the force of it.

"I need to see a neurologist," Sarah said, her voice firm and resolute. "I need to stay out of the field until they can make sure that I'm fit for duty, that I'm not a liability to my team. I won't put anyone in jeopardy by keeping this secret any longer, even if it means I give up my dream of being an agent."

He nodded, his own face shining with pride and respect. "I'm proud of you, Sadler. Damn proud of you for recognizing that, for putting the needs of others before your own."

He reached out, his hand coming to rest on Sarah's shoulder in a gesture of support and understanding. "Your father would be proud too. You're every bit the agent he was, and then some."

Sarah's eyes glistened with tears, a small, tremulous smile tugging at her lips. "Thank you, sir. That... that means everything to me."

"All you need to focus on right now is getting yourself healed because there will always be a spot waiting for you the minute you are ready to come back. And you will be. I know it. Now go get some rest while we sort through this…" He blew out a breath as he shook his head. "Damn. I'm sure glad you followed your instincts and stopped her. This is just…" He slid a hand down the back of his neck, shaking his head as he looked at the sculpture. "Well done, Sadler. I'm proud of you."

Sarah beamed with a soft pride as he pressed a hand on her shoulder then he strode away, his attention drawn by the flurry of activity still swirling around the scene. Mabel and I floated closer to Sarah, our matching smiles growing by the second.

"You did it, Sarah," I said, my voice soft and sincere. "You faced your fears, your doubts, and you came out stronger on the other side."

"I had to," Sarah said on a sigh, the pulled out her phone so we could talk to her. "When I came out of Quantico, I was the toughest, fastest agent there was. There is no way an amateur like Victoria could have gotten the jump on me, and definitely no way that struggle would have gone on as long as it did. But I was dizzy. Disoriented. Hell, I even missed my shot and grazed her shoulder." Her face fell with shame.

"But you still kicked her ass," Mabel noted.

Sarah chuckled. "Yeah. With your help. But if you hadn't been here, or worse, if you had been living, breathing partners that were in real physical danger because I wasn't at my best, I couldn't live with myself if something happened. I already made a mistake that almost got people killed, and it's time to stop trying to prove myself at the cost of endangering others. I'm an FBI agent. A member of a team. And its high time I started acting like one, even if that meant admitting my issues to Donahue and possibly getting myself kicked out of the agency if we can't get these under control."

"You will," I said with certainty. "You're going to go to the doctor, get some help and come back stronger than ever. And when you come back, you're going to learn how to work as a team with them just like you did with us."

Mabel brushed her shoulder with a sly smile. "I mean, not that they are going to be half as fun to work with as a couple of ghostly grannies."

Sarah laughed, the sound bright and joyful even amidst the chaos of the crime scene. "Well, I couldn't have done it without you two," she said, her eyes shining with gratitude and wonder. "Any of this. Found the killer. Learned how to trust partners. You showed me what true friendship looks like, what it means to have someone's back no matter what."

As if on cue, a group of Sarah's fellow agents came rushing over, their faces alight with excitement and admiration. They were led by Agent Collins, the kind-hearted blonde who had always believed in Sarah, and the handsome agent from the bar, his eyes sparkling with something more than just professional respect.

"Sadler, that was incredible!" Agent Collins gushed, her hand coming up to rest on Sarah's arm in a gesture of camaraderie. "The way you took down that killer, the way you never gave up... you're a legend!"

The other agents nodded in agreement, their voices

rising in a chorus of praise and congratulations. I caught the handsome agent's eye, his gaze lingering on Sarah with a mix of awe and affection.

"Looks like someone's got an admirer," I whispered to Mabel, my eyebrows waggling with mischief.

She giggled, her eyes sparkling with amusement. "And look at Sarah, blushing like a schoolgirl. Our little FBI agent, all grown up and catching killers and hearts."

Sarah shot us a look, her cheeks flushing an even deeper shade of pink. But there was no anger in her gaze, only a warmth and affection that made my spectral heart swell with love.

As the agents began to disperse, their attention drawn back to the task of processing the crime scene, Sarah turned to us once more, her expression growing serious and sincere.

"I meant what I said," she murmured, her voicc low and heartfelt. "I couldn't have done this without you. Without your friendship, your support, your unwavering belief in me."

I lump rose in my throat. "We'll always believe in you, Sarah. Always and forever."

Mabel nodded, her eyes glistening with unshed tears. "And we'll always be here for you, no matter what. The Spectral Sleuths, united against the forces of darkness."

Sarah smiled, her eyes shining with a new kind of warmth and understanding. "You know, all my life, I've been a lone wolf. I thought I had to do everything on my own, that relying on others was a sign of weakness. But working with you two, seeing the way you always have each other's backs, no matter what... it's shown me how wrong I was."

She glanced over at her colleagues, a group of agents

laughing and chatting animatedly, their faces alight with the thrill of victory. "I used to think that being part of a team would hold me back, that it would slow me down or get in the way of my goals. But now I see that it's the opposite. Having people you can trust, people who believe in you and support you... it makes you stronger. It makes you better."

I nodded and glanced at Mabel who shared my smile. "And you've got a whole team of people like that now, Sarah. People who have seen what you can do, who know how brilliant and brave and incredible you are."

Sarah's gaze drifted back to the group of agents, a soft smile playing at the corners of her mouth. "You're right. And you know what? I'm actually excited to work with them, to be part of something bigger than just myself. I can't wait to see what we can accomplish together, as a unit, as a family."

Mabel grinned, her face lighting up with a knowing look. "And who knows? Maybe you'll even find a little romance along the way, with a certain handsome agent who can't seem to keep his eyes off you?"

Sarah laughed, her cheeks flushing a delicate pink. "Oh, stop it. I'm not... I mean, I don't even know if he..."

I chuckled, propping a hand on my hip. "Trust us, Sarah. That man is smitten. And why wouldn't he be? You're a catch, in every sense of the word."

Sarah ducked her head, a bashful smile spreading across her face. "Thanks, you two. For everything. I don't know what I did to deserve friends like you, but I'm so grateful to have you in my life."

I felt a rush of emotion, my entire soul glowing with the force of my love and admiration for this incredible woman. "The feeling is mutual, Sarah."

As if on cue, the Crossing Guard beacon began to pulse,

its blue light flashing with urgent insistence. Mabel and I exchanged a glance, our faces tightening with regret and apology.

"Duty calls," I said, my voice thick with emotion.

"Will I… will I see you again?"

Mabel answered, "We still have a few more days before our Crossing Guard shift is up. What do you say we leave you tonight to go be with your friends, and tomorrow we'll find you and spend a little time together *not* chasing down a psycho killer."

Sarah grinned. "I'd like that."

"We've got a job to do," I said, straightening up. Then I glanced over at Sarah's group of colleagues all standing together, talking. "And you've got a group of humans you should go spend some time with. Enjoy your victory with them."

Sarah glanced over her shoulder at them then gave us a little nod. "*Our* victory."

Mabel and I smiled, and as we took each other's hands I said to Sarah, "Enjoy your night with your friends. We'll find you tomorrow."

She gave us a soft nod, then Mabel and I flashed into the vortex, ready to help the next soul on their journey to the afterlife now that we'd stopped the killer.

Chapter Twenty-Five

MABEL

The final episode of *Bridgerton* came to an end as Millie and I clapped our approval. Sarah sat beside us, chuckling at our antics.

"I can't believe this is how you wanted to spend your last morning. Watching TV."

"We couldn't go back without knowing how it ends. Heaven gets every show once the season fully releases down here, but we wanted to watch it NOW, not wait until we got back up there. Plus, it's more fun experiencing it with the living. Kinda makes us feel alive again too! Thanks for hooking us up with it."

"No problem." Sarah stood and walked to the door. "What do you say we go for a walk. Get some exercise. My doctor said it's good for me to do some slow, steady walking every day while I'm healing."

We hopped up and moved to her side. "Lead the way."

The three of us took a leisurely stroll down the street, Sarah talking into her phone so she could speak openly with us, and we recanted the highlights of our adventure. It was nice to see Sarah moving at a slower pace, not just physically, but emotionally and mentally. She was finally going to give her body the time it needed to properly heal, and I knew in my heart that she'd come back stronger than ever.

Sarah, Millie, and I sat on a bench in the park, watching the world go by as we savored our last moments together before our Crossing Guard shift came to an end.

"I can't believe it's over," Sarah murmured, her eyes glistening with unshed tears. "I feel like we just got started, and now you have to go back."

I reached out, my hand hovering just above Sarah's in a gesture of comfort and love. "We'll never be far, Sarah. You know that. And besides, with your new team by your side, you don't need us. You're going to be an unstoppable force for good."

Sarah smiled, a flicker of pride and determination shining in her eyes. "I know. But it won't be the same without you two. Promise me you'll come back and visit, if you ever get the chance?"

Millie nodded, her eyes shimmering with emotion. "Of course we will, Sarah. You're stuck with us, whether you like it or not."

We all laughed, the sound ringing out through the quiet park like a bell.

"You know," I said, my voice low and concerned, "we might not even be allowed back into Heaven after all the stunts we've pulled down here. Breaking the rules, meddling in the affairs of the living... we could be in some serious trouble."

Millie's eyes widened with panic. "Oh, no. You don't think they'd really kick us out, do you? Send us to... to hell?"

"Seriously?" Sarah's eyes widened to match Millie's. "They can do that? But… they wouldn't. Would they?"

I tried to keep a straight face but failed when I burst out laughing. "Nah, I'm just messing with you. They aren't going to send us to hell, silly. We helped a ton of souls cross over, and they probably don't even know what else we were up to while we were down here. They've got bigger fish to fry than keeping tabs on little ol' us. It's gonna be fine."

Millie let out a sigh of relief, but I could still see the worry etched into the lines of her face. Sarah, on the other hand, was grinning from ear to ear, her eyes sparkling with amusement.

"You two are something else, you know that?" she said, shaking her head. "I don't know what I did to deserve friends like you, but I'm so grateful to have had you by my side through all of this."

I felt a lump rising in my throat, swelling with the force of my emotion. "The feeling is mutual, Sarah." But beneath the laughter, I could feel a sense of unease growing in the pit of my stomach, like something was about to shift.

Just then, a familiar sensation began to pulse through my body. I glanced down at my wrist, where the Crossing Guard beacon was flashing, but this time instead of blue, it flashed with a red glow.

"Uh oh," I said, my voice tinged with trepidation. "Looks like it's time for us to head back to the great beyond."

Sarah's face fell, her eyes filling with tears that she bravely tried to blink away. "I'm going to miss you both so much," she whispered, her voice thick with emotion.

Millie and I wrapped her in a ghostly hug, our spectral forms merging with hers in a moment of pure, unfiltered friendship.

"We'll miss you too, Sarah," Millie murmured, her voice

trembling with the weight of her feelings. “But this isn’t goodbye. It’s just ‘see you later.’”

With a final, fierce squeeze, we pulled away. Millie and I clasped our hands tightly together as we prepared to make the journey back to Heaven. Sarah watched us go, her face a mask of bittersweet joy and sadness.

“Give ‘em hell up there, you two,” she called out, her voice ringing with affection and pride. “And don’t forget about us little people down here on Earth.”

I grinned, giving our new friend, our partner, one last look. “Never, Sarah. We’ll never forget you.”

And with that, Millie and I got swept into a shimmering portal that had appeared before us, our bodies fading into the warm, welcoming light then reemerging back in the center of the city street where it had all started, the glowing door beckoning us to step through.

“Wow. Can you believe how much has happened since we were here last?” I chuckled, memories of our first moments as ghosts flooding my mind.

Learning to fly, trying to haunt Howard. How we’d finally started to get the hang of things and met our cherished Sarah. Dancing at the club. Hunting a serial killer. Our trip to Earth had been far more magical than my wildest dreams.

Millie glanced around, sidestepping a car whizzing by. “So much. What an amazing afterlife adventure this has been.”

A heavy thought pushed down on me as we stood on the street looking around. “Do you realize, this could be the last time we ever set foot on Earth?”

Millie nodded. “I didn’t know when I was dying that I was dying, so I didn’t appreciate that moment back then. But now…”

Her voice trailed off as we soaked in the sights and sounds and smells of this imperfect world. I smiled as I watched all the living people buzzing around busy with their lives. Most of them had no idea how special their existence here was, even on the hard days. Even when things were going completely sideways, someday, when they were enjoying their afterlife, how they'd look back on it remember the thrill of emotions that could only be felt when you were truly alive. When things were fleeting and sometimes scary. And how completely, blissfully unaware they were of the supernatural world straddling theirs, of unassuming serial killers living in their midst, or of the tough as nails FBI agent who would work tirelessly to keep them all safe.

And us.

The Crossing Guards who would one day hold their hands and help them pass over into the next life, leaving this short existence of theirs behind them.

"I'm going to miss this." I sighed, giving everything one last glance before I looked back at the door, a sense of nervousness washing over me. "Guess it's time to go back upstairs and see what awaits us."

With a shared look of apprehension, we gripped hands and stepped through the door. As we emerged on the other side, blinking in the soft, ethereal glow of the celestial realm, we found ourselves surrounded by a group of angels, their faces unreadable.

"Oh, crap," Millie whispered, her voice trembling. "We're in trouble. This doesn't look good."

I gave her hand a reassuring squeeze, but I could feel my stomach churning with anxiety. Had we gone too far? Had our meddling in the affairs of the living gone one step too far?

But then, to our surprise, the angels' faces split into wide, beaming grins. Kafziel, the angel who had given us our Crossing Guard assignment, stepped forward, his eyes twinkling with amusement.

"Well, well, well," he said, his voice rich with barely contained laughter. "If it isn't our two favorite ghostly troublemakers. Did you have fun down there on Earth fighting crime and catching killers? When we let you go down thinking you were just planning on a little innocent haunting, we had no idea what an adventure you two would end up on."

Millie and I exchanged a bewildered glance, our mouths hanging open in shock. "You... you knew?" I stammered in my confusion. "You knew what we were planning to do, all along?"

Kafziel chuckled. "Of course we knew. We're celestial beings, remember? We see all, we know all. And honestly, we were quite entertained by your little adventures."

The other angels nodded in agreement, their faces alight with amusement and affection. I felt a rush of relief wash over me, my body sagging with the weight of it.

"But why?" Millie asked, her voice small and uncertain. "Why did you let us go, if you knew we weren't really interested in being Crossing Guards and instead we thought it would be funny to haunt people?"

Kafziel's expression softened, his eyes filled with a warm, gentle light. "Because, my dear Millie, Heaven is about living your best afterlife. And for you two, that doesn't mean endless happiness and perfection. It means a little excitement, a little mischief, and a whole lot of helping people."

He reached out, his hand coming to rest on my shoulder in a gesture of comfort and understanding.

"When you two got to Heaven, you weren't sure if you belonged here because of all the trouble you got into. But what we understood was that all of your schemes, all of your pranks, all of the trouble you two racked up over the decades, was always to help each other or someone else in need. It was never malicious. Never cruel or spiteful. You stood up for people and had a little fun doing it. So, when we discovered you wanted to go to Earth to do a little more mischief, we knew that deep down, no matter what kind of trouble you got into, you would always be there to help those in need. And that's exactly what you did, time and time again."

I felt a lump rising in my throat. "So... we're not in trouble?" I asked, my voice barely above a whisper.

Kafziel laughed, the sound ringing out through the celestial realm like a bell. "Trouble? My dear Mabel, you two are heroes! You saved countless souls, even sent back two extra ones, stopped a killer in her tracks, and brought joy and laughter to so many lives. How could we possibly punish you for that?"

A different angel stepped forward, her long blonde hair flowing behind her. "As angels, we aren't allowed to meddle in the affairs of the living. Free will is paramount, so no matter what atrocities are happening, no matter how much we wish we could step in and save people from the impending disaster, we're forced to sit by and let humans choose their paths… whether it brings harm to others or not. But you two managed to stop a killer without altering anyone's free will, and in doing so, you saved souls from leaving the earthly plane sooner than needed. In fact, we enjoyed watching you down there so much, we're hoping you want to sign up and be Crossing Guards again."

Millie's face broke into a grin, her eyes glowing with

relief and happiness. "So, does this mean we can go back? To Earth, I mean? Whenever we want?"

Kafziel nodded, his eyes sparkling with mirth. "Of course, my dear. This is Heaven, after all. And if being on Earth is what makes you happy, then that's exactly where you belong. You can sign up as Crossing Guards whenever you want."

A rush of excitement coursed through me. "Did you hear that, Millie? We can go back! We can keep solving mysteries and helping souls and causing all sorts of delightful chaos!" I paused, and looked at Kafziel with an arched eyebrow. "That is what you mean, isn't it?"

He chuckled. "The Spectral Sleuths can ride again."

"Yes!" I pumped a fist in the air, then paused, giving him a little smile and a nod. "You liked that name? We thought it was clever."

"Very clever," he laughed. "And we'll all be waiting to see what entertainment you bring us next time you two head back down."

"Well, as much fun as I had down there, I think it would be nice to spend a little bit of time back here in Heaven." I sighed. "I'm exhausted and could use a little rest in the blissful afterlife. Not to mention, I'm dying for a margarita!"

Millie's face lit up like the sun. "Oh, my! Wait. We're back. That means I can...." She held out her hand and a huge piece of yellow cake with chocolate frosting appeared in it. "Cake!"

She squealed as she took a bite, and I laughed and blinked a margarita into my welcoming grip.

"Ahhhh. I missed this," I said, savoring the sweet, saltiness I'd missed so much.

"So good," Millie mumbled with her mouth full of

sugary sweetness. "So, so good. We can go to Earth a lot, but we also need to come back a lot for cake."

The angels chuckled at us as we savored the benefits of Heaven.

"You two must be exhausted. Head on home and stay as long as you'd like. Anytime you want to go to Earth again and be Crossing Guards, just come to the office and we'll send you down."

"Thank you for trusting us," I said, realizing now how this whole adventure could have been missed if the angels hadn't had faith we'd do the right thing even with our wrong intentions.

"You're welcome. Most souls never want to leave the comforts of Heaven, but every now and again, a restless soul like yours slips in, and we'll do whatever we need to do to make sure your afterlife is everything you dreamed it would be. You've earned it."

With a grateful smile, I took Millie's cake-covered hand and we blinked ourselves back to our little stone cottage.

"Home!" Millie rushed to her gardens, happy to greet all of her plants.

I followed her out and then sat on the blue porch swing, smiling as she puttered around her garden greeting all of her favorite flowers. When she was done, she joined me on the swing, and I blinked two new margaritas into our hands.

"Cheers," I said, clinking the salt-rimmed glass against hers.

"What an adventure." She pushed her feet on the ground to start us swinging.

"And can you believe they are going to let us do it again?" I looked at her and grinned.

She matched my smile. "What do you think? Should we

rest up for a few weeks while Sarah is healing herself, and then pop back down and surprise her?"

I nodded, my eyes getting big with the excitement of seeing Sarah again. "I think the Spectral Sleuths are going to be quite the assets for Agent Sadler when she's ready to crack the next case."

Millie shimmied next to me. "I can't wait! I wonder what we'll be going after next? Another killer? Jewel thieves? Bank robbers?"

"And let's not forget, we may need to pause from our crime solving capers to do a little haunting along the way."

Millie grinned wider, kicking her feet with excitement.

I could barely stop myself from blurting out I was ready to go back right now, but then I tasted my margarita again and decided the land of the living could wait a little longer while Millie and I enjoyed the comforts of our hard-earned afterlife.

"Thanks for being my best friend for afterlife," I said to her, and she rested her head on my shoulder.

"Thanks for making my life, and my afterlife, so wonderful. You're the best friend a girl could ever ask for, Mabel."

"Right back at ya, Millie."

We clinked our glasses together, laughing. As we sat there, two best friends on the precipice of another grand adventure, I couldn't help but feel that this—this moment, this friendship, this purpose—was what eternity was truly all about.

Heaven could keep its harps and halos. Millie and me? We had each other, and we had a world below waiting for us with more adventures than we'd ever dreamed.

More by Katherine Hastings

vinci-books.com/TheWilderWidows

It's never too late to start living wildly.

Four widows, one whiskey-fueled pact, and a list of wild wishes. Sylvie, Doris, Alice, and Marge set off on globe-trotting adventures, dodging danger, cops, and expectations—proving their second act might be the boldest, funniest chapter yet.

Turn the page for a free preview…

The Wilder Widows: Chapter One

SYLVIE

"Goodbye, Susie. Thanks again for everything." I waved while she pushed the hospital bed down the walkway to the van parked out front.

"Take care of yourself, Sylvie," she called back. "I really am sorry for your loss. Bruce was a good man."

Leaning against the doorway, I crossed my arms and watched Susie and Virginia lift the bed into the back of the van. With one last wave, they climbed inside. It was surreal watching them drive away, knowing I would likely never see them again. They had been a staple in my life this past month while Bruce slipped away. Their job had been to keep him comfortable, but they'd been as much a support system for me as they had for him. Making it through the horrors of the last few weeks would have been impossible without their comforting words and their knowledge of caring for someone in their final days.

With a heavy sigh, I stepped back inside and closed the door behind me. As it clicked shut, it sealed out the sounds of the engine driving away and the birds chirping at the feeder just outside. Silence settled over the empty house, and for the first time in months, there were no sounds other than my own breathing.

In. Out.

In. Out.

I no longer heard the soft beeping of the machines and the buzzing of equipment keeping Bruce comfortable. No longer did I hear the nurses' hushed whispers while they worked to adjust his medication or the blaring television because Bruce had refused to get a hearing aid years ago when he'd needed it. No one called my name, asking me to change the channel or bring them something to drink.

Silence. Just silence.

But it didn't last long. The doorbell rang and caused me to jump. Craning my head, I peered out the bay window overlooking the entry, but the covered awning hid away the surprise visitors. Part of me welcomed guests to bring noise to my life once again, the silence still unsettling. But the other part of me was exhausted from the past few days of people smothering me with their comfort after I said goodbye to my husband. The doorbell rang again, and I suppressed my groan and went to answer it.

When I opened the door, three older women stood squished together, each gripping something in their hands. Though I recognized them from seeing them around the neighborhood, I didn't know them personally.

"Hello, Sylvie, I'm Doris," the short round one said while she tipped her head and gave me the sympathetic smile I'd grown accustomed to since Bruce passed. "This is Alice and Marge." She pointed to each woman at her side. "We all live just down the road, and we wanted to check in on you."

"Thank you. I'm hanging in there," I answered while I

looked to the other two. They all appeared a little older than me, but the similarities ended there.

Alice, the tall one with sleek modern-styled silver hair and legs up to my ears, mimicked the sympathetic smile. "You have my sympathies."

"Me too," grunted Marge, the one with a face like a pug.

"We're all widows, so we know how you're feeling. In fact, we call ourselves the Wilder Widows because, well, we all live on Wilder Lane." Doris gestured behind her to our suburban street. "Since you're a widow on Wilder Lane now, we wanted to welcome you to the group."

"Oh." I raised my brows. "I didn't realize there was a widow's group."

"We get together and do stuff since we're all bored and lonely." Marge shrugged.

"Lonely? Speak for yourself." One of Alice's meticulously groomed eyebrows rose in a challenge. "I'm not *lonely*, Marge. I've still got plenty of suitors to keep me occupied." She pursed her rose-colored lips and peered down her nose.

Marge rolled her eyes and grumbled beneath a long exhale.

"Anyway," Doris interjected, puckering her face while she scolded Alice with a look. "We just wanted to welcome you to the club." A wide grin spread across her chubby cheeks.

A widow's club? How had I never known such a thing existed? I supposed it was because until five days ago, I wasn't one of them. But now I stood in my doorway with three widows staring at me, awaiting my answer.

"I appreciate the invite. I'm not really sure what to think. I'm still trying to process what to do now that Bruce is gone, but—"

"That's why we're here. To help!" Doris grinned wider and pushed past me into my house. Trying to hide the shock in my eyes at the intrusion, I let her pass before gesturing for Alice and Marge to enter as well.

Marge hoisted the covered dish in her hands. "Where should I put this?" Her rough voice matched her unladylike exterior. Perhaps with a little make-up and a new hairstyle she could pass for a woman in one glance, but that dark grey bowl-cut and her bulging eyes had made me look twice the first time I'd seen her walking around the neighborhood. It had taken several long stares before I'd decided she was, in fact, a woman and not a short old man.

Still trying to process the invasion into my sanctuary, I pointed to the kitchen island. "You didn't have to make me anything, but you can set it there."

"I didn't make it. My mother did. It's lasagna."

Mother? Judging by the look of her, she was easily seventy years old. Either her mother was ancient, or she'd been very young when Marge was born. My own parents both passed away already, and I had only just turned sixty.

"Really, you didn't have to bring anything." In fact, I wished she hadn't. More sympathy casseroles than I'd ever be able to eat in this lifetime took up every inch of my fridge.

"I brought muffins. Fresh baked!" Doris pulled back the embroidered napkin lining her small basket. Steam rose off the muffins, and the intoxicating smell tempted the appetite hiding since Bruce's death.

"They look and smell wonderful. Thank you, Doris."

"Blueberry." She waggled her eyebrows then placed the basket beside the lasagna dish.

"I've got whiskey. You'll need it." Alice pulled a bottle

out of the colorful Vera Bradley bag dangling from her arm.

"Oh!" I appraised it and smiled. "Well, thank you."

"I told you not to bring whiskey, Alice," Doris scolded. "Sorry. She doesn't bake." The last phrase was said in a whisper as if not baking was a mortal sin best not mentioned.

Shaking my head, the first smile in days started on my lips. "No. It's fine. Really. I appreciate it, Alice."

"It's the good stuff. Laphroaig Single Malt Whiskey. Cask strength. This will take the edge right off." She set it beside the muffins and smiled, revealing perfect white teeth fit for someone of her beauty. Even at her advanced age, with her impeccable style, sparkling green eyes, and fashionable shoulder-length silky hair, she likely still turned heads of men half her age. She looked considerably younger than the other two widows standing in my living room, but from the unnatural smoothness of her skin, I suspected it was more medical enhancement than her being closer to my age. But the longer I looked at her, the more I questioned her age, now wondering if perhaps she was younger than me.

"I appreciate you all stopping to check in on me. I'm surprised we've never met, though I'll admit I've seen you around. You ladies walk around the block together some afternoons."

"It's part of our widow's club. We help each other stay in shape… or try, I suppose," Marge said, gesturing to her ample belly. "I eat a lot of lasagnas. I'm Italian, and my mom likes to cook."

"And I love to bake, so that's where this is from." Doris wiggled her large hips and giggled.

"I drink." Alice shrugged.

There wasn't an ounce of fat to jiggle on her fit figure. I wasn't overweight, and I could still turn a head or two, but standing next to that leggy creature had me thinking more walking would do me good. Or perhaps more drinking if that's what was doing it for her.

Rolling her eyes, Marge impaled her with a look. "You even drink *on* our walks, Alice. Don't think we don't know what's in those 'sports drinks' you won't let us try."

Scoffing, Alice returned her scowl. "Only because I don't want your cooties, Marge."

"I don't have cooties. If anyone has cooties, with the way you carry on with your pool boy, it's you!"

"Don't forget the gardener. And my yoga instructor." A sinister smile curved her lips and caused Marge to widen her eyes, though with the size of them in their natural state, it was surprising they could get any larger.

Doris stomped her foot. "Ladies! Behave. You're scaring poor Sylvie here."

She wasn't wrong.

"May we?" Doris asked, gesturing to my couch. Glad she waited for permission this time, I nodded and followed them to the living room.

They sat down and perused me once again with sympathetic gazes.

"I hope you don't mind us barging in, but we wanted to check on you. You're one of us now. We widows need to stick together." Doris touched my leg, giving it a light squeeze. "There will be all sorts of things you'll need to learn. How to pay bills. Figuring out life insurance. Garbage day. Changing light bulbs. It's a lot, but lucky for you, we have it all figured out. All you need to do is ask!"

She pressed her glasses up on her nose, and I realized then who she reminded me of. My grandma Mildred. The glasses were similar, but it was the hairstyle that reminded me of her most. Soft grey hair pulled into a loose bun perched on top of her head was the only way I'd ever seen my grandma wear her hair. Today, as well as the few times I'd seen Doris around the neighborhood, she'd styled her hair exactly the same way.

"How sweet of you all to think of me. But actually, I've been doing most of that stuff on my own for some time. Bruce hated the day to day stuff, so I handled the finances, and he wasn't particularly good at house projects either. I learned long ago how to take care of myself, but I appreciate the gesture."

Doris slapped her leg. "Well, what a modern woman you are! When Harold died five years ago, I was lost. He was the first husband of ours to go, and it took me months to figure things out. That's why I've made it my mission to make sure every Wilder Widow gets the support she needs straight away. We just want to help."

"Well, I don't know how to do any of that stuff, but I have people if you need them," Alice said. "Lots of people."

"Just don't sleep with them like Alice does," Marge taunted.

"Stop it!" Doris swatted a hand at them then turned back to me with her sweet smile. "You'll get used to them. I promise we are a lot of fun to have around. And we could use a new face in our group."

Glancing at their eager faces, my mind raced with a storm of conflicting thoughts. *Do I even want to join this group of strange women?* My first thought was no, but when I contemplated the lonely days stretched before me, I considered it. My life here hadn't exactly turned out like I'd planned after Bruce moved us here from the city for his big promotion. I'd left my friends and marketing career with the goal of starting my own boutique marketing firm here. Those plans had gone up in flames when his health declined shortly after the move. My aspirations got swallowed up while I took care of him, and I'd barely made a single friend since we'd arrived here. Now I had no company to run, no friends to hang out with, and my daughter, Rachel, lived across the country in L.A.

"We meet three times a week and alternate houses," Doris went on. "Though with you in the group, it will be four times a week. Our schedules are flexible since none of us work or have husbands or children at home for that matter. So, let's plan Monday at Marge's, Wednesday at my house, Friday at Alice's, and let's do Sunday after church here."

Struggling to keep my jaw from sagging at her assumption, I bit my lip while I felt the weight of three sets of eyes boring into me. Not wanting to be rude but unsure if I wanted any part of this, I nodded my head.

"Wonderful! You'll need to have treats and coffee for our meetings. Alice will bring her own booze." Doris gave her the side-eye, and Alice just shrugged.

I kept nodding to avoid hurting their feelings, but now I wished I'd shaken my head instead. Although I did miss having female friends to hang out with, spending four days a week with these women might end up being more than I prepared for.

Already planning the numerous excuses I could use to get out of our meetings, I forced a smile. "I look forward to it, ladies."

"We Wilder Widows need to stick together!" Doris grinned. Her enthusiasm labeled her the leader of this crew, and it made sense since she'd been the one to hunt down

Marge and Alice like a widow-sniffing bloodhound. I wondered if, like myself, they'd originally wanted nothing to do with it, but Doris's insistence finally wore them down. Whatever the reason they stayed together, it seemed I was one of them… at least for now. If this went the way I imagined it going, I would need to fade out of the group sooner than later.

"I really appreciate you all stopping by, and I look forward to getting to know you more. But I'm exhausted from the past few days, and I think I need to lie down for a bit."

"Of course." Alice stood quickly. "We'll get out of your hair."

"We completely understand what it's like to bury a husband." Marge rose, but at a much slower pace than agile Alice.

"Say no more." Doris touched my leg again before joining them. "I left our numbers and addresses in the basket with the muffins. Call if you need anything. Since tomorrow is Friday, we meet at Alice's house at eleven in the morning. It's the biggest house on the lane at the end of the cul-de-sac. You can't miss it. We hope you can make it."

"I look forward to it," I lied.

They started toward the door, and then Doris stopped and turned back. "Are you sure you're okay alone? I know I didn't want to be alone for even a second after Harold died, so I'm happy to stay the night if you need some company."

"Thank you for the offer, but I'll be all right."

"Are you sure? We can have a slumber party." Her eyes lit up. "Maybe the girls could stay too! A widow's welcome to our newest member!"

Marge grabbed her arm and pulled her forward. "Cripes, Doris! Leave the poor woman in peace."

Stifling my laugh, I followed behind them. "Really, I'm fine. My daughter stayed the last few nights and flew home yesterday. Last night was my first night alone, but I managed fine. It's time for me to adjust to my new normal."

"It takes a little while, but you'll get used to sleeping alone." Alice grabbed Doris's other arm and tugged her toward the door, then paused and peeked over her shoulder. "Unless you don't want to. I've got people for that as well." She waggled her eyebrows, and I finally let a little laughter escape.

"Thank you for coming by, ladies. I'll see you all tomorrow."

"Goodbye!" they echoed while they stepped outside. I closed the door behind them and stood pressing against it for a few moments before exhaling a breath and walking away. When I passed my bay window, I saw the three of them with linked arms walking away down the street. An odd assortment of women, to be sure, and I didn't know how I fit in yet. But when I turned back to my empty living room, I decided there was no harm in meeting with them a few times. I could always find a way out if it turned out they were intolerable.

Though I'd used the exhaustion excuse to get them out of the house, it wasn't a lie. Burying your husband *was* a lot to handle, both emotionally as well as the logistics of planning everything. Rachel and Bruce had never been terribly close, so she'd handled his death without a ton of emotion, and with her job in upper management, she'd jumped right in to help organize everything from flowers to choosing his casket. But now that he was gone and buried, the hospice workers cleared out, and Rachel and my old friends from the city safely back home, I suddenly had nothing to do but rest.

After letting the quiet settle over me once again, I started through the house. Memories of our life met me with each step I took. Photos on the wall of us with Rachel. That trip he and I took to Hawaii. Our wedding photo. His football memorabilia from when he had won that championship in college; the same night we'd met while he celebrated the win in that bar down on Sealy Street. Our forty years of life together were now only frozen moments of time forever encapsulated in the mementos we'd created. Dragging my fingertips across the trophy, I kept moving while I tried to clear away the fog that had settled over my life these last three years. The three years we'd spent battling his cancer.

Everything looked different now. Our home was no longer a makeshift hospital with nurses and machines scattered throughout the living room where Bruce had spent his last few months. It looked like it did before he got cancer and our lives turned upside down. The floral couch I picked out for our thirtieth anniversary was back in place after I'd stored it to make room for his hospice bed. His La-Z-Boy, the one he'd spent the better part of a decade in, sat alone in the corner where I'd condemned it because of its hideous clashing brown upholstered fabric. We'd argued over it for weeks before our armistice when I'd allowed it in the living room, but not within ten feet of my beautiful couch.

While I looked over the room now resembling a more normal space, I noticed the crooked coffee table. I walked over and tugged the edge to straighten it back out. When I stepped back to examine the room, it appeared as if everything else was back in place. Nothing was missing… except Bruce.

I walked over to Bruce's La-Z-Boy and stood over it, remembering how many times I'd stood right here holding his beer or snacks, sometimes with my hand on my hips demanding he get up and take me for a walk or out to dinner. Usually, he'd waved me aside to get out of the way of the TV, and I'd stormed off in a huff threatening to move us back to the city where I had friends and a career to entertain me. But he'd ignored my pleas, and I'd never made good on my threats. Now he was gone, but that damned ugly chair was still here.

Sliding my hand across the worn corduroy fabric of his recliner, I moved around it then lowered myself into it. Since I hated the sight of it, I'd always refused to sit in it, but while I leaned back against the overstuffed headrest, I realized now why he'd wanted it so badly. Damned if it wasn't the most comfortable chair I'd ever sat in.

While I sunk into the cushions, I closed my eyes and let the tension from the last few days, and months… and even years since his diagnosis, slip away. Like a gentle hug, the chair eased away the anxiety of being on my own. I reached down and pulled the lever, and the footrest popped up. As I reclined, a little groan escaped my lips. For years I'd promised on the day he died I'd have this hideous thing hauled away, but perhaps I'd keep it after all.

Pulling the afghan blanket over my body, I let the exhaustion take me while I drifted off. Visions of my life with Bruce flashed through my mind while the darkness came, but the last thing I saw before falling asleep were the three faces of the Wilder Widows, and I wondered what tomorrow may bring.

The Wilder Widows: Chapter Two

"And *that* is how you make a chain edge cast-on." Doris held her knitted square up like a trophy. "See? Elastic but still firm."

Alice, Marge, and I sat across from her in my living room, each holding our piles of yarn and knitting needles in our laps. I looked down at my own attempt after trying to keep up with Doris's tutorial, but it looked nothing like her example. Glancing over to Marge's work, my eyebrows shot to my hairline. Mine at least resembled the example while Marge appeared to have knit an ugly knot. She caught my expression and furrowed her already sagging brow.

"What? It's close," she grumbled, then jutted her chin at mine. "And it's not like yours is good, either."

Hers wasn't even close to Doris's perfect technique, but she was right… neither was mine. We both looked over to Alice but saw the knitting needle and yarn untouched in her lap. Her hands were otherwise occupied by the martini she'd brought over in a thermos and poured into one of my glasses.

She set aside the untouched yarn and took a drink before answering our stares. "I'll have one of the staff do it for me later."

"Alice! It's not supposed to be for your *staff* to do. It's for you to learn!" Doris shook her knitting needle at her.

"If I want something knitted, I'll just buy it."

"But then you won't learn how." Doris held up her example again. "Don't you want to learn how to do this?"

"Not even a little." Alice scoffed and poured more of the martini from the silver thermos into her dwindling glass.

With a huff, Doris sat back. "Fine. Forget it. I give up. I've tried and tried, but you just aren't interested. No more knitting lessons."

"Whatever will we do?" Marge deadpanned.

Doris scrunched up her face and shoved her project into the small yarn basket she'd brought with her. It was smaller than a purse and had a hand-knit cover over it with a lace and scalloped trim she told us she'd custom created. Making our own matching yarn baskets was next on our lists of projects, and something none of us had any use for or desire to make.

This was my second week of Wilder Widows meetings and the third time they'd been at my house. Each time we got together, we filled the several hours we met with projects and time-sucks. With Doris in charge, we knitted and baked. Each time Marge was at the helm, we watched her ancient mother make Italian food, then sat around the table and ate it. At least at Alice's house, we occupied our hours with massages and pedicures. Once again, it was my turn to entertain, but I had nothing to offer. I didn't knit or bake. There was no one to rub us into comas. Other than marketing, I had no artistic talents or special skills, and there was no sense in teaching these ladies the art of closing a marketing deal. So, with my lack of skills to show, Doris stepped up with knitting.

Again.

While we sat in bored silence staring at the ceiling, I struggled to find the words to tell them this Wilder Widows club wasn't for me. Knitting, baking, and walking around the neighborhood was not how I envisioned spending my golden years. The money I had inherited from my parents, and the money Bruce and I had saved, was more than enough to keep me comfortable for the rest of my days, but I never imagined being retired at sixty. I'd always thought I'd be a career woman until at least my seventies. But now, the thought of starting a new career didn't inspire me the way it once did, and I felt lost with what I wanted to do with all my newfound free time. But the one thing I knew is this wasn't it.

"See. If we don't knit, there's nothing to do," Doris challenged after the silence went on too long.

"There is plenty to do other than knit, Doris," Marge said.

"Like what?" I asked, genuinely interested.

Silence settled over us while everyone contemplated the answer.

"Nothing. That's what's left for us. Nothing," Alice finally said. "I've got my money, my boy toys, and still… none of it matters. I'm bored senseless."

"It's just me and my mom. She cooks, and I eat." Marge slumped forward. "I've got nothing to do either."

"I miss having children and a husband to care for," Doris answered, and a slight quiver shook her lower lip.

I wasn't even sure what I missed, but I knew this wasn't the answer to filling the void. "Is this really it for us?" I gestured to the knitting basket. "Our husbands die, and we spend the rest of our days visiting each other's houses, knitting, and struggling to find something to do?"

"What's wrong with knitting?" Doris stiffened up.

"It's boring as hell," Marge answered, mirroring my thoughts.

"Well, I happen to like it," Doris spat back.

"Good for you, Doris." Alice rolled her eyes. "So knit. But for God's sake, stop trying to force us to do it."

"Force you? I was just trying to give you something to do!"

"We'll do anything as long as it isn't knitting," Alice said, then took another sip.

"Well, fine! I guess I'll just go home and knit alone. Excuse *me* for thinking we needed to be here for each other." Doris started to stand, but I rose first and stopped her.

"I wasn't trying to offend anyone. Please don't go, Doris."

Stopping when my hand closed around her shoulder, she turned back to me. "I was just trying to help."

"I know you were, Doris. Sit. Please. I'm sorry I offended you. It's just… this isn't what I expected to do with my retirement. I'm not really sure what I had planned, but I know it involved more excitement than knitting."

Following my instructions, she settled back down onto the sofa and clutched her knitting basket to her chest.

"This really is boring, ladies." Marge sat back, crossing her arms. "I mean, I appreciate having you in my life, but Sylvie is right. There must be more to life than what we're doing. We're not twenty anymore, but we're far from dead."

"Damn straight," Alice agreed. "I should at least be traveling or something."

"Why aren't you?" I asked, genuinely curious.

Alice opened her mouth to answer but closed it and shrugged.

With a snort, Marge snickered. "Because she'd miss me too much. That's why."

"Oh yeah. That's it." Alice scoffed.

"So why?" I asked again.

"I guess I don't want to travel alone." She paused, and her voice softened as she finished. "And I don't have any friends who would go with me. Other than you ladies, I don't really have anyone in my life."

As I watched the hardness in her eyes soften for a split second, I felt sad for her. Rich, beautiful, and yet still left unfulfilled in her life. I didn't want to end up like that. I wanted to use this time in my life to do amazing things.

Just what they were, I had no idea.

"See. Because she'd miss me." Marge's smirk tightened.

"Well, there must be more than this," I said. "We just need to put our heads together and figure it out."

"Like what?" Doris asked.

"I'm not sure." I shrugged. "But something."

They stared at me with anticipation as I sat down beside Doris.

"It's funny. I spent my whole life raising my daughter, taking care of my husband, and working my ass off to have enough money to retire and live the good life. But now that I'm here, I feel like I missed my life. All those years spent in service to others, and now that it's finally my time with nothing standing in my way, I'm not utilizing the freedom."

"I hear you, sister." Alice raised her glass. "I had dreams—big ones. But then the little bun in the oven pushed them aside, and I never got to live the life I wanted. And now it's too late." She sighed and downed her martini.

"I certainly wasn't planning on being a suburban housewife," Marge said. "I had big dreams myself. Adventures I wanted to go on. But, with Percy's war injuries, and then raising our daughter, we didn't ever go on any."

"Bruce and I traveled every so often, but between our jobs and raising Rachel, we didn't get out to see the world like I'd always wanted."

"Am I the only one who enjoyed just being a wife and mother?" Doris asked. "I never yearned for anything else. I really loved it. All of it."

"It's not that I didn't like being a mother," I answered, "but between being a wife, a mother, and my career, I didn't get a lot of time for just myself to find things I'm truly passionate about. Now I feel like I'm running out of time."

"Running out of time?" Doris laughed. "You're what, fifty-five or sixty?"

I nodded. "I just turned sixty-one."

"You're like a spring chicken! I'm over ten years older than you," she said. "I'm surprised you aren't clucking instead of speaking."

"A babe in the cradle," Marge added, shaking her head. "What I wouldn't give to be sixty-one again. Things really start to go downhill fast once you hit seventy. Everything aches."

"I'm not a spring chicken." I snorted.

"You're not too old to have some fun, Sylvie. I still have fun and," Alice leaned forward and whispered, "don't tell anyone, but I'm older than you."

We all faked a gasp, and Marge clutched her chest. "Say it ain't so, Alice! You're not forty like you've been telling everyone?"

Alice swept a look across the three of us as she lifted an eyebrow. "I can pass for forty."

"In the dark," Marge taunted.

Narrowing her eyes at Marge, Alice continued. "None of us are too old to have some fun."

"We're not all gonna bang the pool boy, Alice." Marge rolled her eyes.

"Don't say bang! Disgusting!" Doris scolded and covered her ears.

"That's not what I meant." Alice shook her head. "Not that I don't recommend it." She waggled her brows.

"Take your hands off your ears, Doris!" Marge shouted so she could hear. Doris pulled her hands down. "You can listen again. We're not still talking about banging."

Her hands shot back to her ears.

"Oh, cripes." Marge waved at her. "Uncover your ears! No more banging talk, you prude!"

Doris peeled one hand from her ear, pausing to make sure the sex talk was over.

"How did you ever manage to make six kids, Doris? The turkey baster?" Alice tipped her thermos upside down, but no more clear liquid poured out. "Shit. I'm out."

"The regular way. With love." Doris lifted her chin.

"You banged. That's how you got babies." Marge laughed.

"Gross!" Doris cupped her hands over her ears again.

"Bang bang bangity bang bang *bang!"* Alice shouted loud enough there was no way Doris's hands blocked out the assault.

Giving up, Doris removed her hands and sat back. "You're all going to hell."

"At least we'll have each other." Alice smiled and reached out, squeezing Marge's hand.

"We'll be warm and toasty. Together." Marge blew Alice a kiss before their sinister laughter merged.

"Laugh now. It won't be funny when the flames of hell are licking at your feet."

"Oh, don't you worry, dear Doris. I'll seduce the devil, and he'll give Marge and me a penthouse suite. I'll be the reigning queen of hell in no time flat." Alice smirked and crossed her legs the opposite way, drawing attention to the lean, long lines that stretched up to her A-line skirt. I'd have killed for legs like that even back when I was twenty. Knowing her legs were one hell of an asset, she rarely covered them up, insisting on skirts and dresses all the time.

"It's *hell*, Alice. Your worst nightmare. You'll be short, fat, and will have a face that not even a mother could love." Doris returned the smirk when she saw the confidence falter in Alice's expression.

"I've been in hell. 'Nam. Whatever's down there will be a walk in the park." Marge pointed at her feet.

"You were in Vietnam?" I asked, startled by the statement.

"Yes, mam. First Lieutenant Margherita Moretti at your service. It's where I met my sweet Percy."

She'd only mentioned her husband, Percy, a few times, but never had she mentioned her time served in war. Interested to hear more, I leaned forward, pressing my elbows into my knees. "If you don't want to talk about it, I completely respect that, but I'm curious what you did over there."

"Two tours, which was two years, I served as a nurse. A lot of that was right in the thick of the fighting."

"Was it scary?" I asked.

Blowing out a puff of air, Marge nodded. "Terrifying. But with my nursing degree, it was my privilege to do what I could, so I enlisted in the Army. 'Nam itself was hell, but I loved the thrill of adventure and even the occasional bullet whizzing past. I miss that rush. I never wanted to be a boring old lady."

"Hear, hear." Alice lifted her empty glass then frowned. "I'm all about skipping the knitting and having some girl talk, but if we're going to chat about our pasts, I will need something else in here."

Excited to hear more about Marge's life, and perhaps have a little fun, I tried to mentally catalog my alcohol. "I'm afraid I don't keep much booze around. Bruce had beer, but after he got sick, he couldn't drink, so I stopped too out of respect."

"Well, shit." Alice's frown deepened.

"Good. You should try water, Alice. It's better for you." Doris gestured to her own glass.

"There's plenty of water in vodka." Alice arched a brow.

"I could go for a drink myself. What about that whiskey Alice brought you?" Marge asked, and three sets of eyes turned to me.

I'd forgotten about the bottle Alice had delivered during their first visit. "You're right! I still have it!"

"Well, then. What are we waiting for?" Alice grinned.

After looking to Marge and getting her confirming nod, I glanced over to Doris. She pursed her thin lips tight, and worry lines deepened on her face.

"Do you want some, Doris?" I asked.

"I don't think I should." She shook her head.

"Oh, come on. Do it!" Alice begged.

"Do it, Doris. Do it." Marge grinned.

She shook her head harder. "I don't think so."

"Come on, you sissy. You know you want the whiskey. It will be fun!" Marge kept on.

"I don't like peer pressure!" Doris looked ready to crumble beneath the taunting stares.

"I'll just pour you a glass, and you can drink it or not drink it. Your choice." I walked to the kitchen and found the bottle in the cupboard where I'd stashed it. After pouring four glasses of whiskey, I carried them back on a platter and set them on the coffee table. Alice snatched hers up without hesitation, and Marge followed suit. Doris and I exchanged a nervous glance before I plucked mine up as well.

"It's been ages since I've drank, much less had whiskey." I gave the glass a sniff. A shudder traveled up my spine when the strong smell of alcohol permeated my nostrils.

"I've never had whiskey," Doris admitted, staring at it like the devil himself sat on the edge of the glass taunting her.

"Go on, Doris. It won't kill you." Unfazed by the straight whiskey, Alice gulped down a swig.

Marge and I took a simultaneous sip, both of our faces puckering while we choked down the fiery liquid.

"Cripes, that's strong!" Marge sputtered.

"It's pure whiskey. What'd you expect?" Alice laughed and took another swig like a pro.

"Wow." I exhaled a breath ripe with whiskey. The warmth traveled through me, and just as Alice predicted when she gave it to me, it already started taking the edge off.

The three of us stared at Doris while she shifted on the couch. "I don't know, girls. I don't think it's a good idea."

"Doris. We can only knit and walk so much. Let's have some fun!" Marge leaned forward, pushing the glass toward her. "Our husbands died. Our lives are nearly over. We earned this shit."

Biting her lip, Doris reached out and slid the glass into

her hands. After one sniff, she fanned her nose and pulled a face. "I can't! It smells like gasoline!"

"That works in a pinch." Alice smiled. "This is much smoother."

"Go ahead, Doris. You won't die." Marge took another sip of her own, this time masking the bitter face I knew she was dying to make.

Plugging her nose with one hand, Doris closed her eyes and lifted the glass to her lips. We watched with bated breath while she took a large swig. The moment it passed her lips, her eyes shot open, and she coughed, nearly spitting out the fiery whiskey I knew burned a trail down her throat.

"Geez Louise!" she shouted.

"Atta girl, Doris!" Marge said.

"Well done." I smiled and lifted my glass in a toast. "To the Wilder Widows."

"To the Wilder Widows!" They mirrored, and our glasses clinked together.

The Wilder Widows: Chapter Three

"Holy cripes, I'm hammered," Marge said, reclining on the sofa. The mostly empty glass dangled in her fingertips, threatening to tip out the last remains of the whiskey.

"I feel funny." Doris teetered beside her, a hiccup punctuating the sentence.

Squinting one eye to see better, I looked to Alice who seemed the only one unaffected by the half-empty bottle of whiskey sitting on the coffee table. "I feel so relaxed." I sighed. "It's been ages since I've been this relaxed."

"I told you girls whiskey was the answer. *Now* I'm into these Wilder Widows meetings." Alice grinned.

"I vote we do this for every meeting." Marge matched her smile.

"I don't think I've ever been drunk before," Doris said.

"Ever?" I asked, turning my squint toward her.

"No. I had wine on occasion and a few sips of beer once or twice, but I've never gotten drunk. My body is a temple, and I don't think the temple should be drunk."

"I think the best way to honor the temple is to bathe it

in booze." Alice waved a hand over her impressive figure. "Like an offering to the Gods."

Snickering, I took another sip of my whiskey. "I've been drunk many times, but it's been a while. I forgot how fun it is. This kind of reminds me of high school when my girlfriends and I snuck some of my dad's brandy and got drunk and told each other secrets."

"Oh! Secrets!" Alice lit up. "Let's do that!"

"Do what?" Marge asked.

"Tell each other a secret."

Doris shook her head. "I'm not sure about that. Secrets are secrets for a reason."

Alice scoffed. "It will be like our Wilder Widows whiskey confessional. Like church, Doris. Just think of us as priests. Wouldn't God want you to be honest?" She arched a brow, and Doris bit her lip while she processed. "I'll even go first."

"You will?" I asked while I tried to think of what secret I wanted to share.

Alice leaned forward, and we followed suit, excited to hear what she had to say.

"When I was younger, I was a showgirl in Las Vegas. And one night after a show, a big Hollywood celebrity invited me to his table. You probably know of him… Harry Hayes."

Of course, I knew who Harry Hayes was. He was the heartthrob I dreamed about when I went to bed in my teens —me and every other teenage girl on the planet.

"Yes, yes. And then you slept with him," Marge said and sat back. "This isn't a secret. You tell this story to anyone who will listen."

Narrowing her eyes, Alice scoffed and sat back. "Well, it's a good story."

"A *secret,* Alice. That's the rule." Marge challenged.

"I have no secrets. I'm an open book." Alice crossed her arms. "You probably don't either."

Marge glared. "I've got secrets."

With a scoff, Alice rolled her eyes. "Like what? You wore a skirt once?"

Marge took a breath and then slammed the rest of her whiskey. When she set the empty glass down, she took a deep breath and blew it out. "I think I'm a lesbian."

"What?" Our three voices merged into one shout while we all whipped around to look at Marge.

"Yep. I think I'm a lesbian."

"You *think*?" Alice asked, her eyes as wide as mine. "Isn't that something you should *know?*"

Marge only shrugged. "I never acted on my feelings, so I can't say for certain, but I definitely think I may be a lesbian."

Doris clutched her chest. "But what about Percy? You can't be a… lesbian," she whispered the last word like she'd head straight to hell with the rest of us if she said it too loud. "You were *married*, Marge!"

"Yeah. I think Percy batted for the other team as well."

"Double beards?" Alice nearly spit out her drink with the explosive laugh. "You two were double beards?"

"What's a double beard?" Doris asked.

"A beard is a woman a gay man uses to make the world think he's straight," I said, still struggling to conceal my shock. Turning back to Marge, my eyes widened. "Did you both know about the other?"

Marge shook her head. "No. I only suspected. We met in 'Nam, and I'm pretty sure he had a thing for boys. But he proposed, and with a face like this I knew I wouldn't be getting another proposal, so I said yes."

"But, you had a *baby!*" Doris was barely hanging on.

"We did it. Twice. That was all it took to make a baby."

"Wait a minute." Alice closed her eyes while she let the sentence resonate. "Are you trying to tell me that in the last, what, fifty years, you've only had sex *twice*?"

Marge nodded.

Alice feigned passing out before sitting straight back up. "How are you even alive? I would *die* without regular sex!"

"Well, considering she's a lesbian and not attracted to men, I can see why doing it wouldn't be high on her priorities," I said.

"No interest whatsoever," Marge agreed. "And neither did Percy. We did it once on our wedding night and once when we decided we wanted to have a baby. Lucky for us, we got knocked up on the first try."

The color started to return to Doris's ashen face. "Heavens to Betsy, Marge! What was your marriage like?"

"Best friends." Her gruff demeanor disappeared behind the sweet smile remembering Percy induced. "We were the best of friends."

"So you, a lesbian, married a gay man, and you two just lived like roommates?" I asked.

"Well, I'm not sure I'm a lesbian. Maybe I'm just asexual."

"I don't believe in asexual." Alice scoffed. "Everyone likes sex. You just haven't found the right person yet."

"I'm not a lesbian, and I didn't like it. I never even had one of those... you know," Doris whispered.

"What?" Our voices rose once again in echoed shock.

"What do you mean you didn't like it?" I asked. "You never had an orgasm? Never?"

Deep crimson crept down her cheeks while she shook her head. "I'm not comfortable talking about... you know. Just forget I said anything."

"Too late now, Doris." Alice grinned like the Cheshire cat. "Spill."

"I'm not spilling!" Doris shrunk beneath her stare. "Let's just focus on Marge. She's the lesbian!"

The statement sent our heads swiveling back to Marge.

"I'm not *sure* if I'm a lesbian. I just suspect."

"Well, are you attracted to me?" Alice asked, leaning forward to give her a seductive stare.

Marge puckered her face. "No."

"Then you're not a lesbian," Alice stated with certainty.

"How do you figure?" I asked.

Her manicured hand swept her lithe body. "Well, hello! Because look at me. If she liked the ladies, she'd certainly want some of this."

Laughing, I shook my head. "That's not accurate, Alice. Just because you look like that doesn't mean she's instantly attracted to you."

"I was the first time I saw you." Marge shrugged.

Alice sat forward, and her face illuminated from the admission. "You were?"

"Then you talked, and that fantasy went out the window."

"Go to hell, Marge." Alice crossed her arms and lifted her chin.

Doris, Marge, and I burst into laughter while Alice feigned her anger.

Leaning forward, Doris whispered. "So, how does one know for sure if they're, you know… a lesbian."

"I'm not sure. I never really thought about acting on it," Marge said. "I had feelings for some ladies when I was younger, and in that day and age, it wasn't acceptable, so when I met Percy, I decided to just get married and pretend they'd never happened."

"That's sad, Marge," I said. "You never really got to find out if you are a lesbian, and maybe could have found a wonderful woman just perfect for you."

"I'm not sad about it. Percy was my best friend. Even though the romance wasn't there, I wouldn't have traded a second of our life together for a tryst with a beautiful woman."

I sighed at her statement, and this time it was my eyes brimming with tears. "That's beautiful, Marge. You two were lucky to have each other."

The waterworks started, and the three of them stared at me with scrunched brows. Every time I tried to choke back the tears, they only came out harder.

"Now look what you did. Your lesbianism made her cry!" Doris huffed.

"No." Shaking my head, I wiped my eyes. "It's not that."

"What's wrong, Sylvie?" Marge reached over and rubbed my back.

While I struggled to shove the secret I wanted to scream back into my mouth, the whiskey took hold of my tongue. "I hated him. Bruce. I hated him so much, and I was happy when he died."

The moment the truth tumbled out, I wanted to shove it back in. For almost forty years I carried it in silence, a weight that nearly crushed me to death.

"Now *that's* a secret." Alice let out a long-exhaled sigh. "You hated him? Really?"

Nodding, I sniffled and peered up at them, terrified to see the looks of shame I was certain would bore through me. They blinked at me in stunned silence.

"I shouldn't have said that. I didn't mean it." I tried to backpedal.

"Yes, you did." Marge touched my back. "It's okay to say it."

"If you hated him so much, why did you stay?" Alice brushed a stray piece of hair from her bulging eyes.

It was too late to take it back, and saying it out loud for the first time in my life lifted the weight I'd shouldered alone and carried for Rachel. "I wanted my daughter to have the family life she deserved. And by the time she left for school, I'd grown complacent. Then we moved here. With no friends and no career to keep me occupied away from him, his volatile personality became even more apparent. I knew I couldn't stay married to such a miserable person any longer. But when I finally gathered the courage to leave him, he got cancer. Then I was stuck. Who leaves their dying husband?"

"Shitty luck." Marge sucked the air through her teeth.

The sentence caused me to snort, and I nodded. "It *was* shitty luck. And it's been three years since he got diagnosed. Three long years living with the man I couldn't stand, a man who's constant complaining and temper only worsened with the illness. Three years watching him deteriorate and praying for the end, then cursing myself for wishing he would die. Three long years."

Doris finally closed her slack jaw. "I'm so sorry, Sylvie. That must have been awful for you."

Nodding, I wiped the last tear drying on my cheek. "Yeah. It's been a long, miserable life with that crotchety man. And now I'm here, sixty-one years old and alone."

"I never really loved my husband either." Alice shrugged. "His money, yes. But him? No. Though he wasn't a bad man, I just didn't love him. He was no Harry Hayes."

"I loved my Percy." Marge sighed.

"Yeah, but like a friend, you lesbo." Alice rolled her eyes. "It's different."

Tears glistened over Doris's eyes. "Well, I loved Harold. With all my heart."

"You're lucky, Doris," I said. "I wish I could have felt that way about Bruce. But I was stuck with him."

"Yeah, kids now these days have it easy with their drive-through divorces and their gay-loving ways." Marge scrunched up her nose. "It wasn't like that for us. You got married to someone of the opposite sex," she said, pointing her finger for emphasis, "and you stayed married. Period. Nowadays, I'd be out of the closet, Sylvie would be divorced, Alice would be a swinger, and Doris… well, Doris would still be Doris."

Doris just shrugged and nodded.

"I was a swinger a couple times." Alice smirked. "Fun times."

Blowing out a breath, I sat back. "There were many times after divorce became more acceptable that I thought about leaving, but I stayed anyway. And then when I was finally ready… cancer."

"Well, now they're all gone, and all that's left is us." Alice took a swig straight out of the bottle. "Just us. Bored old ladies who let their entire lives pass them by."

"I still can't believe this is it for me," Marge grumbled. "Getting drunk with a bunch of old ladies. The adventurous life I had planned is gone. Gone."

"Don't say that, Marge." I tried to comfort her with a touch, but the whiskey made me miss, and I patted the air instead. "We aren't too old. Other women our age still get out there and live their best lives. We've just become complacent in ours, but I'm determined to find fun stuff to do. No more knitting."

"I love knitting," Doris pouted, hiccupping again.

"You knit your little heart out, Doris. That's the point," I said. "These are the golden years. We should be able to do whatever the hell we want. We earned it."

"We *did* earn it!" Marge raised a triumphant fist before her arm went limp and fell back at her side. "All those years living as housewives and mothers, and what do we have to show for it? Nothing, that's what. Now it's *our* turn to do what we want, damn it! Our turn!"

"Amen, Marge. Amen." Alice hoisted the bottle.

"I don't feel like I missed anything," Doris slurred. "My whole life, I wanted a family. A husband. Grandkids. I never even thought of another life."

Marge grunted. "But now what, Doris? They're all gone. Your kids live across the country. They come to visit with your grandkids once or twice a year. And your husband is dead."

Doris's eyes glistened while she stared at Marge in disbelief. Her chin puckered as she fought the tears.

Alice tossed a pillow and smacked Marge in the head. "Christ, Marge! Way to destroy Doris's cheery outlook on life!"

Marge looked to Doris, who had a single tear dripping down her flushed cheek.

"Well, it's true." Marge shrugged.

"It is true," Doris whispered, her voice shaking with the weight of her admission. "They're gone—all of them. And I have nothing left. I'm all alone." The sobs shook her body. "And sometimes… sometimes when I'm feeling lazy, I buy baked goods at the market and pass them off as my own!" The sobs turned to wails.

"You what?" we echoed.

"My secret." She sobbed. "It's that I'm a fraud. A fraud!"

"The scandal!" Alice teased. "Doris, you are a treacherous thing."

"Going straight to hell with us." Marge shook her head, and Doris's sob deepened.

Alice shot Marge a look. "Now look what you did!"

"No," Doris said between sniffles. "She's right. You're all right. I'm a fraud, and we gave up all our good years in service of others, and now they've just abandoned us. We're alone. Old. It's over."

www.ingramcontent.com/pod-product-compliance
Lightning Source LLC
LaVergne TN
LVHW030916080826
845145LV00013B/2927

* 9 7 8 1 0 3 6 7 1 6 4 6 2 *